The
Vanished Bride
of Northfield House

Phyllis M. Newman

To my husband, John M. Newman,

the one person I know who actually sees ghosts

.

Chapter 1

*T*he ghost was my first memory of Northfield House. After taking my coat, a servant ushered me into a small room overlooking the east lawn where the hushed quiet and dim light narrowed the breach between the living and the dead.

In the far corner, a pale blue presence flickered like a flame.

I sat in a high-backed chair, planted my sturdy shoes on the floor, and repositioned my sensible hat. Accustomed to encountering spirits, I focused upon my surroundings—the broad polished desk, the high shelves of books, the clutter of papers, pens, and bottles of ink. The blue glow hovered in my periphery, as specters inhabit the edges of human vision. When looked at directly, they evaporate like mist in the morning sun.

Although such entities had made themselves known to me many times before, I was nonetheless unnerved. My heart thudded, and I felt the urge to flee. But it wasn't fear that inspired this sting of anxiety, this damp, fevered spell of agitation.

Rather, I fought against the worry that I was something *other* than a young, modern British woman. I did not doubt my supernatural perception, but dreaded what it might reveal about me. Was I blessed or was I cursed? Would Father have said this was evidence of evil? Would Mother have called upon the angels to protect me?

After saying a little prayer, I swallowed with difficulty and wondered how long I'd been waiting. I consulted the watch pinned to my bodice. Thirteen minutes past three.

In my trembling hand, I grasped a Liverpool broadsheet, folded to reveal the advert regarding a professional position to which I'd responded weeks ago. It was the possibility of employment that brought me to this elegant estate in northwest England, many miles from home. On the same page was a report about next month's 1922 Women's Olympic Games in Paris and details about the German government's failure to pay war reparations as required by the Treaty of Versailles. I began reading, which momentarily distracted me from the glimmering presence in the corner.

The door swung open without ceremony, making me jump, and admitted an elderly gentleman in a wheelchair.

The blue spirit curled like smoke and disappeared.

A chill danced down my spine despite the warmth of late July.

I stood.

"Good afternoon," he said. "Forgive me for not rising." His gruff voice did not convey apology. He wheeled himself behind the desk. "Please. Sit."

He consulted a document on his desk, his gaze drifting over it. "You are Miss Chatham. Anne Chatham."

"Yes, sir."

"Might you be related to the Chathams of Birmingham? Railroads, I believe."

"No, sir. I don't think so."

He didn't introduce himself, but I gathered that I was in the company of the man I hoped would employ me—Henry Wellington. I tried to relax and accustom myself to his age and infirmity.

"How long have you been a typewriter, Miss Chatham?"

I moistened my dry mouth. "I've completed a full-year course of study with Blount Business College for Women in Liverpool, sir. I can produce forty-five words per minute, error-free."

"There are no references included with your inquiry, Miss Chatham. Am I to understand this is your first effort at employment?"

"It is, sir. But be assured I am . . ." I was about to say punctual, responsible, resourceful, and—at twenty-three years of age—a quite reliable person, when the door flew open.

A dark-haired young man rushed in, bristling with palpable anger. He looked no older than I was. "Father, we must speak again. You should know something more. I—" He glanced at me and fell silent. "Forgive me. I thought you were alone. Is this the new typewriter?"

He glowered with distaste, as though my choice of profession was a character flaw needing correction. Scowling, he left as swiftly as he'd arrived. I felt a swell of apprehension.

The elderly man leaned forwards in his chair, and shadows darkened his face.

A moment of panic gripped me. I felt a terrible impulse to blurt out the facts of my sad story—I was recently orphaned and had invested my meager inheritance on the typewriting course meant to sustain me and spent my last shilling on the train to Northfield, hours from Liverpool.

If I wasn't acceptable to him, I didn't know where to go or what to do.

"Pardon the interruption," Mr. Wellington said. "That was my son, Owen." He gestured towards the open door. "He's impetuous when seized by a strong opinion. I'll have to see to his concern, as it appears to be of some import." He backed his chair away from the desk and wheeled towards the hallway.

My throat tightened, and a sinking sensation paralyzed my chest. I was being dismissed. My knees wobbled as I rose.

He threw his parting words over his shoulder as if an afterthought. "I'll send Mrs. Hadley, and she'll get you settled. We start at nine o'clock tomorrow morning. I expect to see you at dinner, of course."

As he left the room, I whispered a barely audible, "Thank you, sir."

I sat again and tried to settle my stomach. It appeared that Northfield House would be, at last, a refuge, a place to alight, if only temporarily. I closed my eyes and took a deep breath, allowing my shoulders to droop.

Moments later, there was a tap on the door, and the middle-aged woman who'd admitted me earlier stepped in.

"Please come with me. Miss Chatham, is it?"

"Yes, ma'am. Anne Chatham."

"I'm Mrs. Hadley, the housekeeper, as you've no doubt guessed. Welcome to Northfield House." Her words had the rolling r's of Northern Ireland.

She picked up my small carpetbag, which I'd forgotten altogether, and led me down a long corridor to the back of the house and up a set of narrow stairs.

"There are but the four of us in service," she told me as we climbed the stairs. "Cook, Maddy in the scullery, Miz Martha's maid Dolly, and myself is all. We make do. You'll make a pleasant addition, if I dare say it."

"Thank you, Mrs. Hadley."

"Working so closely with Mr. Wellington, you'll be taking your evening meal with the family, you being a professional young woman and all." She looked back at me and smiled, the first sign of friendliness I had seen all day.

I was taken aback by the lack of formality. Before the Great War, these grand country manors bristled with servants and tradition. Nowadays, many grand estates struggled with financial difficulties, so I was not surprised to learn of the skeleton staff. But I was unsettled by the idea I would sit with the family at dinner. A woman in my position was not a servant, but she was not a family member or friend either.

Mrs. Hadley opened a door on the left and led the way into a small, bare room furnished with a single bed, a wardrobe with a mirrored door, and a desk with an armless wooden chair. I looked past the spare accommodations to a pair of large windows. Outside, a rolling lawn led to a vibrant garden and, in the distance, a backdrop of dense trees.

"Oh!" I said. "How lovely."

"Indeed, Miss. The view makes up for what this room lacks in comfort. But surely, you'll manage. It's quiet, anyway, you being the only one back here. This used to be the children's wing, when Northfield housed a large family, including grandparents and maiden aunts. Cook, Dolly, and I have rooms on the far side of the kitchen. Maddy doesn't live in."

I sat on the sagging cot and removed the narrow-brimmed hat I hoped gave me a professional appearance.

"Dinner's at eight thirty sharp, and the family will expect you to join them, if you're not too tired."

Since I'd had only a bit of stale bread and cheese for lunch while at the railway station, the thought of a decent meal roused my hunger. Nonetheless, I was uneasy at the idea of dinner with my employers.

"Mrs. Hadley, I'm not sure I have anything to wear." I imagined dinner jackets and fluttering silks.

"They're not so grand since the Great War, Miss. So much has changed. Your best dress will do. Don't you worry." She turned to leave. "The lavatory's across the hall here. I'll leave you now, but find your way to the kitchen if you need anything." She gestured to her left down the long corridor. I watched after her as she departed and spied the head of another set of stairs and heard the muffled clatter of crockery. Between the stairway and my door there appeared to be several additional rooms.

I listened to the click of her low-heeled, black shoes on the hardwood and then her muffled step as she reached the carpeted hall. I looked once more at the riot of green outside the windows and thought about how far I'd come. I was now many miles inland from my childhood home in New Brighton, a small town on the coast of the Wirral Peninsula in the county of Merseyside, and from the hustle and whirl of seaside Liverpool, where I'd learned my trade. The briny smell of my youthful haunts by the sea had been replaced by the rich fragrance of tilled soil and pasturelands.

I hoped to make a home here, of sorts, or at least to earn my keep. A woman alone with limited skills and no resources could not be too demanding in this unforgiving world. For now, Northfield House looked an auspicious port, with a no-nonsense employer and a friendly housekeeper. If the rest of the household was as agreeable, and the spirits were tolerable, I would count myself lucky. God knew I'd already suffered more than my fair share of misfortune.

Beset by equal parts fatigue and anxiety, I blinked away tears. After unlacing my shoes and placing them neatly next to the wardrobe, I lay across the cot and stared at a cobweb, the collected dust of old memories, in a corner of the ceiling.

Chapter 2

I **must have fallen asleep.** I startled awake in the dark to an intense cold. Something was in the room. A faint light glimmered across the ceiling, and a wayward breath brushed my cheek.

I listened in the silence and then struggled to sit upright and focus on the gathering shadows to make sense of where I was. Then I remembered.

Northfield House.

Someone was outside my door. I felt this unseen being as one perceives impending rain on the breeze. Swallowing my unease, I wrenched open the door and swept into the corridor. At the end of the hallway, something disappeared around the corner. Did I hear the whisper of bare feet, perhaps the rustle of satin? Was my visitor a member of the household, intent on spying? Or had the ghost lingering in the study below decided to seek me out?

It wouldn't surprise me. Often, where I settled, spirits gathered. Ever since my illness, I'd found myself with one foot in the other world. The visitations did not speak, or at least, I couldn't hear them. Sometimes they showed me scenes; sometimes they revealed symbols. They wanted me to know their story, to speak their names.

Most only communicated their sadness, anger, or despair. A bouquet of flowers wilting before my mind's eye or tears falling upon a lock of hair expressed loss; a flaming sword communicated rage. But I'd come to believe that some spirits wanted my help to comfort the living or resolve something left undone. When I was able to find a piece of jewelry secreted under a loose floorboard or a lost letter between the pages of a book—and then return the keepsake to a loved one—my belief was strengthened.

I learned more and understood better with the passage of time. But there was no way I could really be sure. After all, interpreting random signs as having significance is one of the most profound impulses of human nature.

Shaking off my disquiet, I checked my watch. Three minutes after eight. I steeled myself to meet the rest of the household, hunger adding to my distraction. I shed my plain linen skirt and limp blouse and hung them carefully in the wardrobe, wire hangers being among the few amenities the room provided. I opened my bag and decanted a few things, including my only good dress, a dark gray serge worn to my father's funeral two years ago. My employer would surely forgive its unfashionable length and approve its simplicity as befitting an amanuensis on hire.

I pulled on the dress, donned my shoes, and smoothed my black, glossy hair into its least attractive arrangement, a knot at the back of my head. As the hired help, I felt it was inappropriate for me to accentuate my femininity or any beauty that might be mine.

Hastening across the hall to the lavatory, I filled the rust-stained sink with tepid water from a humming tap. I stared into the faded mirror. My dark eyes were swollen with sleep, my cheeks pale. With my broad forehead, long straight nose and well-couched chin, I looked a serious female, older than my twenty-three years. At precisely eight twenty-five, I took a deep breath and descended the back stairs to the hallway that led to the front of this imposing building.

I passed the study, morning room, and library before entering the large formal hall, full of dark oil paintings and polished wood. As I approached the broad stairs leading upwards to private areas of the house, the weight of some unknown sorrow settled over me. My steps slowed until I stood completely still in the gloom.

I paused as if captured by something hanging in the atmosphere. After several moments, the murmur of voices claimed my attention, leading me towards the dining room at the other end of the great hall. I moved on, shaking off the strange melancholy.

When I reached the closed double doors, I clearly heard a woman and a man speaking. Unsure whether to interrupt the conversation, I hesitated with my hand on the doorknob.

"But it's tedious to have her here. I don't care for it." The woman spoke in rich, cello-like tones.

My heart sank. I suspected she was speaking about me.

"Now, darling, don't be difficult." The man cajoled her, his voice warm and humorous. Definitely not Mr. Wellington or his rude son, Owen. Someone else.

"Am I not the lady of the house?" The woman sounded insulted. "Do I not get to decide upon . . ."

"Of course, Mother, but you think only of yourself. Consider Father and his feelings, won't you?"

"Your father? As if it mattered to him."

Rather than stand there like a sinful eavesdropper, I gathered my courage and pushed the door open. To my dismay, the speakers—a beautiful middle-aged woman seated at the head of the table and a well-dressed man of about twenty-eight years—became silent, looking at me with surprise. My face prickled with the heat of embarrassment.

I opened my mouth to speak, but nothing came out. I must have looked like a cod.

The man hesitated only a moment before taking my elbow to usher me into the room. He glanced at the woman. "Careful,

Mother, or you'll scare away Father's new typewriter with your ill temper. I'm sure Miss, ah . . . ?" He gave me a charming smile.

"Chatham. Anne Chatham." I found my voice and nodded, eyes lowered.

"I'm sure Miss Anne Chatham," he said, sweeping me forwards, "doesn't wish to play audience to our little family squabbles."

"Ignore my eldest, Miss Chatham." The woman rose to greet me. "He amuses himself by being troublesome. I am Lavinia Wellington. Welcome to Northfield House. We are delighted." She sat again, her mouth a grim line of disapproval.

Despite thickening into middle age, Lavinia Wellington was as lovely as her voice was melodious. Her face was a perfect oval, accentuated by full lips and high cheekbones. Tall and dark, she was corseted into an exquisite violet gown with flounces and pleats, her one adornment a blue rosary tucked at her waist. Although, like me, she hadn't adopted the new look—short unstructured sheaths and dropped waists—I felt dowdy by comparison, in my plain frock. Her only concession to current styles was a jeweled lace headband.

"And I am Thomas Wellington." The young man bowed in an exaggerated fashion. "At your service." His sleek blond hair was brushed back from a handsome face; a mischievous smile played upon his lips. Despite broad shoulders and heavy musculature, he moved with grace.

He also stood a bit too close to me, exhibiting a disturbing familiarity.

Before my discomfort became a blush, the door opened again, and my employer was wheeled into the room by his grim-faced son Owen, who had interrupted my interview earlier. Mr. Wellington looked grayer and more shriveled than he had earlier in the day.

"We're finished with this discussion for now," Mr. Wellington said to Owen, then waved a hand at me. "Please be seated, Miss Chatham. You've met the rest of the dinner party, I see."

Thomas pulled out the nearest chair for me, and I sat. He then took a place between me and his mother.

Owen wheeled Mr. Wellington to the far end of the long table. Tall and slim, he walked with a slouching posture, as if some invisible weight rested upon his shoulders. After carefully positioning his father at the table, he stepped forwards and bowed slightly to me.

"I am Owen Wellington, Black Sheep." He was as dark as his older brother was fair.

His father frowned. "Don't be churlish. I will consider your suggestions. But I promise nothing." He wheeled his chair closer to the table. "All tedious business we leave outside the dining room. We have a new member of the household."

Owen silently took a seat opposite his brother.

"What shall we make of you, Miss Chatham?" Thomas teased, looking me up and down with an insolence I was unaccustomed to.

All eyes turned in my direction. I felt a burning blush crawl from my throat to my hairline. Had I been expecting grace or familial warmth in the bosom of this home, it was not to be found this evening.

Chapter 3

*M*y throat constricted as I struggled to speak. My chest felt hollow. Four pairs of eyes appraised me, expecting something.

"I'm pleased to be here and to meet all of you," I stammered.

To my surprise, Lavinia Wellington came to my rescue. "You must be tired, my dear. Don't submit yourself to questioning by these ruffians."

"Oh, I like *that*," Thomas said, feigning hurt feelings. "After I spent the day doing your bidding. Brought you flowers, too."

"From my own garden." Mrs. Wellington gave up a tight little smile and favored him with an approving glance.

"Is Aunt Martha coming down to the table?" asked Owen, brooding like Heathcliff.

"She'll take dinner in her room," said Mrs. Wellington.

Mr. Wellington turned to me. "Martha is my sister. Widowed. She's often unwell and doesn't always grace us with her company. Your paths will cross at some point. And that is the extent of our happy family."

To my ears, his tone suggested the opposite of happiness.

Mrs. Wellington's expression soured as a young girl carrying a soup tureen backed into the room through the swinging door. Maddy, no doubt. My mouth watered as the aroma of onions and mushrooms scented the air. As she served, Thomas kept the conversation going.

"Father, Mother is being difficult," said Thomas. "It appears she doesn't fancy a visit from cousin Charlotte next week."

"You don't wish to see your grandniece, my dear?" said Mr. Wellington.

I was much relieved to learn the conversation I'd interrupted had *not* been about me. I relaxed a bit as the girl ladled soup into my bowl.

Mrs. Wellington aimed an exasperated look at Thomas. "Charlotte is so—so disruptive. My nerves."

"Nonsense. Charlotte is high-spirited and lively. It will be nice to hear a gay young lady's laughter about the place," said Mr. Wellington, shooting a glance at me before a troubled expression clouded his eyes.

Mrs. Wellington, her face pinched, withdrew into silence.

"So, it's agreed." Thomas chuckled at his mother's expense. "You don't mind a visit from Charlotte, do you, Owen?"

"Why would I?" Owen shrugged.

Thomas turned his gaze to me, his blue eyes lingering to scrutinize my hair, my face. "You'll like Charlotte, Miss Chatham. She hits the ground like a bomb, changing the landscape. And if you ask me, this stodgy old pile of stones could use a bit of rearranging."

Cousin Charlotte sounded forbidding rather than agreeable, but I said nothing, unable to formulate a comment that was both inoffensive to Thomas and supportive of Mrs. Wellington.

"Thomas, your metaphors," Mrs. Wellington said. "Haven't we had enough of wars and the various methods of mass destruction?"

Everyone glanced at Owen, who kept his head down. I detected unspoken meaning behind her words but could not decipher their significance.

Silence fell as we brought our soup spoons to our lips. I focused upon the meal like a starving mongrel but tried not to betray my hunger or soil my bodice. The soup was followed by sweetbread pate with peas, then fried smelts with sauce tartare. After a few minutes, the family continued chattering about the fields, the tenants, and the servants, all issues that did not include me, while my attention was trained on the food. I hadn't eaten fish or veal for many months. I savored every morsel.

Between each course, Maddy removed empty plates with a good deal of clatter and clang, whispering, "Pardon me," repeatedly, before bumping open the door with her elbow and hip and exiting the dining room.

"That girl," Mrs. Wellington complained, without bothering to keep her voice down, "doesn't belong in the dining room."

"We do the best we can, Lavinia dear, under the circumstances," said Mr. Wellington.

"Surely we can once again afford to hire a proper staff," she said. "Hostilities are well past, and there must be trained footmen looking for employment now the war no longer engages all our young men."

Beyond thinking with sadness about all the young men who had perished in the worldwide conflagration, I regretted learning my employment at Northfield House might represent an unwelcome expenditure of limited funds.

Owen, who seemed to wake from a trance, said, "If Father would only . . ."

"Give it up, Owen." Thomas's voice boomed with good humor. "Hash it about later. We've come through a war. England has fallen upon hard times. The least we can do is be of good cheer, grateful some other bloke took the cannon fire."

Owen's posture stiffened. "If we intend to manage the tax bill, we must implement some changes."

"Mind yourself, Thomas." Mr. Wellington was stern.

Something flashed between the brothers. Was it sincere dislike or merely a momentary anger? Clearly, they disagreed about something important. The war was a point of contention, perhaps.

I wondered if either of them had served. Thomas had a military bearing, but his jocular manner suggested he'd never been in harm's way, and indeed, he didn't possess the temperament of a soldier, particularly a battle-weary one. I could discern nothing about Owen. He might have been too young during the war to join the armed forces. Contemplating their situation did not minimize the suffering I felt in my own losses. I placed my fork upon my plate, suddenly unable to eat another bite.

Mr. Wellington looked first at Thomas, then at Owen. "Leave the discussion about taxes and war for another time."

"But, Father," said Thomas in his teasing manner, "perhaps Owen should discuss his ideas about the estate with me."

Mr. Wellington said, "Not now, Thomas."

Owen's expression darkened.

I had a flash of clarity. The tension in the room must relate to the laws of entail. Thomas, as the oldest son, would inherit Northfield upon his father's death. Owen would receive much less from his father's estate.

"I suspect that Owen is hoping Parliament will change things." Thomas, self-satisfied, wouldn't let it go.

I was aware of the latest political intrigues. New laws being considered by Parliament would abolish primogeniture and enable estates to be divided among heirs or sold off in parcels. The traditionalists had been fighting against these proposals. Henry Wellington appeared to be nothing if not traditional. If Owen did support these changes, his opinions could be in direct opposition to his father's beliefs.

Owen remained silent, his face an unreadable mask. A tic began to worry his left eyelid as an awkward stillness enveloped the room.

I felt uneasy being exposed to private family issues. The deep divisions and thinly veiled frustrations troubling this house felt like a swell beneath my feet. I feared that I would be expected to take sides. Still, they did not know real hardship, this fractious family that seemed so eager to reveal its conflicts. The fine china and silver were in use. Their meals still magically appeared upon the table without any effort on their part.

Mr. Wellington shook his head. "We're forgetting," he said. "We have a newcomer with us this evening."

"Of course, Father." Thomas once again turned his probing eyes to me. "Tonight, Miss Chatham, you're an honored guest. Tomorrow, you'll be yet another of us unfortunate creatures scrabbling about the earth to earn a living."

I didn't wish to participate in whatever machinations he devised, which felt like some trap designed especially for me. Yet, I found myself saying, "Indeed, that is true, sir. I must make my own way." *Unlike you, Thomas, who will inherit your livelihood.*

"That's enough, Thomas," Mr. Wellington said with a weary sigh. "Miss Chatham, you're from Birmingham, if I remember correctly. Your family is in railroads?"

"No, sir. Not at all." I kept my tone light to hide my embarrassment at having to correct him once again. "I come from New Brighton and, of late, Liverpool. My father, now deceased, was a Presbyterian clergyman."

"Ah, a Calvinist. Unfortunate. I mean your father's death, of course," he said.

Thomas smirked at his father's correction. "And your mother, dear Miss Chatham?" he asked. "Are your labors supporting a widowed mother?"

Startled to be confronted with such insolence, I hesitated for a moment. "I'm afraid I'm orphaned, sir."

"Dear, dear," he continued in a jocular vein, "to lose one parent is unfortunate, but to lose two looks like carelessness."

"Thomas! The words of Oscar Wilde are hardly appropriate given the circumstance." Though she chided her son, Mrs.

16

Wellington's face revealed only admiration. "Please don't tease. Miss Chatham will find your behavior boorish."

Clamping my jaws while fighting tears, I remained silent.

Thankfully, Maddy entered with a tray.

Mr. Wellington smiled at the dish she placed before him. "My favorite, bread pudding. Compliment Cook, will you, Maddy?"

"Yes, sir." She curtsied and continued around the table, placing a bowl of currant-studded dessert at each place setting.

I silently thanked Maddy for diverting attention from my unfortunate circumstances. Owen shot a glance at me while I composed myself.

"Speaking of railroads," Thomas said, "what are we to make of the companies consolidating into the Big Four? Will this combat the unions?"

"I would think that's the main purpose," Owen said. "The bigger the railroad, the smaller the worker."

"And we should hope so," said Mr. Wellington. "Strikes everywhere. Not only in Britain, but across Europe and the Americas. Not just railroads, but mines, harbors, textiles, public transport. Why, in Amsterdam, the typographers are striking. What are we to make of all this unrest?"

"The workers are demanding a fair share of the wealth they create," Owen said. "They've seen nothing but wage cuts since the war."

"They're Bolsheviks, the lot of them." Mr. Wellington frowned.

Thomas leaned back in his chair. "Railroad strikers should watch out. Belgium is preparing to launch an airline. Might be the end of the railroads." He looked smug.

"And a boon for the leftists," Owen shot back. "Unemployment will feed working class unrest. What's happening in the east will spread."

Mr. Wellington sighed. "You may be right, Owen. The Bolsheviks are gaining strength. We mustn't underestimate their influence."

"The Americans support us in refusing to recognize them," Thomas said. "We have power, too."

Owen shook his head. "If our governments want stability, they must provide certain protections to the disenfranchised workers."

"No one willingly gives up power," Thomas spoke with authority. "We're looking at world-wide insurrection, if we listen to you, Owen. Do you side with the Bolshies, even after the czar was murdered?"

"The Romanovs were fools. If you want peace, promote justice," said Owen.

"No more politics." Mrs. Wellington ended the discussion with a wave of her hand. "None of the world's problems will be resolved around this table." She stood, prompting the rest of us to take to our feet as well.

I assumed Lavinia Wellington was regularly dismissive of any problems not directly concerning her and her family. I also saw where the political lines were drawn and where the family's various sympathies lay. Thomas spoke like he had been handed everything. Owen had the opinions of a man whose future was uncertain in a changing world. Perhaps I alone could identify with the working class, having recently counted myself among their ranks. The only thing I knew about the Bolsheviks was they advocated equality for women.

"Miss Chatham," said Mrs. Wellington, "will you join me in the drawing room for coffee?"

Sensing her invitation was born of courtesy rather than enthusiasm, I said, "That is kind of you, Mrs. Wellington, but if you don't mind, I'll retire. I've had quite a long day."

"Of course, my dear. As you wish."

Mr. Wellington said, "You've been made comfortable, I trust?"

"Yes, sir. Mrs. Hadley has seen to it."

Thomas placed a bottle of port and two glasses next to his father.

Mr. Wellington poured a glass of the ruby liquid. "I'll meet you in my study, Miss Chatham—you know where it is—promptly at nine tomorrow."

"Of course. Good evening."

Owen mumbled, "Good evening."

Thomas affected another exaggerated bow. "Until tomorrow, Miss Chatham, I await with bated breath."

Leaving the dining room with a stifled sigh of relief, I returned the way I'd come. The formal hall was now shrouded in darkness, except for a narrow path of moonlight filtering through large windows on the landing.

A shadow moved. I halted my step. Holding my breath, I felt eyes upon me, a presence so palpable it made my flesh crawl.

Someone was watching me.

Chapter 4

*H*ello?" **Heavy carpeting** and draperies swallowed my words. "Who's there?"

A rustling sound, like heavy silk, came from the stairway. I peered into the gloom. Something dark flickered, thickened, and disappeared into the blackness beyond the landing.

A chill ran down my spine. I stood as still as the moonlight before taking a deep breath to calm the sting of fear. Whoever or whatever had lingered there was now gone.

The encounter suggested a furtiveness not present when I was confronted by the dead. Therefore, I suspected one of the inhabitants of the house had been watching me. Perhaps it was the maid, or maybe Mr. Wellington's widowed sister was stirring about and didn't fancy an encounter with a stranger on the stairs. I must take care. The events of the day should not be allowed to overwhelm me and mislead me into assigning to the spirit world what might be easily explained by this one.

The upstairs lay in total darkness. These rooms harbored mysteries, untold disappointments, and lurking tragedies that splashed upon the past, bleeding into the present. A flood of heartache, of layers of sorrow, of deep and abiding longing, swept through me. This house held secrets. And someone, or something, wanted them told.

I steadied myself before hurrying along the long dark corridor towards the backstairs. My shoes echoed on the bare steps as I ascended to the sanctuary of my room. Closing the door, I was disquieted to find it had no lock.

I hesitated, my hand on the doorknob. I was being fanciful. Why should I have need of a lock? I tried to dismiss an uneasy sense of vulnerability. Taking a deep breath to settle my nerves, I allowed my body to relax for the first time since arriving at Northfield House.

I looked about the small room and accepted that the space within these four walls was mine. At last, my new life would begin. I was no one's daughter, no one's sister, no one's wife. I must make a life of my own. Now that the worldwide war had decimated the marriageable male population, many young women of limited means and no family shared my fate.

After washing up, I put on my nightdress and placed my meager belongings in the wardrobe. A shelf and one drawer accommodated my white cotton shifts and stockings. Several blouses, all in shades of beige and each softened with wear and repeated laundering, took their place beside two skirts, one a dark tweed, the other brown, both bereft of ornamentation. In the bottom of the carpetbag, I left the last remnants of home, including a package of letters and cards I'd received throughout my childhood, my father's personal Bible, and my mother's wedding band. The rest of the carpetbag's contents were not as precious, but comprised the only other things of value that I owned: two tortoiseshell combs, a pair of black cotton gloves, and lace trim from a dress I'd outgrown years before. Also left inhabiting the bag were a card of darning silk, a packet of needles, and tiny gilt-washed sewing scissors. With these I would no doubt ply my tediously acquired womanly skills to repair or alter hand-me-downs or second-hand clothing found at church bazaars.

At last, I extinguished the one guttering candle and lay on the narrow bed. The springs protested under my weight, but the crisp bedding smelled of lavender.

I contemplated the view outside the large windows, noting the rolling landscape, a study in black and white. In the distance, a light breeze soundlessly tossed the treetops. Before I reflected upon the stars in the heavens, my mind wandered. Images washed over me—the narrow, cobbled streets of Liverpool, black water lapping the docks, and dark boats creaking in the harbor. I shook these memories from my mind, shedding the ghosts from my past like tears.

My slumber was deep and dreamless. I emerged after what seemed like days, realizing I'd hardly moved during the night. The brightening sky was rouged pink in the east. A light fog drifted over the fields. For a brief moment, I felt a wave of homesickness, recalling the narrow, shadowed rooms of the parsonage, the comforting quiet.

Turning towards the door, I saw it open a crack. About three feet above the floor a pair of large blue eyes shadowed by a fringe of bangs stared back at me. Unlike the ghost in the study, it seemed a benevolent being.

"Hello," I said.

The door opened a bit wider to reveal a girl of about six years of age. She was spindly and pale, like a volunteer seedling. Her narrow, dirty face was obscured by stringy blonde hair.

"Who are you?" I asked.

When I sat up, she darted off. I opened the door and looked after her but saw only the edge of her dress as she disappeared beyond the end of the corridor.

I dressed quickly in a shirtwaist blouse and narrow ankle-length skirt. Attaching my watch to my lapel, I noted it was after seven, later than I'd thought. Rather than take the stairs to the long corridor leading to the front of the house, I decided to see where the back stairs led. I took the passageway to the left, walking past half a dozen small, sparely furnished rooms much like my own. Opening a door at the top of another flight of stairs, I heard the clatter and clang of dishes mingled with voices below. I'd found my way to the kitchen.

Warmth and the aromas of baking greeted me as I descended. The smell of cinnamon instantly evoked my mother, her laughter chiming as she busied herself at the breakfast table, setting out bowls of porridge for me, my sister, and my brother. I stood in the entry until Mrs. Hadley noticed me.

She rose from the large table in the middle of the room. "Good morning, Miss. Did you sleep well, now?"

"Quite well, thank you."

"Come in." She motioned to a chair across from her near the fireplace, which was cold this time of year. "Let's get you a bite of breakfast."

A large woman with a ruddy face appeared. "I'm Cook, Miss. Pleased to meech yer." She did a little curtsy as she set a cup of tea in front of me. "Yer've met Maddy?" She motioned to the girl who'd served dinner the previous night.

"Not properly, no. Hello, Maddy. I'm Anne Chatham."

"Miss," she said shyly as she arranged dishes on a silver tray.

"And Dolly, Miz Martha's maid," said Mrs. Hadley, indicating a stout young woman who nodded in my direction as she left with the tray Maddy had prepared.

I assumed that Martha, Mr. Wellington's sister, must take breakfast in her room.

Cook put a plate with bread, jam, and clotted cream before me. The realization that I'd now eat regularly caused an overwhelming swell of gratitude.

As I prepared a bit of bread, movement near the fireplace caught my attention. I turned to see the Little Seedling huddled there, staring. "Hello, again," I said.

PHYLLIS M. NEWMAN

"Have yer met our lit'l un, then?" said Cook.

"Earlier this morning." I added more jam to the bread, then held it towards her.

She inched forwards and, after a moment, took it with a grubby hand.

"What's your name?" I asked.

She retreated behind the fireplace, where I could see only her bare toes.

"That's Katherine Marrible. Kitty, we call her. Poor wee bairn," said Mrs. Hadley. "She doesn't speak. We don't know how much she understands."

"More'n yer'd think," said Cook.

"She came here a babe with her mother, she being in service during the war. Died soon after, poor dear. We look after the girl, we do," Mrs. Hadley said, smiling. "Kitty's no trouble. Like a cat, she is. Silent. Steals in and out unnoticed and sees but everything. No one in this house can get anything past Kitty, don't you know."

I included Kitty on my list of possible Northfield residents who might have been lurking outside my door and on the dark staircase last night.

"I've got to go on now." Mrs. Hadley stood. "Are you in need of anything, Miss?"

"No. Thank you, I'm fine. But I've a quick question, if you would?"

"Yes, Miss?"

I considered how to pose it. "Thomas Wellington. He has the look of the military about him. Did he serve?"

"Oh, no, Miss. That would be Mr. Owen. He joined the armed services. Mr. Thomas was too important here at home, to look after the farm. Food production being so essential to the war effort," she hastened to add.

"I did wonder, Mrs. Hadley. Thank you," I said as she labored up the stairs towards the dining room. So I had been wrong. Thomas had remained at Northfield House during the Great War, and Owen

24

had gone off to fight. I admonished myself for making assumptions about the Wellington family, as neither hasty conclusions nor my uninformed opinion would benefit me as I tried to adjust to my new circumstances.

I finished breakfast while Cook and Maddy bustled about preparing the morning meal for the household. Kitty huddled in the corner. From somewhere about her spare skirts, she had produced a small wooden box, which she now clutched in one hand.

"What have you there, Kitty?" I asked. Her gaze darted from mine as she hid her hands behind her. She ducked her head and backed away.

Consulting my watch to find it was only ten after eight, I decided to explore the grounds before reporting to the study. The kitchen door opened onto a courtyard. On my way outside, I motioned for Kitty to come with me, but she withdrew into the clutter in the pantry. I smiled and stepped into the pale morning sunlight of late summer. The day was fresh and clear with but a hint of autumn in the faint breeze.

I took the kitchen path past the vegetable garden, the stables, and other outbuildings, and drew near the grove of ancient oak trees visible from my second-floor window. Laboring up a small incline, I surveyed the house from a distance, taking in its massive proportions. Northfield was larger than it looked from the front. Two wings projected from the main structure to form the rear courtyard. The north wing was bordered by hedges and flower beds, and I identified the location of my own room on the upper floor, where I'd left the window open and white curtains shifted in a stir of air.

The south wing appeared to have fallen into disuse. The windows were shuttered, the veranda and surrounding grounds neglected. That degree of deterioration did not surprise me. Since the Great War and changing economic fortunes of England, many fine houses of the landed gentry had slipped into disrepair. It struck me anew how scarce revenues and increasing taxes led to penury, limiting service staff and changing social mores. Certainly, these circumstances explained my own situation.

I looked across the rolling hills and fields surrounding the manor. Livestock dotted the landscape. Tenant farm houses nestled in a valley. I made my way down a gentle slope to a narrow path beside a deep, meandering stream that burbled through the weeds and rock at its edge. Following it past the trees and along a short expanse of meadow, I approached a wooden footbridge where the gathering water churned over large rocks below. The weathered bridge, shaded by weeping willows on the opposite bank, spanned a deep divide, making a charming picture. A tangle of wild roses and gorse tumbled down both sides, ending in an outcropping of jagged stone.

Once upon the bridge, I found my footing unsteady. The boards were black and slick with damp, and the half-rotted railing fell below my center of gravity. I stood in deep shade, the trees forming a thick canopy of gloom. Beneath me, the rushing stream formed a seething caldron. Yet, just a few feet downstream, the water calmed and continued on its way.

I was struck by the loneliness and isolation of this spot, despite its beauty. The ravine, wet with spray, supported bright moss and tendriled vines, giving the place an ethereal quality. I found myself staring into the coursing water below, mesmerized, my blood humming, until I felt disoriented. I shivered and hurried back towards the house.

Once again on the footpath, I was startled to see Kitty behind a nearby tree. Indeed, she was like a cat. I hadn't seen her follow me.

"Walk with me, Katherine." I put out my hand.

She drew back.

"Kitty?" I tried again.

She hid behind the tree once more. She needs time, I decided, strolling forwards as she trailed after me, but I will make this child a friend.

Chapter 5

*M*y work at **Northfield House** began in fits and starts. Although I'd arrived at the study before the appointed hour, hoping to impress Mr. Wellington with my diligence, he didn't appear until after ten that first day.

While waiting for him, I assumed the smaller desk near the window for myself. Upon it sat a newer model Remington portable typing machine with locking carriage. With some difficulty, I repositioned it (luggable rather than portable would be a more apt description) to suit me and proceeded to tidy the working space. I located paper, carbons, and other necessary materials in the drawers and felt a pleasant sense of anticipation.

When Mr. Wellington finally appeared, he explained the nature of my duties.

"Nothing taxing, Miss Chatham," he said. "You'll typewrite as I dictate at times, but more often, you'll simply transcribe."

He handed me a sheaf of papers covered in his crabbed handwriting. His major interest lay in agrarian land reform in Britain across the centuries, particularly as compared to other nations. A self-taught scholar, he was working on his eighth manuscript on the subject of agricultural production. I was struck by his secular interests. My father had been devoted to study of a religious nature, naturally, and had directed my own studies accordingly. Now, it would seem, my devotions would take a back seat to practical research.

Most days, we labored together companionably enough, but I was often alone, typing up his copious notes, my strong fingers, swift and sure, playing over the keyboard. The Remington's action was not as stiff as that of the old Underwoods we used in school. I felt privileged to have such a sophisticated machine, with its bold letters and easy strike.

My employer gave me a short break in the early afternoon, during which I went to the kitchen for tea. In the evenings, I took supper with the family. There, as well, considerations of a spiritual nature rarely emerged, aside from a rather perfunctory grace uttered before the meal. This, more than anything, emphasized how my life had changed. From the sheltered existence of a clergyman's child, where reading from scripture each morning and observing vespers during the sixth canonical hour was a daily ritual, I entered a world of dubious values. The Wellingtons were beset with more mundane concerns, profits and losses from their land, cost of rentals, and tenant relationships.

For a week following my arrival, Thomas did not join us for dinner, due to some errand not revealed at table. Without his cheerful banter, as unsettling as it was, we sat in stony silence after the required pleasantries. The clock over the mantel kept up a monotonous count of the endless seconds.

Owen was an indecipherable, taciturn figure. He appeared to dislike me and made no effort to be welcoming or to engage me in conversation. His dark eyes focused on his plate as resolutely as my head remained bowed.

I thought perhaps his war experience weighed heavily upon his psyche. No outward signs of that burden were obvious, however. Most soldiers who survived the Great War returned bearing visible scars, permanent reminders of the hideous consequences of human folly. But Owen's broad shoulders lolled casually, and he moved with easy grace, not unlike his brother.

Mr. and Mrs. Wellington, when they spoke, held forth only about household issues and petty disturbances with the servants. Despite the grandeur of Northfield House, both elegance and charm were in limited supply. I inwardly prayed to be invisible, not even daring to hope for casual conversation. The easy, comfortable chatter about the events of the day that characterized mealtimes during my childhood was surely lost to the past.

Three times that week, I glanced up from my plate to see a foggy being hanging upside-down from the ceiling several feet behind Mrs. Wellington. Gleaming silver threads snaked across a vaguely human form.

Each time, I declined to look at the apparition. I focused my attention instead upon my dinner. Sometimes, ignoring a specter dispelled it; other times, a ghost persisted and forced unbidden images into my head—symbols that rarely meant anything to me. As I sat in the dining room at Northfield House, the spirit prevailed and unsettling visions appeared. A hand opened to reveal something dark crawling out of the palm, which metamorphosed into crushed violets. Something shiny and iridescent like fish scales swam in my peripheral vision. A bouquet of white roses wilted in my mind's eye.

Despite the disturbing experiences during the evening meal, my work day took on a pleasing routine. Mr. Wellington was patient and generous. I found myself to be accomplished at my job. I looked forwards to filling my days with competent effort as endless pages of type flowed from my fingers, attesting to my skill and industry.

The intellectual nature of the work was exciting as well. Mr. Wellington was, for the time being, detailing the agricultural successes in the States. I learned about the record wheat crops being produced in America's breadbasket, the Great Plains of the Midwest.

"Indeed," my employer said, "the grasslands of Oklahoma and Texas have yielded to the plow. The American farmer can take great pride in those straight lines, which I imagine will soon run from coast to coast."

Apparently, livestock grazing had been abandoned as agricultural mechanization and high grain prices during the Great War encouraged aggressive exploitation of the land. The sea of grass characterizing Middle America had all but disappeared in less than a decade.

"So you think it advisable, man's triumph over nature?" I asked before I thought better of it.

"And why not?" said Mr. Wellington. "God gave man dominion over the earth, did He not?"

I wasn't sure it was quite right to challenge the natural world in this way. "Such hubris might offer unforeseen challenges in the future," I dared suggest.

My opinion made him thoughtful. Our different ways of seeing the world often resulted in lively discussion. I believed I challenged him to think deeper on his subject matter.

Having ended my first week of gainful employment with a growing sense of satisfaction, I retired early. I looked forwards to my first day off but lay in bed, tossing about. Sleep wouldn't come. Finally, at half-past midnight, I gave up. I pulled on my wrapper and, in search of a book to lull me into slumber, crept downstairs to the library.

The wood-paneled room had the stale odor of disuse, like an attic, and the stillness of a tomb. I closed the door behind me and, in the bright moonlight streaming through the tall windows, ran my fingers over a shelf of books. I selected a slim volume and slipped to the windows in the dark. Lingering there, alone with my thoughts, I contemplated the stars hanging just above the trees.

"You're getting on well, I take it," said a man's voice from the shadows.

"Oh!" I jumped, my heart lurching.

Owen materialized from out of the gloom. "I'm sorry. I didn't intend to frighten you."

I caught my breath and took a step backwards. "My apologies for intruding. I shouldn't be here." Relief surely showed in the set of my shoulders. For a moment, I'd feared it was Thomas who had discovered me alone in the darkness. But then I asked myself why I should entertain such a feeling of dread about Thomas.

"I'm the only one ever in this room, and rarely this late," said Owen. "So why shouldn't you avail yourself of the amenities?" His arm motioned to the towering shelves of books as he stepped into the light spilling across the carpet. His white shirt was untucked and open at the neck. His dark hair, more disheveled than usual, fell into his eyes and curled over his collar.

I suddenly realized my own dishabille and pulled my wrapper close. "Please forgive my wandering about."

"Unnecessary." He stepped closer and reached towards me.

I stifled the impulse to withdraw. His fingers only brushed mine as he took the book from my hand.

"*The Poetry of Samuel Taylor Coleridge,*" he read aloud, surprise in his voice. "So you're a romantic. How extraordinary."

"My mother's favorite poet," I said by way of explanation.

"She walks in beauty, like the night."

"That's Lord Byron." I smiled and lowered my eyes from his face to his bare throat.

"So it is. You're more than meets the eye, Miss Chatham. More than the cool, efficient typewriter."

I couldn't think of anything to say. He returned the book to me and moved towards the windows to stand with his back to the room. The shadows darkened his countenance, and he looked a quite dashing figure in his loose shirt. I realized his feet were bare and blushed to the roots of my hair.

"Thomas will be surprised," he said.

"Thomas?"

"My brother is not intellectually inclined, is all. Therefore, he never expects it in other people."

I glanced at the corner where Owen had been sitting. His own reading material lay upon a table. The gold lettering on the spine glowed in the moonlight. He had selected *Abraham Lincoln*, the Godfrey R. Benson biography.

For an uncomfortable moment, I struggled for something to say. "Is Thomas often away from his duties on the farm this long, with all the responsibilities he must carry?"

Owen's smile was rueful. "Indeed, he is."

"Is he returning soon?"

"You'll be happy to know he returns home tomorrow."

I was startled. I feared I had given the impression I was somehow interested in Thomas and was anxious for his presence. "It's none of my business, of course. I was only curious."

"Women are always curious about Thomas."

I was mortified that Owen might think I was preoccupied with his brother. I had no doubt where Thomas's schemes regarding women would lead, so nothing could be farther from my mind. I feared any protestations on my part would only strengthen Owen's mistaken assumption. "I didn't mean to imply . . ." My posture stiffened, and I took a step backwards.

"I've made you uncomfortable," he said, dismayed. "It was not my intention. Please excuse my clumsy attempt at humor." He made a conciliatory gesture, his hands open and palm up as he shrugged.

"Not at all." I relaxed my posture, hoping to project casual disinterest. "I'm just making an effort to understand my employer and his family, since I'm now living here among you."

"Well, you're in luck, Miss Chatham. Thomas is bringing our cousin with him. You'll learn more about all of us through exposure to Charlotte. You'll find her quite a challenge."

Challenge? The discussion was just getting worse. "Surely you don't think I perceive your cousin to be a rival."

"Of course not! I–I know you weren't suggesting . . . I didn't intend to . . ."

His presumption that I might see Charlotte as competition for Thomas's attention or that there was some sort of contest was offensive. "Really," I said, "it's absurd. You misunderstand. I have no personal interest in your family, if that's what you're suggesting." I squared my shoulders, projecting my displeasure.

Owen straightened and withdrew behind a mask of formality. "I fear I've caused you agitation," he said with exaggerated courtesy. "I apologize." He strode towards the door. Turning to face me, he paused. "Mother keeps cousin Charlotte in check. She is more likely to engage in battle for Thomas's affections. I cast no aspersions upon you."

With that, he departed, leaving me to stare after him.

Chapter 6

*T*he encounter with Owen left me unsettled. I reviewed our conversation in my head, but I could not determine whether he had intended to suggest a rivalry between his cousin and myself. I feared I had overreacted and said something I shouldn't have. As a result, I couldn't focus on Coleridge or fall asleep until past three.

In the morning, I was groggy, overtaken with weariness after a restless night. I walked to the village with Mrs. Hadley and Dolly to attend church. Seated in the dim sanctuary, I could barely stay awake as the clergyman lectured about sin and salvation. I could not help thinking of Father and the parsonage that had always been my home. For a moment, I smelled the lilacs in bloom at the kitchen door and saw the sunset glinting in the leaded-glass windows of Father's study. It occurred to me for the first time that it was unlikely I would ever see the haunts of my childhood again.

On the walk back to Northfield House, Dolly talked nonstop, apparently making up for little opportunity otherwise.

". . . and Mr. Henry and the Missus, they take the motorcar to Melling for services every Sunday, they do." She walked with a flirtatious skip to her step.

"And they attend the Catholic church there?" I asked, remembering Mrs. Wellington's rosary.

"That they do, Miss," said Dolly. "They some of the times stay all day long, don't they, visiting family and friends in town." She wore a saucy, rather fashionable hat—a little straw bonnet with purple ribbons, at odds with her dour dress.

Mrs. Hadley gave me a tolerant, understanding smile as Dolly chattered on.

"The Missus' sister lives thereabouts. Elderly, she is," Dolly continued, delighted to impart personal information. "Sometimes they don't come home at all, but stay the night."

Mrs. Hadley remained silent, seeming to glide along as she walked in her Sunday best, a simple dark dress with a high, lace-trimmed collar.

"Are they staying the night today?" Dolly asked suddenly, turning to Mrs. Hadley. "Or will they be wanting supper?"

"They'll be along early today, Dolly," said Mrs. Hadley. "Cook will take care of supper, and I'm sure you'll be grand help, as usual."

"Missus Wellington's sister has a fine house, though not as fine as Northfield," Dolly continued without pause. "Such doin's they have there, with the finest food and such."

As Dolly gossiped, my mind wandered until we reached the gravel drive of Northfield House. The servants went on their way, and I, having nothing to occupy my time, found myself in the garden alone. I ambled through the neatly maintained beds surrounding the north wing, where time and attention had produced a well-manicured formality. Boxwood and privet edged trimmed swaths of grass and patches of hydrangea and cultivated roses.

I walked as far as the south wing gardens, where it was clear no gardener was assigned. The grounds were untamed, taken over by invasive violets and unfettered rhododendron. The overgrown wisteria, entangled with clematis and viburnum, might have created a pleasing nonconformity, if not for the chilly air and the profound sense that I was being watched. Looking upwards at the grimy, vacant windows and the shutters hanging askew, I became uneasy. The deep shadows were oppressive, and I hurried to the house.

At tea time, with the staff off, I availed myself of the kitchen. It was a welcoming space, where glowing orbs slipped cheerfully out of sight whenever I entered, as happy spirits do. I sat alone at the table until Kitty appeared. She crept in and settled on the hearth. Close beside her, she laid the tiny wooden box.

"How are you, little Kitty?" I didn't expect an answer.

She had a blue ribbon tying up her hair.

"Your ribbon is pretty. It matches your eyes." I leaned forwards a bit, and she didn't move. *Progress.*

I offered her tea, but she did not respond, moving backwards almost imperceptibly, like a cat. We sat in companionable silence for several minutes.

"What do you keep in your little box, Kitty?" I ventured to ask at last.

She hid it in her pocket, her eyes never leaving mine.

"Shall we go to the veranda and take the air?" I stood and held out my hand.

She didn't take it, but followed me through the house and out the French doors on the south side.

"Shall we go to the stream and pick wildflowers? Would you enjoy that?" I asked, aware that I was drawn to the footbridge and its wild beauty. I had found myself making a daily trip there in the early evening before dinner.

Kitty stood back, declining to accompany me.

I walked alone in the soft air filled with the fragrance of drying vegetation. Wispy clouds sailed through the watery sky. I took the narrow path beside the creek, its calm surface belying the deep, rapid currents. Insects buzzed, and the weak afternoon sun warmed my back. When I stooped to run my fingers through the timothy, I noticed Kitty well behind but following along. I turned to the swift water pouring over mossy rocks and looked for small fish and damselflies in the shallows pooling along the bank. As I plucked blue cornflower and pink asters, I saw that Kitty also had made a small nosegay that she clutched in both hands.

After an hour of dawdling, I approached the footbridge. If Kitty followed still, she was hidden by the slim trees that gathered along the water's edge. I picked my way through the high grasses and across slippery stones, gripped the handrail, and inched to the center. I watched as the rushing water, sparkling in the pale sun, poured from its shaded depths. The roar of the swollen stream drowned out all other sounds of nature. It was the only place I felt completely free, perhaps like a wild animal might feel, with awareness but no identity.

I don't know how long I stood there, mesmerized. After what seemed a good bit of time, I came to and tore myself away. As I crested the high ground to the footpath, I saw Kitty almost lost in the shifting patterns of dappled sunlight glistening on dew-spangled clover.

"Come, Kitty," I said, although she declined to look my way. "We should be getting on home."

As I climbed the veranda steps, with Kitty trailing several paces away, I heard the guttural puttering of a motor car. In the distance, I saw it stop, and two colorful figures stepped from gleaming metal and disappeared into the stables.

I turned from the scene as Lavinia Wellington swept majestically through the double doors on the billowing fragrance of lilacs. She was handsome in lavender lace. Her ever-present rosary occupied her hands.

"Good day, Mrs. Wellington."

"They've stopped to see the horses," she said, staring in the direction of the barns. "Charlotte would want to see Delphic Oracle." As if answering a question she expected from me, she said, "The mare she always rides."

I turned to speak to Kitty, but she was gone.

My eyes shifted to the dazzling black automobile parked in the distance. As I imagined having the glorious freedom to travel anywhere at my whim, Thomas and Charlotte emerged from behind the outbuildings. They ambled up the tree-shaded path towards us. Moving through intermittent sunlight and shadow, Charlotte's red hair flashed like a warning beacon.

Mrs. Wellington, looking stiff and implacable, radiated tension. She took a deep breath as they grew near. As they emerged into the garden, I had a clear view of Charlotte.

A wild sunset of hair, untamed by combs or braids, framed a flawless face. I had never seen a more beautiful creature. She was as tall as Thomas, her figure willowy under a bare skim of bright blue silk. Her avant-garde dress with dropped waist, pleated hip band, and fluttering sleeves made me feel dowdy in my long heavy frock, my black hair constrained into a severe knot.

"Hello, my dear." Mrs. Wellington favored her niece with the lightest possible embrace. "I trust you had a good trip. It's such a long distance, London."

Thomas kissed his mother's cheek. "Hello, darling." He turned to me and deepened his voice dramatically. "Charlotte, this daunting figure is the new typewriter."

"Anne Chatham." I offered my hand and met her amber eyes, ignoring Thomas's suggestive smile. "I'm pleased to make your acquaintance."

From Charlotte's hand hung an old lace parasol, its Victorian primness in jarring contrast to her fashionable dress. It swung to and fro from her delicate fingers.

"I'm Charlotte Darwell. So you're a typewriter, Miss Chatham?" Her smile revealed perfect teeth.

I saw her take my measure. "Yes, Miss Darwell."

"How very daring of you. An independent working woman." She opened the parasol and held it aloft to frame her shining hair. "I'm envious."

"You needn't be. My work is a necessity."

She stepped into the shade and lowered the tip of the open umbrella to the floor of the veranda, the lace creating a web of shadow on the stone. "I commend you for being the model of a modern female."

Absorbed while Charlotte twirled the parasol between us, I said, "My situation is hardly praiseworthy." My mind slipped to the home I no longer had and the penurious life I looked forward to.

The parasol spun, its patterns blurring. I watched, spellbound.

"Of course it is. And you are the first self-supporting woman in my acquaintance." Charlotte smiled.

The parasol spun faster.

"Should you ever require my assistance, you need only ask," I told her.

"How kind of you to offer."

The whirling web of shadow was hypnotic, the delicate lace patterns dancing. For a moment, I felt dizzy and closed my eyes.

"Where is Owen, Aunt Lavinia?" Charlotte's voice echoed as if from an empty chamber far away. "Shall I have to hunt him down?"

I opened my eyes. Whatever spell had been woven was suddenly broken.

Mrs. Wellington, followed by Thomas and Charlotte, moved into the cool, dim interior of the house. I trailed behind, noting how Charlotte shimmered against Northfield's deep colors and dark polished wood, as if she glowed from within.

"It's wonderful to be here," Charlotte smiled, looking around. "It is so very good to see you, Aunt Lavinia."

"I'm sure Thomas will amuse you. But please excuse me, won't you, my dear?" Mrs. Wellington said, striking an exhausted pose. "I'm feeling quite unwell. Anne?" She motioned to me to accompany her, like a servant.

I was disconcerted at being ordered about in a way unrelated to my employment, but I submitted without protest.

We abandoned Thomas and Charlotte in the gloomy light of the parlor. Once in the corridor, Mrs. Wellington whispered a directive. "Please inform my husband that his son has arrived with Charlotte.

I have a terrific headache and will be unable to join the family for dinner."

After giving Mr. Wellington the message from his wife, I escaped to my room as well, hoping I wouldn't pay a price for witnessing family discord. Both Thomas and Owen had intimated that Charlotte was a force to be reckoned with. Now that I'd met her, I agreed that she would be a source of conflict.

High emotions were likely to motivate more than one inhabitant of Northfield House.

Chapter 7

Mrs. Wellington's attitude was in full sail, banners flying, so I needn't have worried about being privy to family squabbles. Not only did she decline to join us for dinner that Sunday, she rarely emerged from her room for the next several days. With Thomas and Charlotte in attendance, however, the evening conversation was once again lively, if not exactly cheerful.

Charlotte made a preliminary effort to include me, starting with "May I call you Anne?" She followed with a string of questions, barely giving me time to answer one before she asked another.

"How long have you been working?"

"What does your family think?"

"Do you eschew marriage?"

"Did you know, in America, authorities have ruled it legal for women to wear trousers anywhere?"

But soon enough, she dismissed me to attend to the adoration of the men. Mr. Wellington doted on her. Thomas was loquacious. And when Charlotte spoke to him, Owen's face took on an animation I'd not seen before, although he was no more talkative. Charlotte hopped from topic to topic, pulling us along like fish on a line.

Oddly, for the duration of Mrs. Wellington's absence, there was no sign of the inverted ghost that sometimes trembled in the shadows behind her. The only peculiarity in evidence was a pale violet aura that occasionally bathed Charlotte. When she laughed exuberantly or probed too forcefully, the color deepened and was flecked with black.

I felt awkward at the dinner table, unsettled by the thought I had no right to be there. Their family connection and childhood history made me feel even more the outsider. And I hadn't forgotten Owen's humiliating suggestion that I had set my sights on Thomas. Defenseless against their teasing humor and discomfiting questions, I kept still when not spoken to directly. A niggling little drop of dread dampened any pleasure I might have had in their company.

One evening, the talk turned to plans for the estate, the nature of which I didn't entirely grasp.

"Father, has Owen won your approval?" said Thomas. "Has he finally sold you on his version of Frankenstein's monster?"

Owen stared into his wineglass and said, "No. We haven't discussed it lately."

"Your brother has his own ideas about cultivation, Thomas. We differ, that's all. Let's not start a disagreeable discussion."

"It's just some harmless baby-brother teasing, Uncle Henry," Charlotte laughed. "Thomas doesn't mean it. Owen—you don't mind, do you?"

"Owen's the resident pacifist." Thomas grinned. "He doesn't mind anything."

This revelation surprised me. If Owen went off to war, why would Thomas call him a pacifist? After all, it was Thomas who stayed home with a deferment.

Owen looked as though he'd just awakened. "What's this talk of Thomas? There's no one in the room except you, dear Charlotte. I can't even think what else I might have on my mind." He smiled.

I suddenly realized he was quite handsome underneath that brooding glare, the planes of his face angular and sharp.

Charlotte rewarded Owen with a bright laugh, and the family wandered into a discussion of distant relatives. While they talked, Charlotte leaned into Thomas, her hands caressing his arm, her gaze darting across his face. I diverted my eyes, uncomfortable with the inappropriate display of affection. Owen also looked away, focusing his gaze on a crystal pitcher of water.

That night, I realized that Charlotte now ignored me because she deemed me no threat. But I suspected she was capable of great cruelty. I spent every evening on edge, fearing I might be made an object of derision, if not by her, then perhaps by Thomas.

Days later, Mrs. Wellington remained secluded. However, long-standing neighbors—Mr. and Mrs. Hansford from Melling—joined us for dinner on Friday evening. Dr. Termeer, who regularly came to check on Mr. Wellington's sister Martha, stayed for the meal as well. Earlier in the day, he'd also looked in on Mrs. Wellington and announced she had a malady of the sinus cavities and should take bed rest, along with tincture of laudanum. The evening was much more subdued, given the dignified personages in attendance. Thomas and Charlotte were on their best behavior, and Owen managed to be amicable. No one remarked on my silence.

After dinner, we filtered into the hall. I could now escape to my room, so I turned to take the hallway to the back stairs. As everyone else sauntered towards the parlor, I glanced over my shoulder, only to see Charlotte and Thomas linger behind. I saw him pull her into the shadow of a large palm, out of sight of the others.

She arched away from him. I heard Charlotte's throaty laugh as she said, "Don't!" and Thomas's humorous pleading as he grabbed at her.

"Forget the lip paint. Allow me to kiss you," he begged.

"You'll muss my hair," she giggled, deftly avoiding his embrace. "And Aunt Lavinia will take my head off!"

Just as Thomas put a hand on her body in a way no lady should allow, they disappeared—but not in the direction of the parlor where everyone else had gone.

A ripple of shock coursed through me. The darkened stairs I ascended felt suddenly like a tunnel that separated me from the world of light and laughter. Swallowing hard, I scurried to the privacy of my room, where I couldn't wait to unbutton my confining clothing.

I faced the possibility that I was a prude. I didn't want to be judgmental. Perhaps I made too much of Charlotte's behavior. I must remember that she was a cousin, even if a distant one. Many families were more physically affectionate than my own, and expectations of feminine deportment were changing. However, it underscored my loneliness, her belonging so thoroughly to this family, this social class, and this sensational age.

Later, after attempting to read for over an hour, my room felt as constricting as my clothing had earlier. I sought relief on the veranda, sitting atop the steps in the growing darkness. From my vantage point, I admired the garden, with its backdrop of splendid twilit sky. Pink hydrangea grew in profusion along the low walls. Phlox, aster, and purple dahlias crowded the walks. From this distance, the blossoms created an impressionist's palette of pastels. My daydream was interrupted when Mrs. Wellington and Thomas walked into my line of sight from a far corner of the garden.

I withdrew into the shadows as mother and son strolled arm in arm along the path. He stopped to pluck a late rose from the climber on the low stone wall; she accepted it and put her head on his shoulder. I felt like a voyeur and stole back to my room, their intimacy making me feel uneasy.

Chapter 8

*F*or the next few days, Charlotte disrupted everything. Her laughter wafted like chimes through Northfield's rooms. She squealed with pleasure at beating Thomas at cards and shrieked with mock anger when she lost at chess. Her cheerful, teasing manner was loosed upon the household and everyone—including the servants—was gayer because of it. Even Owen was cajoled out of his glowering moods in her company.

It seemed I was the only one wary of Charlotte's charms.

During the day, I found myself alone in the study, diligently working, while Mr. Wellington committed himself to entertaining Charlotte. He accompanied her into the village on shopping sprees and visits to neighbors. She went horseback riding with Thomas in the mornings and touring in his new motorcar in the afternoons. When I caught sight of the car, a black and silver blur, Charlotte was always in the passenger's seat, her loose, gleaming hair lashing in the wind.

Most of the time, Owen was nowhere to be seen except at dinner, and I imagined he was off somewhere sulking over his glamorous cousin's attentions to his brother. Mrs. Wellington kept to her room, and my only glimpse of her was the moment of affection with

Thomas in the garden. I began to wonder if we would see her at all during Charlotte's visit.

I envied Charlotte's carefree life. But, given my upbringing, I was ashamed of my feelings. I should be grateful for my gifts and my current position since I knew, as the orphaned daughter of a minister, I would always be on the wrong side of the haves and the have-nots. My circumstance required devotion of my time and effort in service to others. I accepted this, but my surrender did not soften the sting of loneliness.

I spent my free hours in the kitchen with Kitty or in my room, washing and mending my clothes. Otherwise, I went to the footbridge, as though drawn by some siren song. This spot had a strange grandeur, a mysterious solitude that invited lingering contemplation. Its rushing water and lush greenery drowned out thoughts of sadness and regret. It became my refuge.

In the study, I became accustomed to the seclusion, and there was much to occupy my time. I had a growing stack of typed pages to my credit. One morning, Mr. Wellington had left careful instructions, including a request that I proofread and retype the corrected materials on changing agrarian policies in Tudor and Stuart England. He'd indicated that he left them on his desktop, but I searched it in vain.

Not to be discouraged, I pulled open the center drawer where he stored pen nibs and paperclips. Not finding what he'd asked me to take care of, I peeked into the others. In the bottom drawer, I riffled through papers that looked private in nature and happened upon a small, framed portrait hidden in its deep recesses. I picked it up and stared.

At first, I believed it was Charlotte. I recognized her perfect oval face, wide-set eyes, generous mouth, and cloud of flowing tresses. On closer inspection, I realized the picture was old. The clothing and hairstyle were from the last century. And the photograph itself was a faded tintype. Perhaps it was her mother or another close relative. The initials engraved on the silver frame were *EG*.

Once again, I felt I'd intruded on the privacy of my employers. Disappointed in myself, I replaced the photograph and closed the drawer. Despite being unable to locate the papers he'd left for me, I continued working on materials related to the agrarian revolution during the Georgian period. If nothing else, the steady tap of the typewriter keys lulled me into a restful calm, and time passed quickly.

Mr. Wellington did not appear in the study that day. The family left the house early to gather at the home of nearby friends for dinner and an evening's entertainment. I ate a light meal with Cook, Mrs. Hadley, and Kitty in the kitchen. I eventually sat alone in my room, where I read a few pages of Coleridge and took comfort in having the quiet time to myself. Inevitably remembering soft summer evenings at home, I sorely missed the family I no longer had.

At that moment, I realized that I would be the last person to remember them, the only one left who could speak their names. A terrible ache filled my chest. I closed my eyes and forced myself to accept God's will, to remember that Heaven was our reward. I tamped down feelings I could not name, something akin to anger mixed with sadness and longing. I leaned my head against the spare desk and prayed for the time when this raw wound would leave behind an insensible scar.

By nightfall, I returned to my stalwart self, mended a pair of stockings, and laundered a blouse in the lavatory sink. After polishing my shoes, I washed up and brushed my hair. By a quarter after ten, I crawled into bed and fell into a deep sleep.

In the darkest part of night, I bolted upright, startled.

Had someone screamed?

Chapter 9

I **strained to hear,** barely breathing, certain I'd heard a shrill cry. I felt it was the outburst of someone in mental anguish, rather than physical pain.

Pulling on my dressing gown, I glanced through the windows. The gardens lay silent, and the still trees stood like sentinels in the dark. No movement, not even a breeze, disturbed the view. The scream had come from inside the house.

I crept into the corridor. At first, I saw nothing. No air stirred, nor did additional sounds reach my ears. I stood as motionless as the pattern in the wallpaper. Then I felt, rather than saw, a shadow fall— and then, at the end of the hallway, a tiny light flickered like a candle flame.

I was not alone.

Hesitating but a moment, I inched down the corridor towards the pale light. It had disappeared by the time I reached the back stairs, and I stood at the top, peering into the darkness below. There it was again, glowing in the hall leading to the front of the house. It pulled me forwards, almost against my will. My bare feet swept along the polished floors, then upon the deep carpet, until I stood before the formal staircase in the great hall. I turned in all directions, seeking the glimmering flame. Moonlight spilled through the windows on the landing, creating a path upwards to the long dark passageway leading into the depths of the house.

A faint orb bobbed against the shadowed ceiling on the second floor, encouraging me to mount the steps to where I'd never been before and had no purpose. Halfway up, the orb vanished. I shifted my gaze from corner to corner, searching. Reaching the top of the stairs, I paused, listening. I heard nothing. Tiptoeing forwards, I found myself before ornate double doors, pulled open to reveal a formal salon. Curiosity overcame my reluctance as I stepped into the center of the moonlit room.

It was as though I'd gone backwards in time. Gleaming leaded glass windows and mahogany furniture, dark and heavy, surrounded me. Rich color danced across the floral carpet as I took in fringed pillows, velvet draperies, and brocade upholsteries. Memories of my grandmother's parlor, where I helped her put out tea and ginger cookies, washed over me. Before I was enveloped in sadness, an aged voice whispered from the dark.

"We meet at last."

I whirled about, an unladylike squeal caught in my throat.

"You're the new typewriter." The voice was confident.

Half-hidden in the gloom, a thin, elderly woman leaned against a velvet settee. She was swathed from head to toe in heavy nightclothes, stiff lace about her throat.

"Forgive me." My voice quavered. "I didn't intend to intrude. I thought I heard someone cry out."

"Oh, these old houses and their ghosts." She dismissed my concern with a flutter of her fingers. "Since neither of us is able to sleep, perhaps you can spare an old woman a visit." She moved stiffly to take a seat and motioned to a chair across from her, on the other side of a small table, in front of the moonlit windows. "I am Martha Langtry."

Henry's widowed sister.

"Go ahead now," she said. "Sit."

I considered it a command and did as she asked. My eyes sorted the collection of shadow and light until I could make out her form. Her pale skin was like old stone, her hair like ancient lace. If the spirit also sat with us, I was unaware of it.

"They're right," she said. "You're a pretty little thing."

I was suddenly aware of my disheveled appearance—my loose hair, unshod feet, and threadbare shift. "I am Anne Chatham and, as you say, the typewriter."

For a moment, I wondered what she could possibly know about me, but of course, Dolly and Maddy saw her daily. In my experience, elderly invalids kept up with gossip through the servants. Apparently, the situation was no different at Northfield.

She chuckled. "I'll bet the boys are taken with you. Maybe not Thomas, now that Charlotte is here, but Owen."

I considered defending myself, but decided not to take offense. The old woman likely had little else to do than wonder about romantic liaisons. Dolly probably speculated freely with her mistress regarding the various goings-on in the house. Martha Langtry probably knew my entire short history at Northfield.

She had a book in her hand. "Have you read Freud, Miss Chatham?"

"Freud? The Austrian neurologist? No, indeed, I have not, Mrs. Langtry."

"You should." Her smile was inviting, her manner gracious. We might have been having tea in the kitchen. "It's very enlightening. He reads minds, you know."

I wondered if she was serious or if it was a metaphor. "I don't understand."

"If you could read minds, you'd understand the sexual dynamics of this troubled household."

I was shocked by her casual reference to the personal lives of the family and how easily she took me into her confidence. Maybe she was not really aware of who I was. My grandmother, in failing health at the end of her life, had behaved oddly and shed her inhibitions.

Sadly, Mrs. Langtry appeared as though she might suffer similar indignities. Perhaps she, like Grandmama, would eventually wear her bedroom slippers to church and embrace the gardener as he trimmed the roses.

"And trouble besets Lavinia and Thomas especially," she went on. "Oedipus complex."

I shook my head. "I am familiar with the Greek tragedy, but I'm afraid I don't understand the reference."

"A pattern of behavior in which a boy loves his mother in an unnatural way, precisely Sophocles's theme." She nodded knowingly, offering an impish grin.

The image of Mrs. Wellington and Thomas in the garden sprang to mind. A doting mother, a loving son—surely this was not so unnatural? Not in my experience, but perhaps Mr. Freud thought so.

"They appear to be close," I said. Unsettled, I wanted to make my excuses and return to my room.

"It's more than it seems, mark my word. A tangled web of deceit eludes us, an evil spider's web." Her rheumy eyes suddenly glittered with malice, her fingers curled like claws. "And then there's Charlotte."

I could imagine Charlotte as either the spider or the prey. "Sometimes," I said, thinking of Mrs. Wellington's attitude towards her grandniece, "it's easier to love family members than to like them."

The old woman's face creased with a venomous smile. "This goes deeper."

My scalp prickled as a chill wound about my ankles. For a moment, the shrouded, shrunken old woman took on the aspect of a gremlin. Martha Langtry leaned forwards out of the shadows. Moonlight reflected off her piercing eyes, giving me the distinct impression she'd been waiting a long time for the opportunity to share these revelations.

"Charlotte, the grandchild of Lavinia's oldest sister, is the very image of Eleanor Granville," she said.

"I'm sorry, Mrs. Langtry, but who is Eleanor?"

"Have you not heard about her?" The old woman's expression softened, and in the darkness, I could see the beautiful woman that she must have been.

I shook my head. "No one has mentioned her."

"Lavinia had two sisters. Eudora is the eldest—and grandmother to Charlotte. Eleanor was Lavinia's younger sister."

I thought of my own sister with sadness. "Was? Am I to understand that Eleanor has passed?"

Mrs. Langtry ignored my question. "It's ancient family history by now, of course. It's been thirty years. But still very much alive in Lavinia's mind, I can guarantee. Because she was the second choice, the second wife, second to Eleanor." Her cruel eyes narrowed with glee. The graceful woman I'd glimpsed for a second disappeared.

"Mr. Wellington married Mrs. Wellington's sister?" The words fell out of my mouth before I could stop myself. My own forwardness shocked me. I was taken aback, wondering why Mrs. Langtry would share such intimacies with a stranger.

"Yes, indeed he did."

I remained silent, remembering the old photograph in Mr. Wellington's desk, initialed *EG*.

Eleanor Granville. Perhaps to reveal this was the reason the spirit guided me here.

Martha Langtry prattled on. "My little brother Henry was the most eligible bachelor in these parts at the time. The heir to Northfield House, rich, handsome. The best family." She preened, offering this opinion without humility. "And he adored the ladies, enjoyed flirting, toying with affections, as you modern girls would say today."

I had difficulty seeing wheelchair-bound Henry Wellington, with his balding head and gray pallor, as a dashing young rake. But in his youth, before succumbing to age and infirmity, he must have been the very image of Thomas.

Martha continued, "Both Eleanor and Lavinia vied for his attentions. As the older sister, Lavinia assumed she would receive the proposal. But my headstrong brother was never one to do what was expected, to conform to what the family would consider the right and proper thing. Lavinia may have been the obvious choice, but Eleanor captured his heart."

The smile that lit Martha's face reflected a fond memory. It faded to a cunning grin when she added, "Lavinia was livid when Henry finally asked her father for Eleanor's hand—her *younger* sister's hand. She tried to hide her fury, but everybody knew."

I should have remained silent and not encouraged the disclosure of family secrets, but overwhelmed with sadness for Lavinia, I couldn't help but respond. "And Henry married Eleanor?" That had to have been deeply humiliating for Mrs. Wellington.

"Yes. Mother and Father got over their shock and, of course, conceded to Henry's wishes in the matter of love. After all, one Granville girl was as good as another. Lavinia just had to swallow the disgrace." Martha then got a wistful, far-off look upon her face. "The wedding of the century, they called it. Eleanor's parents invited three hundred guests, weighted an altar with the sacrifice of fields of flowers, had the church bells pealing throughout the county." She turned wistful, sinking into the past. "She carried my childhood Bible and Lavinia's blue rosary."

Something old, something new, something borrowed, something blue . . .

As Mrs. Langtry contemplated the consequences of tragic young love, her eyes filled with tears. I barely breathed, wondering what had gone wrong. Something must have happened to Eleanor.

"The wedding breakfast and ceremony were at the bride's home, but the reception was here at Northfield. Champagne flowed, music and laughter floated on the soft spring air. This house was glorious in those days." She sighed and then struck a coquettish pose.

Through Martha Langtry's eyes, I saw the sparkling glamour of a Naughty Nineties wedding, the splendor displayed by the Wellington family, no expense spared for their firstborn son. I imagined the wedding party, drunk with happiness, delirious with spirits and rich food, frenetic with feverish energy, frolicking into the night.

"In those days, I was a married woman with children. My husband and I left the merrymaking by midnight and retired to my former bedroom in the family wing. The last time I saw Eleanor and Henry together, they were waltzing by candlelight."

The last time. For a moment, I was unnerved by the scent of decaying flowers wafting on the stale air.

"The next morning, I was awakened along with everyone else by a frantic Henry. Eleanor had disappeared. Vanished."

Vanished? Surprise jolted through me. "How could that be? In a house full of people?"

"I asked the same question. The wedding party had been up all night, drinking, eating, laughing as they played the games of childhood. Blindman's buff, tag, hide-and-seek, I spy." Her voice took on a quality of reverence, like a poet reciting favorite lines. "It was during the games that Eleanor went missing."

"Poor Mr. Wellington." I felt a sinking sensation in my chest.

"Henry was distraught. His beautiful bride was gone. Her absence, by that time, had gone beyond a practical joke or a fit of pique if she'd had her feelings hurt." Martha frowned, shaking her head as though she still struggled with the reality. "He and I roused all the guests at Northfield, and they joined in the search. We combed through the house, the gardens, and the fields."

In my mind's eye, I saw the rumpled wedding party and hastily dressed guests swarming the countryside like bees.

"I was up for days. We found nothing. After forty-eight hours, even the still waters beyond the footbridge were dredged."

I shivered. "Has no one seen or heard from her since?"

"Not I, nor anyone in the family ever heard from—or of— Eleanor again. No one knows what happened. Except Eleanor. Or her abductor. Or, I have always suspected, her lover." Her tearful voice faltered.

I tried to reconcile this startling theory with the rest of the story. "I'm sure I don't understand, Mrs. Langtry."

"It could have happened." She eagerly promoted her more optimistic premise. "There was another suitor before Henry. It might have been serious, but Henry was the real catch. Eleanor was so proud of the proposal, of being chosen by the richest, handsomest man. And I always believed the competition with Lavinia was the thing that most recommended Henry. The chance to best her older sister."

Finding it difficult to believe that Eleanor Granville had abandoned her husband for someone else on her wedding day, I was puzzled by Mrs. Langtry's astounding conjecture.

Martha's eyes softened. "Perhaps I am wrong. I could see those two were in love, Eleanor and Henry. But what else could have happened?"

I envisioned Eleanor, in a cloud of bridal white, disintegrating into a mist of timeless memory. I leaned over and touched Martha's hand.

She blinked and shook her head. "Henry and the Granvilles searched everywhere, interviewed family and friends time and again, placed advertisements, and eventually hired detectives. They could think of nothing other than she'd been taken against her will. It was the only thing they could accept."

"And no one could provide insight? Not even her former suitor?" I dared to ask.

"Jonathan Cavanaugh? He professed no knowledge of the disappearance and was engaged to another by the time Eleanor vanished. He was unimpeachable."

I sat quietly, not knowing what to say.

"There was not one shred of evidence of treachery. At least, nothing was ever found." Mrs. Langtry stared into the distance, her watery eyes focusing on events of long ago. "Henry gave up his inquiries after two years—although her parents searched until they died—and after a respectable interval, he married Lavinia."

I had a new understanding of Mrs. Wellington's hauteur. Becoming the mistress of Northfield House must have been a bitter success for her. She had attained her heart's desire, but only after her sister lost or rejected it. This knowledge must have haunted her.

"Henry believed he owed something to the Granvilles. Lavinia knew the marriage was more an obligation than a desire to possess her."

This put a harsh face on the conclusion to such a sad tale. Mrs. Wellington would not appreciate the pity I felt at that moment. "But surely Mr. Wellington grew to love her?" Perhaps I was being romantic, but I wanted to believe that Henry Wellington had felt something more than duty when he proposed to Lavinia Granville.

"I doubt love was ever Lavinia's purpose, but she's managed to make a life," said Martha, staring at her shriveled hands, folded upon the book by Freud in her lap. "Does it not occur to you that Lavinia has recreated the adoration that should have been hers, and that she wanted desperately from Henry, in her son, Thomas?"

This seemed to me an unfortunate, even unhealthy, outcome.

Martha turned her shrewd gaze on me. "And now," she said, "Charlotte, who looks like Eleanor returned from long ago, still young and fresh, appears to have captured Thomas's heart. It must rankle Lavinia."

If what Martha Langtry said was true, then I imagined Mrs. Wellington would be appalled that someone threatened to displace her once again. "How difficult that must be for her," I said. "The lamentable past repeating itself."

I looked about the gloomy room, which held the past, present, and future of Martha Langtry. The scene evoked another age, as though my companion were mired in time. Old photographs lined up on a table like ghosts, capturing memories in shades of gray. Velvet-draped Victorian tables sat atop an ancient Axminster Rose carpet. Martha Langtry's lace cap and shawl must have dated from her youth. I wondered if she ever stepped out of the house—or out of her past.

"You've been kind to suffer my intrusion, Mrs. Langtry," I said.

She sat in utter stillness. After a moment, she blinked and started. "What, dear?"

"I apologize for having disturbed you." I stood.

"No problem at all, my dear. It's nice to see young folks, especially someone Owen's taken a fancy to." She frowned. "Now don't let him take liberties," she said, her voice stern. "Men don't respect girls who let them do as they please."

I was unsettled by her assumptions but let it pass. She obviously thought I was someone else. Her mind had taken her to another time, another place.

"Good night, Mrs. Langtry," I said as I stole away.

On the retreat to my bed, I hesitated outside the study before stepping in. I pulled the heavy drape aside to allow the weak light of dawn to brighten the room. Opening the bottom drawer once again, my hand found the tintype.

I stared at the beautiful face. *Eleanor, is it you who haunts Northfield House?*

Chapter 10

By the end of the week, Mrs. Wellington joined us for dinner once again. Perhaps she'd decided her absence accomplished nothing more than delivering her son into the arms of the red-headed enchantress. Whatever her reason, she reappeared at the head of the table.

Charlotte and Thomas were subdued in her company. Owen was as enigmatic as ever, it seemed, finding everything disagreeable. I felt a pang of sympathy seeing Mrs. Wellington, having just learned of her heartrending past. Now I understood her habit of wearing gray or lavender—the colors of mourning—and the constant presence of the blue rosary, its crucifix a symbol of torture and pain. In her own way, she continued to remember her sister. One might think she was doing penance, haunted by the past.

"Are you feeling better, Mother?" Thomas asked.

"Yes. Much better."

"We missed you, Aunt Lavinia." Charlotte lowered her eyes as she uttered this untruth, unable to banish the sly smile upon her lips. "This big old house is just a bore when you're not around."

Mrs. Wellington said, "No doubt you were able to amuse yourself, my dear."

"So, you've decided to join us, Lavinia," said Henry as he wheeled in. "Will the meal sit well with you? It may be a bit heavy for the weather."

"Thank you, Henry, I'll be just fine." Her tone suggested annoyance.

Owen maintained his silence, as did I. He cast a glance at me, his eyes darting away the moment they met mine. I hoped he'd forgotten our encounter in the library, where he practically accused me of setting my cap for Thomas. The memory still caused me a sting of humiliation every time I thought of it, not to mention the unfortunate impropriety of our bare feet and my loose hair.

Tonight, Charlotte's beautiful hair was dressed in Grecian-style ringlets that trailed down her bare back. Her slip of a dress was deep emerald, and a diamond necklace lay against her bare throat. She glittered like candles on a Christmas tree, while the rest of us were unadorned and clad in dark, earthy tones.

"You've been shopping, my dear," said Henry, openly admiring Charlotte's attire.

Suddenly, all eyes were on the stunning girl in silk and satin. "I didn't pack much to bring with me, Uncle Henry," she said. "Cousin Thomas just swooped down and carried me away."

Thomas grinned. "I am Apollo to your Daphne, dear Charlotte." His eyes danced with mischief.

Mrs. Wellington cleared her throat and said, "I understand you've also spent some time at the stables."

I suppressed a smile. *Touché, Mrs. Wellington.* Horse flesh was young womanhood's foremost challenger for male attention.

"How did you find Delphic Oracle, Charlotte?" she asked.

"Still spirited despite her advanced age," Charlotte said.

Mrs. Wellington bristled visibly at the shot over her bow, taking it as an affront. "Age has its compensations, my dear. You might remember all our young horses were conscripted for the war effort."

"And not one survived," Thomas said with more good humor than seemed warranted. "It appears our thoroughbreds were no match for German artillery."

In an effort to reduce the tension, I asked, "Weren't the horses used for logistical support? Transport of provisions, that sort of thing?" I had assumed horses stayed behind the battle lines.

Owen broke his silence. "Indeed, they were better in deep mud and over rough terrain than wheels. But as horses were no defense against cannon fire and mustard gas, we quickly abandoned mounted cavalry, except in the Middle East. There our adversaries were less technologically advanced."

I imagined Arabs in long robes, throwing stones. "How many animals did you contribute to the cause?"

Thomas answered, "Twelve. All except for my mare, Catspaw, who was foaling at the time. And Delphic Oracle. She'd gotten a bit long in the tooth, lucky duck. During the war, hundreds of thousands of animals died of disease and starvation. Even when they were well behind the front lines. Poor brutes." His smile never dimmed.

Owen gave Thomas a surprised look and said, "Losing a horse was a greater tactical concern than the loss of a soldier."

"Only a bloody pacifist would care about that little detail," said Thomas.

"Give the valiant beasts their due," Owen said. "Germany was defeated in part because they couldn't replace their lost horses."

Perhaps bored with the turn the conversation had taken, Charlotte brought it back to herself. "Delphie is the same old dear, still agile and responsive. Thomas and I raced to the village, and I won."

Mrs. Wellington's countenance darkened. She turned her face to her oldest son. "It's because my son is a gentleman, Charlotte." She smiled. "Of course he would let you win. You are not only his cousin, but a guest in our home. He would do everything necessary to ensure the success of your visit."

Charlotte, for once, looked chastened by the rebuke.

In the silence that followed, I assessed my companions. Thomas was well aware of the undercurrents between his mother and Charlotte. He took pleasure in his mother's dismay and Charlotte's goading. He looked polished and self-satisfied, wearing a jacket with the latest cut, a sharp contrast to Owen's haphazard attire.

Mrs. Wellington's frock captured the grace and elegance of a time that had come and gone, with its handmade lace and stiff whalebone stays. I suddenly had a glimpse of a more prosperous Northfield House before the war: young girls in their large hats and corseted gowns, stables full of sleek mounts, the house chaperoned by white-gloved servants.

Now everything had changed. Charlotte and Thomas seemed to have inherited the future, with its promise of automobiles, aeroplanes, and jazz bands. The rest of us embodied the past: Owen with his passion for the croplands, Mr. Wellington with his outmoded ideas of farm management, and his wife and I with our heavy skirts and confined bodies.

Thomas stepped into the pause in conversation. "Mother, shouldn't we plan an entertainment while Charlotte's visiting?" He grinned. "We've been all over the county seeing old friends. We should have people here."

Charlotte arched an eyebrow, suppressing laughter.

Henry spoke before his wife could reply. "Splendid idea for you young people. It'll be good to hear some silly chatter around here for a change." He looked at Owen sourly. "Get your mind off agriculture and on cultivating a yen for a girl."

"Sounds better than plowing fields, Owen," Thomas said.

Charlotte giggled at Thomas's suggestive words. I felt my face heat and glanced at Mrs. Wellington, who wore a grim expression.

"If a party's what you want, Thomas, just address Mrs. Hadley. She need only clear the date with me," she said.

I felt certain, had Mr. Wellington not spoken so quickly in support of a party in Charlotte's honor, his wife would have discouraged it.

"Thank you, Aunt Lavinia," said Charlotte. "It's very kind of you."

"I know!" Thomas said, excitement in his voice, "Let's have a masquerade ball!"

Charlotte almost squealed with joy. "Oh, let's do! What fun!"

I saw no corresponding enthusiasm among the others and kept my head down.

"Whatever you wish." Mrs. Wellington looked bored.

"Odd to wear a mask in my own home," mumbled Mr. Wellington.

"Don't worry, Uncle Henry. If you wear a costume, a mask isn't necessary," Charlotte reassured him.

"You mean I won't be recognized if I'm wearing outlandish clothing?"

Charlotte laughed. "A costume is intended to bring out a different side of your personality, a hidden part of yourself. Disguise isn't really the point." She turned to me, "Is it, Anne?"

I was caught off guard. "I . . . I'm not sure." I swallowed hard. "I've never attended a costume ball."

"Never?" Charlotte gasped.

Her disbelief annoyed me. She must realize someone of my background wouldn't have had such an experience. "Of course not. I was reared in a parsonage."

"Well, then, you *must* come," she said, with exaggerated camaraderie.

"Surely, I cannot."

"Oh, Thomas, Uncle Henry, make her come!"

I could not imagine that Charlotte's plea had any other purpose than to humiliate me. I wasn't a member of the family. I was an employee, and without the resources to obtain a costume.

"You are thoughtful, but I must decline." I said.

Thomas flashed a smile at me. "Come on, Anne. Things have changed. It's a new world, and a young woman may cross the boundaries of the past. Nothing prevents you from attending a ball anywhere you're invited."

His egalitarianism surprised me. "That is very gracious of you. But it's not appropriate. And I don't have a costume."

"I can lend you one." Charlotte beamed. "I have a wonderful outfit from last year, which I've not worn here. Dolly can take it in or let it out. I'm taller, but we look to be the same size."

"That's kind, but—"

"It won't be any fun at all if you don't come," Charlotte persisted, her hands clasped in prayerful pleading. "If we have to think of you reading a book or darning a sock in your stuffy old room, we'll have a dreary time." She shook her curls and frowned. "Do come! I insist."

Owen interrupted. "Oh, hash it all. Anne, if you go, I'll go."

The table fell silent.

I couldn't have been more surprised. I looked from Owen, to Thomas, then to Charlotte as they awaited my response. "Since you put it that way, I guess it would be churlish of me not to accept." The moment the words passed my lips, my heart sank.

Charlotte and Thomas cheered at their success as the conversation moved to themes for the party and whom else to invite. As soon as possible, I excused myself from the table and practically ran to the veranda for a breath of air. The evening light was soft as the sun smeared its brilliance across the western sky. I leaned against the banister. Trying to walk the tightrope of my existence was exhausting. I was neither fish nor fowl, neither a family member nor a servant.

The footbridge beckoned. I found myself sweeping down the dirt path towards the stream, the water glistening in the pale light. I stepped lightly on the slick boards, holding carefully to the handrail. I relaxed and let the rushing water soothe my nerves. I heard grasses rustling on the bank behind me, then footsteps, and saw a shadow move. Much to my surprise, Owen was almost at once standing at my side.

For a moment, we watched the water pour over the rocks below in silence.

"I sincerely regret getting us caught up in that," he said at last.

Owen probably hated the idea of a costume ball more than I did. "Whatever were you thinking?"

"That I'd have to go, and you should suffer through it as well." He smiled.

"Thank you, sir, for thinking of me," I said in a facetious tone.

"Glad to be of help, Miss." He tipped an imaginary hat. "I suppose you're aware that Charlotte only wants to ensure that you see her in her own elegant costume."

"And assumes I'll make a poor comparison beside her exquisite beauty." I sighed. "I guessed as much."

He chuckled and said, "You come out here often?"

"When I want to think. Is this still Wellington property?"

"Yes. All the land on either side of the ravine is ours. The fields beyond here," he pointed to the right, "are the ones I do my work in. The barn you see above the trees is where I spend most of my time. There's a greenhouse beyond."

"What is it you do there, Mr. Wellington?"

"Owen. Please." He seemed to relax for the first time since we'd met. "I'm developing new cultivars of grain to resist drought and disease."

I was surprised to learn his work was botanical in nature. "You cross-pollinate varieties of grain?"

He nodded. "I'm now crossing several strains." He looked perturbed. "If only Father would understand what it could mean to Northfield."

So this was the work about which they disagreed. "I see. Now I understand Thomas's reference to Frankenstein's monster."

"My father sees these experiments as interference with nature. Or maybe he doesn't see it as part of God's plan. He's reluctant to abandon the old ways. It's unfortunate, because we need to expand yield to survive."

I was reminded of my earlier conversation with Mr. Wellington, and his belief that plowing coast to coast and controlling nature was acceptable. Apparently, Owen's work fell outside what was considered proper. "So your work is an attempt to preserve Northfield?"

"Yes, but I see it as more than that. My ultimate purpose is to address hunger. The Great War has exposed so many shortages."

He has not only a scientific mind but a social conscience, I thought, suddenly warming to him. "I understand that you went to war?"

Even in the darkness, I could tell he was discomfited.

"I tried to do my bit, bloody good that did."

"It is odd, is it not, that Thomas refers to you as a pacifist?"

"It's because I refused to carry a gun. I volunteered for the Royal Army Medical Corps."

Ah, a conscientious objector. How strange that Thomas would deride him, since he himself had not served at all.

"You have medical training?"

"No more than a competent nurse. I oversaw food and other provisions for the field hospital, something which was more in my line."

"Does Thomas share your passion for crop science?"

"Thomas is not at all interested in farming. The estate will be his, however, so he's happy for me to make whatever advancements I can."

Owen sounded bitter. I felt uncomfortable treading on intimate family concerns and sought another subject. "Can you reach your greenhouse by way of this footbridge?"

"Yes, see the path cleaved into the stone on the far bank? That's one way to get there." He looked at the jagged rocks and roiling water beneath, clutching the dangerously low handrail. Then he pointed behind us. "Back upstream, there's a branch of the road that crosses the creek. Takes longer, but it's far less treacherous. Would you like to see the greenhouse sometime?"

I hope he doesn't think I've invited myself for a visit. I've gone too far. "Of course," I replied coolly. "Sometime."

His posture stiffened, and he fell silent. After a moment, he released the railing and stepped away. "It wouldn't be very interesting to a city girl with professional aspirations, I'm afraid," he said. "Good evening, Miss Chatham." He left as quickly as he'd come, fading into the darkness.

I hadn't meant to offend him, but I had been worried about appearing too presumptuous. I stifled the urge to call after his retreating figure. Instead, I closed my eyes and listened to the falling water.

Chapter 11

O
h, Miss Anne, a fancy-dress ball!" cried Dolly the next morning, as soon as I sat down to breakfast at the kitchen table.

"You won't be near so excited once you find how much more work it is," said Mrs. Hadley. After thinking a moment, she smiled. "It'll be lovely, though. Like the old times, before the Great War."

"Surely it will be the event of the season," Dolly said. "All the best people will come, and it'll be talked of across the whole county."

Mrs. Hadley flashed me a knowing look and said, "Now, Dolly. It's just a party. King George himself isn't coming."

"I didn't say he was," Dolly said, miffed. "But society folk will be here."

Cook placed bread, butter, and jam before me, along with a cup of tea. Mrs. Hadley sat and poured another cup for herself.

"What can I do to help, Mrs. Hadley?" I asked.

"Nothing at all, Anne. You're a professional young woman, not a servant."

I heard an echo of Thomas's words from the night before. I felt once more the distinct sense of living between two worlds, not a comfortable inhabitant of either. "I'm a typewriter. I could do the invitations, perhaps?"

"Engraved, them'll be," said Cook. "They'll do 'er up right, mind you."

"Mr. Henry gave us leave to have additional hands from the village." Mrs. Hadley sipped her tea. "I'll need girls to ready the ballroom. Cook will have help in the scullery."

"Glad I am of that." Cook nodded, her face red from pulling bread from the hot oven.

"Perhaps we can have the cakes brought from that new bakery in town. The one on Oxley Square?" Mrs. Hadley said.

"Nothing like it in my kitchen," Cook said. "As long as I'm responsible, I'll be doin' the bakin'."

The staff already knew the date, not quite a month hence, and had plans for the menu and decorations. Mrs. Hadley and Cook, being old hands of Northfield, were familiar with the requirements.

"It'll take all that time to manage the preparations. We don't have the help that we once did," Mrs. Hadley said. "You should've seen us before the war, Anne. Footmen, a butler, and maids on every floor. We had the greenhouse thriving, and we decorated with our own flowers. Tables laden with meats, cakes, candies, all made in our own kitchen." She looked wistful.

I envisioned creamy freesia and stephanotis, pink roses, and even exotic orchids. I could almost taste the sugar plums and *crème glacée*, and hear the music of violins fill the air. "That must have been lovely."

"Yes, it certainly was." Mrs. Hadley gazed out the window. "I wonder if there are enough young men left to mount a proper party."

I thought of the young men no longer available for parties, service, or business—not to mention marriage. It was only because of the war that women like me found work, and only because of the war that we needed to. A lump rose in my throat.

"I should get upstairs. Thank you for breakfast, Cook." I patted Kitty on the head as she sat on the hearth peeking into the small box she carried with her always. She gave me a distant look, as though she were elsewhere. Perhaps she was. None of us knew what transpired in the mind of that child.

❧

After lunch, Charlotte and Thomas left us to visit her parents in London. They sped out of Northfield in the gleaming touring car, both wrapped in dusters and wearing goggles. The rutted roads would take them only so far, and they'd have to board the train at Birmingham for the rest of the journey.

Charlotte and Thomas planned to return on the morning of the ball. I imagined that, in the meantime, Charlotte would be preparing the most exquisite costume ever to grace a party at Northfield House. She might choose to be a regal queen in gold velvet, or Scheherazade dripping in gemstone-colored silks, or Ophelia in pristine white. Almost anything I could dream was possible for Charlotte, a girl with such a confident and ambitious nature.

With Charlotte gone, the entire house was not just quiet, but still. I spent the rest of the day in the study with Mr. Wellington. His book was nearing completion, and we were already mapping out plans for the next one. My duties had expanded to include research and retrieval at local archives and libraries, and I was developing a certain confidence of my own with regard to ferreting out obscure information and drawing reasonable conclusions.

"Does Owen ever help you with your scholarship, sir?" I ventured to ask. "You appear to have common interests." Ever since the night on the footbridge, Owen seemed to be exiting any room I stepped into. I hoped it was happenstance and not intention. I had the sinking sensation that the sight of me was now an embarrassment to him.

"Owen is not interested in historical or current agrarian practices, more's the pity. He's got newfangled notions about farming methods."

"You disagree with his ideas?"

"Some are acceptable. His concepts about conservation and cultivation seem appropriate to our way of life."

"And other ideas are not?" I asked.

"He crosses different types of seed, experiments with newly developed varieties. I cannot believe God intended man to fool with his creation," Mr. Wellington said.

"Don't natural pollinators, insects and birds, do the same?"

"Then we should leave them to it," he said with a scowl, ending the conversation.

Chapter 12

Over the next week, the dinner hour was strained with desultory conversation since Thomas and Charlotte had gone. Owen withdrew into his taciturn self, declining to participate in banal exchanges. I, however, grew a bit bolder at the table.

One evening, Mr. Wellington and I carried our discourse on Britain's agrarian revolution from the study into the dining room. He had actually begun to seek my opinion.

"There were many important changes benefiting our country, my dear," Mr. Wellington said, taking his seat. "The introduction of farm machinery, like the wheeled seed drill which mechanized the tedious work of scattering seeds, was one of them. And the horse hoe, used to eradicate weeds between rows of crops, made an enormous difference."

I placed my napkin in my lap and voiced my position as delicately as possible. "But these innovations created real hardships for peasant farmers. Poor farm laborers were rendered redundant. Most lost their land and their livelihood."

"But you support progress, don't you? Surely you accept the replacement of wooden tools by iron ones, which are so much more efficient."

"Of course I do." I avoided pointing out that only the wealthy benefited from these efficiencies. "I'm only saying our government passed new laws regarding enclosure without regard for the devastating impact on broad swaths of the poor. That should have been foreseen. They could have prepared the dispossessed with education and training."

"Surely that was unnecessary. The poor moved on to urban areas to find work. The factories were both schoolroom and training ground."

"That I know very well." I had watched children trudging to the textile mills and canning plants in the early dawn, their clothes merely blackened rags. I had seen young girls begging on street corners in the dusk. "But these people lost homes, families, communities, and sometimes even their health."

"But they gained new opportunities," said Mr. Wellington, sipping wine from a crystal goblet.

Owen cleared his throat, the first sound he'd made in two days. "As a minister's daughter from Liverpool, Anne has firsthand experience of the dispossessed migrating to industrialized cities. She witnessed the breakdown of the social structure. We denizens of Northfield House were spared that awareness, Father."

Mr. Wellington scowled.

I gave Owen a grateful smile. He looked away.

"Enough of this talk about things over which we have no control," Mrs. Wellington said. "We have problems enough here at home with the price of tea and inadequate staffing." She shot a disapproving glance at Maddy's retreating form. "And no goods are handmade any longer. Those awful machines will soon take over everything. Have you seen the lace they produce? I won't wear it."

I fell silent, biting my tongue. I hoped for additional support from Owen, who was clearly in sympathy with me regarding the perils of economic disruption, but he returned to his quiet, distracted state.

After dinner, I passed the grand staircase on the way to my room and was startled to see Martha Langtry standing at the top. She was barely a shadow in the lamplight.

"There you are!" she said, her voice lilting. "You've come at last."

Her greeting was so familiar I almost looked over my shoulder to determine if perhaps she addressed someone else. But we were alone. "Hello, Mrs. Langtry. It's good to see you again."

She came halfway down the steps and motioned for me to come closer. I mounted the stairs and she embraced me, tears filling her eyes.

"Why, Eleanor," she said. "Where've you been?"

"What?"

"It's been such a long time."

"Mrs. Langtry. It's Anne Chatham."

"I'd know you anywhere, even after all these years," she said. "Now, tell me. Whatever happened to you?"

Senility. I recalled once more the ravages of this condition on my grandmother. Her mental confusion and lost dignity still weighed upon my heart, especially given the many other losses that followed. I tried to dispel the sadness that threatened to grip me.

I put my arm around Mrs. Langtry and led her to the room where we'd first met. She sat with exaggerated caution on the velvet settee. I settled next to her, near the faded photographs.

Now I looked more closely at them and saw images of her younger self, her children, and a distinguished gentleman, presumably her husband. And there was one of Eleanor, sitting with the picturesque footbridge in the background, peering into the camera. It startled me, that Mrs. Langtry so valued a candid print of a distant in-law, one gone so long and yet kept close in memory. They must have been friends. That, perhaps, explained the wistful longing she revealed the night we met. And the pointed dislike aimed at Mrs. Wellington. Perhaps it was also the reason Martha existed on the periphery of Lavinia Wellington's home. There was a wariness there, I then realized, between Martha and Mrs. Wellington. I wondered if Mrs. Langtry was another uncomfortable reminder of the false start that Mr. Wellington made with Eleanor as his wife.

I picked up the picture and stared. It didn't seem possible that the exquisite face hid a merciless, cruel heart. She didn't appear capable of abandoning her groom and her whole family, never to return. Any answers to that enduring mystery seemed sadly out of reach. I leaned towards Martha and took her gnarled hand.

Silvery moonlight pooled on the carpet, and Martha Langtry waded into her youth. "Have you seen Papa's Portland Damask roses?" she asked. "The red ones? They're my favorite, but Mother decorated the house all summer with Blanc de Vibert. The Damasks are so fragrant, you'll love them." She squeezed my fingers.

"I'm sure I will," I said, feeling like an imposter.

"When are you coming to Lancashire, Eleanor? You must see the garden before autumn. Everything will be gone if you delay." She stared into a vacant corner. "We can make ice cream for the children. They've gotten so big you won't recognize them."

My heart ached for the elderly woman. Surely, there would be no harm in allowing her to believe me to be Eleanor for a few moments. "Yes, I'm sure. How old are the children now?"

Martha ignored the question. "Did you know Jonathan Cavanaugh married Jane Barrett? They took their time," she said with an edge of scorn. "I imagine he was waiting for you, dear, hoping you'd change your mind and return. He never did get over losing you to Henry. Everyone's talking."

"Are they, Martha?"

"You, my dear, are the object of much speculation." She smiled like a child, whispering behind her hand. "The gossip and wagging tongues, you wouldn't believe how they chatter. They mean to be cruel, but they're actually jealous. You've gone off on a grand adventure. You're free from all these irksome rules. I like to think you made it to America, to the Wild West."

I envisioned Eleanor, a proper Victorian beauty just entering womanhood, bouncing along with a wagon train towards the red rocks of Utah. A sudden wave of grief gripped me—I felt, in my heart, no such hope for the missing girl.

"Your life has been exciting, while the rest of us languish in 'lives of quiet desperation.' You read Thoreau, don't you Eleanor, in America?"

"I guess everyone in America knows Thoreau."

"I always wonder if you're wearing a fringed deerskin like an Indian squaw or a calico bonnet like a pioneer woman."

The idea that Eleanor might have shed her old-world limitations and embraced freedom in the form of a practical head covering made me smile.

"Of course, Henry is beside himself, and your parents do suffer." She turned suddenly to me. "Did you know Daniel Hargrove died? Fell off his horse. His fiancée eventually married that Durrant boy, the younger one. I've forgotten his name."

"I'm sure I don't know him," I said.

"I met him once at a spring ball. It was the year lavender was so popular with the girls. And fresh flowers to decorate their hair."

As I sat beside her for the next half hour, she rambled on about people and places lost to time. She evoked images of horse-drawn carriages, summer picture hats, and pastel silks. The breezes were warmer, the sky bluer, and happiness was a glittering bubble.

I looked at Martha Langtry with pity, but also understanding. She went happily to a place I hoped never to go. Born of age or anguish, senility had erased recent memory, leaving her safely in the past.

Chapter 13

A nother cry in the night had me vaulting out of bed and racing down the corridor in the dark. This time, I didn't question what I'd heard or wait for a spirit to show me the way to the second-floor corridor. Ghosts walked tonight, and I needed to bear witness. I was on the back stairs before I became fully awake. Dashing full tilt towards the grand staircase, I blindly plowed into someone with a thud and a sharp yelp—and found myself sprawled on the floor.

"Damn it! What the hell!" Someone stumbled over me, nearly falling.

It was Owen. He grabbed me roughly by the shoulders and pulled me upright, while I struggled with my modesty and my nightdress.

"Anne!" His whisper was hoarse. "What are you doing?"

The pitiful sound of weeping echoing from above captured our attention. Owen released my shoulders and stepped closer. We both stood still in the shadows, listening.

Silence.

Could he hear the thudding of my heart?

A stir of air swept past us and up the stairs. *Had a door been opened?*

A faint knocking noise reverberated through the house. *Was it the wind?*

Then, there it was again, a stifled cry sifting through the dark.

"Do you hear that?" Caution laced Owen's voice.

"Yes." I said, barely able to breathe.

Standing motionless at the base of the stairs, I strained to catch any fragment of sound. I'd almost decided it was nothing but a dream when there it was again. Not the anguished cry that had awakened me, but a tearful moan. It was more than the wind in the trees. Despair struck me to my soul.

As we stood shoulder to shoulder, Owen whispered, "What is it?"

I shook my head. "I'm not sure."

"Where's it coming from?"

I wrapped my arms across my chest. "Upstairs?"

"Shhh." He grasped my elbow.

Leaning close, he took the initiative and guided me up the staircase. We took slow silent steps upwards. Clouds obscured the skies for the moment, so no moonlight paved our way.

At the top, Owen turned right into the long passageway. The eerie murk engulfed us. We passed doors standing open to expose unoccupied rooms, the furniture crouching in the gloom. He put his arm protectively about my shoulders, moving us both into the darkness. We crept past the double doors, now closed, to Mrs. Langtry's sitting room. I heard nothing but our soft footsteps on the hallway carpet. Near the end of the broad passage, we halted as if stayed by an unseen hand.

Feeling a rising sense of horror, I closed my eyes. I saw a bouquet of white roses again, a white Bible with gold lettering, rosary beads spilling forth from the throat of a lily. These visions battered my poor brain, as if trying to force me to grasp their meaning. I trembled and opened my eyes, hoping to dispel them.

"Anne? Are you all right?"

I dared to take one more step. Then fear paralyzed me. "I don't think I can go any farther."

"Look." He stared at something ahead. "Do you see that?" Owen breathed the words in my ear. "What is it?"

Before another set of ornate doors draped with cobwebs, the hinges rusted, something hung suspended in the air.

"Fog?" I whispered, for that is what it looked like, but not what it was. "Something foggy—or a cirrus of smoke." I didn't want to admit to Owen that I perceived a spirit. I had never revealed my secret to anyone.

"But it has a form. Do you see that? It looks . . . human."

My throat constricted. So he could see it, as well. "Like a silhouette behind frosted glass."

Without warning, the misty substance drifted towards us. My heart lurched. His arm still around my shoulder, Owen held me tighter. Then the cloud-like thing began to swirl. It thickened and darkened, pulsating rhythmically. Taking on a blue cast, it flattened against the floor, writhing. Owen wrapped me in his arms, and we drew back, huddled together.

My mouth was dry and my pulse hammered. Owen's body shook, and I felt his jaw against my skull, working as if he might speak. Or scream. I wanted to flee but couldn't tear my eyes from the specter before us. It stilled for a moment, as if waiting. I smelled hot candle wax and felt the sluggish blood in my veins, warm and thick.

Suddenly, the miasma stirred again with a languid twisting motion that caused my heart to seize. Owen's fingers dug into my shoulder. Sweat prickled my scalp. The ghostly form rose, elongated, then seeped into the crack between the double doors and disappeared.

Owen dropped his arms, and I took a deep, shuddering breath. The heavy atmosphere that had immobilized us lifted. I was exhausted, but the terror I'd felt was gone.

"Owen, what did you see?" I asked softly.

"A shadow. Something dark. It was more a sense I had, a distinct feeling, not what I could see. But it was there, I know it."

"You're right, it was real." I considered telling him about my encounter with whatever haunted Northfield House on my first day, that blue shade in the study, but decided against it. He could easily dismiss the limited images he'd witnessed tonight. I was not yet ready to trust him with my deepest secrets resulting from my enhanced perception. No one ever saw what I did. I shivered. Suddenly aware of my state of undress, I wrapped my arms tightly around my bosom, my face hot with embarrassment.

Owen whisked off his silk dressing gown and draped it over my shoulders. The soft fabric carried the warmth of his body and his woodsy scent. I became acutely aware of standing so close to him and having shared an intimate moment of panic. I could still feel his protective arm across my body, sheltering me from harm. His loose pajamas, the top unbuttoned to the waist, heightened my discomfort.

For an awkward moment, I looked about. "Where are we? Where do these doors lead?"

"This is the south wing. It hasn't been used for decades."

I had seen the crumbling exterior and derelict gardens of the south wing during my walks on the estate. So here was the entrance to the rooms with the shuttered windows. "It's locked up, you mean?"

"Precisely. It's been closed since my father was a boy."

"Do you know why?"

"The cost of upkeep. There was no need for so many rooms. Not since the last century has Northfield entertained so many guests that these rooms were required."

"May we enter?" I asked, emboldened by our shared experience.

"Of course we may." He shrugged his shoulders. "Certainly I can find the key in Father's desk. But let's return tomorrow, in daylight." He looked sheepish, his unruly hair hanging in his eyes. "I've seen enough of ghosts for one night. I have no desire to follow this one beyond these doors."

He startled me, so casually admitting that he'd seen a ghost. As I wondered whether Owen was speaking metaphorically, we returned to the ground floor with dispatch, putting distance between ourselves and the troubling vision. We stood awkwardly at the bottom of the staircase.

"Anne, why were you wandering about in the middle of the night?"

"I heard a scream. Or, I had at least the sense of one. Did you not hear it?" I wanted with all my heart to share what I knew about the spirits who lingered here.

"No. But I've not been able to sleep of late," Owen said. "I was on my way to the library when I encountered you, as you'll undoubtedly remember."

I massaged my elbow to relieve the soreness there. "But you'd heard nothing? Nothing attracted you or compelled you to approach the stairs?"

"Not until we stood here in the darkness. I heard what sounded like sighs. Then a woman weeping. At that moment, I did have the most overpowering sensation of something beckoning me upwards and towards the south wing. When I saw that shadow in front of the doors, I was almost powerless to resist."

My pulse quickened. Owen's perceptions seemed less acute than my own, but perhaps he was a kindred spirit—someone who could not only confirm my visions, but share my ordeal. "Have you ever experienced this in the past?"

"No, never."

I checked my excitement. "Have other residents of the house ever spoken of strange occurrences?"

"Not at all."

I plunged ahead, throwing caution to the wind. "You've had no thought that ghosts roam the halls of Northfield?"

"If there were signs, no one has paid any attention. Although now that you suggest it, things have been odd since *your* arrival."

"Odd?" I had a moment of panic, fearing I'd been found out.

"I don't know how to describe it. A stirring in the air, an unsettled quality about the shadows, a whispering through the darkened halls."

He looked past me, and his face softened as if, for a moment, he was lost in thought.

I quite suddenly entertained another reason for feverish bother.

To my surprise, a yearning awakened deep in my breast. For a moment, I wanted to feel Owen's arms about me once more. Then I stepped back and drew his robe more tightly around me, remembering I was a girl alone in this burdened house. "I must get back to my room."

"But, I am willing to explore the south wing in your company, if that would please you."

"My pleasure has nothing to do with it." One of the spirits of Northfield House had lured us to the south wing. In my experience, only desperate spirits made such bold overtures. Owen—rational, dispassionate Owen—believed he had also seen that presence tonight. There would never be a better time to disclose the truth. Emboldened, I made a sudden decision to reveal something of myself. "I believe a ghost walks at Northfield, and nobody will rest until someone discovers why."

With a wry smile but no hesitation, he said, "That is quite obvious. Are you suggesting that *we* make the effort to free both the spirit and my ancestral home?"

"I am," I said, deciding to stand by my revelation.

He paused a moment. "But it's best we keep our ghost hunting to ourselves, to avoid ridicule, don't you think?"

I couldn't tell how serious he was, but at least the issue of ghosts was out in the open. "Of course, it wouldn't do to share what we have seen with anyone."

I indeed believed he was right about keeping our resident spirit a secret, but for the moment my only concern was returning to my room. The dawn light attenuated the darkness, and the servants would be up and about soon. The fact that Owen and I were roaming the halls at night would be a scandal. I turned towards the back stairs. "We should talk another time."

"Allow me to accompany you to your chamber."

"I assure you I know the way," I said, trying to dismiss him.

"Nevertheless." Owen struck a respectful posture and offered his arm.

Shooting a nervous glance towards the other end of the house, I uttered, "Thank you."

I proceeded as quickly as possible to my room. Before parting at my door, Owen and I made plans to meet that afternoon.

"Shall I see you in the study at the time you typically take tea?" he suggested.

"That would be fine, Owen."

"Get some rest, Anne."

"You do the same," I said, although I doubted either of us would sleep any longer that night.

Chapter 14

*T*he morning dawned damp and gray. I rose early and dressed quickly. After depositing Owen's robe on a chair in the library before anyone saw me, I entered the kitchen. As usual, Cook was bustling over a hot oven, Kitty was hovering about the hearth, and Dolly was preparing a tray for Mrs. Langtry.

Before making her way upstairs, Mrs. Hadley handed me a note. "Mr. Owen left this for you."

I opened it with trembling fingers.

Anne,

I was called away today to take delivery on a shipment of seed. I'm unable to keep our appointment but will return by late afternoon.

Owen

P.S. I have the key. Meet me in the library before dinner.

I felt like a conspirator! We had a scheme afoot, but I had to admit *my* feet were getting cold. My enthusiasm was dampened by the very real consequences that could befall me. It was all well and good for Owen to do as he pleased, but I had no business meddling.

I thought of the displeasure that such an endeavor would create, and I could not afford to risk angering my employers. Neither Mr. nor Mrs. Wellington would look kindly upon an outsider involving herself in family matters. And I believe it was, indeed, a family matter. Now that I could take a breath and consider the clues I'd been given, I knew. The images shown to me, the childhood Bible, the rosary, and the white roses that were certainly a bridal bouquet, convinced me beyond a hair's breadth of doubt that the spirit who sought our attention was Eleanor Granville.

I worked through the morning, my nerves jittering. Mr. Wellington read over the papers I produced, sorting and making the typical changes. To avoid unnecessary mistakes, I typed more slowly than I was able. Keeping my mind on issues like crop rotation and enclosure proved challenging.

By noon, the skies darkened, and a great storm brewed. Black clouds bruised the horizon and rolled across the distant hills. When the rain came down in sheets, I worried. If Owen was out in the deluge, travel would be difficult, if not dangerous. In wet weather, the roads became muddy and some of the streams impassable. I feared he wouldn't make it home this evening as planned.

As the dreary afternoon wore on, my doubts multiplied. Increasingly, I felt it unwise for me to venture beyond those locked doors. I had no right to explore the abandoned wing of Northfield House. Very little escaped the staff, or even Mrs. Wellington. Surely, my employer would learn of my presumptuous behavior.

By the time I covered the Remington and placed my typed pages on Mr. Wellington's desk, I was even wondering if this would be the grand adventure I anticipated. Perhaps I was being fanciful. Did I really expect to find the ghost of Eleanor Granville in the closed south wing of Northfield House? We were more likely to find moldy wall hangings and mouse droppings than mystery.

I needed to be sensible. My natural curiosity could imperil my employment. The thrill of last night's adventure had muddled my rational thinking. I could not let my emotions or the messages from the spirits control my behavior. When Owen arrived, I would inform him that I couldn't investigate the closed wing. That would be the right and proper thing to do.

At that thought, my heart sank. I left the study in low spirits and headed towards my room. As I approached the stairs, a commotion at the front of the house reached my ears.

I backtracked along the corridor and stopped just before the turn leading to the main hall.

". . .and I had the misfortune to get caught at Melling and spent an hour in a pub before venturing on." Owen's voice was unmistakable.

I felt an odd flutter of excitement.

"I was worried the bridge might flood," said Mr. Wellington.

"I left the samples in the boot. They should be fine until morning."

Mr. Wellington cleared his throat. "I wish you'd give up this ill-conceived study of yours."

I strained to listen as the voices moved away.

". . . important," Owen's words strayed to me.

". . . waste of time . . ." his father said.

Their quarreling faded as they entered the study and closed the door. I was unsettled by the discord between them, but breathed a great sigh that Owen was safely home.

To my surprise, I was beginning to find him more agreeable. The experience last night gave us a secret to share. I remembered his hand on my shoulders and his breath against my cheek. I could still feel the warmth of his body pressed against mine and smell the earthy scent of his skin. My face heated with shame at the thoughts I allowed myself to entertain.

Once again upstairs, I washed my face and primped too long, arranging my hair into a pleasing pile of loose curls atop my head, secured with the tortoiseshell combs. I opened my window and attempted to read the Book of Ruth in my father's Bible. Despite this tale of constancy, I was determined to back out of ghost hunting with Owen. He would understand. Unable to concentrate, I peered into the distance at the growing twilight. A dark bank of clouds obscured the sky even though the rain had stopped. The fragrance of damp soil, decaying vegetation, and new-mown hay wafted into my room.

Although Owen hadn't designated a time, at six thirty I rushed downstairs to the library. I searched the shelves for a moment. Then I slid the second volume of *Remembrance of Things Past* off the shelf, sat, and waited.

Chapter 15

*B*y seven, Owen hadn't yet appeared, and I felt a strong urge to return to my room. My stomach was unsettled. He would forgive me for not waiting. Perhaps he, too, had changed his mind. Beyond that, I was sure he had better things to do, like attending to the seedlings or bags of grain or whatever he'd left in the boot of his car. I swallowed my unease and stood before the cold fireplace holding the book I was unable to focus upon.

My resolve to withdraw from pursuing the spirit in the south wing had strengthened over the half hour I'd waited, and I saw no reason to maintain my vigil. I replaced the volume of Proust and reached for the door.

It suddenly swung open wide.

I yelped and stepped backwards, startled.

"That'll never do, if we're to be ghost hunting." Owen stepped into the room and wagged an old-fashioned iron key in front of my face. His eyes held all the good humor and anticipation that had dissipated in mine during the preceding hours.

"Sorry I'm so late. I had to get out of my wet things, and I'd made it all the way to the main hall when I realized I'd left the key in my room."

When I did not immediately respond, he said, "I hope you haven't been waiting long."

"No." Flustered, I gestured towards the bookshelves. "I was reading, that's all."

"Come on, then. What are we doing, standing here in the library? Let's go," he said, his excitement palpable.

I hung back. "Owen, perhaps we need to reconsider what we're doing."

"You're not losing your nerve?" His gaze probed my face.

"No, not at all. It's just not my place to get involved in . . ."—I shrugged while I searched for the right words—". . . a private family matter."

"Not your place? Then whose place might it be?" His shoulders sagged with disappointment.

"I fear your parents would find my meddling offensive."

"But you are the very reason this mystery has thrust itself front and center. You're the catalyst. Nothing will be resolved without you."

"I hardly think that justifies action on my part, Owen."

"And why not? You are the chosen one, the one who can get to the bottom of whatever this is."

His perspicacity startled me. "Still . . ."

"You don't understand, Anne, why this might be important. I never gave much thought to my family's painful past until you arrived, but there was a tragedy in their lives. It's something you wouldn't know about, but now I see how the mystery surrounding it burdens my parents. This entity we've discovered may reveal answers."

He was, I believed, thinking of Eleanor and her disappearance, but I remained silent, feeling it inappropriate to admit I had already learned about this sorrow from his Aunt Martha.

Owen beseeched me. "My father suffers. Can't you see how not knowing the truth about an event of import weighs upon his very soul? It makes it difficult for him to move into the future and to embrace a changing world. He is frozen by the past. Mysteries, secrets, the great unknown eats away at his very core. You can't deny him—and my mother—relief from these tragic memories."

"I don't feel right about this." I doubted that discovering Eleanor's fate would endear me to those who might benefit from the knowledge.

"Anne, you have a gift. For some reason, God has given you this ability to see ghosts and, I imagine, to learn from them. How can you refuse to help?"

"Oh, Owen." I felt tears gather. He understood more than I'd thought possible.

He clasped my hands and pulled me closer. "If you will not think of the living, then consider the dead. The ghost needs your help. And, somehow, I know that putting this ghost to rest will help my family," said Owen.

I believed the pitiful wraith we had seen last night was what remained of Eleanor Granville on this earthly plane. She wanted release from the purgatory in which she languished. She wanted the truth known. Only then could she rest in peace. I was at once overwhelmed by a sense of duty.

Owen looked deep into my eyes with a dark frown. "I know that you can help without reservation, not even understanding how I know. And you know it, too."

I let down my guard with a sigh. "You're right, Owen. This ghost needs our help. I'm sorry I doubted the obligation."

He grinned. "So we're on?"

I nodded and stood straighter to show my firmness of purpose.

He offered his arm and I took it. We dashed into the great hall to the stairs and up, only slowing when we reached the head of the long passage we'd explored the night before. Silence met us as we paused, then moved stealthily ahead. The rooms we passed looked less menacing in the pearlescent light of early evening. In one of them, a clock chimed, suggesting the monotonous passage of time.

We found ourselves again before the double doors where something otherworldly had beckoned the previous evening. The doors looked just as forbidding now as they had then.

Owen said, "Are you still willing to explore where a wraith blocked our path last night?"

I nodded. "But I believe that the spirit wasn't so much blocking our path as showing us one."

Owen inserted the heavy key and the lock responded with a rusty squeal. He turned the ornate knob and pushed the door, its hinges groaning as he applied pressure with his shoulder. The bottom dragged on the floor as it was forced open a few inches, just enough for us to enter.

For a moment we stood in the gloom. I was aware of Owen's nearness as I took in our surroundings. We were in a large gallery, its length broken by pillars on either side. Pale evening light streamed through tall windows. Our footsteps echoed. Dust stirred with each movement. Ancient portraits still hung on the walls.

"How long has this wing been closed?" I asked, leaning close to a painting of a scowling man.

"Fifty years or more. Since my father was a boy."

It occurred to me that perhaps no one living here now had ever entered this space.

Owen continued, "It's hard enough keeping up the main house, especially since the war."

He used a handkerchief to wipe the grime from a brass label I was trying to decipher. The engraving read *Charles Harold Wellington, 1772–1841.*

He frowned. "This must be my great-great-grandfather. Either he was quite an unattractive fellow, or this is a very bad painting."

"The ones of the women appear to be better." I approached another portrait and peered at the plaque. "*Euphemia Alice Holmes Wellington, 1733–1750.* She died so young and looks so lovely."

"No doubt the women demanded a more appealing likeness."

This strange space didn't seem to inspire in Owen the awe I felt. The family history appeared to be discarded in this abandoned place. "Why aren't these portraits in the main house?"

"My mother probably wouldn't allow it. She wouldn't like these sourpusses staring at her from the dining room walls." Owen dismissed any question of value, sentimental or economic. "Grandfather Wellington's portrait hangs in the great hall with his contemporaries, including Mother's family. Where would we hang all these?"

I'd been aware of more recent paintings decorating the formal rooms of Northfield, none of them older than two generations. The distant family history resided here, locked away. I felt the passage of time like a surge beneath us.

"Shall we see the rest?" Owen grabbed my hand and pulled me towards another entryway at the far end.

A tingling sensation ran from my fingers to my toes. Heat spread from my face through my limbs. Feeling once more the closeness we'd shared the night before, I boldly grasped his hand in return. At the far entrance, double doors led to a broad hall with rooms opening on either side.

"This appears to be a parlor," Owen said as we peeked in the first door.

The room was festooned with cobwebs and filled with sheet-covered furnishings arranged in groups echoing their use decades ago.

"A music room," I said, opening a set of French doors, their glass panes dulled by time. The pianoforte, its teeth-like keys grinning, faced scattered rows of empty chairs as delicate as the dust that embraced them.

We entered room after room of drooping draperies and peeling wallpaper. Bare bedchambers devoid of decoration sat next to rooms furnished right down to rugs on the floors and candlesticks on the mantels. Empty trunks occupied shadowed corners. Water stains marked the walls. The smell of mold, wood rot, and mice was everywhere. No footprints but our own disturbed the dusty floors.

During the next hour, we explored the entire south wing of Northfield House, picking our way through dim, shadowed spaces stained with damp. The rising half-moon shot silvery light through the dirty windows.

When we reached the last room, Owen pushed the door open. He stopped abruptly, and my body collided with his.

"Apologies!" he muttered. "Mildew seems to have gotten the better of this room." His hand rose to cover his mouth and nose.

I recoiled at the faint, fetid odor. "More than just mold, I think."

I held my breath while taking in the furnishings in the dim interior: the sagging bed, the trunk at the foot, paintings askew on every wall. The chamber was darker than the others. Or perhaps the moon had found a cover of clouds.

Owen turned to me. "Did you hear that?"

I strained my ears as we stood like statues in the doorway.

"It's the wind, Owen."

Thunder growled in the distance.

"No, I heard something inside. A thumping or pounding overhead."

I whirled about suddenly, my arms in front of me, as if for protection.

"What is it?" Owen asked, startled, looking down at me.

"Something touched me." It was more than my heightened imagination. Owen drew me against him, his hands on my shoulders, and I felt the blood course through my veins as palpably as the air that filled my lungs.

I turned up my face to look at him. We were standing closer than propriety allowed. Owen bent nearer.

Knock. Thud. Knock. Thud. Knock. Thud.

A stab of fear nailed me where I stood. Owen wrapped a protective arm around my shoulders. I leaned into him.

"What is it?" he asked softly. "Is she here?"

"Maybe," I whispered.

Knock. Thud. Knock. Thud. Knock. Thud.

The noises first came from directly overhead, then surrounded us, coming from the walls and the floor. The sounds of something trapped—a thing desperate and struggling—repeated every few seconds.

"Where's it coming from?" he hissed.

"From everywhere. And nowhere."

Owen pulled me closer. I was terrified, despite taking shelter in his arms. My shoulder pressed against his warm chest and my head tucked under his chin.

After a moment, the sound changed. I heard scratching—fingernails or claws or beaks on wood. The shadows in the corners thickened and seemed to pulsate. Or was something breathing? I felt an overwhelming sense of dread. The scratching was followed by the rustle of wings, a soft fluttering. Perhaps a bird had gotten trapped on the floor above.

Knock. Thud. Knock. Thud. Knock. Thud.

Then nothing.

I waited for the thumps and scratches to begin again, but heard only Owen's rapid breathing.

His grip on my shoulder softened. Before we could step away from each other, I heard something else. Whispers. Not words, but sibilance. A faint weeping.

I could pretend no longer that the sounds issued from a bird or animal. I had heard crying and scratching from spirits before, but none had ever filled me with such horror.

Owen shuddered, and I tried to swallow.

My sight darted from the floors to the ceilings, from corner to corner, searching for additional signs of a spirit. I saw none. The bed, its elaborate draperies, and the pictures on the walls were all mute, but a plaintive lament—a mournful sobbing—suddenly filled the space.

When the weeping stopped, I found my hand pressed against Owen's chest. I could feel his heart beating, hard and fast, under my palm.

"I think it's over," he said, releasing my shoulders.

I withdrew my hand and took a step away.

Owen looked at me and opened his mouth to say something but stopped before he spoke. An otherworldly silence descended. At that moment, the cold came. Soundless. Chilling. It brought a foreboding greater than terror.

"Do you feel that?" Owen asked.

"The cold? Yes." I shivered.

"Is she coming again? Like last night?" Owen looked about the room and drew closer once more.

"I don't know. Listen," I said, and released a shuddering breath.

The room was unnaturally still. The cold didn't blow, drift, or seep, but settled around us. Still, I saw nothing as I had the night before.

Making a concentrated effort to quell my fear, I vowed to face whatever this was and to know it. I could not deny that a ghost haunted Northfield, and I had to understand it and, if possible, lay it to rest. Memories from another life could not harm me. Longing from the past could not wound me. Looking up at the ceiling, I raised my hands in front of me, palms up, appealing. "Eleanor?"

Everything snapped back to normal. The last room at the end of the long hall was once again stuffy and damp, with dim moonlight outlining the still furniture and candle smut on the walls. The only sounds were the wind and our ragged breathing.

Owen took my hand. "Let's get out of here."

We turned our backs to the forlorn bed and the large trunk that anchored the room. We dashed down the passageway, through the gallery and out the double doors. Owen shut the doors firmly, then pulled the rusty key from his trouser pocket and locked them once again.

How foolish, I thought. Locked doors will not keep Eleanor in.

As we took the stairs, Owen said, "You're a cool one. So you've heard about Eleanor?"

I wasn't sure what he'd expressed was surprise or admiration. I said, "Of course, Owen. Secrets are always difficult to keep when specters roam." I didn't want to discuss how I knew about the family tragedy, and said, "Owen, we must record what we've seen and compare our experiences. Shall we go to the study?"

He nodded without speaking as we swept down the hall.

I sat at my desk, retrieving a fountain pen and a fresh steno pad.

"Please relate to me what you heard, everything you can remember." I poised my pen above a blank page.

"Nothing until we approached that final bedchamber. A thumping noise. Faint, but definite, at least a dozen times."

"I heard that as well," I said, scribbling notes.

"That was followed by whispers. I couldn't distinguish any words. Just whispers."

"Did you not hear weeping? A heartrending sobbing?" I asked.

"No. Did you? Were words spoken?"

"I heard no words but most definitely a mournful weeping."

"The room seemed darker than the others." Owen concentrated, his eyes closed.

"There may be nothing supernatural about that," I said, taking care that our imaginations didn't assign otherworldly explanations to understandable phenomena.

"The cold came next," he said. "A bone-chilling, dismal cold."

"Yes."

"But Anne, it was more than just cold. There was something distressing, woeful, or disheartening about it." He shook his head, frowning. "It's difficult to convey how it made me feel."

"I felt that as well. Melancholy is the only description I would ascribe to it. Something that struck clean to the heart."

Owen said, "You called out 'Eleanor.' Do you believe, as I do, that we have encountered the spirit of Eleanor Granville, mother's lost sister?"

I lowered my eyes, not daring to look him in the face. "I am sorry, Owen. I don't wish to intrude upon a lamentable past that is none of my business."

"But you believe it, don't you? That we are searching for Eleanor?"

I hesitated. I dare not tell him of the images that appeared to me when ghosts materialized. I was not yet ready to reveal everything. Once Owen learned the entire truth, I feared he would look at me as peculiar—a freak.

I spoke slowly, measuring my words. "I felt a presence—*Eleanor's* presence, I believe. You have felt this spirit as well, even though you may be less certain of the identity."

"I have no reason to doubt you, Anne, if you believe it."

"But we both saw it, didn't we? We both experienced it." Knowing that I was not alone in this was important, although I did not doubt it was real.

Owen took a deep breath. "Yes, certainly, but you more so than I. You are clearly more sensitive, seeing more distinctly whatever was in the passage last night, hearing more just now."

You have no idea, I thought. Still, it was a great relief that another person experienced even a small part of what I did. It wasn't validation that I sought, but a soul in harmony with my own. Keeping such a secret was painful.

I finished writing and put the pad into my desk drawer after dating the entry, thinking that perhaps if we kept a careful record, we could solve this mystery together.

"Do you think we can ever confirm who or what this is?" he asked.

"I don't know. But, Owen, the only possible way to resolve this enigma is to find out what happened to Eleanor." I knew this in my heart without understanding why.

"How do we do that?"

"Find the records of events at the time. News reports and diaries or letters, if any exist. And people who were directly involved—your father and mother, and your Aunt Martha—may be able to help."

"How can we discover anything after all these years, when others were unable to find answers at the time?"

"I don't know. But someone is trying to tell us something."

"Clearly," said Owen.

I frowned with concentration. "I have an idea. The day after tomorrow, I'm scheduled for a trip to the library, related to my work with your father. While there, I can look into this. I'll start with the newspaper accounts of the day Eleanor disappeared."

"Yes, that's an excellent plan," he said.

"Do you know the date of your father's marriage to Eleanor?"

"No, I don't. But my parents married in June of 1895."

"So I'll also go to the church and look up the marriage banns."

"Good thinking," he said. "It's a solid start."

I saw admiration in his eyes, and something in the center of me seemed to melt.

We stood and looked at one another. We were on a mission and nothing would deter us. I felt a deep camaraderie with a kindred spirit, something I had never before experienced.

Owen reached out and lifted the watch pinned to my lapel, to read the time. His touch caused a little thrill to course through me.

"It's eight thirty," he said. "They'll be expecting us."

Chapter 16

*T*he following day dawned fresh and clear, the rain having cleansed the air. I woke anticipating all manner of possibilities. I looked forwards to tomorrow's trip into Melling, where I could use my research skills to unravel secrets. Owen and I had a mystery to solve, which excited me. We would not let the matter sleep as long as restless spirits walked the halls of Northfield.

This endeavor also meant spending time with Owen. My mood lifted with the thought of him. Then my better judgment dampened my spirit.

Careful, Anne, don't be a goose.

I distracted myself by focusing on the secrets of Northfield House. Even if Melling yielded no answers, the principals related to the disappearance of Eleanor Granville were, after all, still here to inform us: Mr. and Mrs. Wellington and Martha Langtry. Perhaps there were staff members still living who could cast light upon past events as well. No one simply disappears from the face of the earth without leaving a trace, even if that trace is but a phantasm from the next world.

How to approach the subject with reluctant witnesses was the challenge. I was sure no one would tolerate inquiries from me. Owen and I needed a scheme. He would know best how to appeal to his family regarding unpleasant facts they would rather leave buried.

I spent the morning in the study with a sheaf of papers Mr. Wellington handed to me, typing furiously. This new manuscript centered on different varieties of grain adopted in Britain. It also detailed the practice of crop rotation—rather than allow fields to lay fallow, farmers could plant turnips and clover to restore the soil. The discovery of new ways to increase food productivity reminded me of Owen's scientific experiments.

Once again, my mind wandered to my trip to Melling and what I hoped to find. Considering our goals, I decided to see Owen privately once more before going. We needed to discuss how best to delve into the secrets that burdened this dark house. That afternoon, rather than take tea in the kitchen, I snatched an apple and ate it on my way to the fields.

In the interest of discretion, I didn't take the road around the front as Owen did. Instead, I decided to travel the path leading from the footbridge, remembering the evening he'd pointed out the roof of the barn. The sounds of autumn provided a cheerful backdrop as I hurried towards the stream. Birdsong and the buzz of insects mingled with the rattle of drying grasses dancing in the gentle breeze. Fields of golden wheat gleamed in the distance, undulating like the sea.

The pale sun had dried the dirt path leading to the footbridge where the stream, now swollen by the rains, roared below. The tumult emphasized the excitement in my breast.

I held tight to the handrail as I darted across the old bridge. The path on the other side was steep and slick with spray, dampening my shoes and stockings. I labored up, pulling myself along the narrow cleft in the rocks by finding footholds in the stone. This route shortened the distance to the fields, but I now understood why it was not often used.

When I emerged from the ravine, I saw the barn, whitewashed and topped with a thatched roof, rising before me. On the other side was a greenhouse made of stacked field stone, covered with a curved network of metal spines and glass.

Walking round to the front of the barn, I entered an open sliding door. The dim interior was strangely still and smelled of hay and dust. Bales of straw rose high on one side. Bins of grain, each tagged with numbers and a date, were lined up against the other wall. From outside, the distant drone of farm machinery and male voices drifted to me. A calico kitten wrapped around my ankles. I picked up the kitten and took a weed-choked path to the greenhouse.

Under the glass roof, low tables covered with flats of seedlings filled the space. The bright green shoots grew in shallow trays, in two tiers. Overhead, narrow water lines threaded across the interior for irrigation. The weak sun filtered through the panes, making the air steamy. The kitten struggled, and I put her down.

Near the door was a waist-high, roughhewn wooden table scattered with books and pencils. An open ledger revealed a series of entries, dates, and codes of some kind. No doubt, this was where Owen did his scientific work, made his calculations, and kept his records.

I attuned my senses to the atmosphere. In these outbuildings bathed in golden light, I felt no spirits stir. Whatever specters troubled the house did not linger in this open, airy space where Owen found happiness in his daily occupations.

A creased, faded photograph tacked to the wall above the table caught my attention. I leaned close. As my eyes sorted darkness and light into an image, I was startled to see Owen, Thomas, and Charlotte as adolescents. Dressed in summer whites, they stood in their bare feet beside a horse-drawn carriage. Thomas looked defiant, a fist raised towards the camera, a cocky grimace on his face. Owen, his face half-turned away from the camera, wore a wistful expression. Only Charlotte was smiling.

Seized by a sharp pang of envy—or maybe it was loneliness—I felt the distant otherness of one who had nothing and belonged nowhere. My thoughts were burdened by the weight of irrevocable distance between then and now, the fundamental pathos of the photograph. My eyes filled with tears. The people I loved, and who had loved me, were all gone.

But these three had grown up together. They were family, had always known each other, had always been friends. Sharing a past, they belonged to one another in a way that could never be altered or duplicated. And I could never be a part of it.

With a start, I realized that Owen was holding Charlotte's hand.

Feeling as if I'd been prying, I hurried from the greenhouse, hoping I hadn't been seen. Outside, I listened for voices and set off towards them. Picking my way through the high grasses that bordered the field, I saw several men working on a steam-powered tractor—a huge black barrel of an engine supported by four red wheels. One of the men had stripped to the waist, exposing a muscled back and sinewy arms glistening with sweat. When the slim figure stood, I realized with a shock it was Owen.

At the same moment, one of the other men caught sight of me and said something. Owen turned and looked around in the pale afternoon sun. Broad-shouldered and lean, he stood for a second, staring as if to make sense of me.

"Anne!" He moved with precision, taking long strides in my direction, grabbing his shirt on the way.

I averted my eyes, but not before noticing several angry red scars on his chest and abdomen. I had seen such injuries before, on men returning from the war. These were shrapnel wounds, only recently healed.

Queasiness clutched my stomach. I now more fully understood his emotional withdrawal and his silent moods. Previously, I credited a critical father, a neglectful mother, and a natural inclination to solemnity. Now I also saw that the blight and hopelessness of war were etched in those ugly scars.

The kitten had followed me, giving me something to concentrate my attention upon, rather than stare at Owen's bare chest. By the time I picked her up and turned to face him, Owen had pulled on his shirt and begun to button it. The thin, rough fabric stuck to his damp skin. Before I met his gaze, I saw that his dungaree cloth trousers were stained with mud. Dressed this way, he looked like a different person, and I was reminded of the costume ball. "The tractor's broken down. My apologies." He gave me a sheepish grin as he tucked in his shirt. "I didn't know you were coming." He took a large handkerchief from his back pocket and wiped his brow and hands.

"I'm sorry I interrupted your work," I said, hoping my face wasn't red. "I should've let you know."

"Not at all. I'm glad you're here."

He immediately launched into a description of the fields surrounding us, pointing in one direction and then the other. "I'm experimenting with wheat, oats, millet, barley. I even have a plot of sorghum."

I stooped to release the struggling kitten and snagged a bright blue chicory blossom as I stood. Remembering the grains detailed in the manuscript I'd typed up that morning, I asked, "What about rye?"

"Sure, we've grown several varieties."

I twirled the blue flower between my fingers as he walked me towards the greenhouse. "And maize?" I asked.

Owen hesitated. "Are you actually interested in this?"

I nodded.

He grinned. "Maize doesn't do well in our soil. The American staple eludes Britain, I'm afraid. I'm working with hard varieties of wheat now, durum especially."

He talked about the species he'd crossed—einkorn, emmer, and spelt. Taking me through the greenhouse, he described the process, what he had discovered, and how he kept his records. It amused me to see him so animated, his guileless face lit with pleasure.

Following him from one row of flats to another, I was enchanted by his immersion in his work and pleased he wanted me to understand and appreciate the science involved. As we left the greenhouse, I dropped the chicory blossom on the wooden table below the old family photograph.

Outside, I glanced at my watch and was startled to realize how long I'd been gone from Northfield House. "Owen, thank you for showing me around and helping me to understand the work you do, but I have to get back."

He looked disappointed. "Of course. I understand. I didn't mean to keep you."

"Not at all." I laughed. "I'm flattered you think me capable of grasping the intellectual intricacies. That's a rare thing to find in a man." I wanted to make sure he didn't misunderstand, as he had the night on the bridge. "Your father expects me. I'm late as it is. See you at dinner?"

"As usual," he said, his smile friendly.

I returned the smile. "I'm still going to Melling tomorrow."

He glanced at the workers in the field. "If I can get the tractor repaired today, I'll go with you."

My heart beat a little faster at that possibility. But, I reminded myself, such arrangements might arouse Mrs. Wellington's disapproval. "That's not necessary. I'm accustomed to traveling alone. I'm quite capable."

"A fair point." Owen walked with me towards the stream.

As we passed the white barn, I remembered the task that had brought me to the greenhouse. I wanted to encourage Owen to speak to his parents about Eleanor's disappearance.

Owen spoke first. "I've been thinking how to approach Father— what questions to ask."

I glanced at him in surprise. We had both been thinking about the same thing, at the same moment. "That seems a much larger challenge than a trip to Melling. Perhaps speak to him after dinner and a glass of brandy or two? It's a matter of family history, so why wouldn't you, his son, want to know? Surely he'll understand."

He regarded me as though considering it. Then he turned towards the laboring men in the distance, who had managed to get the tractor moving. Owen waved, trying to attract their attention. Then he put thumb and forefinger to his lips and emitted a shrill, earsplitting whistle.

I laughed. "Sir, you are most surprising."

"Just one of my many talents." He grinned, crossing into the field to join his men. "Take care getting back." He called over his shoulder. "I'd rather you take the path through the fields. The rocks near the bridge are always slippery."

"I managed on the way here," I said. "But I'll be careful."

"You had better be," he said. "It's more treacherous than you think."

"Until tonight." I turned towards the ravine, pleased that he had expressed care for my safety.

The kitten was nowhere to be seen as I returned to the footbridge. I was not surprised, however, to see our other Kitty waiting for me. Perhaps unwilling to brave the slick boards or maybe the rocky path in her bare feet, the Little Seedling sat in the shadows, obscured by wildflowers on the other side of the ravine.

Chapter 17

*A*fter the work day ended, I visited the kitchen with questions for Mrs. Hadley that, should she be kind enough to answer, would shed light on the Wellington family. I sat at the table with a pot of tea near Kitty, who shied away. I appealed to her with a nod of my head, admiring a jelly jar filled with cornflowers she'd picked. A moment later, Mrs. Hadley arrived to supervise the dinner preparations.

"Good evening, Miss. And Little Kitty." She smiled at us.

"How are you, Mrs. Hadley? This is the first time we've crossed paths today. Would you care for tea?" I raised my cup, motioning to the squat little pot on the table. "We could talk for a moment."

She studied me with her sharp blue eyes. "No tea, thank you, but I might sit a spell." Patting her graying hair into place, she took a seat across the table and looked expectantly at me. "What is it you're wanting to know, Miss Anne?"

Apparently, I was as transparent as glass.

"If you don't mind my taking liberties . . ." I paused.

"You may ask what you will. Your words will not leave this kitchen," she said, reminding me that we shared a high level of trust.

I plunged ahead. "Was Owen wounded in combat?"

"Indeed, he was. Most grievously. Why do you ask?"

"I just had that impression," I answered, hesitant to admit I'd seen the angry scars on his body. There was no way to explain that I'd seen him undressed that wouldn't embarrass both of us. "It's just that I didn't want to put my foot in it, as they say."

"It was a terrible thing. Metal fragments from some sort of explosive contraption ripped open his chest. It's a wonder he's alive. He was in hospital for months."

"How did it happen?"

"He's never spoken a word about it. All we know is he was near the front, too close to the cannon." She shook her head and wore an expression of sorrow. "He recovered, at least physically. He's quieter now, less hopeful." She looked wistful. "He was the most optimistic child, full of passion and commitment. He's different now, but it's still the early days. I do hope he recovers himself more as time passes."

There was a long pause where I hoped she'd say more. In the silence, I recalled the serious, thoughtful adolescent boy in the picture tacked upon the greenhouse wall. I understood his longing for change, how he dedicated his efforts to doing the right thing, and why he devoted himself to the land.

I chose my next words with care.

"Knowing him a bit now, it seems odd that Thomas didn't join the fighting. He strikes me as the military type."

"Mr. Thomas was needed on the farm. Essential services, you know." She looked uneasy.

I was certain the farm was an expedient for Thomas, to avoid putting himself in harm's way. "That is strange, is it not, since he seems so uninterested in running it, while Owen is so committed?"

She sighed. "Nothing much escapes you, Miss Anne. 'Tis true. But it was a good excuse, you might say."

"Why did Owen not do the same?"

She shook her head, sadness in her eyes. "Mr. Owen was young and idealistic to a fault. He had no lust for the fighting but was wanting to do his part for King and country."

I didn't need to ask if Owen harbored any resentment about his sacrifice in the face of Thomas's avoidance of it, or if Thomas begrudged Owen his bravery. That I could determine for myself. Perhaps the strain between them had nothing to do with Charlotte. For my own reasons, I hoped it was so.

"You knew them as children," I said. "How long have you been with the Wellingtons?"

"Since Mr. Thomas was a babe, nigh on thirty years."

My spirits flagged. This meant Mrs. Hadley had arrived at Northfield House after Eleanor's disappearance. "So you didn't know Mrs. Wellington's sister? Eleanor Granville?"

Mrs. Hadley neither hesitated nor showed surprise at my question.

"But I did, Miss. You see, I was the upstairs maid in the Granville home when Miss Eleanor and Miss Lavinia were still girls. 'Twas Miss Lavinia, after she married, who brought me here to Northfield House."

Chapter 18

*T*o hide my excitement, I refilled my teacup and paused before my next question. I decided to be direct. "Mrs. Hadley, what do you think happened to Eleanor?"

"No one rightly knows, Miss. That was the most joyful day, in the beginning. Mr. Henry so in love with that beautiful girl. She was too young to really know her own feelings, but she was determined about the marriage. It's just not possible, what some say, that she planned all along to leave."

"So you don't believe she left of her own free will?"

"I knew her well, Miss, and I don't believe her capable of such cruelty. After all these years, it seems odd, don't you think, her not getting in touch with her folks, if she were still living?"

"When did you last see Eleanor?"

Her gaze, full of sadness, lowered to her hands lying upon the kitchen table, mute testament to her helplessness. "I remember like 'twas yesterday. She and the other young people were playing hide-and-seek. A children's game, no less. So cheerful, they were. At the time, I thought it right silly."

"Do you recall your last image of her?"

"She was tying a handkerchief about Miss Lavinia's eyes. Miss Lavinia was 'it' and everyone else scurried to hide. I was about quite late, cleaning up. It was after one. All the staff from both houses were committed to working the day. I was young, too, not yet twenty, and taking in the festivities, living it through them."

"And when did they realize she was missing?"

"Hours had passed when they became anxious about her disappearance. At first, they thought she was playing a practical joke, but by five o'clock that morning her absence had ceased to be amusing—or even suggest pique if she'd had her feelings hurt. It was near dawn."

"Did anything else go missing? If Eleanor had planned to leave, I imagine she would take clothing and money. Or jewelry."

"That's a funny thing, Miss. Not a stitch of clothing was gone, her trousseau all packed and ready, her other clothes still hanging in the wardrobe. I know, because I prepared her trunks myself. I had even embroidered her new initials on her silk camisoles. They were neatly folded on top, undisturbed, and everything else—her pantalettes, cotton chemises, skirts, bodices and stockings—were all where I'd placed them. None of us could think of anything taken. 'Twas just her gone, in her bridal gown."

An uneasy conviction gripped me like a cold wind. Eleanor Wellington, née Granville, didn't leave Northfield House of her own accord. *Where was she? What happened to her?*

I thought of something else. "Mrs. Hadley, what day was it? The day of the wedding?"

"June 26, a Sunday. The year of our Lord 1892." The date rolled off her tongue as though she repeated it daily, like a prayer.

This saved me a trip to the church in search of the marriage banns. I placed a hand on Mrs. Hadley arm. "It is wretched of me, Mrs. Hadley, stirring up sad memories. It was not my intention to tread on tender wounds."

"I'm the one to be regretful, Miss." She wiped a tear from her eyes. "I'm an old fool, getting emotional after all this time. But back then, it was a nightmare. For days, I awoke in the night, fancying I'd heard her crying."

"You've a right to mourn, Mrs. Hadley," I said, with the realization that unless this mystery was solved, everyone would continue to grieve.

❧

At dinner that night, I reminded everyone I was going into Melling to the library to do research for Mr. Wellington.

"My work will take up most of the day, but is there any additional errand I can do?" I addressed Mrs. Wellington.

"Thank you, Miss Chatham, for asking, but no."

It appeared Mrs. Wellington would not be beholden to me under any circumstances.

Owen glanced my way, catching my eye. "Good luck with your search, Anne. I hope you find what you seek."

"Fine researcher, this girl," Mr. Wellington said, appreciation in his voice. "Good head on her shoulders. I am relieved that I don't have to sift through dusty records."

"Perhaps that will give you enough time to contact your solicitor," Mrs. Wellington said. "If your resources can manage an assistant like Miss Chatham, Northfield House should be able to hire a proper butler, as well."

"Next week, Lavinia," he said.

Owen winked at me.

I could not take her comments so lightheartedly. Mrs. Wellington never missed an opportunity to remind me that my employment presented certain hardships for her. I knew that I'd better manage my expectations. No matter how inspired Owen might be, there was no future for me in this household. I was naïve if I thought I could get too comfortable here.

Early the next morning, I walked into the village and boarded a public bus. Two hours later, it deposited me on the outskirts of Melling, a civil parish within the borough of Sefton in Merseyside. I walked a half mile to the registry office at the town hall, the repository for county records and historical documents. After hours of looking for land titles, deeds, and mortgage reports, I had extensive notes on the information important to Henry Wellington.

By three o'clock that afternoon, I was able to devote my attention to my self-assigned task, which also involved my employer, and walked to the local library.

"Where might I find archived newspapers and periodicals?" I asked the librarian, a young, agile man dressed in yards of black gabardine.

He led me to another room, asking, "What year do you wish to review?"

"1892." My heart began to race.

The librarian ushered me through a door and up a set of metal stairs. He snapped on an electrical bulb overhead that shed a dim light and created deep shadows.

"Each shelf is labeled." He ran a long, bony finger down the side of the wooden shelving unit. "You can find the year here—and here, each month."

He turned and left me alone in the cavernous room, trailing behind him a faint odor of camphor and witch hazel.

Suddenly, my task seemed daunting. I stood before piles of broadsheets. *The Standard,* the daily morning paper was there, as well as *The Melling Bulletin,* a weekly. I found the year I was searching for, and then the month of June, and lifted a stack of dusty newsprint from its resting place. I began with the daily, carrying several days' production to the long, narrow table behind the shelves.

I thumbed through the old, brittle papers until I unearthed June 27, 1892. I scrutinized each page and found nothing. I kept going forwards from that date.

June 28, nothing.

June 29, nothing.

Not until June 30 did the paper report the story of the missing bride. A short article appeared at the bottom of page 1 surrounded by bold black lines:

Village of Northfield: Eleanor Louise Wellington, née Granville, 19-year-old wife of Henry Addison Wellington of Northfield House, Merseyside, disappeared presumed kidnapped between 1:00 a.m. and 6:00 a.m. on 27 June.

During the festivities following her wedding and reception, the bride disappeared from the home of her husband. Authorities were notified of the disappearance by 12:00 noon after a thorough search of the house and grounds.

Anyone having information of Eleanor Wellington or the presumed crime is asked to contact the Constabulary in Melling.

The report of Eleanor's disappearance had taken three days and was written in dry, matter-of-fact prose. I suspected that the news had been suppressed by the family until they were desperate for information and resorted to this short news article. The kidnapping of a beautiful girl, a member of the landed gentry, on her wedding day would have been sensationalized fodder for the yellow press, had someone's palm not been greased. Eleanor's parents, or the Wellingtons, had likely paid reporters to look the other way.

After arching my aching back and relaxing my stiff shoulders, I continued searching through copies of *The Standard* for a month after the disappearance and found only the same simple, straightforward news article, repeated a week later.

Digging into three months of *The Bulletin* turned up the same article, printed twice in July.

I continued to peruse *The Bulletin* until something else emerged. In January 1893, an ad appeared in the classified section:

MISSING PERSON Seeking information regarding the whereabouts of Eleanor Wellington, formerly Granville, wife of Henry Wellington of Northfield House, Merseyside. Please contact Michael St. George. **Post Office,** West Kirby.

After scribbling down the contents of both notices, I leaned my head upon my arms and closed my eyes, tired of hunching over papers and breathing in book mold. I'd learned nothing new. I'd merely confirmed information that Martha Langtry and Mrs. Hadley had already made known to me.

I looked at my watch. I had but twenty minutes to catch the last bus from Melling to Northfield. I gathered my handbag and steno pad and sped towards the stop in the gathering twilight.

Chapter 19

I returned home after ten, too late for dinner, and ate a simple meal of cold mutton and bread in the kitchen instead. After cleaning up after myself, I headed upstairs to my room. Just as I reached the door, Owen stepped from the shadows in the corridor. I jumped in surprise.

"Anne," he whispered. "Tell me what you found."

"You frightened me!" I took a deep breath to calm my fluttering heart.

"My apologies. I've been waiting all day."

Nervous about being alone with him in my bedchamber, I said, "Meet me in the library in ten minutes."

"Of course," he said and turned to the back stairs.

After bathing my face in cool water and tidying my hair, I grabbed my steno pad and proceeded to the library. There, Owen and I sat in a pool of yellow light shed by an oil lamp while I shared my handwritten copies of the news report and the advertisement I'd uncovered in the local papers.

"Anne, this is wonderful."

Surprised he wasn't disappointed, as I believed I'd come away with precious little, I said, "Why?"

"Don't you understand?" he said with admiration. "This confirms everything we believe so far. Now we know when and from where Eleanor disappeared. We also know that the authorities must have been stymied, since the family eventually moved on to a private detective. You're remarkable."

I tried to see from his point of view. Was this, perhaps, meaningful information after all? I hung on his words, too willing to receive his praise. But I became suspicious of his sincerity. Was I being manipulated? Once again, the world looked like a lonely place, too thick with obstacles for me to be comfortable with anyone.

"Let's keep pushing on," he said. "We need to talk to the man mentioned in the papers, this St. George."

The hunt excited him. But why, after more than thirty years?

"Owen," I said tentatively, "have you never been curious about your Aunt Eleanor before? It's such a dramatic story."

"Strangely, no. I've never been compelled to wonder about it."

"You've never felt her presence?"

"As I said the other night, only since you arrived in this house."

So my presence at Northfield had opened a portal or stirred an unseen, tortured soul that lingered there.

"Do you think we can find St. George in the telephone listings?" Owen asked.

"Perhaps. If he still has a business. He may not even be living."

"You're right, of course," Owen said. "Not a very promising thread to follow."

"We could check the deeds registry. He might own property."

He brightened. "It's a place to begin. Anne, we'll turn up something. We simply must. I've begun to realize how important my family history might be."

His mood was infectious, and I felt an unaccustomed affinity with this strange, dark young man. This emotional connection and his recognition of the relevance of the past in his life made me bold enough to inquire about something even more personal.

"Owen," I said, recalling my glimpse of angry, red scars on his body. "You were wounded in the war, were you not?"

"Indeed, I was." He turned his face away.

"I'm sorry if the memory is painful."

"It's not that. Actually, the war and my military experience were a godsend."

"There are few who would say that about such a frightful ordeal."

"It changed everything. My whole perspective on life."

"Seventeen is a tender age to encounter the worst of humanity. It must have altered everything you understood about the world."

"There's nothing like a sucking chest wound to sharpen your faculties."

"My God." I suppressed a wave of nausea.

He bowed his head and leaned towards me. "I'm sorry. Forgive me. I needn't be so explicit. I shouldn't burden you with—"

"I don't mind," I said quickly. "I want to understand. I want to know. I can't fully explain it, but the more I know, the more effective I can be as we unravel our mystery. You can never tell what information may be useful." This had been true more than once in my experience. I suspected that Owen's near-death event made him susceptible to connections with the world beyond this one.

He looked at me with trust and then swept his gaze about the room. Hesitating only a moment, he said, "It happened near the end of hostilities. I was working in a field hospital near the front lines during the battle of the Vardar."

"This was in September 1918?" I asked, knowing Vardar to be the decisive battle on the Balkan front.

"Yes." Owen's countenance darkened as he remembered. "British forces joined Allied troops at Salonika, where they met Turks and Huns on the battlefield. My detail was near the front lines of the battle of Doiran. The day I was wounded, the British reached Strumitza."

I recalled that it was after this offensive that the Bulgarians began armistice negotiations. Owen had almost made it to the end of the war without injury—physical injury at least.

"They told me an artillery shell hit the hospital compound. All I can truly remember is flying through the air. I awoke in excruciating pain. It seemed like the awful gurgling of my lungs came from someone else."

I tamped down the bile in my throat as he recounted his story.

"They pulled me out of the mud and did the best they could. Infected tissues were cut away and the wounds sealed repeatedly. Even today, I can't stand the smell of carbolic lotion."

I was aware that doctors now used both carbolic lotion and bismuth iodoform paraffin paste to prevent infection of severe wounds. Neither was especially effective. Owen was fortunate to be alive.

"After I survived ministrations in the field, I was transported across the continent by horse cart and train. Then I endured additional surgeries in France, until finally I was able to convalesce at the Pavilion in Brighton."

Many fine homes and public buildings across Britain were repurposed to house the wounded during and after the war. I couldn't imagine what it took to get him there in one piece.

Finally, Owen offered a rueful smile. "I had hours of electrical therapy, massage, and bed rest. Finally, after two years, they sent me home. I was one of the lucky ones. At least my face wasn't blown away by shrapnel, nor any limb amputated by guillotine."

"Oh, Owen. How did you survive?"

"I didn't think I would. I spent endless hours in hospital, alternately thinking how alone I was, or how lucky. More importantly, it seemed to me the only reason I was spared was to do something meaningful."

"Your agricultural experiments."

"Yes. Don't you see? Many ills of the world could be resolved with a safe and adequate food supply. War typically revolves around the need for natural resources—water most importantly, but also minerals, seaport access, and arable land."

"So adequate food production is a means of preventing war?" I said.

"One of them, anyway. I joined up as a simple act of defiance. I needed to get away from here, from Father and Thomas. I had to become my own man. Then I realized how important my skills were. My wartime experience taught me that an army moves on its stomach. Being a farmer, I thought I could make a particular contribution once I returned home."

I visualized a romantic boy going off to war to help his fellow man. "But you joined the medical service?"

"With the medics, I was at the front, but wouldn't be in combat, carrying a gun. And I was in the essential position of getting provisions to the field hospitals. Everywhere around us, people were starving."

I imagined the blockades and a ravaged Germany, where more people died of starvation than in battle. I said, "You must have witnessed such misery."

"I believed I could make a difference in England's fortunes after the war. At least I'd talked myself into that during my long days in hospital." He shook his head. "I wanted to accomplish something important."

So Owen was an idealist. His role in feeding the armed forces had transformed into a desire to feed the world. "And don't you think you have?" I asked.

"No one ever comes out of a war feeling proud. Or vindicated. It's just an enormous waste."

"But that didn't discourage you. You should be gratified by that."

"Anne, you're the first person who's understood." He put his hand upon mine.

My heart skipped a beat. We shared a long, silent moment of communion. A shadow darkened the doorway, startling me. I snatched my hand away as we jumped apart.

Thomas leaned against the doorjamb with a smirk upon his face. "Is this Romeo and Juliet I see?" He laughed. "Are you two getting in the mood for tomorrow's costume ball?"

"I'd almost forgotten that damnable party," Owen muttered. He looked squarely at Thomas. "I'm convinced that Anne is the only person who might make it halfway tolerable."

I was both chagrined and gladdened by Owen's compliment. I was also reminded that I could not forget myself. I had no doubt that Mrs. Wellington would hustle me out of Northfield at the first suggestion of an inappropriate relationship with her son.

Owen asked, "When did you and Charlotte return?"

"Just now." Thomas winked. "You were no doubt too busy to hear the motorcar."

"My ear is tuned to more important concerns," Owen said, stealing a glance at me. "Did you want to see me for some reason?"

"Father sent me," Thomas said, taking a step backwards into the hall. "He wants both of us, actually."

Owen turned to me as Thomas moved out of earshot. "It's late. We should continue our conversation about Michael St. George tomorrow."

"I hope so." I was swept up with the notion that lifting the weight of this tragedy from the Wellington family was important to Owen's future. With growing trepidation regarding my unfortunate attraction, I realized it mattered to me as well.

Before I could think of anything to say that would recreate our moment of affinity, he was gone. I listened to his swift step as he crossed the great hall towards the other end of the house.

Chapter 20

*T*he next morning, I stood in Charlotte's bedroom as she lifted a scarlet satin gown from its box.

"A flamenco dancer," giggled Charlotte. "Isn't it daring?" She held the dress against her body, smoothing the bright fabric across her bosom and hips.

"It's lovely. But it's so . . . red."

"Yes," Charlotte crowed. "It's exactly your opposite, so it's perfect!"

I wasn't sure this was a compliment. "You're very kind."

"A costume reveals your innermost, secret self, Anne, the persona you are afraid or unable to let out," Charlotte said. "Except in this case, it may not be you at all since the dress is mine."

For some reason, this annoyed me. "Then perhaps you should wear it. I don't think I could." I still wasn't convinced my going to this party was a good idea.

"Don't be silly. You can't go to a costume ball without a getup. The whole point is to become someone else. Don't you think *not* dressing for the ball would be inconsiderate?"

"I'm afraid I don't follow."

"Not wearing a costume shows you don't care, that you didn't bother to take a go at it. Don't be a spoilsport, Anne," her voice took on an edge. "Everyone's expecting you."

"That sounds ominous," I muttered under my breath. I realized that her desire for my presence had nothing to do with me. She wanted an audience for yet another moment in the sun for herself. I would be but a dim satellite reflecting her glory.

"If you find it too revealing, I'm sure Aunt Martha can lend you a shawl." Charlotte blithely dismissed any concerns I might have.

So this was her challenge. And, of course, it was a competition that I was meant to lose. I smiled brightly and took a step towards her.

She piled the red satin into my arms. "You can't see mine until tonight. It's a surprise."

I left with the dress—and matching slippers, a small pot of rouge, and a deep sense of foreboding. In my room, I laid the dress out on the bed and studied it. It was narrow in the waist and hips, with a ruffled hem pinned up above the left knee in front. And it was a scandalous shade of crimson. Bordello red, my mother would have called it, whispering so Father couldn't hear.

I should not have let myself be talked into this. My employers might judge me as frivolous, while it was my instinct to maintain the image of the consummate professional.

But many people would be attending the ball. I could get lost in the crowd, and eventually make my way to the sanctuary of my room at the first opportunity. Quite likely, I was making too much of this evening's event. It was merely a party, and as unused as I was to such merriment, it was quite ordinary to the Wellington family and their friends.

After hanging the dress in the wardrobe, I returned to work and finished typing something begun the day before. Now that Charlotte was here, Mr. Wellington would be scarce, and I'd have the study to myself. I luxuriated in the solitude while, at the same time, felt engulfed by loneliness.

I'd achieved a comfortable rhythm, the keys clacking with my precise movements, when something outside the window caught my attention. I stopped the relentless movement of my hands to watch Charlotte and Mrs. Wellington walk towards the garden, dodging rain puddles. Charlotte took long, easy strides, swinging her hips, trailing a brightly colored scarf from her fingertips. Her delicate skirts rippled in the light breeze. Mrs. Wellington looked stiff by comparison, her back straight in her dark, corseted dress. Perhaps they were burying whatever hatchet they tossed back and forth between them.

The animosity Mrs. Wellington displayed towards her own sister's granddaughter was troubling. They were family, after all. But perhaps Martha Langtry was right, that Charlotte's designs on Thomas, whether trifling or not, and her striking resemblance to Eleanor, Henry's first choice for a wife, were threatening to Mrs. Wellington's sense of herself. Charlotte could not help but be a constant reminder to Mrs. Wellington that she was second, not only in Henry's eyes, but in Thomas's as well.

They passed beyond my line of sight until I stood, leaning across the Remington to peer out the window. They were going beyond the garden to the path leading to the footbridge.

I felt a pang of anxiety. Would Owen change now that Charlotte was here once more? Our ghost hunting might not hold his interest any longer. With Charlotte charging the atmosphere, perhaps he'd succumb to his brooding self, recalling an unrequited love, his passion reawakened.

And there were other reasons for concern. Owen and I had developed a budding friendship, with the mystery of Eleanor and the haunting spirit of Northfield to unite us. We shared a moment of intimacy last night. Where could this possibly lead? Encouraging a man of his station to dally with my affections would be disastrous, as it could lead nowhere.

Mrs. Wellington and Charlotte moved behind the trees, and I sat again, feeling once more like a voyeur. I was being entirely too negative. I would always be an outsider, but surely Owen was still committed to our ghost hunting. His parting words to me last night confirmed it.

I pondered where Owen might be at that moment. Perhaps he was laboring in the fields or, because of the rain, being fitted into his costume for this evening's festivities. I recalled his claim last night— that I was the only person who might make the ball "halfway tolerable." I, too, felt *his* presence would be the only thing that might bring me enjoyment.

I was too restless and edgy to continue working and went to my room. I took a warm bath, washed my long hair, and perched in the windowsill while it dried in the setting sun, which finally appeared between storm clouds. I again contemplated the dress hanging in the wardrobe. I should try it on in case it required some alteration.

I pulled the gown over my head and tugged the clasp locker closed. Smoothing it over my torso, I turned to the wardrobe mirror and gasped.

The dress revealed a stunningly low décolletage, edged with a deep ruffle. More ruffles barely covered my shoulders. The fabric cinched tight around my slim waist and hugged my hips. Gathered high on the knee, the triple-flounced hem exposed my legs. At first glance, I was appalled. This dress was unsuitable.

Then, just for a moment, I let myself enjoy the picture in the mirror.

I had been transformed into a seductress, the scarlet dress flattering not just my figure, but also my dark coloring. Still loose, my thick, black hair fell in waves across my shoulders. Charlotte might well be surprised if she assumed I couldn't do this costume justice. I looked like a completely different person, released from my customary drab uniform. I ran my fingertips over the silky red fabric. Perhaps Charlotte was right about costumes. As she'd insisted to her Uncle Henry on that night not so long ago, a mask was unnecessary if you could conjure another personality with the right robes, like an actor transforming into a character on the stage.

I danced towards the mirror in a tight little pirouette, my skirt fluttering behind me. Who might I become, clothed so? Circe with her magical powers? Leda, all innocence and sensual mystery? Hippolyta, warrior queen, conqueror of men?

Tonight, the house would be filled with strangers. Most of the revelers would not know me and would have no preconception of who I was or how I should behave. Perhaps, just for this evening, I could be free from the constraints of my upbringing, my current circumstances, and my limited future. Tonight, I could set aside my true nature to become something else, someone with boundless opportunity.

Viewing my figure from every angle, I felt powerful. I embraced the femininity that the dress revealed, the potency of my sex. The woman who stared back at me from my mirror was not only confident, but also shockingly brazen. Had I finally come into my own?

I looked forwards to making an entrance, to flaunting this hidden side of myself. This sensation felt like a dangerous drug. This must be the way Charlotte and women like her felt every day. Why should I not join them, even if my freedom was but a mirage for an evening?

I imagined Owen admiring me, whirling me about the dance floor, his hand at my waist. Then I saw his mother watching from the crowd, an angry frown upon her disapproving face. At this, my small bubble of optimism burst. Was I possessed? I could never wear such a costume. Although London society might find it acceptable for someone like Charlotte, here in the country, it would be a scandal for me. And I could not so blithely change who I was or how I felt about myself.

I undid the dress and slipped it off, along with my bravado. I felt I must withdraw. I was too cowardly to show myself as anyone but who I was. For a moment, I sat on my bed with the silken garment draped across my lap. What would I do now? Borrow an outfit from Maddy and go as a scullery maid? I could make an excuse, tell everyone I couldn't close the clasp. Or that I felt ill.

But Owen would be looking for me, I was sure. He would be disappointed. It would be like breaking a promise.

I smoothed the gleaming satin. "It is your desire, Charlotte, that I dare wear this dress, projecting a pale reflection of you, a sloppy carbon copy of the glamorous adventuress." The very thought galled me. I stared at the ruffles filling my hands, felt the smooth fabric beneath my fingers.

I was loath to let Charlotte embarrass me, but I hated the idea of disappointing Owen. I considered the dress that lay in my lap once more. Perhaps, I could make an alteration or two. It might work.

I dragged my bag from under the bed. With the gilt-washed sewing scissors, I ripped out the ruched seam that gathered the hem to above the knee. I inspected the neckline and carefully drew up the ruffle with tiny stitches at the shoulders. The slippery satin tested my talents as a seamstress, but I persevered. Finally, I had the courage to try it on again.

Now the mirror showed me a different woman. The skirt flowed softly to the floor, and the bodice was higher and lay flat, covering fully the cleavage of my breasts. More modest now, the dress was perhaps even more alluring.

No one could fault me in this altered frock. If Charlotte was hoping to humiliate me or put me in a compromising position, it would not work. If she expected to show me at a disadvantage to her own beauty, she would fail.

"I accept your challenge, Charlotte. I can do this." I dressed with care, compelled by an excitement I'd never felt before. Just before departing my room, I posed before the mirror once more. I stood tall, swept my hair behind my shoulders, and lifted my chin with confidence.

Perhaps I drew strength from the resident ghost, for I felt Eleanor with me. Poor Eleanor, who disappeared in her prime before life truly began and missed the balls and the admiration which was her due, would dance once more.

Tonight, I was the embodiment of the ghost that haunted Northfield House.

Chapter 21

*A*n hour later, feeling quite unlike myself, I rushed down-stairs. With my lips rouged, I sidled into the darkened study and sat near the window, watching as guests arrived.

Shiny automobiles puttered in one after another, lined up in the drive, and disgorged their passengers. A steady rain, abating just as the first visitors appeared, had cooled the evening and weighted the atmosphere with a luxurious damp. I paused until the house was well populated before attempting my own entrance.

The click of my high heels gave me courage as I breezed down the passageway and into the artificially lit ballroom. Tonight, I was one of them. In the hand-me-down gown, I was not the harlot to be shunned as my questionable benefactress might have expected, but an enchantress capable of magical spells. As I stepped across the threshold, a heady sense of enthusiasm seized me. My bosom swelled with expectation.

The entire room was ablaze with color. Silver and crystal sparkled in golden candlelight as the soaring notes of *Rhapsody in Blue* filled the air. Faces turned in my direction. While poised at the entry, I noted appreciative stares from several young men.

Our hosts were positioned just inside the ballroom, in a receiving line. Costumed in Elizabethan dress, Mrs. Wellington and Mr. Wellington smiled and chatted, greeting new arrivals. With his wheelchair draped in dark velvet, my employer wore a maroon doublet and cape. His garb paled in comparison to his wife's purple brocade gown, trimmed in satin and covered in pearls. An elaborate linen ruff, decorated with gold threads, encircled her neck. Her hair was woven into an intricate chignon studded with multicolored jewels.

Standing near his mother, Thomas noticed me first. He registered my unexpected appearance and approached to take my hand. He was dressed as a South American gaucho in black satin detailed with silver embroidery, and he carried a braided whip at his side. He swept me into a corner. For once, I felt emboldened by Thomas's admiration and met his challenging look with a saucy one of my own.

"My dear Miss Chatham, you have unsuspected talents," he said with a laugh. "You should expose yourself to society more often."

"I never think of myself as an object available for public consumption," I said with a smile.

"You look dangerous," he said, with a glance at his weapon. "I'm glad to be armed."

Catching my image in the mirrored French doors, I saw my cheeks flushed pink and my eyes shining with excitement. "You have nothing to fear from me, Thomas, as long as your mother is chaperoning this party." I glanced about the room for Owen.

Thomas looked abashed. "Don't tease. You take unfair advantage. There's no peace in the house if I don't behave myself."

He escorted me into the room and introduced a middle-aged couple in medieval garb, she in a bell-sleeved peasant shirt and he in a tunic with leggings. When the music started again, the gentleman asked me to dance, earning a disapproving look from his wife. Thomas looked delighted with my predicament and returned to the reception line, abandoning me to be spun onto the ballroom floor.

"So, you're old Henry's typewriter," my partner ventured, running his eyes over my face and hair. "How does Lavinia feel about his spending time alone with you?"

It hadn't occurred to me my aspect might stir jealousy. My employers could judge me harshly for such a display of hubris. This concern added to my hesitant movements and halting feet, as the last time I had danced was some years before and with my father, who had officiated at a wedding. Fortunately, my partner was adept, and we moved with other couples about the room in a counter-clockwise sweep, swirling in a sea of gleaming costumes.

When the music stopped, a young man dressed as Robin Hood introduced himself, and we began to twirl about when the orchestra started again. As we circled the room, my hand rested lightly on the shoulder of his deep green vest, while his hand, sheathed in a leather gauntlet, grasped my waist. I looked again for Owen. Perhaps he wasn't coming after all. When another young man stepped up, I realized there was a line of gentlemen, watching and waiting their turn. I suddenly felt uncomfortable in the limelight.

As I was backed across the dance floor in step to the music, I was surprised to glimpse Martha Langtry seated in a corner with other elderly women, all wearing either black or deep purple Victorian-style frocks as if in mourning.

They might have been wearing costumes, or merely old clothing from their youth. I then reprimanded myself for my uncharitable thoughts. When the band started playing *Lady, Be Good*, I took it as a sign I should step away from the crowd.

"Please," I entreated my partner, outfitted as a musketeer from the age of Louis XIII, "I must speak to Mrs. Langtry."

We stopped and stepped outside the whirling dancers. He bowed with the élan befitting a king's guardsman and, with a little smile, took his leave.

I turned to Martha. "Mrs. Langtry, how nice to see you."

She gave me a blank stare. "Have we met?" In her lap, she balanced a plate littered with the remnants of an artichoke-olive canapé I'd seen Cook preparing earlier in the day.

The other women, who nibbled on the canapés and smoked salmon on toast, watched us closely.

"Yes, but it's been a long time. I'm Anne. I work with Mr. Wellington."

"How are you, dear?" She looked past me into the crowd. "Have a seat and talk to an old lady." She made a shooing gesture to the tiny woman in black sitting next to her.

The little woman shot me a look of disdain before vacating her chair.

Martha opened an elaborate fan and fluttered it before her face.

Feeling warm, I wished for a fan of my own. But what I really wanted was a mask to hide behind. The scarlet dress made my desired invisibility impossible. I scanned the guests and spied Thomas again, but not his brother.

"Have you seen the bride?" said Martha.

"What?" I asked, assuming one of the revelers was dressed as a bride.

"Just lovely," said Martha. "All those flowers."

I searched among the tumult of guests, both the originals and their doubles reflected in the mirrored doors.

"Eleanor has never looked more beautiful," Martha said, beaming.

I was engulfed by a wave of pure pity. Martha was at another party in another time.

She eyed me with disapproval. "That *dress*, dear. I hope you don't think ill of me if I suggest it is most inappropriate." She shook her head. "Quite improper."

I felt a stab of humiliation. My confidence wavered. But I called upon Eleanor's supporting presence and decided to humor my elderly companion. After all, her suffering trumped any discomfort I might feel.

"I must apologize, Mrs. Langtry." I bowed my head with mock contrition. "I'm a simple country girl and didn't know what I should wear."

She laughed. "There, there, my dear. Don't be disheartened. No one's looking at you, anyway. They'll all be looking at her."

"Of course!" I agreed. "Do you need anything, Mrs. Langtry? May I get you a glass of water?" I touched her hand.

She jerked away from me and snarled, "Don't do that. How dare you touch me!"

My face stung as I looked about at our companions. No one seemed to notice that Martha was unstable. I said as softly as possible, "Would you like to go to your room? Lie down for a while?"

"Why should I? I'll miss all the fun."

I was wondering how much fun she could possibly be having when she turned to me, leaning close, and whispered like a conspirator.

"You forget," she said. "I know. I know everything. I saw what really happened." She drew herself up with smug hauteur. "I'm telling."

Telling what? She might have been thinking of Eleanor's wedding—or another event tangled in her jumbled mind.

Martha closed her fan. We sat in silence, peering at the assembled throng as they paused with the music.

A hush fell.

For a moment, anticipation hung in the air.

Then an excited murmur ran through the room.

All heads turned towards the entrance. Charlotte stood at the top of the steps. She was dressed as an ethereal moth. A shimmering white gown rippled across her body, falling from the high collar at her throat to the floor. Her hair was hidden under a close-fitting, beaded skullcap. A pair of gossamer wings with fluttering ribbons completed the effect. The translucent fabric revealed every alluring curve of her body, unaltered by any foundation garments. She looked like a silken goddess, lit from within by moonlight.

The crowd broke into spontaneous applause at her appearance, and Charlotte beamed a glorious smile at her adoring admirers. Cries of appreciation bounced about the ballroom like reflected light.

It was only then I saw Owen. Dressed like Edgar Allen Poe, he wore a close-fitting black suit with a silk bow tied loosely around a high white collar. With his dark, tousled hair and solemn expression, he most assuredly recalled the famous poet.

He stood at the edge of the dancers, his eyes devouring Charlotte.

Something inside me withered and withdrew. With Charlotte's arrival in her diaphanous costume, I felt sure I looked garish and overdone. Whoever or whatever infused me with confidence had fled.

Perhaps this was just what she'd planned. Her image was that of heavenly angel, otherworldly sylph, ethereal sprite. Mine was smoking demon with my tumble of black hair and crimson gown. I might as well have been holding a pitchfork.

As I watched Owen, who looked mesmerized by Charlotte's silvery figure, a young man appeared before me, extending his hand. I rose without thinking, without seeing his face, and we spun awkwardly about the floor. A jazz number gripped the crowd, and another man stepped forwards and pulled me into the circle of revelers. I moved to unfamiliar music, rocking and bouncing, ungainly and clumsy, back and forth and around.

Drums pounded, and horns blared in propulsive syncopation. I continued to dance and dance, unable to catch the tempo. The beat of the music pulsed throughout the room, the rhythmical throb vibrating the floor, and we swayed and dipped around the whirl of sparkling color and grinning faces. I feared I was making a spectacle of myself, but felt trapped in the crush of dancers.

Charlotte drifted through the mob like a cloud, bestowing kisses, dancing with one admirer, and laughing with another. I heard a babble of praise follow her whenever the music paused.

Everything tilted for a second when a waltz seized the room and rolled over the dancers. Another man took my hand and we eddied and swirled, round and round. Yet another man cut in. I hardly acknowledged my partners, barely felt their hand in mine, the other resting at my waist.

Owen appeared suddenly, grasping me and pulling me close. We spun around the dance floor, his dark, brooding face hovering above mine until I was breathless. I felt his excitement, but was aware of an undertone of hostility.

"You are quite the surprise, Anne," he breathed heavily against my cheek. "I thought my darling cousin would dress you in a nun's habit or perhaps a shroud."

My cheeks stung with shame because of my absurd costume. He was making fun of me. He'd also been drinking, but I couldn't tell how much. Perhaps that is why he showed up so late. He had to muster the courage to be in the same room with Charlotte. He glanced over my head in her direction.

Was he interested at all in me? I thought not. It was not I who stoked this passion, this desire, this heat. It was not I who antagonized him, but Charlotte.

"Owen," I stiffened against him. "Let's sit this dance out."

He couldn't hear me and swung me faster across the floor. He buried his face in my hair. "Anne, you're ravishing."

He pointedly ignored Charlotte, as she glided through the crowd like an apparition. But I still believed his every move, his every breath, was for her. I was an easily sacrificed pawn in the game they played.

"Owen," I said, pulling us out of the arc of dancers as he tried to hold on to me. "Please, let me go."

I tore myself from his embrace. He looked startled and stepped backwards. I could only imagine what deep emotion seethed within his heart, but I was sure it had nothing to do with me. I ran from the room, and Owen didn't follow. I took refuge on the veranda outside the mirrored doors and gasped to catch my breath, blinking away tears.

Leaning against the balustrade in the heavy humid air, I plumbed my feelings. From the shadows on the veranda, I watched the dancers. Charlotte stood out like sparkling ice in a dark sea of velvet. Now in the embrace of a beautiful young man, she swept across the ballroom floor, luminous as candlelight.

I looked for Owen. As he stood at the edge of the frenzied revelers looking dejected, he was approached by a young girl and pulled into the stream of dancers. Grim-faced, he bounced about the floor with a laughing partner, all golden curls and blue satin. Little Bo Peep. They disappeared into the crowd.

My eyes searched the room for them and found Thomas standing at the far side of the dance floor against the bar. He threw back a whiskey, wiping his mouth with the heel of his hand. His gaze followed Charlotte as she danced with the beautiful stranger. He looked not only sullen but angry.

Behind Thomas, Mrs. Wellington sat with Martha Langtry. As if the two were old friends. Neither of them registered concern, seemingly unaware of the emotions churning about them. So deceptively calm and gracious. I knew better. I had no doubt that Mrs. Wellington kept a watchful eye on Thomas and Charlotte. I was left to wonder if she felt the same about the possibility of Owen and her grandniece. If she could orchestrate the play of emotions and their outcome, I imagined that Mrs. Wellington would pair Charlotte with any other man in the room. Anybody but one of her precious sons.

Maybe I was the only one deceived, a simple girl brought up in a parsonage. I knew little of the machinations of the landed gentry. Perhaps every young person was controlled by scheming parents, anxious about their marital prospects and the social and political gains to be made.

When another round of dancing started, I skirted the dance floor and fled to the study. Taking refuge there, I could hear the stormy music and raucous laughter without being part of it. No one would miss me. I sat at my desk in the quiet starlight for a very long time, both my heart and my eyes closed.

❧

The motor cars left, one by one, just as they'd arrived. The earlier dignified greetings were replaced by joyous voices in retreat, tongues loosened by alcohol and exhaustion. After I heard the last automobile depart, I remained in the study, gazing out the back window at the star-spangled sky.

Something flickered in the darkened woods beyond the gardens. Pale and luminous, a floating figure moved in the shadows near the path to the footbridge.

Someone was out there. I stood and leaned close to the window in the dark. I stared, riveted, trying to distinguish the shadows in the moonlight, desperately needing to dwell on something other than the disastrous evening.

All was breathlessly still until I saw it again—something as fine as mist, as faint as fog. My rational side reminded me that rain had fallen all week, leaving the grounds soaked with damp. Perhaps this was nothing more than miasma forming among the trees. Or maybe Kitty was out there in the woods, watching the revelers, just as I was.

And yet . . . I felt a prickling of my face, and a chill raced down my spine like a spider.

Eleanor! Is that you?

Chapter 22

*M*y head swam with thoughts of Eleanor. Eleanor in her wedding dress, Eleanor dancing by moonlight, Eleanor disappearing like the stars at dawn. What passions had been stirred by fevered emotions tonight, disturbing the haunts of the lingering dead? The ghost in the south wing had tried to speak to me more than once before—to communicate something of great importance. I believed it with all my heart. I might yet again be a witness, if Eleanor walked tonight.

I swallowed the lump in my throat and grabbed Mr. Wellington's woolen shawl from a desk chair. Wrapping it around my shoulders, I hurried through the now-quiet halls to the veranda. As motivated by thoughts of impressing Owen as by encountering our ghost, I stepped outside.

The starless night enveloped me. The path to the footbridge shimmered like a twist of pale ribbon, banked by a solid wall of black shadow.

I dashed across the wet grass in the dark to the trail leading to the ravine, towards the apparition. My delicate slippers and the bottom of my skirt were almost immediately soaked through. The wet silk wrapped about my cold legs, hampering me. I gathered my skirts and swept forwards, feeling as if I teetered on the edge of the truth. I felt the possibility of grasping the knowledge that would unveil the mystery shrouding Northfield House.

Eleanor! I wanted to call out. *Stop! Wait for me!*

Sliding on rain-slicked stones, I reached the footbridge and looked in all directions. The pale figure I sought was nowhere to be seen in the inky black of night. But emotion charged the atmosphere. Some palpable sensation hovered, suspended in the air. I was certain something watched me as I paused at the edge of the bridge.

It had begun to rain again. The dense vegetation draping the ravine glistened with damp. Rushing water drowned out all other sounds. I kicked off my shoes to cross the ancient boards, worn smooth by a century of use. Holding tight to the wooden handrail and inching forwards, I saw that something was wrong. Just an arm's length before me, the raw, broken ends of the railing glowed white in the darkness. Another step, and my hand would have encountered nothing but air.

My first thought was a tree branch had broken off in the storms, fallen, and torn through the guardrail. I halted, aware of the dizzying height, fearing I might lose my grip and go over the side.

My attention drawn to the rocks far below, I spied what looked to be a large bundle of rags. The swift water worried at its edges, tearing and grasping. My vision sorted the image, and the bundle came into focus. I recognized Charlotte's shimmering silver dress, her gossamer wings, and their trembling ribbons.

Dear God.

A fearful dread paralyzed me where I stood. For a few seconds, I was frozen with shock, my heart pounding. I screamed, "Charlotte!" But the word was barely a breath caught in my throat. Panic throbbed in my chest, but I forced the breath into my lungs.

"Help! Please, help!" I shrieked into the dark night, my cries lost on the wind.

I backed away from the broken boards and shrugged off the shawl. Taking care not to slip, I scurried to the other end of the bridge to a spot where the drop was not as steep and the climb appeared less treacherous. Pulling my skirts close, I clambered over the side, clinging to the vegetation anchored to the cliff. Halfway down, I lost my grip and slid down the ravine, finally catching myself. I grasped at the wet rocks, scraping my palms, breaking my nails, and slipped again. Unable to find purchase, I fell to the bottom, landing in the stone-strewn mud on my knees and elbows. My gown was soaked, and my palms burned.

I pulled myself upright, and took unsteady steps forwards, nearly tripping over a downed tree. Making my way over the sharp boulders, I scrambled to the water's edge.

Once within reach of Charlotte, I stared at her still form, broken upon the rocks.

I knew without touching her that she was dead. Her head was twisted at an unnatural angle, half in and half out of the raging waters. Charlotte's amber eyes stared upwards to the black sky. Rivulets of rain ran from her cheeks and chin and slack mouth. The skullcap was gone. Her long red hair tangled like seaweed in the foam.

My vision telescoped, showing everything in bright clear detail as if from a great distance. I reached for Charlotte's hand. The torrent was clearly growing stronger with the increasing downpour. As I clambered into the water and reached to pull her away from the raging stream, I saw something gleaming and familiar twisted in Charlotte's fingers.

I opened my mouth yet again to cry out, and a rush of water hit me from behind, knocking me against a boulder. The force of the surge pinned me against the stone and pounded my head hard. For a moment, I lost consciousness. Or perhaps, I slipped away from the horror confronting me to a comforting place, a place of grace, for I saw the image of my father wavering before me, reaching for me in the water.

"Daughter, it's not your time. Fight."

With all my strength, I pulled on the hand I grasped in mine and heaved myself upwards out of the rushing waves and onto sharp rock. When I opened my eyes, I was holding onto Charlotte.

I heard someone screaming. *Was it I?*

Then, out of nowhere, Owen was beside me in the driving rain. *He must have heard my cries. Or he followed me.*

Or maybe he was already here.

He emitted that shrill, commanding whistle, sounding the alarm, and I was vaguely aware of two men from a nearby tenant farm at the broken bridge. Owen shouted orders to them and grabbed me as I held tight to Charlotte's hand, grasping at her body snagged upon the rocks. In desperation, I tried to pull her out of the churning waves.

"Let her go," Owen shouted above the pelting rain. "Let go!"

"No!" I screamed, tightening my grip on Charlotte's cold, limp hand. "We need to save her."

"We can't help her, Anne!"

He tightened his arm around my waist and peeled my fingers from Charlotte's hand. The torrent of water rose higher, flowing ever faster over the rock, tugging at her. Her head lolled to the side.

As Owen held on to me, I lost my grip, and Charlotte's body was wrenched downstream. She went under, bobbed back up like a sleek mermaid, and was swiftly borne away by the swollen river.

Dragging me from the water's edge, Owen embraced me.

"No, Owen!" I cried. "She'll be lost!"

"Anne, Anne. I thought I'd lost *you*," Owen said, holding me tight.

Chapter 23

Charlotte's body was found the next day, once the rains stopped, in a quiet ponding of water downstream between Huyton and Melling. She floated face up, like Millais's Ophelia, her hair tangled with blossoms. Not daisies nor rosemary, but forget-me-nots.

Life at Northfield house turned somber and hushed. Members of the household went about their ordinary business in silence. I was excused from my duties and lay in bed, the cuts and abrasions on my chin, hands, and knees slowly mending. My head ached, and my memories of that night felt muddled. I remember shaking with cold as Owen wrenched me up the steep cliff. Then I recalled being pulled from the ravine by the tenant farmers, who had responded to Owen's whistled signal and run to help.

I must have been in shock, for I remembered little else. The blow to my head addled me, making me faint and confused. My most persistent image from that night was of stars swimming above me in the black sky.

After that, I no doubt lost consciousness. I recalled nothing else until I found myself in my own bed, dry and warm, while Doctor Termeer tipped a draft of bitter liquid into my mouth.

"You've had a great shock," he told me. "The laudanum will help you sleep."

҂

Four days later, Mrs. Wellington lent me a raven-feathered hat and a long, dark coat for the funeral. I believed they were the only things propping me up that day as I walked, stood, and sat. I recalled only vague impressions of the solemn rituals. The eulogy did not reach my ears. As the mourners stood at the grave site and drifted towards their motor cars, I saw them only as shadows. Stiff black coats, rustling black dresses, black veils rising in the air like wings. They sounded like birds chattering, the tears and cries of anguish penetrating a sorrowful calm, until they all dispersed like a murder of crows.

Upon returning to Northfield House, I sat in the morning room with Mrs. Wellington, who held my hand, offering the unlikely touch of kindness.

"How grateful we all are, Anne, for your presence at the footbridge." She leaned forwards, whispering as though I might find the spoken word painful.

"But," I stammered, "I was useless. I couldn't help her." I stifled tears.

"If not for you, dear," she said, "we'd still be looking for Charlotte, or perhaps even assume she'd left with a . . ." She paused and looked away. ". . . a friend. We might not have realized for days that she'd had a fatal accident."

"Oh," I blinked and tried to clear my mind. "I see." Still, it took no particular skill or bravery on my part to be present at such a fateful moment. Had I arrived two minutes earlier, I might have been able to save her.

I did not voice my dismay, as I was still unable to express myself well. In the days following Charlotte's death, I existed in a fog of melancholy tinged with anxiety.

❧

The inquest, delayed for a week until I was able to give testimony, was held in Melling at the county seat where silent onlookers packed the courtroom. As I answered the coroner's questions, an unmanageable tremble altered my voice.

"No, I did not see her fall."

"No, I had not seen her leave the party and go to the bridge."

"No, I don't know if she had planned to meet someone."

"No, no one else was there. Not that I saw. I was too shocked to take in my surroundings."

Mrs. Wellington, dressed in deep mourning and having exchanged her elaborate blue rosary for a simple one of black beads and silver filigree, gave testimony as well. "The footbridge was a favorite place. Charlotte would retreat there as a child, to daydream. I can't recall her going there recently." Tears dampened her cheek and her fingers moved from bead to bead on her rosary.

Thomas was distraught, his face drawn. He added nothing to the straightforward information gathered. "I don't recall what time I last saw Charlotte, but I'm certain it was in the ballroom. She was dancing, always so gay and . . . alive."

Mr. Wellington wore a mask of grief. "I'd left the dance early, about eleven, I think, to retire. The partiers were still ploughing around, too noisy for me. My niece, my dear Charlotte, was the center of attention, milling about and laughing when I departed." He shook his head while staring at the floor, as if he could see her image there.

A bereft Owen testified as well. "I came running when I heard Anne's screams." He offered no explanation for why he was in the vicinity of the footbridge, and the coroner did not ask for one. "Before descending to the rocks, I saw Anne huddled over Charlotte. I raised the alarm, calling out for help."

Several men from neighboring farmsteads also spoke at the inquest. They told of hearing Owen's sharp whistle, something they were attuned to from working with him in the fields, and rushing towards the footbridge to assist him.

The questioning was very thorough, and no one could shed light on why Charlotte was at the footbridge so late at night. When asked for my thoughts, I could only posit a guess. "It was so hot," I said, "with the crowded dance floor and the ballroom lit with candles. She may have sought respite from the noise and the heat. It was typically cool there, above the flowing water."

No one could know why the railing broke, or how Charlotte fell through it. My assumption was the most likely. "The boards were always slick, the handrail shaky. She must have slipped and fallen against it." My voice caught with the horror of it.

The inquisitor asked, "Why, Miss Chatham, were *you* at the bridge at that hour?"

"I saw someone from the study windows—I'd gone there to escape the frenzied excitement of the ball—and I thought it was Kitty, out there in the dark. But it must have been Charlotte." My voice dropped to a whisper. "It—it was of course Charlotte I'd seen." No one pressed me to be more forthcoming.

I did not admit I thought the pale figure in the shadowy distance might be the ghost of Eleanor Granville.

"And, Miss Chatham, what did you see as you arrived at the scene of the tragedy?"

"What?" Distracted by my memories for a moment, I asked for the question to be repeated. "Oh. I saw the broken handrail. When I looked below, past the missing crossbeam, there was Charlotte, lying at the bottom of the ravine at the edge of the water."

"What happened next?"

"I—I panicked. I don't remember climbing down the side of the cliff. But the next thing I knew, I was clutching at Charlotte. Trying to get her off the rocks. Away from the water." My mind, confused as it was, went back to images at the footbridge. "She was missing her headpiece. Her hair spilled into the stream. Her wings—one of them was broken—fluttered with the twisting ribbons, like an injured bird. And she had something in her hand."

I couldn't remember what was clutched in Charlotte's cold fingers. When he was questioned, Owen said he hadn't seen anything. Sunk deep in my subconscious, it skittered away each time I tried to remember. Whatever it was, it avoided my grasp, escaping to a dark, safe place in my mind.

The verdict was swift and definite: death by misadventure.

Chapter 24

*F*or two weeks after the inquest, I felt as if suspended in a dim liquid that distorted sound and vision and permitted only languid movement. Baffled by my confusion, I turned inwards to a blessed nothingness.

Following Charlotte's death, Mrs. Wellington sat with me every afternoon in the library. During those endless days, as I struggled towards normalcy, she was gracious and thoughtful.

"I've brought you some broth, dear. And some strong tea. You must take care of yourself." As she attended to me, she kept up a cheerful monologue about mundane concerns regarding Northfield House and its inhabitants, both of us sipping at amber liquids intended to warm and nourish.

"Mrs. Hadley is taking down the light drapes, exchanging them for the heavy winter ones, and the summer slipcovers have come off the furniture."

"The garden yields only root vegetables this time of year, before they turn the soil."

"There was frost on the lawn this morning. It'll be the last of our roses."

At other times, she read aloud to me from *The Odyssey*. Its familiar story of trials, tribulations, and thwarted yearning seemed somehow to mirror my own troubles as I tried to regain my balance. It required enormous effort just to stay upright for part of the day.

Eventually, Mrs. Wellington spent our time together knitting in silence for long hours, her fingers working ceaselessly. The click and clack of the needles were punctuated by sudden thoughts she expressed like demands.

"You must smile more, Anne," she said as we watched autumn leaves sail outside the windows. "You are lovely when you do so."

"Thank you, Mrs. Wellington. You are so generous."

"Call me Lavinia, dear. We are to be friends, are we not? I am so grateful to you." She set aside her handwork to offer me a teacup. "How can any of us thank you for trying to save our Charlotte?"

"No, please, I did nothing." Her tributes made me feel helpless and ineffectual.

"At the risk of your own life, dear Anne. We can't ever forget." She never failed to laud me and express her profound gratitude.

"It was what anyone would do, Mrs. Wellington." I hesitated. "Lavinia."

It surprised me, her complete change of heart. But no one knew better than I how grief and loss can alter your attitude towards the world. Mrs. Wellington seemed to call up some other version of herself that permitted the empathy she bestowed so freely.

By Remembrance Sunday, I felt more myself and told Mrs. Wellington that I wished to join them for church and the wreath-laying ceremony.

She hovered close and peered into my eyes as if to view my soul. "You look wan today, Anne. Best that you wait another week."

"I'm fine, really. Just a bit of lingering fatigue." It was encouraging that I felt less inclined to lie still, withdrawn from the world, and desired to join the living in honoring the dead. That distant sorrow was something more easily grasped. My memories of our many parishioners, mostly school boys, lost in the Great War stood in stark contrast to the shadows of recent events, as vivid as red poppies blooming against white headstones strewn across Europe.

"You mustn't tire yourself." Mrs. Wellington dismissed my request. "I'll sit with you during the two minutes of silence on Saturday. That should suffice."

Perhaps it was also a good sign that I chafed against Mrs. Wellington's supervision. I had grown accustomed to my independence during these months at Northfield House. My confinement had grown tiresome. Now I imagined smothering in the pillows she plumped around me.

Full recovery of my psychological strength lagged, to my great dismay. A lingering agitation manifested itself in strange ways. The sound of running water made me gasp. Rain in the night startled me awake. Silence filled me with dread. When I did attend church the following Sunday, claustrophobia gripped me as I sat between the Wellingtons. My insides rippled with panic, and I grasped the hard edge of the pew before me to remain seated. Of course, I went nowhere near the footbridge.

And I dreamed of Charlotte with her wild hair and gossamer wings. From the depths of still waters, she reached out to me, grinning and skeletal, and tried to take my hand, to put something in it from her own.

More than once, startled awake by these images, I watched a specter float across the ceiling above my bed. It flickered like candlelight before moving into the hall and down the stairs. I was unable to determine if this was Eleanor once again, or if Charlotte's spirit now haunted Northfield as well. I mentioned my night terrors to no one, lest I be thought mad.

❧

The members of the Wellington family, particularly Mrs. Wellington, were ever present as I recovered, but there was little contact with the rest of the inhabitants of Northfield.

When I felt up to it, I joined the family for dinner but otherwise took my meals in my room. Mrs. Hadley, Cook, Dolly, and Maddy went about their work like shadows. Martha Langtry stayed in her chambers. I began to feel I was being kept from mingling with the rest of the household. A shroud had fallen over every facet of my life, separating me from anything commonplace. I missed the calming habit of breakfast with Mrs. Hadley, the chatter of staff in the kitchen, and my one-sided conversations with Kitty.

During my convalescence, Owen often stopped by the library in the afternoon, but our interactions were limited by his mother.

"You mustn't excite her, Owen." Mrs. Wellington stood between us as Owen hovered at the entrance. "Dr. Termeer has ordered complete rest and quiet."

He abided by her wishes and withdrew at first. But when I became stronger, he persisted. One day he paused at the door on the way to the fields. "You're looking well, Anne. It's a relief to see you more yourself."

"Thank you, Owen. I'm better every day." I saw regard in his eyes and found his physical nearness uplifting. If Charlotte's death troubled him deeply, he gave no overt sign, for which I was grateful.

"Go along now, Owen," said Mrs. Wellington, drawing my hand into her lap. "You'll try poor Anne's strength."

"Just allow me to give you this." He handed me a book—*Sonnets to Orpheus* by Rilke.

"Thank you," I said softly and clutched it to my breast, worried that Mrs. Wellington might disapprove, thinking the tome her son offered me suggested an inappropriate romantic interest.

After I left Mrs. Wellington and returned to my room, I examined the volume. The sonnets were in the original German, which Owen knew I was unable to read. Our conversations had touched on our talents at foreign languages, and I'd mention mine extended only as far as rudimentary French. So the title itself was the message. I let myself imagine that I was his Eurydice, whom he'd rescued from Hades. Smiling, I tucked the book beneath my pillow.

Other than these efforts, Owen and I were reduced to seeing one another during the occasional family dinners that I was able to attend. We sat in silence, and I was content merely to be in his company. Whenever Mrs. Wellington was distracted from the conversation by Maddy's minor transgressions, clattering the china or dropping a spoon, he gave me a furtive smile.

During this time, Thomas grieved openly. I caught sight of him from my chamber window, sitting alone in the garden. He was taciturn at dinner, his old jocular manner replaced by a stormy scowl. We spoke but briefly one day, encountering one another in the hall outside the library before his mother arrived.

"Anne, I depart for London tomorrow."

"I'm sorry for this awful trouble," is all I could think to say. I imagined he wished to banish recent memories, displacing them with the sights and sounds of the bustling big city. We shared a moment of silence before he spoke again.

"Do you wish to leave this place, Anne? It must be difficult, rising each day to remember." All his swagger had fled. "Come to London with me. Or I'll see you get back to Liverpool."

I couldn't plumb what was behind his gentle insistence. Going with him anywhere was fraught with peril to my reputation. "I can't possibly, Thomas."

"I'll assist you with whatever you need." His eyes searched mine.

I couldn't help but think about how Thomas behaved the night that Charlotte died. I remembered his anger and bitterness, his excessive drinking as he watched her flirt with other men. It was possible he had planned to meet her at the footbridge and was too late. I wondered if his grief might be laden with guilt.

"Thank you, Thomas. But I feel I must stay, at least for a bit." I didn't admit there was no one in Liverpool to receive me. I had nowhere to go. As dark and sinister as this house had become, I did not wish to trade Northfield for a lonely room in a squalid boarding house.

Kitty also managed to penetrate the fortress of my loneliness. She left wilted bouquets of wildflowers at my door and slid twigs or smooth stones from the creek under it. From my window, I caught glimpses of her hiding in the garden or weaving through the fields of waist-high grasses.

Finally, by the third week of November, I'd regained balance enough to return to work in the study for a few hours. With a manuscript before me, I operated the typewriter keys, my fingers flying over them, as I concentrated on the written pages. Typing not words but letter by letter, I often could not recall the content of my labors. The miasma that clouded my mind ebbed and flowed, but I had full faith that in time it would permanently recede.

That morning, Mr. Wellington was kind, if withdrawn. Despite his own sadness and sense of loss, he couldn't have been more generous. "Miss Chatham, should you be up and about? There is nothing so important it can't wait until you're fully recovered." He laid a comforting hand upon mine.

"It's actually good for me to have something to do, Mr. Wellington, to fill the time. The effort isn't taxing."

"Occupy your mind with a cheering book to distract you from all this," he said.

I was startled when he handed me Wilke Collin's *The Woman in White*. Instantly, I thought of Charlotte, standing at the top of the ballroom stairs in her pearlescent, gossamer gown.

It wasn't until later, after he'd strayed elsewhere in his creaking wheelchair, leaving me to my typing, that I recalled the book's major themes of look-alike girls, mistaken identity, and the suspicious death of an innocent young woman.

Later that week, I crept to the study earlier than usual and discovered my employer, silent and brooding, contemplating the picture he had secreted in his bottom drawer. Unaware of my arrival, he looked longingly upon the likeness of Eleanor before returning it to its resting place.

I gave no sign that I'd witnessed this, and wondered how often he gazed upon the picture since Charlotte's death. It troubled me to think that the loss caused him to relive the original tragedy of Northfield House.

By the end of the day, after Mr. Wellington had left, Owen materialized at the study door. "You appear to be functioning well," he said, smiling. "I've missed you."

He lingered in the doorway, looking hesitant, even sheepish. "It's good you're downstairs every day now, even if it's just sitting with Mother between intervals of frenzied typing." He glanced right and left down the corridor.

I assumed he was looking about for his mother, who had wrung from him a promise to not bother me. Or perhaps he was embarrassed, remembering our encounter under the footbridge as we grappled with Charlotte's body, and the bold words he'd whispered in my ear: "Anne, Anne. I thought I'd lost you."

That black night, Owen had cradled me in his arms. He rescued me at some risk to himself and held me close as we were pulled from the bottom of the ravine. I hoped he didn't regret this admission in the light of day. I even questioned that I remembered it correctly. And it still troubled me, his sudden appearance at the scene of Charlotte's death, giving credit to the possibility that he'd planned a rendezvous with her.

"You're very kind. I am doing considerably better." My words rang with formality. I wished to speak more freely but struggled to recapture our former ease. "And of course, thank you for pulling me away from the high water. I'm so sorry my futile efforts put us both in danger."

Owen took a step into the study. "Anne, of course. Think nothing of it. Saving Charlotte, well, you and I . . ." He stammered.

I felt the heat of humiliation. Maybe he'd been on his way to the footbridge to secretly meet Charlotte when he heard my cries for help. I wondered if he needed to confess this, but couldn't find the words.

ॐ

I continued to work for several hours a day, slowly increasing my time at my typing machine. I was quite a sturdy soul, so my prolonged weakness was not only surprising, but troubling. I had no idea a head injury could be so debilitating.

Even as I gradually improved, Mrs. Wellington still insisted we sit together each afternoon in the library, where the sun shone through the high windows while she served tea. Or we took walks on the grounds, keeping to the north side of the house, avoiding the gardens and the path to the footbridge. She talked about the village and its history and of her children growing up in that enchanted place. She also continued to be obsessively concerned with my recovery.

"You're regaining your strength, my dear," she said. "We're so relieved."

"You've been very kind. There are no words to express my gratitude."

"Hardly, Anne dear. What you've been through, I cannot imagine. Your efforts to save my niece were heroic, and we will do whatever necessary to help you heal after such a harrowing ordeal."

"You've done so much."

She tilted my face with a finger, studying the scrapes I had suffered on my cheek and chin. "Your injuries won't leave a scar," she said.

"I'm not concerned." A minor set of scars was the least of my worries.

"I have been meaning to ask you." She hesitated. "That is, I've been concerned about something."

"Of course, anything, if I can help."

"Do you think," she began delicately, "I mean, did you see Kitty at the bridge that night? At the inquest, you said you thought you saw her." She quickly added, "She's been not only silent but withdrawn. It's hard to know if she, too, is suffering. Was she there, watching? It's horrible to contemplate, but do you think she saw something?"

"No, I didn't see her. As far as I know, she wasn't there." Once again, I declined to reveal that I thought the moonlit creature I followed down the path might have been a specter from another world. *Eleanor.* "I only feared it might be Kitty, out in the dark. The only person I saw was . . ." I stumbled over Charlotte's name, unable to speak it aloud.

"No, no, don't dwell on it." She took my hand, placing in it a red chrysanthemum she'd plucked from a planter on the veranda. "Banish those images from your mind. You need to forget it ever happened." She smiled and leaned close.

"I will do my best." A flash of irritation stung my cheeks. Mrs. Wellington spent her days trying to control my actions, and now she was telling me what to think. She might be surprised to know that my mind was often preoccupied with thoughts of Owen. I missed our friendship. I suspected that our ghost hunting and our efforts to solve the mystery of Eleanor might have dissolved in the tears shed over Charlotte.

Still, I often caught Owen watching me—glancing across the dining room table, turning his face towards my window while walking in the garden, or slipping past the study door as I worked. But we spoke little. I feared he would now become an irregular figure in my life because I was irregular myself, spending long evenings in my room or sitting in the shadows with his mother.

Charlotte's death had cast a pall over everything. It seemed as if the rushing waters of the ravine had swept away more than Charlotte's life that night.

෪

I awoke one morning feeling much more myself. Perhaps the strain that burdened me had been relieved by Mrs. Wellington's absence. She was spending a long weekend in Melling with her ill sister, rather than fussing over me in a darkened room at Northfield House. For two days, I had been free from her suffocating attention and the constant worry of offending her.

The smothering malaise that fogged my brain had lifted for the moment. I rose quickly and dressed. For the first time since the ball, I went to the kitchen.

Kitty sat on the hearth. A genuine smile lit her face as I entered. Cook turned her friendly grin in my direction.

"Why, Miss Anne! What a wonder to see yer down here agin. And yer lookin' so thin and pale, luv. Sit and lemme get breakfast into yer." She bustled about and placed toast and jam before me.

My appetite had returned, and it pleased her to see me eat.

Mrs. Hadley entered from the courtyard and embraced me. "Miss Anne! How good it is to see you sitting here once more." Her careworn face was shadowed with despair.

I shared her dismay. Everything had changed. "I never meant to stay away."

She busied herself fixing us both a cup of tea. "Well, you're here now."

"I can't remember now why I did. I mean, stay away."

"You've just been a bit addled with all the goings-on and your head injury, is all. You were overwhelmed with grief."

Dolly, who came out of the larder, smiled and nodded. She clearly wanted to tarry, but Mrs. Hadley gave her a nod to dismiss her, indicating she should take Kitty with her. The housekeeper waited

154

until they'd gone before saying, "We were right worried about you, Miss Anne."

"Thank you, Mrs. Hadley. Your consideration means a great deal to me."

She glanced over her shoulder before continuing. "Things aren't right here, in this house. There's a darkness that's fallen."

"Death, especially of one so young, can have such an effect." Sadness weighed upon my heart.

"It's more than that. There are secrets."

"Secrets, Mrs. Hadley?" I was not really surprised. My own mind was agitated with some unidentifiable unease.

"You know things when you've been in a house long as I have," she said, keeping her voice low.

"Yes, Mrs. Hadley, I think one does. What bothers you so?"

"Why did Mr. Thomas leave so sudden like?"

"This does not seem to me unusual. Thomas was close to Charlotte."

Mrs. Hadley nodded. "He was smitten with that girl."

"Leaving Northfield seems to be an appropriate response to grief, to having lost her, especially in such a gruesome way." For the first time since the inquest, I allowed my conscious mind to project a picture of Charlotte lying broken on the rocks, the rushing water fluttering her torn wings with their rippling ribbons.

"But it's not only that," Mrs. Hadley said "There's Mrs. Wellington. She encouraged him to go, fairly hustling him out of here. It's just not natural, her being needy and self-centered as she is. She's so fond of the boy, t'would be more likely she'd cling to him."

I listened thoughtfully but failed to see any real reason for concern. Mrs. Hadley had only her intuition to trouble her. Still, something worried at me as well, something that burrowed deep into my subconscious. Visions of Charlotte lying at the edge of the water never included her hands.

"And Mrs. Wellington gathered up all Charlotte's belongings and discarded them. Did the packing herself rather than have the staff take care of it. We've not even been allowed in the room."

"Mrs. Hadley, we all respond differently to sorrow." I imagined Mrs. Wellington lovingly touching all her niece's effects, an act of consecration. A snippet of poetry came to me: *the sweeping up the heart, and putting love away* . . .

"And there's Owen," she said.

I swallowed hard but did not look away. "What about Owen?"

"He was in love with Charlotte, since they were children. I fear he's lost his senses, the way he's dealing with her death. He hasn't been himself at all, mooning about like a sick cat."

So I was right. There had been something between Owen and Charlotte. I had picked up the undercurrent of frustration whenever Owen and Thomas were in the same room with her. I recalled the night of the costume ball, when Owen and Thomas had both been cursed by jealousy. Charlotte had clearly played with Thomas, but I wondered if she had also toyed with Owen. I visualized the faded photograph Owen had tacked above his work bench in the greenhouse. Charlotte and Thomas were looking into the camera. And Owen was staring at Charlotte.

I grasped Mrs. Hadley's hand. "What are you trying to say?"

Tears trembled in her eyes. "Miss Anne, I'm afraid one of the boys was . . . ," she said, struggling to continue, ". . . was with Charlotte when she fell."

"You think Thomas or even Owen . . ." My mouth was dry. "You believe one of them was a witness? And failed to reveal what they knew?" Unsettling suspicions felt like a fist gripping my heart. After a moment of reflection, I couldn't believe Owen knew anything more about Charlotte's death. He wouldn't have lied at the inquest. He would never have kept such a secret.

"And Mrs. Wellington knows more than she lets on." Mrs. Hadley wiped away a tear. "Otherwise, she wouldn't have done it."

"Done what?" I could feel the heat crawl up my face.

Mrs. Hadley looked behind her and then leaned close, whispering. "She burned the costumes that Thomas and Owen wore that night."

My blood ran cold. Mrs. Hadley seemed to be saying that Mrs. Wellington destroyed evidence of some kind. "Do you believe Mrs. Wellington knows something she hasn't told?"

"She must. I feel it in my soul. But she would never implicate one of her sons." Mrs. Hadley buried her anguished face in her hands. "My poor boys. Poor Charlotte."

I took a deep breath and considered the facts. Perhaps Charlotte had intended to meet Thomas . . . or Owen, although it pained me to think of it. But neither man would have witnessed her fall and then vanished. Owen would have moved heaven and earth to save her. He would have been the first one down the ravine had he been present. None of it made any sense.

"Mrs. Hadley, what exactly did you see?"

She dabbed at her eyes with a handkerchief. "I couldn't sleep that night. I imagine none of us could, after, you know. It must have been just before dawn when Mrs. Wellington crept down the hall beyond the kitchen to the boot room."

"And?"

"She was there until first light, stoking flames in the fireplace. As soon as she left, I scurried down there and found the boys' costumes, burnt and smoldering."

I tried to think of some reason for Mrs. Wellington to have done such a thing. I recalled cleaning up my father's study after his death, because it was the only thing I could do. From the outside, it might have looked like I was erasing him from my life, but that is not at all what I felt.

"Grief and distress can make us act oddly in another's eyes, Mrs. Hadley," I said.

"And there's more." She looked about her again and gripped my arm. "Among the tattered fabric of those costumes was something else. At first, I didn't recognize it. A handful of blackened beads and shriveled cloth."

"Could you determine what it was?" I asked

"Oh, yes. It was Charlotte's skullcap. And beads spilled out of one of the trouser pockets."

For a moment, I was speechless. But I shook my head and closed my eyes, considering the myriad possibilities. "Please calm yourself, Mrs. Hadley. Charlotte could have dropped the skullcap anywhere, and Thomas or Owen—or even Mrs. Wellington—could have found it." But, even as I spoke, I envisioned a struggle on the footbridge, angry words, a shove.

"I can't shake the fearsome thought, Miss Anne, that someone was with Charlotte when she fell." She hung her head.

I fought to control my own suspicions, to be sensible, and I wanted to relieve Mrs. Hadley of her distress. "You're boxing with shadows. There's nothing to be gained with these conjectures. There's no way to know if Charlotte wasn't alone. We can never know."

Mrs. Hadley raised her reddened eyes to mine.

"But we can, Miss. Someone saw Charlotte being followed that night. Someone knows the truth."

Chapter 25

I was shocked into silence once again, my mouth gaping. At last, I said, "Is that true? Did someone see Charlotte go to the footbridge? And saw she was followed?"

I thought of Kitty. She was the most likely witness, given her habit of being everywhere, watching everyone. But there was no way for her to communicate with clarity. And no one would believe so young a child. I looked about for Kitty, thinking perhaps she'd stolen nearby. The housekeeper sat huddled before me.

"You've come this far, Mrs. Hadley." I took her hand and looked into her eyes to provide encouragement, compelled to know the truth. "You must tell me everything."

She frowned and spoke as though she might choke. "Dolly heard Mrs. Langtry tell Mrs. Wellington that she saw something that night."

Martha? Martha was suffering from senility. People would no more believe her than they would Kitty, wondering what decade she was mired in. "What did Mrs. Langtry say she saw?"

"Dolly said she was taunting Mrs. Wellington with what she knew. She was going on about standing in the shadows and watching Charlotte make her way past the garden and someone else out there in the dark. And she made reference to family secrets and lies, what she knew and what she'd seen. Dolly said Mrs. Wellington called her wicked, insisting that she knew nothing. Dolly felt sure Mrs. Wellington was intent on protecting someone."

"How can you be certain Dolly interpreted it correctly?" I asked.

"Well, when you put it that way, perhaps not," said Mrs. Hadley. "Dolly has a habit of putting more meaning to things than she ought. And she overheard. She wasn't a party to the discussion."

"So she may have misunderstood what was said," I replied. Dolly was always spinning broken threads into a whole fabric of misinformation. She didn't mean anyone ill, but she usually got it wrong.

"Maybe she did. But Dolly said Mrs. Wellington was right anxious about what Mrs. Langtry was saying. She pressed Mrs. Langtry, insisting upon details, then refused to believe her. She spoke harshly, called her a crazy old harridan."

"Those are cruel words. But I'm sure you've seen how confused Mrs. Langtry appears at times." I sat back in my chair, becoming thoughtful.

Mrs. Hadley rose with a look of distress. "Mrs. Langtry does get a bit mixed up. Her memory is jumbled, you see. But Dolly was sure that Mrs. Wellington was angry with her. She wouldn't have used such ugly words to her sister-in-law otherwise."

And I believed that Dolly wouldn't have made up such words either. "These are all troubling events, Mrs. Hadley. Destroying the costumes, the discovery of the skullcap, the arguments. Still, the facts surrounding that night remain the same. If you can, try not to speculate. You'll make yourself sick with worry." I patted her hand before making my way upstairs to the study and to the distraction of work.

I tucked Mrs. Hadley's revelations away and spent the rest of the day typing, working in a kind of lockstep regimen, as if to blot out the world. I escaped the troubling questions swirling within through mindless busywork. Late in the afternoon, Mrs. Hadley suggested that I stop for the day and join the others for dinner. After I declined, Maddy brought me a tray of food, which I picked at without interest or appetite.

When I did pause, questions about that night came flooding back. Surely there was some rational explanation for events that followed. It was folly to assume anything based on unsubstantiated conjecture and gossip. Also, Mrs. Hadley's disclosure about Owen's attachment to Charlotte worried my battered heart. I hoped with all the fiber of my being that we could recover our friendship.

I recalled my memories of the costume ball—Thomas's excessive drinking, Owen's fevered attentions and distracted dancing, Charlotte's heartless flirting, and her manipulation of everyone, including me. Against my better judgment, I imagined Charlotte's death. My assumption—that she slipped and fell through the railing—made the most sense. However, it was also possible she struggled out of an embrace, stumbled, and fell.

But what monster would have abandoned Charlotte on the rocks? And even if that was what happened, I had seen no one on the path or the bridge. And I was the first one down in the ravine.

Mr. Wellington showed up in the study only briefly. He asked if I needed anything, looked wistfully out the window, and wheeled away without another word. He looked unkempt, as though he couldn't quite concentrate on his routine toilette. Perhaps he, too, worried the details of Charlotte's death.

It was quite late by the time I placed my neatly typed pages on Mr. Wellington's desk and plodded towards my room. I paused on the stairway to the back corridor. The house was dark and silent. Restless and suddenly loathing the prospect of being confined by four walls, I returned swiftly to the first floor and rushed to the veranda. Once there, I took a deep breath. The night was black and devoid of stars.

I looked towards the path to the footbridge, and a shuddering chill swept through me. Perhaps I would never again go to the footbridge, or take comfort in its wild setting among the black rocks and raging waters. This house was no longer a refuge.

Dark forces lurked among the shadows. Even I had withdrawn into the dim recesses of Northfield, remaining ever watchful. I didn't know why. There was no reason the tragedies of this house should touch me in a more meaningful way than they did the servants or other outsiders who plied their trade among the privileged classes. I had no responsibility to understand, to unravel the mysteries, or to resolve the sadness that lingered there. Yet I felt compelled.

With sudden clarity, I knew what I must do. I had to talk to Martha Langtry myself. If she truly knew something about Charlotte's last hours, she might be able to help me dispel the shadows that obscured the events that night. I made my way to the bottom of the stairs in the great hall and stood as still and silent as the portraits surrounding me, listening for voices. The household had retired hours ago, and no one would see me approach Martha's rooms. I stole up the stairs and stood before her door.

Tap, tap, tap. No answer. *Tap, tap, tap.*

I pushed the door open an inch. "Mrs. Langtry? Miz Martha? Are you awake?" I opened it wide enough to sidle through. As my eyes adjusted to the dim light, I saw her sitting in her rocking chair, a dark silhouette against the windows.

"Miz Martha?"

She turned her face towards me as I slid to her side, saddened by the small form huddled there. She had the fusty smell of age, the watery eyes of old memories.

"Miz Martha, are you well?" I knelt beside her.

A tear tracked down her cheek. "Where is everyone?"

"To whom do you refer?" I asked. "Who are you thinking of?"

She turned again towards the windows and the darkness beyond. "Everyone's gone. Where did they go?"

What ghosts did she miss, sitting tucked away in her rooms day after day?

"I had a yellow gown," she said, smiling. "Yards of ruffles. It was the very finest muslin. So lovely."

I kept still, not knowing what to say.

"And this large-brimmed chapeau with pink ribbons." She lifted her hands to an imaginary hat.

"Where did you go in the beautiful bonnet, Miz Martha?" I decided to accompany her on this visit to her past. I pulled a footstool near and sat.

"I was a great beauty." She glowed with the memory, lifting her chin like a coquette. "I had my choice of beaus. I had what they called *style*."

Along with family distinction and a great deal of money, I thought. "Of course, Miz Martha."

"Were you at my wedding?" She looked at me, her eyes sharp. "We imported the flowers—orchids and white freesia. And my gifts. My in-laws presented me with a complete set of Tiffany silver, including all the serving pieces. The pattern was Chrysanthemum."

"It must have been quite wonderful."

"And I'm sure Jimmy Westlake stole a piece. A spoon, I think. I'll have to talk to his father, make him give it back." She expelled an angry breath.

I tried to imagine the faraway place she occupied—the silk-clad women and top-hatted men arriving in grand carriages, leaving engraved calling cards.

"Father gave us the house in Preston. The gardens were small but still quite lovely. I was surrounded by beauty."

"Did you raise your family there, Miz Martha? You must have been so very happy."

"George bought the surrounding farmland later." She looked at me as if suddenly realizing I was there. "Yes, we were happy. At first." She paused. "Then the baby died."

I took her hand in mine. She stared quietly into her lap.

I shifted my gaze to the faded photographs lined up like gravestones. My sight came to rest on a small silver frame holding the image of a tiny girl. The other pictures were of boys who, as their many portraits revealed, became men.

So she lost her only little girl.

"Grief's a peculiar thing," she said. "George didn't take comfort in me."

"He took consolation in your other children?"

"No," she said. "Maybe." Her voice trailed into a whisper, the words swallowed by thoughts of long ago.

"I'm sorry for your loss, Miz Martha." Finding solace after losing a loved one is often a difficult journey. I bowed my head, missing my parents. My thoughts veered to my childhood, to my mother's hands as she braided my hair.

Martha turned a gimlet eye to me. "What do you care? Who are you?"

Taken aback, I opened my mouth, but nothing came out.

"I know. You work for wages. Why don't you get married? Find a man to take you to bed."

I felt as though I'd been slapped. Then I remembered my purpose. Clearly, Martha had returned to the present, so I carefully posed a question. "Mrs. Langtry, the night of the costume ball, when did you last see Charlotte?"

"The boys were buzzing around her, weren't they?" A sly smile played upon her lips. "That see-through thing she wore. She knows how to get a man." She looked at me sharply. "Better'n you, chippie."

I sat upright, shocked at such a word applied to me.

"Eleanor knows, too, how to get what she wants. But she's a lady. She plays within the rules, never crosses that line. Not like Charlotte. Or you."

I wondered by what game she assumed I profited. Perhaps she saw my profession, or a woman in any profession, as improper. But she was certainly right about one thing. Most women beguile to get what they need, if not what they want, and manipulate within the narrow path of acceptability available.

I peered at Martha in the gathering darkness. Was she lucid? She spoke of Eleanor and Charlotte in the present but maybe at her age, time had lost its meaning and past, present and future were all the same.

I tried again. "Did you have a pleasant evening at the costume party, being able to see family and friends?"

"I don't know if it was pleasant," she said. "But it was interesting to watch."

And what did you see, Martha? I thought, becoming anxious. "Mrs. Langtry, did you make note of Charlotte leaving the party?"

She paused, as if remembering, and said, "I'd just returned to my room, desperate to get out of that hot velvet. The ballroom was a steam bath."

I recalled the warmth of my face, perspiration tingling on my scalp that night. I silently willed Martha to stay focused on that evening.

"Dolly helped me unhook the bodice and to remove those high button shoes. I shooed her out and stood in the dark with the lamps out. The rain had stopped. I threw the windows open to the damp and the breeze."

I remembered the sensation when I stepped outside that evening, the cooling currents that washed away the sultry air of the ballroom.

Martha said, "I closed my eyes and thought myself a girl again. It's so easy to recall, feeling young, getting past my old bones and yellowed skin. I stood alone and allowed the cool air to plaster my shift to my body."

Impatient, I said, "And Charlotte? You saw Charlotte?"

She sighed, having relived the freedom of blowing in the wind, having shed her age as she had her dress. "Yes. I saw Charlotte, unmistakable in those wings and glittery headdress. She must have torn herself away from that party and crept through the house to the south veranda. I saw her step off the porch and dart like a shadow towards the bridge."

"She was alone?"

"She was. But I knew it was unlikely she expected to remain by herself, where she was going," she said, her smile grim.

"And did you see who followed her?" I asked with bated breath, my mouth dry.

Turning her piercing eyes to me, Martha Langtry said, "I saw you, Anne Chatham." She recalled my name with no difficulty. "I saw you follow Charlotte to the bridge."

Chapter 26

Of course. I was the one racing after Charlotte. She was the phantom I thought I saw, and it was I who followed.

And if Charlotte was indeed wearing her skullcap, something else became clear as well. No one other than I trailed after Charlotte to the footbridge. If someone was there, they were already waiting for her. I closed my eyes. Something swam up through my memory of that night but quickly darted away.

I was awash with fear. Something wasn't right. Something evil pervaded this house, and I was lost in its shadows and secrets, trying to find my way out. I could not remain a moment more with Martha Langtry, mired in her suffocating rooms and wretched despair.

Closing Martha's door behind me, I headed for the stairs. I stopped at the top with a start. Cool air drifted from somewhere. For a moment, I was frozen—pinned to the spot like a butterfly to paper. As if mesmerized, I turned to the left and took a step into the passageway leading to the abandoned south wing of Northfield.

A musty odor accompanied by a chill came from the direction of the ornate double doors. I was drawn like a bird of prey to an exhaled breath. Perhaps I was chasing a mirage, a phantom of my afflicted mind, but I could not be deterred. Sweeping deep into the hall, I approached the doors Owen had locked weeks ago, before Charlotte plunged into the ravine, before everything changed.

The doors were ajar. Both swung silently open at the touch of my fingertips. The smell of damp, of decay and mold, of pale things that grow in the dark, engulfed me. I entered the picture gallery without hesitation and scurried to the end of the room. There, as the eyes of those long dead watched from their sagging picture frames, I paused and listened. The quiet hung in the air like dust.

The door opened soundlessly without my having to touch it. I slid through to stand in the broad corridor opening into room after room, spaces Owen and I had explored not so long ago.

I felt the pang of loss. The sense of excitement and common purpose we'd had failed us. We'd abandoned our determination to unravel the mysterious secrets of Northfield House.

I edged forwards in the dim moonlight seeping around shuttered windows towards the room at the end of the hall, where everything seemed to gather and hover in the dark.

The ticking of a clock came from one of the chambers. I don't recall having heard it the first time we probed here. Perhaps some subterranean shift caused a pendulum to swing again. Holding my breath, I crept towards the inky blackness.

Something moved. At the far end of the passageway, past thirty feet of peeling doors and rotting floorboards, a shadow stirred. A coil of terror curled through my body, and I stood rigid with fear.

By the pricking of my thumbs, something wicked this way comes. I imagined a thing far more sinister than a Shakespearean witch.

I shook off the panic that throbbed like a heartbeat. *Screw your courage to the sticking place.* I thought of Lady Macbeth at her moment of decision. To discover what inhabited this place required a spine of steel, a fearless resolve.

"Eleanor?" I whispered, my voice constricted by dread.

The smell of spent matches and dried roses washed over me. I took a step backwards.

Hands like talons griped me from behind. Horrified, I opened my mouth to scream, emitting only a strangled gasp.

"Be still, Anne!" Owen hissed in my ear, pulling me hard against him. "Don't move!"

We stood pressed together, anchored by terror, as something began to pulsate in the darkness ahead.

Chapter 27

*A*n unnatural silence enveloped us. Trembling, we stared as the door to the last room creaked open, moving almost imperceptibly.

I felt a pulse beating in my jaw.

Owen stood still, as if holding his breath.

The hallway became even blacker.

I was held spellbound. Something watched from the darkness.

Then the atmosphere changed, becoming so heavy it was difficult to breathe. Cold seeped from that last room, filling the corridor.

The chill brought a soul-wrenching melancholy, despair so thick it was almost visible. I smelled dead bugs, dried grass, and spring mud. A stinging sensation crawled up my face, and sweat dampened my brow.

From out of nowhere, a wisp of fog appeared in the air. Hanging in front of the farthest wall, this pale, filmy substance whirled and gathered, growing denser. We stood like stone statues, and I felt bolted to the floor.

The empty space around us began to vibrate, as if breathing.

The wispy thing hanging before us quivered, and then twisted in slow circles. Dark eyes, piercing in their awareness, materialized in the thickening mist. The miasma coalesced and elongated. Around the eyes appeared the oval of a face, and following that, the outline of a female form. She seemed much taller than I, and very slim.

Owen clasped me tighter. I shrank into his embrace. Neither of us could speak as the atmosphere became even more oppressive, its heaviness sapping my strength. Caught in the path of this wraith, I could not move.

Time passed—whether seconds or minutes, I could not tell—as the being became fully manifested. It transformed like something captured with binoculars, a blurred image resolving into a sharp, clear figure.

It appeared almost skeletal, sharp bones masked by the sheerest of substances. The slender body was shrouded in draperies in various shades of white, silver, and gray, like a cloud, but with the weight and fluidity of fine cambric. The flesh, the tangle of tresses, and the eyes had no color, much like the tones of an overexposed photograph. As the vision became complete, I saw clear and distinct features and detailed clothing.

The specter paused in the thickened air, hung motionless for a heartbeat, then shifted her smoldering eyes to gaze at us. I cowered, paralyzed. Owen gasped, his fingers digging into my arms. Her skirts billowed, and she floated slowly towards us down the long passageway, swaying rhythmically, undulating like a deep-sea creature.

Courage, I told myself. A ghost has no power beyond the ability to terrify. My horror was overwhelmed by the desire to know why she walked, why she haunted Northfield House.

Collecting my will and standing tall, I shook off Owen and took one step forwards. I swallowed my panic and found my voice. "Eleanor. Why are you here? What keeps you mired on earth? What would give you peace?" My questions were barely a whisper.

The apparition continued towards us. Owen stepped beside me, shaking. I felt a shudder of fear trace through my body. The ghostly figure stretched her long fingers in our direction, and I resisted the urge to scream.

Her face altered. It appeared she was struggling to speak.

"Tell us, Eleanor," I said, my voice trembling. "Speak to us. Help us understand."

The ghost, suspended in the air, halted several feet before us. We stood, riveted by terror to the spot. Slowly, deeper shadows gathered, and the sharp-edged clarity of the figure softened. The dark eyes disintegrated like smoke. Fading once again, the specter receded and spiraled towards the ceiling, forming a small cloud that swirled and pulsated. With a sharp flash of blue, it disappeared.

Owen expelled a ragged breath and sagged against the doorjamb. "Dear Christ! What the hell was that?"

My legs trembled, and I struggled to stay on my feet. "What did you see?"

"A fog that swirled and, I swear to you, Anne, eyes that burned like coals."

"I saw her face, clothing, the skin of her hands. Everything." I took a great shuddering gulp of air.

"You called her Eleanor. Was she really Eleanor?"

"I believe so. Still, the spirit I saw was so ravaged, she didn't resemble Eleanor's picture. She looked like no one. Or anyone." I meant to be practical and keep my mind open to other possibilities.

"So it could be any of the ancestors whose pictures hang in the gallery?"

"I suppose that's true. But it's definitely female."

He looked uncomfortable. "Could it be—?"

. . . *Charlotte?* I shook my head. "No. It's the same presence we saw the first time. I'm certain of it." I could never mistake those eyes.

"Let's get out of here," he said, grabbing my hand.

We dashed through the gallery and the double doors. He produced the key from his vest and locked them once again.

"What were you doing in the south wing?" I asked.

He looked sly. "Same thing you were." He stared at the doors and shivered. "Shall we go to the study?"

Once there, we turned on all the lamps to dispel the darkness. The study had a homey quality that calmed me. Owen produced a small flask from his back pocket and offered it to me, but I declined. He swallowed a mouthful before we settled ourselves in front of his father's desk. I didn't bother to make notes this time as we shared what we had seen, heard, and felt. I would never forget what I had witnessed.

Owen said, "I saw but shadow and light, and could only distinguish the dark eyes clearly. The phantom quivered as it hovered at the end of the passage until it moved towards us. I thought my heart would fairly stop." He took a deep breath. "A menacing cold rendered me powerless—sapped all my strength."

I drank in Owen's presence, feeling his comforting warmth, as we sat facing each other in front of his father's desk. He was still wearing his work clothes and smelled vaguely of soil, green grass, and the liquor from his flask. His eyes, reflecting familiarity and regard, rested on mine. Our old camaraderie had returned, if only for that moment.

"I wanted to scream like a girl," Owen continued, offering a quirky smile. "But you *are* a girl, and I note you did not cower the least bit."

"Don't be absurd. I was terrified."

We both laughed, shaking off our fear.

I relaxed my guard, in spite of believing I should keep my emotional distance. There were still too many unanswered questions about the night of the costume ball, how he felt about Charlotte, and how he felt about me. But my heart did battle with my head. "It's good to laugh with you."

Having exhausted discussion of our ghostly encounter, Owen shifted gears. "How are you feeling?"

"Quite well." I looked at the floor.

"I regret it's been so . . . awkward these last weeks. I've been hesitant to talk to you since that night."

The moment he said this, I knew it was true. "But why?"

"I felt guilty."

"About what, exactly?" I steeled myself for the answer.

"I'm not even sure. That Charlotte's dead. That you were first down the ravine. That Thomas left. That Mother's so smug."

"Your mother? Why, Owen, she's been lovely." *In her own peculiar way.*

"She hated Charlotte."

"That's a bit strong. She may not have liked Charlotte, but she certainly didn't wish her ill."

"Thomas was a bit too keen on Charlotte for her comfort. Her death appears to resolve Mother's most vexing problem."

"What are you saying?"

"Nothing." He relaxed with a sigh. "Nothing at all."

For a long moment, I pondered this tragic accident. People succumbed to so many merciless killers—pulmonary tuberculosis, scarlet fever, diphtheria, typhoid, pellagra—that one more untimely demise shouldn't have shocked me.

Yet, something still troubled me about Charlotte's death.

"Anne, don't you feel something's off?"

Once again, it seemed as though Owen had read my mind. I felt emboldened. "I do. Since you brought it up, help me understand something."

"Of course, if I can."

"Why would your mother burn the costumes that you and Thomas wore that night?"

"Did she?" He looked startled.

"Yes. Someone," I said, wishing to protect Mrs. Hadley from any unpleasant questions that might ensue, "found remnants in the fireplace in the boot room. And saw your mother as she left."

He shrugged. "I can't imagine. Mine was in muddy tatters, so why not? But Thomas's as well? And she did it herself?"

"It appears so."

He was thoughtful for a moment. "Maybe she found the costumes a painful reminder of that awful night, and it represented some sort of ritualistic cleansing."

"And Charlotte's skullcap was also among the burnt tatters." I decided to put it all out there, hoping he had some clue.

That information gave him pause. "Where do you suppose she found it?" He frowned, concentrating.

"I have no idea."

So the skullcap hadn't been in his pocket, but it might have been in Thomas's. Or Mrs. Wellington might have discovered it somewhere and added it to the pile to be discarded after the disastrous costume ball. Or perhaps someone had found it at the ravine and returned it to her.

There was a long moment of silence. I imagined we were both thinking about Charlotte lying upon the rocks at the water's edge, her loose hair tangling in the stream.

"Shall I ask Mother about it?" he said.

I felt a little jolt of embarrassment. "No, of course not. That would only distress her, I imagine." I was certain Mrs. Wellington would be offended that her actions were a subject of discussion by the servants. "We'd better let it be."

"Probably."

"Owen," I said. "There's something else."

"Of course," he said. His face was open as a choirboy's.

"Why were you at the footbridge the night Charlotte died? How is it you arrived at the scene so quickly?"

"That's not difficult to answer." He looked sheepish. "I was following you."

Chapter 28

S hock must have shown on my face. "Following me?"
This disclosure forced me to revisit that night—and my last glimpse of Owen as he swung around the dance floor with a blonde swathed in blue, possessed of more than a shepherdess's crook with which to snare him.

"I saw you leave the ballroom and waited for your return—in vain, as you know. I decided that you must have retired for the evening. When the guests began to depart, I escaped the ballroom by stepping onto the second-floor balcony. Then I glimpsed you, beyond the garden, racing towards the bridge. So I followed you."

Caution crept up my spine. *Be careful.* "To what end, might I inquire?"

He hesitated, looking away. "Curiosity."

"Curiosity?"

He stared at the floor. "I was startled to see you out in those woods so late. And, I wondered what had attracted you there."

"You were spying?" I blurted, only half-joking.

He looked dismayed. "I thought you were meeting someone . . . I wanted to know who it was."

I was rendered speechless with embarrassment. I wondered how he could think this of me, that I was capable of meeting a man under such compromising circumstances. Instead of revealing my discomfort, I decided to tell him the truth.

"After I left the ballroom that night," I said, "I withdrew to the study. I saw something pale moving through the gardens towards the woods. At first, I believed it was Kitty, just as I testified at the inquest, and I was concerned for her. But then I thought of Eleanor."

"Eleanor?" He looked surprised.

"Of course. That vision of glowing white resembled the specter we'd seen. So I left the house in pursuit. I'm now mortified, given what actually happened." I didn't disclose I'd hoped to earn his admiration for chasing down Eleanor's ghost.

"I guess imagination got the better of us both," he said.

"It would appear so. Neither of us expected the tragedy awaiting us at the footbridge." I had a sudden vision of Charlotte bobbing in the water.

"I must apologize, Anne." He looked deep into my eyes. "I fear I'd said too much at the scene of . . . the accident."

He was referring to his declaration as he pulled me from the water's edge. *"Anne, I thought I'd lost you."* I was stung, thinking he regretted the feelings behind those words, and remained mute. I could not make my gaze meet his.

"After that night, I felt sure you'd leave us." He picked at a patch of mud on the knee of his breeches. "But you stayed at Northfield. At the same time, you seemed to have drifted away. Gone to another place. Somewhere I couldn't go."

Owen had been watching more closely than I realized. "It wasn't intentional, to be so distant. My head injury made it difficult to focus."

"I know that now, but then I interpreted your withdrawal as rejection. I assumed you wanted nothing to do with . . . the Wellingtons after such an experience."

Or with him *particularly* was his unspoken implication.

I turned towards him. "Owen, you're wrong." I hovered on the verge of confession about my poverty, my utter and complete aloneness, and my feelings for him which were totally inappropriate considering my station in life. But I could not bear to see him look at me with pity. My courage crumbled.

Rather than trust him with the unvarnished truth, I hid behind Eleanor. "I'm still committed. After tonight, more than ever, I want to continue probing the mysteries of this house—to discover the facts behind Eleanor's disappearance." I held my breath, praying that my reassurances would be enough to reestablish our friendship, bringing us into harmony of purpose once more. I knew I could not offer him more than this.

He looked relieved. "Given the fantastical display of the paranormal upstairs just now and your response, I guess you're strong enough to do so. I admire your mettle. I wanted to wail like a banshee and take refuge behind your skirts."

I couldn't help but smile at the picture he painted. Owen smiled too, and we sat companionably for a moment with only the meticulous ticking of the mantel clock to fill the silence. It announced one o'clock with a subtle grinding of gears and a single soft bong.

Surprised at the lateness of the hour, I stood. "So we'll continue our search? For the answers?"

He stood as well. "Of course. I'd like that."

We moved awkwardly towards the door.

"I'm away tomorrow," he said, "but will be back by evening. We'll talk when I return."

I nodded, suddenly exhausted. Owen and I parted, going to our respective ends of the house. On my way upstairs, I pondered the attitude of members of the family towards me. Some of them obviously thought me capable of indiscretions I would never contemplate in my circumstances. Owen believed I might meet a man at the bridge. Martha accused me of contemplating sexual escapades with one of her nephews. Mrs. Wellington imagined I had designs upon one, or both, of her sons.

I was unsure whether to laugh or be angry. My life wasn't nearly as exciting as others supposed.

Entering the shelter of my room, I caught my dim reflection in the spotted wardrobe mirror. Dark hair spilled across my shoulders and framed an earnest face. My drab shirtwaist revealed my slim figure, but hid my warm and sturdy heart. I admitted, for once and all, that it belonged to Owen. The thought that we were still friends buoyed me, despite the fact we were fated never to have a future together. Still, I could give him a gift no one else could. I could lay to rest the ghosts that lingered here, darkening the world of those still living.

Chapter 29

*T*he following day was foggy and cool, making the study a comfortable cocoon. Heeding my own advice to Mrs. Hadley, I set aside troubling conjectures about the accident at the footbridge and focused on my work. I spent both morning and afternoon searching records borrowed from the courthouse for land transfers and leases. Mr. Wellington was inconvenienced with a nasty head cold, Owen was in Melling representing the family's interests at a meeting related to farm subsidies, and the house was astir with its regular hustle and bustle.

Late autumn required the inhabitants of Northfield to ready the house for cold weather. Mrs. Hadley aired the blankets and comforters stored away during the warm months. With Kitty's help, Maddy harvested the last of the kitchen herbs from their raised beds. Dolly washed, folded, and put away Martha's summer frocks, replacing them with woolens and heavy twills.

I sought a breath of fresh air in the garden before nightfall. The hazy fields that had once been abuzz with large harvesting machines lumbering like bumblebees now lay fallow. Someone had attended to the flower gardens and deadheaded the hydrangeas, mums, and roses. A large mound of faded blossoms had been piled alongside a rake that leaned against the naked lilacs.

I turned the corner at the buckthorn bushes and nearly ran into someone coming the other way. I stumbled backwards and was steadied by a hand at my elbow.

"Thomas?" I was startled. "When did you return?"

"Just this morning," he said, smiling. "It's delightful to see you, too."

I was at once irritated. "I didn't know you'd come home. I'm surprised, that's all." I looked towards the front of the house for his car.

"I parked near the stables," he said as though reading my mind. "Should I have notified you first?"

"Of course not. Please forgive me," I said, trying to hide my annoyance.

"Just teasing." He put an arm through mine and walked with me towards the house. "You're such a good audience, Anne, always so obligingly disconcerted."

I hated that he was right. And I noted how thin he'd become. His tailored suit hung much too loosely. Other than that, he appeared to be the same man I first met in the dining room a mere five months ago.

"If you don't mind my saying so, you should always wear your hair that way."

His appraisal was admiring, but I feared he was laughing at my expense. Flustered, I regretted my decision to dress my hair loosely with the tortoiseshell combs. Believing none of the family would be home, I had been lax about presenting a professional appearance.

As Thomas reached for the veranda door, it swung open. His mother stood at the threshold wearing a look of surprise edged with hostility.

"My dear Thomas, you look tired." She embraced him and planted a fond kiss upon his cheek.

So the chilly expression was for me.

"Have you been eating well?" she asked, not acknowledging my presence.

"I was just on my way to the study," I excused myself. "Welcome home, Thomas."

As if I'd become invisible, neither of them responded. "You weren't in your rooms, so I went looking in the garden, Mother," he said as they began walking together.

I glanced at them as I scurried towards my allotted corner.

"How good to have you home." Mrs. Wellington pouted prettily. "It was deadly without you. I've done my best to see to everything. It's been so wearing."

Thomas had a reassuring arm around his mother, and she rested her head upon his shoulder.

I knew better than to come between Mrs. Wellington and her sons, particularly Thomas. Their affection for one another made me uneasy, but I doubted I'd have thought so had Martha not planted such an indecency in my mind.

As I stepped inside, I met Mrs. Hadley on her way downstairs.

"Are you quite all right, Miss Anne?"

"Of course. It's just . . ." I hesitated, but knew I could confide in her. "I don't know how to feel now Thomas has returned. He unsettles me with his slights. And he's unkind to his brother."

"It's just his way. He's always been of a teasing nature, dismissive-like, so to put one at a disadvantage. He treats everyone with that superior manner, even Mr. Henry and his mother. Don't you mind him."

"I'm sure you're right, Mrs. Hadley. I make too much of his jokes." I kept to myself that I found Thomas's personality distasteful. His sense of his prerogatives and the belief that the rules of society didn't apply to him were irksome. And his arrogance was not only vulgar—it was menacing.

"If you'd known him as a boy," she said, smiling, "it'd be different." She gave my arm a pat and went on her way.

I pondered the mystery of Thomas. He had lofty expectations, making many demands upon the world. What if he had decided that if he could not possess Charlotte, no one could?

His return caused me to dwell upon that night, provoking a need to resolve questions that I should have put behind me long ago. And once again, that niggling little forgotten fact about Charlotte's death worried at me. I concentrated, trying to remember what she grasped in her hand, but it slipped away each time it surfaced, like smoke on the wind.

The early evening dragged by. I was relieved when the mantel clock tolled seven, and I could cover the Remington and escape to my room. An hour later, I wandered to the kitchen for tea and a buttered scone.

"Dolly, please tell Mrs. Wellington I won't join them for dinner tonight. Since Thomas is home, I'm sure they'd prefer to be alone."

"As you please, miss."

With Mr. Wellington ill and Owen away, I didn't want to feel like an intruder. I had one ear cocked to all movements in the house, waiting for Owen's return.

That evening, as I sat at my bare desk mending the hem of a skirt, a light tap on my bedroom door startled me.

"Please come in," I said, expecting it to be Dolly, or maybe Kitty.

Instead, the door opened to reveal Mrs. Wellington, standing in the hall with a tray.

I dropped my mending in surprise.

"I apologize for disturbing you, Anne, but I believe I was rude earlier today." She glided into the room and set the tray, which held a pot of tea and some china, on the desk. "I hope that's not why you declined to join us for dinner. I won't sleep if I don't apologize."

"No. Not at all," I stammered. "Time to myself is rare, and you and Thomas must have much to discuss that doesn't concern me."

"Well, you understand then. I'm relieved you didn't think me ungracious."

"Please don't worry on my account," I said. "You've been more than kind."

"I want to make sure you're comfortable and bear me no ill. It's just that I was so grateful to have my boy back, and no one else exists for me when he appears."

Truer words were never spoken. I wondered if she really saw herself.

"And, of course," she added, "we've missed our tea together these past few days, haven't we?"

I glanced at the tray and was relieved to see only one cup. Besides, there was nowhere else to sit in my spare room except upon the narrow bed. Mrs. Wellington looked distinctly out of place in her elegant dress, all mauve lace and satin rosettes. I felt as though she filled the room, taking up all the space.

"I value our little talks." Her smile didn't reach her eyes. "Let's sit for an hour tomorrow after you finish your work. We'll make up for lost time."

"Of course, as you like." I tried not to sound dispirited. I had hoped she felt she'd done her duty and would dispense with the social hour on my behalf.

"I don't want to keep you, dear." She gestured towards the tray. "Enjoy the tea and get your rest."

She slipped through the door and down the stairs. She left in her wake the scent of violets and chamomile.

I sipped the tea while watching the moon rise. Afterwards, I read from the dim light of the candle while sitting in bed. I thought I would ask if I might have an oil lamp for the desk. That was my last thought before the cool evening air and pervasive silence lulled me into slumber.

❧

When I awoke sometime later, my book upon my breast, the candle was out and my door ajar. Comfortably nestled against my pillow, I chose not to rise and dress for bed but fell asleep once more.

I don't remember waking again. Nevertheless, I found myself stumbling outside my room, disoriented in the dark. No sight, sound, or touch guided me. The sensation of a feverish dream, of clawing through a thick and oppressive atmosphere, was overwhelming. I waved my arms about, searching for something to ground me. After taking several tentative steps into the inky blackness, I felt myself launched forwards, tumbling in the air. My hip hit the hard edge of a step, and I went sliding and bumping down until I sprawled on the floor below. I must have cried out. After a moment of silence, I heard raised voices and footsteps running in my direction.

"Anne! What happened?" Thomas bent over me.

I struggled to sit upright. "I . . . I don't know."

Mrs. Hadley put her hands on my shoulders. "Don't move a bit. Is she hurt, Mr. Thomas?"

"No, really. I'm fine." I wiggled my toes and flexed my legs and arms. "I don't think anything's broken."

"Stay still," said Thomas. "Are you sure you haven't injured yourself?"

I lay down again and took a deep breath. Taking inventory, I decided the fall had merely bruised my hip and shoulder blade. Although somewhat addled, I was otherwise unhurt.

Thomas slid his arm beneath my shoulders and carefully helped me sit up. "Can you stand?" he asked.

"I believe so," I said.

With their help, I stood, and at once, my head swam.

Mrs. Hadley said, "Did you slip on the stairs in your stocking feet, Miss Anne?"

I tried to remember the sequence of events. I had been cautiously moving forward—and then suddenly falling. I wondered if someone might have pushed me. Or placed an obstacle at the head of the stairs. I looked behind me to the top of the staircase. No shadows or movement suggested anyone hidden there. And I saw nothing on the steps that might have tripped me.

"Sure, 'tis a wonder you were close by, Mr. Thomas," said Mrs. Hadley, "to raise the alarm. I'm not certain I'd have heard the fall from downstairs."

Where was Thomas when I fell?

"How do you feel, Anne?" He looked into my eyes. "Can you move your head and neck?"

"I'm fine. Thank you for coming to my aid." I brushed my hair off my face and shook my head. "I cannot remember leaving my room. I don't know why I was in the corridor. What time is it?"

Thomas glanced at his pocket watch. "It's just after midnight."

"How unfortunate, you with another bump on the head. You must be more careful," Mrs. Hadley said, clucking like a mother hen.

I wondered if I'd been sleepwalking, but I'd never done that before. "I'm usually asleep by now."

Thomas supported me with a hand on my elbow. "Shall we step into the library? You should stay awake for a while. There's a risk you've suffered another serious head injury. That's especially dangerous since you've just recovered from the first one."

I limped down the hall leaning on his arm. Mrs. Hadley opened the door and lit a lamp. Thomas deposited me in an overstuffed chair and turned to a cabinet, where he found a bottle of brandy and two glasses.

"Mrs. Hadley?" he gestured to her with the bottle.

"No, Mr. Thomas, not for me. I'll sleep poorly. I'd best be leaving unless you need my assistance?" She looked at me closely.

"Everything is fine, Mrs. Hadley, thank you," I said as Thomas handed me a glass of amber liquid.

"Please feel free to retire," he said. "I'll remain with Anne until I know she's suffered no ill effects."

The housekeeper left, softly closing the door behind her.

"I regret being such a nuisance," I said with dismay. "I'm entirely too much trouble."

"Not at all." Thomas took a seat across from me, holding a glass of brandy in his hand. He raised it with a nod in my direction. "Cheers."

We both took a sip, but only I coughed as it burned my throat. "I really don't know what I was doing up at this hour. I don't even recall waking or leaving my room."

"But you're dressed."

I became aware of my disheveled clothes, undone buttons, and stocking feet. "I fell asleep reading. The next thing I knew, I was falling in the dark."

He frowned. "Has this happened before? Awakening somewhere, not knowing how you got there?"

"No, of course not." I was irritated. It wasn't a fair characterization of the situation at all.

"I had a roommate at school who walked in his sleep. Nervous little fellow. Given recent events . . ." He paused and looked down at his drink. "Perhaps you're overwrought."

"I assure you that is not the case in the least. I'm a quite sensible and sturdy person."

"At ease, Miss Chatham," he laughed. "This is not an inquisition into your character."

How absurd. Thomas was the most exasperating man. But it was possible he was right—I hadn't yet fully recovered from my traumatic ordeal.

He rose from his chair, put down his glass, and knelt in front of me, peering closely into my eyes. "Pupils normal. Any headache?" He raked the fingers of one hand through my hair and probed my scalp, putting me ill at ease. "I don't detect any lumps or bumps. Any painful injuries?"

"Only to my pride." I shrank from his touch.

At that moment, the door flew open. Owen stood at the threshold, startled at the little tableau we presented—Thomas kneeling at my unshod feet with a hand in my hair, and me holding a drink.

We both gaped at him. He turned three shades of pink, mumbling, "Pardon the intrusion. Excuse me . . ." He left as quickly as he'd arrived.

I was aghast.

Thomas burst out laughing and adopted a dramatic pose, his hand at his throat. "Do you think he'll gossip with the servants?"

"It's not at all funny." I pushed him away, trying to imagine what Owen must think, finding us together late at night. I also couldn't imagine trying to explain.

"Drink the rest of that," Thomas motioned to the brandy in my glass as he stifled his laughter. "It'll help you sleep."

I doubted that. The entire bottle wouldn't calm my mind.

He downed the rest of his glass in one swallow. We both stood, and after an awkward moment, he walked with me to the bottom of the stairs. "Shall I be a gentleman and show you to your door?"

"That is utterly unnecessary," I said.

"I was quite sure it would be," he grinned, mocking me.

He bowed melodramatically and backed away as I went up. Before I closed my door, I heard his unbridled laughter echo through the house.

Chapter 30

*S*ince it was nearly dawn before I fell into fitful sleep, dragging myself out of bed at eight took concentrated effort. Before standing upright, I took stock of my bruised body and decided it would function adequately. My blemished reputation might be something else. I felt a pang of deep unease, remembering Owen's sudden appearance in the library the previous night.

In the lavatory, I washed and pulled on the freshly ironed shirtwaist I'd hung from a rack the day before. A button on the sleeve popped off and bounced upon the floor. As I retrieved it from under the claw-foot tub, I spied something. Reaching deep beneath, I dragged out a wadded-up bath towel. It was large, pale green, and one I had never before seen.

I could not explain its appearance in a lavatory I exclusively used. Thinking of last night, I felt myself stumbling about the hallway in the dark and losing my footing at the head of the stairs. A chill ran down my spine. If this green towel had precipitated my fall, either it had been innocently dropped unnoticed—or someone had purposefully placed it at the top of the stairs. Either scenario was possible, with the first being more plausible.

However, it was beyond credulity that the towel could have been shoved under my bathtub in some accidental fashion. Someone had hidden it.

I closed my eyes and shook my head, trying to piece together the events of last night. It wasn't so simple. I couldn't even remember leaving my room, so it would be foolish of me to depend wholly on my memories.

After staring at the towel for a long moment, fishing for any forgotten fact, I folded it and laid it across the edge of the tub. I would ask Mrs. Hadley at the first opportunity how it might have come to be there.

I went to work and had the study all to myself. Mr. Wellington was still in bed with his head cold, and I was therefore able to favor my stiff hip and shoulder, walking and sitting gingerly, without generating unwanted concern. A purple bruise bloomed on my elbow, and frustration grew at the thought of the night before. To my chagrin, Owen had made himself scarce. I wanted to explain, although I had no idea what I might say.

Each time I rose from my desk, my head swam. I felt like crying. During the past few days, I'd finally felt recovered from the calamity at the footbridge, and now I was struggling with discomfort and confusion again.

By the end of the day, I was exhausted. Feeling a bit of nausea, I took the opportunity to sit on the veranda to watch the lowering sun. Apparently, Mrs. Wellington had forgotten her magnanimous gesture of the previous evening. She wasn't available to seek me out at the end of the workday, having gone into the village with Thomas to visit friends early in the afternoon. My only feeling was relief.

The veranda was awash with soft air and pale twilight. I was thinking of Owen and where he might be and how I could explain last night when Kitty, like a shadow, stole near.

"Hello, Kitty. Where've you been?"

She bowed her head with a smile. Sitting at the edge of the porch, she twisted her dirty bare feet, pulling her too-thin dress over her knees. Her worn canvas slippers were sitting neatly on the step below us.

I wondered if the child had a proper pair of shoes. With the colder weather coming on, I was concerned with her well-being. And beyond her physical health, I wondered if Kitty was being taught her letters and sums.

As if to answer my questions, Dolly appeared behind me. "Little Missy Kitty, there you are," she said. She held in her hands pieces of heavy fabric. "Come let me see how long to make this." She turned to me. "This is from an old dress of Miz Martha's she no longer wears. Fine wool and good enough for our Kitty's winter garment, am I right, girl?"

The child rose and before standing in front of Dolly as asked, handed me her precious box. I was startled but touched by this act of trust. I did not violate that confidence by looking inside it.

Dolly held Kitty to her bosom as she measured the length of cloth against her thin body. "You've grown like a weed this summer, you have."

I thought back to midsummer when I first met the Little Seedling.

"Dolly, isn't Kitty of school age?"

"We do teach her here, Miss." Dolly smiled as she fussed with the fabric and pins. "She don't talk much, but she's a smart 'un. She does her fractions as she learns to bake. She can read recipes, double or halve ingredients quicker'n Cook."

I was surprised. Perhaps Kitty was older than she appeared. "When's Kitty's birthday, Dolly?"

"That'd be next month—January. Don't recall the exact day, as her mom left us kind of sudden-like. Kitty's nigh on eight years. Don't seem possible."

She was older than I'd thought and still very precocious, it seemed, for so young a child. No wonder I had the sense she saw and understood everything.

A shadow fell between Dolly and me. I turned to find Lavinia Wellington standing at the steps wearing a light wrap and a veiled hat.

"There you are, Anne. You haven't forgotten about our talk, have you? We cut our visit short just to get back."

I'd gotten used to these suggestions that I was somehow inconsiderate and didn't apologize for something not within my power to control. I said instead, "How thoughtful you are." I was going to suggest Kitty come inside with us, but she'd disappeared, taking her box with her. I wasn't the only person uneasy in Mrs. Wellington's company.

She put her arm through mine. "Dolly, tell Maddy we'll take tea in the library."

As we strolled in that direction, she chattered about her day in the village and the friends she'd seen. When we reached the library, we sat at opposite ends of the leather couch behind the low table.

"Thomas tells me you had an accident last night."

I might have known he couldn't keep it to himself. "It was silly of me. Well, clumsy anyway."

She peered at me as if to determine my truthfulness. "What were you doing up so late at night?"

"I don't know. That is, I don't remember getting up and leaving my room." I dared not reveal thoughts that I might've been ambushed, if not by someone secreted in the darkness, then by something, such as an errant towel, at the head of the stairs.

"Were you sleepwalking?"

"I have never done so before and cannot imagine that I was," I said, hiding my irritation. Of course, Thomas would share every thought in his head with his mother.

"But you weren't hurt?"

"Not at all," I lied, ignoring my sore body.

She adopted an exaggerated look of concern. "I'm troubled by another incidence of bad luck for you at Northfield, Miss Chatham." How easily she reverted to a less convivial manner of speech, eschewing my Christian name. "We don't like to think it's not healthy for you here."

I understood this as a challenge, if not an actual threat, and was rendered speechless. This comment forced me to weigh my limited options, for staying here or leaving this house. My chest tightened.

The rattle of the tea tray announced Maddy as she struggled down the hall. Mrs. Wellington pressed her lips into a tight line of displeasure. Maddy opened the door with a hip and awkwardly swung the heavy tray into the room.

Out of patience, Mrs. Wellington said, "Just set the tray down, Maddy, and leave."

"Yes, Missus." Maddy avoided eye contact but managed a quick bob of the head and ducked out the door.

Mrs. Wellington turned a strained smile to me as she picked up the teapot. "I'll be mother. Just relax, my dear."

I doubted I would ever feel relaxed in Mrs. Wellington's company. "Thank you. You're very kind."

"Not at all." She handed me a cup and saucer. "We enjoy our little talks, don't we?"

The pinnacle of my day. I suppressed a sigh. "It's lovely to sit and chat before dinner, yes."

"Especially with a fond companion." Mrs. Wellington patted my hand. "How have you filled your time today?"

I often felt she pumped me for information, with the hope of uncovering some hidden desire or ulterior motive. The competition I presented for her sons' attentions was the likely reason for her veiled comments. I felt vulnerable and tried to allay her fears with a display of interest in my work. "Compiling documentation on historical rules regarding leases and rents, transcribing manuscript to type, as usual. We've discovered a great deal recently."

"Did you see Mr. Wellington?"

She hadn't listened to my response. "Apparently, he continues to feel unwell," I said. "He didn't come to the study today."

"Poor Henry. I must stop in to see about him."

The milk of human kindness. I stifled a frown. Struggling to make conversation, I asked, "Does Mr. Wellington discuss his scholarship with you?"

"Oh, my dear, why would he do that?"

I spoke carefully. "It would be only natural, an interest in his work."

"It bores me, the history of land contracts, laws, regulations, customs of ownership. All I need to know is Thomas inherits Northfield."

"But what of Owen?" I blurted out, unable to stop myself.

"Owen has many interests." She dismissed him. "He's a scholar, like his father."

"I see." I tried to fathom what this meant for the family. It belatedly occurred to me it was unwise to reveal to the lady of the house that I had any personal interest in Owen. I backed away from the subject.

Mrs. Wellington said, "I'm not worried about Owen. He's sensible and knows how to work. It's Thomas that troubles me. He's so impetuous." She turned her smile on me as she changed the topic. "Boys are much less mature than women their own age, don't you think? They're likely to make such unfortunate choices."

I understood the implication. That her sons might set their sights on an impoverished minister's daughter was not to be endured. She stared closely at me, watching my reaction, no doubt gauging the extent to which I was a threat.

She tilted her head with an attitude of wistful regret. "That is why the loss of our Charlotte is so tragic."

Her concern struck me as disingenuous, but I nodded.

"Thomas and she were so well-suited." Mrs. Wellington looked longingly into her cup.

It is possible they were an ideal couple, as I thought they were two of a kind, but she would never have accepted Charlotte as a daughter-in-law. Mrs. Wellington had chosen to recast Charlotte as the ideal mate to send the obvious message that I was totally unsuitable. The independent working woman in me was offended. It appeared most members of the Wellington family thought me a gold digger, trolling for a husband.

Much to my dismay, there was no way to defend myself from such a charge. To declare my innocence was to confirm Mrs. Wellington's worst fears. I sighed and placed my teacup on the tray.

"Thank you, Mrs. Wellington, for your kindness. Now I must lie down. I think I'm coming down with Mr. Wellington's cold." As I stood, a wave of nausea washed over me. I didn't feel like myself at all.

"Shall I have dinner sent to your room, dear?" She was quick to exclude me from the supper table.

I acquiesced without hesitation. "Yes, that might be best." If Mrs. Wellington wanted me out of the way, she would have it. She could easily undermine my position here if she wished to do so. One critical word to Mr. Wellington and I might be sacked. It was up to me to decipher her desires and fulfill them. In our cat-and-mouse game, I was most assuredly the mouse.

Back in my room, I collected items to launder in the sink while I awaited the evening meal. As I hung my stockings and under-garments across the racks in the bathroom, I noticed the pale green towel was gone. I took a quick peek under the tub and in the cupboard. It was nowhere to be found.

I immediately felt uneasy. Then I noticed that my own soiled linens had been gathered up as well. The closet had been stocked with fresh items. Perhaps Kitty had a new set of chores, which included collecting dirty laundry for the household in anticipation of tomorrow's weekly wash. I made a mental note to ask Mrs. Hadley about the mysterious green towel tomorrow.

Chapter 31

*M*rs. Wellington sent a supper tray to my room that evening and every evening for the rest of the week. Thus, I was deftly banished from the only formal family gathering. For the next few days, I had no opportunity to speak with Owen or Thomas.

It was just as well—I didn't want to heighten Mrs. Wellington's suspicions that I sought to ensnare one of her sons. Still, despite my better judgement, I had hoped to see Owen. I worried that he had misunderstood the scene with Thomas after my fall, and for that reason was avoiding me. I also knew, however, that this was the busiest time with the harvest. I tried to catch a glimpse of him in the fields, but to no avail. By the end of the week, Thomas came by to lean on my desk and question me.

"We miss you at dinner," he said. "Whatever are we to think?"

I couldn't tell him that his mother had decided I was too much of a distraction for her sons and wished to separate us as much as possible. Even a hint of that would send him dashing off to argue with her. I would gladly allow his mother to win this battle if it meant keeping my employment.

"You know where I am, Thomas." I gave him a smile. "You can't miss me if I'm always here."

"True. But try to explain, for my sake."

"If you must know, the cooler weather has brought on a malaise of some sort. It sends me to bed early. It'll pass soon, I hope." This was a half-truth—I did suspect that I was fighting off Mr. Wellington's cold.

"Come for a walk in the garden, why don't you? Take a break from all this." He waved his hand, indicating the books and papers surrounding me.

"You should ask your mother for a walk, Thomas," I said, trying to make my concern clear.

He relented. "Right. Understood. I'll leave you to your work."

I didn't want Lavinia Wellington to imagine me a competitor. Each evening, she continued to produce a tray of tea, and we sat for a few minutes after I ended my work for the day. As always, she attempted to peer into my soul.

"How are you getting on, Anne? Feeling better?"

I told her what she wanted to hear. "I'm so grateful for your kindness. I'm bothered by exhaustion by day's end, and it's comforting to sit quietly in my room."

Again, a half-truth. It was a relief to rest my aching head in the evenings, and lying down quieted my vague feelings of nausea. Unfortunately, loneliness also plagued me. I missed Owen, and truth be told, I missed even the tangential relationship with the family at the dinner table, which had given my life some normalcy.

"Is there anything you need? Anything I can do?"

I paused. "A small oil lamp for the desk would make my room more comfortable," I said. "I spend my evenings immersed in a book, and the candle is so dim."

"How delightful. What are you reading, my dear?"

"*The Beautiful and Damned.*"

A little taken aback by my language, she looked askance, grasping her hands at her bosom.

"F. Scott Fitzgerald, the American author," I said to answer her unspoken question. "He wrote *This Side of Paradise.*"

She was dismissive. "I don't read new novels. Classics are the only books worthwhile. Ask Henry. But yes, of course, a lamp is a good idea," she said as though she'd thought of it herself. "I'll see to it."

If a lamp would keep me away from her sons, it was a small concession to make.

❧

The next day, Owen came to see me. I looked up suddenly to find him standing in the study doorway.

"I haven't had a chance to talk to you this past week," he said.

"Nor I you."

"Sorry for that. I've been beastly busy. And you shouldn't let Mother bully you."

"I hardly have a choice."

"Can I assume you don't wish me to say anything? You prefer to handle the situation yourself?"

At this, we both smiled. It was reassuring that Owen understood precisely what was going on. I didn't have to explain or pretend that I preferred to eat my evening meal alone.

"Mrs. Hadley told me about your topple down the stairs." He looked grave. "She assured me you hadn't injured yourself again."

"No, Owen. I'm fine except for a bruise or two." I took a deep breath, relieved to know that he had inquired after me. His question also reminded me that no satisfactory explanation existed for the presence of the mysterious green towel. When I inquired of her, Mrs. Hadley looked puzzled and said, "I don't rightly know, Miss Anne. There are several old towels of that color piled in the boot room, but I'm at a loss to explain how one of them ended up in your bath."

Tucking the niggling worry about the towel in the back of my mind, I focused upon Owen. Since I wanted there to be no shadows between us, I gathered my courage and spoke plainly. "But I do worry that you might have misunderstood something that night."

198

"You sharing a brandy with Thomas?" Owen said.

"Yes, yes, exactly," I spoke too quickly, nervous about addressing such a delicate subject. "He was being attentive, making sure I wasn't hurt. There was nothing more."

Owen brightened. "I figured as much. Thomas is always about to assist a pretty girl."

My heart warmed at the compliment, and my breath caught. "I'd hoped you hadn't gotten the wrong impression."

A small smile broke over his solemn face. "No, not at all." His gaze held mine.

And in that moment, all was right between us again.

He blinked as if to remember himself. "By the way, I have something for you." He stepped from behind the door and, with a shy expression, produced a rectangular maroon box. It was about sixteen by eight inches, no more than an inch deep, and had "OUIJA" written in golden Gothic script across it.

I stared at the object in his hands. "What is it?"

"It's a device enabling communication with the spirit world."

I perked up. So Eleanor was not to be forgotten.

"I thought we'd try it," he said, smiling. "Why not?"

I took the box from him, puzzled. "Seriously? What does 'Ouija' mean?"

"It's pronounced '*wee-jah*' and means 'Good luck,' they say. It's used during séances to contact the dead and has become quite popular since the Great War. Percival Gilliam claims they were able to speak to his brother who was killed in the Argonne."

Opening the box on my desk, I frowned as I fingered a small, triangular piece of wood with three tiny legs attached to the underside. A circle of magnifying glass was embedded at one corner. A glance at the instructions indicated it was called a "table."

"I'm skeptical, too," he said, "but thought it might be interesting."

I withdrew a bifold board covered with the letters of the alphabet, numbers from zero to nine, "YES" in one corner, "NO" in another, and "GOOD BYE" at the bottom. We read the directions together, Owen's head bent over mine.

> *Fold the board across the laps of two persons, a lady and gentleman, and place the small "table" upon the board.*

I glanced up at Owen, imagining us sitting in the dark.

> *Place the fingers on the table without pressure, so as to allow it to move easily and freely. In one to two minutes, the table will commence to move, at first slowly, then with more force. Spirits will be able to talk or answer questions by choosing the printed words or the letters necessary to spell out sentences, which will show through the glass on the pointed end of the table.*
>
> *Great care should be taken that only one person at a time presents questions, to avoid confusion, and the questions should be put plainly and accurately.*

I felt a small tug of alarm. I wasn't sure Owen understood what we might be getting ourselves into.

> *To obtain best results, it is important that those present should concentrate their minds upon questions and avoid other topics. Have no person present who will not sit seriously and respectfully. If you use it in a frivolous spirit, asking ridiculous questions, laughing over it, you may generate an unwanted response.*

Since I was already subject to unbidden, undesirable activity of spirits, I felt a growing unease.

> *The Ouija is a great mystery, and we do not claim to have exact directions for its management; neither do we claim that at all times and under all circumstances it will work equally well. But we do*

claim and guarantee that, with reasonable patience and judgment, it will more than satisfy your greatest expectations.

Following the instructions for its use, there were directions for putting the table together, which Owen had already done, and an admonishment to keep the board smooth and free from dirt and moisture. Then printed below was the address of either the inventor of the device or the manufacturer: *WM. FULD, 1306 N. Central Avenue, Baltimore, MD.*

"I'm willing to give it a try if you are," he said, looking up into my face, displaying more enthusiasm than I felt.

I put my misgivings aside, heady with the nearness of him. I'd tried to put Owen out of my mind, and thought I had, until he was near once more. I closed my eyes for a moment and took a deep breath.

Focusing my mind again on the ghost hunting, I let excitement and new possibilities grip me as I considered the exotic board game. I had never been able to conjure specific spirits—like someone I loved, my parents or siblings—at will. Perhaps this would be a way to do so. And for the first time, sitting there with Owen at my side, I wanted to trust someone with the truth about myself.

"Have you encountered our ghost since the last time we saw her?" he asked.

"No. Have you?"

"I tried going into the south wing again but lost my nerve. Standing at the doors, I felt nothing. Besides, we both know you're the catalyst for any spirit activity."

I was startled by his words, feeling my true nature was exposed. Swept with the freeing sensation that someone knew me at long last, relief spread through my chest. Owen might understand and accept my deepest secret. But I kept my head about me. He spoke only in generalities. He didn't know anything specific.

"That's why we might be successful with this," he said, indicating the Ouija board.

We agreed to meet in the library at ten that evening. Owen departed, while I went about my work with renewed vigor. I rolled fresh blank paper into the machine and set to tap-tapping, sending pages covered with type spilling out. By the time my transcription was finished for the day, and Mrs. Wellington and I had shared our cup of tea, I was giddy with excitement. Alone in my room, I barely ate, for my stomach was still a bit delicate. I couldn't concentrate on my book, either. I spent the last hour before my designated meeting with Owen staring at the same page.

At last, I abandoned my room and crept through the house to the first floor. Owen was waiting in the dark library. He'd already opened the board atop a low footstool and lit a candle. The little pointed piece of wood, the table, was placed on the surface of the board. A bit breathless, I had to remind myself this was not a romantic assignation. Shadows surrounded Owen, the light and dark emphasizing the angles of his face. We kneeled on the floor on either side of the board, which was turned towards me.

The candle bathed us in soft light. We remained silent at first, as though we might disturb the spirits we sought with the spoken word. For a long moment, Owen's gaze held mine.

"Put your fingers on the table," he said as he placed his own upon the wooden triangle. We bowed our heads over the board, just a whisper apart. In a hushed voice, he asked the spirits to speak, pausing and waiting between each question.

"Are you here?"

"Who are you?"

"Where are you?"

Our fingers were poised, ready to respond.

Nothing happened.

"Are you here?" Owen asked again. He looked at me. "Maybe you'd better ask."

I posed the same series of questions.

"Are you here?"

"Who are you?"

"Where are you?"

Nothing.

Again, I beseeched the spirits to come.

We even moved the table around the board, spelling out *"Eleanor,"* and after a moment of hesitation, *"Charlotte,"* but without our obvious efforts, the table was motionless.

After several minutes, I relaxed my shoulders and breathed a disappointed sigh. "I'm sorry. I'm not feeling anything."

"But you do, don't you?" said Owen.

"What?"

"Feel ghosts. Receive messages from beyond. Perceive things. That is, you've seen into the world of spirits," said Owen. "Am I right?"

"Yes." With that one simple word of admission, I felt a knot of tension loosen deep within me. Yet, I dared not meet his eyes. I wasn't sure how much to say. I again felt exposed.

He leaned close. "It's doubtful the ghosts of Northfield have been at rest all these years. A catalyst or some kind of medium was necessary for communication to take place." He reached towards me and took my hand. "That medium is you. You are a conduit from that world to this."

I didn't know what to say. "It's not something I want. It's not intentional." I stood, and he stood with me.

"No apology necessary, but you must admit you've shaken things up. It was pretty dull until you brought an awareness to this house. This whole story of Eleanor lay dormant for decades."

My eyes filled with tears.

"Anne?" He frowned with concern. "Anne, what is it?"

I turned away, but he caught my wrists and forced me to face him.

"Don't, Owen."

"What's happened? What's wrong? You must tell me, Anne. I can see the melancholy that weighs upon you, and has, ever since your arrival. You appear to shoulder an unbearable pain."

"I can't."

"Trust me, Anne. I'd never do anything to harm you. What troubles you? Why are you so alone?"

I emitted a shuddering sob, and Owen caught me in his arms, soothing me like a child.

"I am alone, it's true, yet not alone," I whispered. "I have no parents, family, or friends to depend upon." Owen held me while my tears fell, and I surrendered to my grief. Feeling vulnerable, I shared what I'd never told anyone. "I do . . . see things. I see the dead." Barely a whisper escaped my trembling lips.

Owen held me tighter. "That much is already clear."

"I mean, they are with me, often, not just here in this house. And usually they're unbidden. And the reason for that is . . . I can't say it."

"Don't you understand I'm a friend, Anne? You can trust me with your deepest fears. Revealing them is the only way to unshackle yourself from the pain they cause," said Owen. He held my chin in his hand and tilted my tear-stained face towards his.

Our eyes met.

"Tell me," he said. "Tell me everything."

I took a deep breath and sat upon the couch. He took a seat beside me and held my hand. Swallowing with difficulty, I told my story.

"Owen, I'm a survivor of influenza."

The look on his face told me I didn't have to explain. The terrible pandemic that ravaged the world at the close of the Great War touched every family in Britain. Ultimately, it killed more people than the Black Death of the Middle Ages, and no city, village, or town had been unaffected.

"I lost my mother and my brother and sister. While I lay on my sickbed struggling to breathe, almost everything I loved was taken away in a breath." My face felt frozen with grief, my jaws clenched.

Owen nodded. "I was in a field hospital in France. Ten times as many men died of flu as on the battlefield," he said. "Fine lads, many friends. At the time, we thought it was a German biological warfare tool. Only the Huns could have devised such an ugly, insidious weapon."

Owen knew what I had suffered. He would have seen the blood-tinged froth that filled lungs and airways and choked its victims to death. But he didn't yet know everything.

"I died, Owen. I died and left my body."

A frown creased his brow, but he remained silent. Only his unspoken support could have enabled me to go on.

I continued. "I felt my spirit drift away, far away, into another dimension. I saw my body lying below me, pale and still, until my consciousness burst upon another world. Both light and darkness, music and dissonance, the beautiful and the grotesque were present in that place." I shuddered.

"How can you be sure it wasn't a fevered dream? A hallucination?"

"It's impossible to explain, but I know. I actually went somewhere. And returned."

"And since that experience, you've had some special insight?" he asked.

"If you want to call it that. From that time, I've been in touch with the souls of the dead, as though a doorway has been opened. Some special access has been granted me, a portal to those who have passed on." I wiped tears from my cheeks. "Some speak, some want something, others simply hover in my awareness. But I am convinced they exist everywhere should I choose to see."

"You can suppress those visions?"

"Most of the time but not always." I shook my head.

"How terrifying," he said.

I turned towards Owen and leaned close, appealing to him. "Yes, but only at first. Once I was able to control my fear, I wondered what they were, what they wanted. It's the unexpected that's so unnerving. Ghosts inspire fear because we don't understand."

"And you've learned what?"

"Most are simply lost. They don't know they're dead, and they continue to haunt this world, unable to satisfy their needs and desires, not knowing where to go. It's their frustration they express. They are but an imprint on the physical plane, like an echo or a shadow."

"Most but not all?"

"Some entities have awareness and purpose. They want something from me. These are the spirits I am wary of. I feel quite distinctly that our ghost—the one we call Eleanor—wants something very specific."

"Should we be afraid?"

"Maybe. If our specter wants revenge. Or if she is malevolent, seeking to destroy."

"I see," he said. "Well, at least this explains why there's suddenly spirit activity in the house. Your presence makes our expanded consciousness possible."

A great weight lifted from my heart as we sat in the candlelight. Owen touched my fingers with his, we breathed as if with one breath, and I no longer felt alone. He accepted my confession more readily than I'd thought anyone would.

"I saw our ghost my first day here, Owen. I knew nothing about the Wellington family or your history, yet she was there." It was important that he knew I wasn't merely projecting some personal pain of my own upon his family mysteries.

"She spoke to you?"

"Not in words." I glanced at his face. "Her shadow, rippling with somber color, hovered in a corner of the study. Even without any knowledge of her story, I felt her melancholy. Only later, when we encountered her spirit together, did I grasp the heartless tragedy suffered here."

"Yes," he said. "I feel that, too. Something deeply disturbing."

I explained to him the images that inhabited my head when ghosts walked and what I thought they conveyed. I told him of the flowers and other wedding symbols that accompanied our encounters with Eleanor.

After a moment of silence, I said, "You were right, Owen. Having spoken about my story, the burden is lighter. Thank you. I'm grateful for your friendship."

"I know a bit about burdens, Anne. And about bearing them alone," he said.

Of course, I knew his as well. Owen suffered through the war only to return to a disinterested family, everyone dismissive of his dreams. The angry scars marring his body flashed upon my mind.

We sat in comfortable silence for a moment while I remembered Owen's dedication to something bigger than himself or the Wellingtons, something that his family roundly ignored.

"How are your experiments going, Owen, after all these weeks?"

He seemed pleased to confide his own feelings after my rather shocking disclosure. He leaned back against the leather couch where his mother and I had tea earlier that evening.

"We've had more success than I'd dared dream." He smiled. "The spring wheat yield was much greater than expected." He talked about the new thresher and issues with getting the grains to market.

"If it weren't for the falling prices, income would soar," he said, shaking his head over the vagaries besetting the farmer.

"And your father? Is he coming around to your way of thinking?"

"I cannot say he is." He looked worried. "Partly because the science offends him, but even more so because the estate isn't mine."

I didn't want to bring Thomas into our discussion. "What will your future be, Owen?"

He looked at me. "My future is as uncertain as your own. You will struggle to work with the living residents as well as the spirits wherever you may be engaged. I will have to find my place, farming certainly, but where that might be is still a mystery to be resolved."

Then we both heard it.

Voices.

Whispers.

Unintelligible words, but words nonetheless.

We knew it wasn't somebody elsewhere in the house. We'd heard this before—in the last room of the south wing. Owen rose, pulling me to my feet. We tiptoed towards the closed door leading to the hallway and listened.

Heartrending, mournful cries of sorrow reached us, as if coming from a great distance. Owen looked at me and I nodded. We stood shoulder to shoulder, and he opened the library door.

Chapter 32

*T*he whispers grew louder in the hallway.
I was drawn towards the study. Grasping Owen's warm hand, I pulled him down the hallway to the study door, where we stopped and listened once more.

Without warning, I felt an electric current whip through my body and seize my limbs. I snatched my hand from Owen's, pushed open the door, and entered as if forced by an irresistible impulse. I pulled the cover off the Remington and sat before it.

I began striking the keys.

Owen stood across the room as though unable to move, staring at me.

My fingers flew across the keyboard while the carriage rattled to the left. Then I slammed the return rightwards. The bell pinged repeatedly as I typed at remarkable speed. I stared straight ahead, not looking at the paper or the keyboard.

I have no idea how long I was at it, but suddenly my hands fell to my lap. At the same moment, Owen flew to my side and looked at the paper on the roller.

"Anne! You were in some kind of trance. Look!"

The paper was filled with the same word over and over, in capital letters.

ELEANOR ELEANOR ELEANOR ELEANOR
ELEANOR ELEANOR ELEANOR ELEANOR
ELEANOR ELEANOR ELEANOR

We gaped at one another, shocked. Owen's hand shook, and I couldn't move. The atmosphere was heavy, pressing down upon me. After a moment, something snapped, making my ears pop. I took a deep breath, and my shoulders slumped forwards, nearly toppling me from the chair.

Owen caught me around the waist and helped me stand. "Are you all right?"

I shook my head to clear it and looked at Owen. "What happened?" My legs trembled.

He helped me sit back down in the chair again, and then knelt beside me, his arm around my shoulders. With his free hand, he pulled the paper out of the machine and held it before me. "Look at this! Do you remember writing it?"

"Of course," I said. I hesitated for a moment, befuddled. "I mean, I remember typing. Hitting the keys. But I had no words in my head. Maybe all our talk of spirits inflamed my imagination? It's unlike me to be so impressionable, but I don't know how to explain it. I just wasn't myself."

Owen said, "That's it! Maybe this really wasn't you." He gestured to the paper.

I frowned at him.

"I mean, maybe you were simply the medium for something else. That someone, or a kind of foreign entity, occupied your body to get this message across. And who else would it be but Eleanor?"

"Is it possible?" I asked, sick to my stomach. "That game, the Ouija board? Did we do it? Make a connection with the spirit world?" It was frightening to me that a spirit could possess my body.

"There was *some* kind of connection," Owen said. "Read the end of the message."

He shoved the paper into my hand and pointed. The last words were "FIND ME."

Chapter 33

"We did it, Anne!" Owen was so excited his voice shook. "We've not only seen Eleanor, now she has spoken to us." He leaped up in his enthusiasm.

I stared at the paper in my trembling hand. "A clear directive, to be sure." My voice wavered as if on the verge of tears. "But 'find me'? I wish she'd given us something more. A clue of some kind."

"She would, if she could have. You said yourself that spirits have difficulty communicating, that they are confused, bewildered."

"We need more to go on." I felt uneasy.

"But, this is fantastic. It validates what we've been doing. It's what we've been hoping for. This is everything and more. She's telling us we're on the right track."

"Yes, of course." I couldn't embrace his enthusiasm, as I felt I had been physically violated.

Owen was practically skipping about the study, unable to keep still. "This is a giant leap forwards," he said. "We'll keep going, step by step, until we find all the answers. I know it. I know we're going to resolve this mystery."

A tear volunteered at the corner of my eye. I was all at once exhausted and swept with a sense of deep foreboding. "Owen, I must go to my room. Let's think about this and how to go forwards tomorrow."

"Are you quite all right?" He took the paper from my hand and laid it aside, kneeling beside me once more. "I'm an idiot, babbling on about this instead of tending to you. Shall I get you a cup of tea? Something else?" A troubled frown replaced his giddiness.

"No, please don't bother." I smiled for his benefit. "It often happens, you see, when entities make themselves known. My strength is sapped by these experiences," I said, pointing at the typewritten paper, "as though this otherworldly being uses my energy to communicate."

"If you're sure," Owen said. He seemed dejected.

I hated to be a wet blanket. "It's over now. I'll be fine." Without explaining further, I rose.

Owen offered me his arm, and I took it gratefully. My weariness felt bone-deep. We slowly took the stairs to my room as if accompanied by a funeral dirge.

At my door, Owen took my hand. "You sure you're all right?"

"Of course."

"Then I'll see you tomorrow?" he said. "I'll come by the study, probably early morning before I leave for work."

All I could manage was a wan smile.

I listened to his footsteps recede down the passage. Not bothering to disrobe, I collapsed upon the bed.

For hours, dark shadows and a suffocating fear inhabited my dreams. Eleanor hung on the periphery, beckoning. Even worse, the horrifying ordeal of discovering Charlotte's body loomed once more. Memories of that night swam forwards and receded as I grasped at them, trying to understand something. Like the mythical creatures of a fantastical merry-go-round, images leaped towards me and spun away as I tried unsuccessfully to board. I awoke in a panic, struggling to remember some detail just beyond the reach of my tortured mind.

❧

Well before dawn, I rose to sit upon the window ledge and watch the morning light reveal the gardens silvered with frost. A pale monochrome had enveloped the world. I could smell the cold.

I feared our search, Owen's and mine, into the world of the spirit inhabiting Northfield House had provoked an unhealthy instability in my personality. In addition to being afflicted of late with a queasy stomach and dull headache accompanied by debilitating exhaustion, a dark melancholy had taken hold of me.

After last night's experience with the Ouija board, it took all my strength and concentration to manage my responsibilities to Mr. Wellington and maintain normal interactions with the household. Even Owen, when we saw one another before he left for the fields, could not penetrate my distraction.

"Have you thought more about what to do next regarding our ghost, Anne?" He looked about to make sure we were not over-heard. He was still gleeful about the success of the night before.

"No," I said, concerned that he expected too much of me. "Please understand, Owen, I cannot conjure spirits at will. I may be able to ignore them when they appear or suppress their messages, but I cannot call specific entities forth."

"But last night—"

"—was an anomaly," I insisted.

Frankly, I was terrified at the thought of using the Ouija board again. I could not in all good faith encourage his enthusiasm, not feeling at ease about our prospects.

"I'm sorry, Anne. You do look tired. I feel I've burdened you."

"I need to recover from the experience, is all." I tried to be reassuring, although I was not confident myself.

"Are you well, my dear?" Mrs. Wellington asked as she poured tea at the end of my work day. "You look pale."

"How kind of you to ask." I did not divulge that I hadn't slept well, awakening at the oddest times. "It's only that my dreams are troubled." I struggled to focus on our conversation.

"Troubled dreams? We're so distressed to hear that," she said as if speaking for the whole family. "Might your torment be related to our unfortunate tragedy, my dear?" Mrs. Wellington looked into her steaming cup. "I hate to think it."

"I would like to believe I'm made of sterner stuff," I said.

"Perhaps, Anne, you would benefit from some time away from Northfield."

My distress at this suggestion must have played across my face because she followed quickly with, "Just for a few days, to rest and relax. Would you like to visit relatives? Go home to Liverpool for a while?"

I sat like a stone. I had no friends or family in Liverpool. There was no respite for a woman in my precarious position.

"I'm sure Henry could manage. And your job will be waiting for you when you return."

"That is kind of you, Mrs. Wellington. Allow me to think about it, after reviewing my work schedule."

I didn't trust her. She might take the opportunity to be rid of me. A short trip to Liverpool or London could be followed by a note informing me my services were no longer needed.

Perhaps paranoia was a symptom of my malaise. That assumption was rational, but I also had sufficient reason to doubt Mrs. Wellington's support. It worried me that she might be aware somehow of the interest Owen and I pursued. I dismissed that thought, as our ghost-hunting adventures were surely known only to ourselves.

However, I had no doubt our meddling would have met with her deep disapproval.

❧

That evening, I was taking a solitary turn in the garden hoping for Owen to find me, when Thomas popped up out of nowhere.

"Mother's right. You do look pale. You're unwell."

"Nonsense," I said. "Why wouldn't I be pale? I sit at a desk all day."

"But you still decline to join us for dinner? For another week?"

"The time alone suits me, Thomas." I kept to myself that, for the most part, it suited his mother. "The dinner hour is a time for the family."

"You're not going to leave us?"

Uneasiness gripped my stomach. "Why would you suggest that?"

"Mother thought you might want to return home for a visit."

I felt a hollow sensation in my chest. "Not for some time. After all, I've not been here for six months yet. I can hardly think of taking off."

"Given the circumstances, everyone would understand should you do so, but I am pleased to hear you've no plans," Thomas said. "It's lonely enough at Northfield. And if you're not here, Father will commandeer Owen or me to visit those drafty archives."

He took my arm as we moved along the path. I looked uneasily behind me for Owen or his mother.

"How was your visit to London?" As soon as I spoke, I wanted to withdraw my thoughtless question. Thomas had gone to London to escape the reminders of Charlotte's death.

"Diverting," he said. "I'm afraid I spent too much time with the lads, drank spirits to some excess, and attended racy theatre. Well, Noel Coward, actually."

I made no response, looking away from him.

"You're disappointed?" Thomas stopped and turned to face me.

"Why do you imagine so?"

"Your silence speaks volumes."

"It isn't my place to have an opinion, Thomas. Aren't you projecting your own feelings?"

He looked sheepish. "I imagine I expected more of myself than drowning my sorrows with wine, women, and song, as they say."

It saddened me to think Charlotte might so easily be put to rest. I remained silent.

"You must think me quite shallow," he said.

"I don't think of you at all." I didn't intend to be rude but spoke my mind.

Thomas burst out laughing. He placed an uncomfortably familiar arm around my shoulders, which I wanted to shrug off but did not, as we continued walking. "Quite so, Anne. I like you for putting me—a randy cad whose response to tragedy is a fling with another woman—in my place."

I unclenched my teeth and said, "Are women so interchangeable? One will do as well as another?"

His eyes narrowed. "That's hardly fair, Anne. I was fond of Charlotte and enjoyed ribbing Owen about her, but I wasn't in love. Beyond that, she was family. Her death was a shock, but life goes on after all."

His confirmation of Owen's feelings for Charlotte made my heart ache. But I pushed my emotions aside and recalled the times I'd seen Charlotte and Thomas together. I'd seen him pawing her in the hallway after dinner during her first visit. At the masquerade ball, Thomas had been drunk, and if not smitten, he was at least covetous of Charlotte's attention. Regardless of how he felt about her, he had wanted her favors and was competitive enough to vie for them.

He wasn't being truthful now. Her death *had* to have been more disturbing than he cared to admit. The only question was *why* he would deny it.

That night, Charlotte had been teasing all the men, bestowing her glance on one after another. A man's desire was nothing to play with. I could easily believe she lit a fire and got burnt. I was reminded of

Charlotte's skullcap and wondered if it might have been in Thomas's pocket.

It harrowed my mind, the thought that Charlotte was not alone at the footbridge the night she fell. She was not a tender soul who would seek solace by wandering to the ravine. She wouldn't have left the ballroom without plans for an assignation. But I knew Owen wouldn't succumb to violence. I wasn't quite as sure about Thomas.

All at once, I felt faint. My head swam with images of that night, of the swirling water, the driving rain, slick mud, and sharp rocks. And Charlotte's twisted body and her fluttering wings and her hand bobbing in the current. And something else I couldn't grasp, a memory that slipped through the water like a fish catching the silvery starlight.

I forced myself to concentrate. Whatever was in Charlotte's hand, it might reveal something about Owen, or maybe Thomas. I tried to imagine what I couldn't bear to remember.

My head throbbed, but I didn't want Thomas to think me weak. Being vulnerable, depleted of physical strength, seemed dangerous in his company. I leaned against the garden wall to steady myself. To hide my debility, I bent to cup a white rose with my hand. When I rose, I could see he was angry.

"Perfect," Thomas said, almost hiding his sneer, "that you should select the white rose rather than the red. Do you know how prim you are?" He took a step forwards and, placing a fingertip at my chin, traced a line down my throat to my collar bone.

I struggled to quell the shiver of revulsion but stood my ground.

He stepped back, looking frustrated. "A gentleman would accompany you to the house. Is that necessary in this instance?"

I said nothing, unsure how to deal with his sudden change in attitude.

"As you wish." He spun on his heel and trod down the gravel path, his heavy footsteps quick and decisive.

I sagged against the wall, exhausted but grateful for his departure. I determined not to make an enemy of Thomas. I was already engaged in a delicate dance with his mother, trying to stay in her good graces.

❧

Deep in slumber, I sprawled across the bed, my foot dangling almost to the floor. All at once fully awake, I listened for whatever had disturbed my sleep. The house was silent.

A foul odor filled the room. Sour milk. I pulled the coverlet over my nose and mouth.

I heard dripping water.

Then I detected a slithering beneath the bed.

Icy fingers grasped my exposed ankle.

Panic swept through me. I jerked my leg up onto the bed and scrabbled to the other side of the mattress. I cowered against the wall, gripping the blankets against my breast, the sheet knotted in my fists. I swallowed the bile that rose in my throat, fearing Owen and I had opened an evil portal with our meddling.

Something crept to the corner across the room. Shadows gathered. A dark thing huddled there, breathing. It moved like a large bird, awkward, hobbling on foot. I heard a flutter and a scratch. Shuffling sounds followed, then scuffling. Dread rippled through my body.

It can't hurt me, it can't hurt me, it can't hurt me . . .

My door creaked open a few inches. A small, solid black figure stood at the threshold. Frozen in fear, I felt my heart lurch as the shadow swept towards me.

Kitty crawled into my bed. With a cry of relief, I pulled her to me with both arms, and we clutched one another. I wondered what she saw, and if she felt what I did.

The dark, breathing thing in the corner began to evaporate. At the same time, a spark of pale light appeared overhead. Tearing my gaze away for a second, I saw that Kitty watched it, too, the light reflected in her eyes. It wavered and danced like flame.

As it moved across the ceiling, Kitty buried her face against my neck. She trembled, and I held her close.

I detected a scurrying in the walls. Hundreds, if not thousands, of tiny feet. Then a wave of scrabbling things washed across the floor, flowing like water. Not mice. Not bugs. Then silence fell once more before I heard mournful cooing like that of doves and low muttering as if crows roosted in the trees. The pale flame flickered.

"Go away!" I finally found my voice. "Go! Now!"

The light faded to black, leaving only a whiff of dried roses.

"There's nothing here, Kitty. You're fine, everything's fine." I soothed her until she relaxed and, after an hour or more, fell asleep.

She seemed as fragile as a baby bird, her eyelids blue. I clasped her to my breast, perhaps the closest I would ever get to motherhood. Her fine hair was damp, her body hot. Her delicate limbs hung limp like those of the newly dead.

Chapter 34

nne. Anne!"

I awoke to an urgent tapping at my door the next evening. I'd fallen asleep after work, fully dressed, an open book upon my lap. Smoothing my disheveled hair away from my face and securing the button at my throat, I rose and cocked open the door.

Owen was standing in the dim evening light. "May I come in?"

Against my better judgment, I stepped aside, allowing him to enter.

"What time is it?" I looked behind him towards the stairs. I feared his mother might show up unexpectedly again with a tea tray. It would play rather badly if she found her son alone with me in my room.

"About half past seven." Owen gazed about my chamber. "Where exactly was that shadowy creature huddled?" he asked in a whisper. He was the only person I dared share my experience with, and clearly, he'd been mulling it over in his mind since we'd crossed paths earlier in the day.

I pointed to the northeast corner of the room. "There."

He inspected the spot closely, looking disappointed. "I see nothing but a bit of dust."

"Be grateful you don't share my visions. They're disturbing."

I gestured to the desk chair and he sat. Since there was nowhere else to perch except upon the bed, I continued standing. I feared a misunderstanding if someone, particularly Mrs. Wellington, found us in what could be judged as a compromising situation.

"What do we know about Eleanor?" he asked.

I paused to think, sweeping the cobwebs of sleep from my head. "That she was your mother's sister, and that she married your father first."

"And," Owen said eagerly, "she disappeared on her wedding day. And what has been deduced from that?" Impatient, he didn't wait for my answer. "That she either ran away or was abducted. For my father's sake, the entire family settled on the latter."

I nodded. "That seems to be the case."

Owen said, "How do we know that when Eleanor vanished, she was abducted?"

"Well, we don't know for sure," I said, "but if she'd left of her own free will, don't you think she'd have eventually written her parents?"

"And, since she didn't, everyone assumes she died," said Owen. "But isn't it possible she left willingly but died accidentally?"

"I suppose. That would have produced the same results—Eleanor disappearing without a trace and never contacting her family." I couldn't understand what he was getting at.

"Or she might have died at the hands of her lover. Perhaps he was insanely jealous," he posited.

"It strikes me as odd that a lover would whisk her away only to kill her," I said.

Owen shook his head in frustration. "She might have joined the circus and died while on the flying trapeze."

Now he was being silly. "Well, that seems unlikely. We could spend hours spinning stories because there's no way to know the truth."

"Precisely. We only know the mythology that has grown up around her. And from those who promote the myths. Why should we take their word for it?"

"Why not?" I was skeptical. "What would they have to gain by lying?"

"Protecting the family, their pride, their dignity. Think of how appalling it must have been for the Granvilles. And how could Father ever admit that the woman he loved abandoned him?" Owen stood and paced the room. "There's so much we don't know."

"You're not suggesting we return to the south wing . . ." I suppressed a shudder, imagining us bent over the Ouija board set out upon the trunk in that dark, cold room at the end of the corridor. "I can't go back there. Not yet."

He took my hand in his. "No, no of course not. I wouldn't ask you to."

"But what can we do?"

"We engage in an unemotional, factual investigation of our own, like a science experiment. We collect the evidence ourselves and come to conclusions apart from emotions, embarrassment, fears, and wishful thinking—all those hidden motives."

"How would we go about that?" I asked.

"Father, Mother, Aunt Martha, and perhaps others are still alive and can give account," Owen said, his color rising with his excitement. "There's also Jonathan Cavanaugh, Eleanor's first love." He sat again.

I finally perched on the edge of the bed and looked levelly at Owen. "You do realize that I, the lowly typewriter, can't ask them these questions, don't you?"

"But no one could fault me for asking. Curiosity and all that. They'll understand I'd want to know about it, the family history, before they're all gone."

"Your Aunt Martha's account would not be reliable."

Owen dismissed me with a wave of his hand. "You're wrong about that. She can't seem to retain anything current, but her memory of the past is faultless."

"Before we go opening up old wounds, tell me what makes you think we don't already have the truth?"

"This." He produced from his pocket the paper I'd typed the night we used the Ouija board and shook it open. "Don't you see? It has to be Eleanor. And she says, 'FIND ME.'"

I was awash once again with the feelings of dread that gripped me that night.

"Anne, there was *never* any evidence that Eleanor was abducted. Given that she vanished without a trace, I find it difficult to believe she left voluntarily. Her message to us is a clear invitation to solve the mystery that surrounds her disappearance. Given this," he glanced at the typewritten paper again, "I don't believe Eleanor Granville ever left Northfield House."

Chapter 35

What do you mean—never left?" I asked, confounded.
He paused. "Eleanor is still here, at least in spirit, inviting us to discover what really happened. Doesn't it stand to reason she isn't anywhere else?"

"I'm not sure I follow."

"Well, you tell me. You're the ghost conductor, or whatever you call it. How does it work? Doesn't a spirit haunt the last place they existed in life? Or do they return to happy childhood homes or favorite vacation spots?"

Exasperated, I said, "I have no idea, Owen. I'm not sure what they do, or how or why ghosts inhabit their haunts." But his questions posed an interesting question. Why would Eleanor's spirit be here in Northfield House if she abandoned her husband, if she'd run off with a lover?

Owen persisted. "All I'm saying is that we don't have enough evidence to come to any conclusions."

I could not disagree. "You may be right."

"First thing tomorrow, I'll speak with Father. That may open up some ideas. With luck, he'll provide a thread that will lead to something else. That's how police work is done. Methodical attention to detail and follow-through."

I refrained from reminding him that a thorough investigation probably *was* done at the time of Eleanor's disappearance. "Yes, that might work, Owen."

"But asking Mother will have to wait until she returns from Melling."

Only then did I remember that Mrs. Wellington left that afternoon to visit family and would be away for a few days. "Of course, we must try." I tried to rally my enthusiasm, which was dampened by my usual fatigue.

"Tomorrow, then," he stood and hesitated. He looked awkward, as though he wanted to speak of something else but said only, "Have a good night, Anne. I hope Eleanor rests easily as well," as he left.

The next morning, I awoke early from a fitful sleep. Owen's certainty of discovering decades-old secrets kept me unsettled throughout the night. A cool bath restored my energy but didn't relieve my doubt. More sophisticated investigators than the two of us had put their best efforts towards solving the mystery of Eleanor Granville's disappearance. Admittedly, Owen's belief that the family had intentionally buried the facts was plausible. I dressed and went downstairs.

As I approached the study, angry words drifted out into the corridor. I stopped and waited. It was not my intention to eavesdrop, but the raised voices carried to where I stood.

"Confound it, boy, I don't care to discuss it. What you now know is what we all know, and that's all there is."

I heard a drawer slam.

"Father, it's just that—" Owen said, most of his appeal lost to my ears.

"There isn't anything else to understand. And don't be bothering your mother about this nonsense. New methodology, my foot. You'd better keep your head in your confounded wheat bins and think about something other than this foolishness."

Owen said, "I regret to have distressed you, sir."

I stepped back into the corridor to remain hidden until Owen left. After he vanished at the other end of the great hall, I lingered for a moment, then entered the study as I normally would and took my seat behind the Remington.

"Good morning, sir." I fixed my sight on the papers cluttering my desk.

Mr. Wellington didn't answer. His bottom desk drawer was open, and he held the picture of Eleanor in his palm. I pretended not to notice, and he appeared to be oblivious to me. Owen's inquiry had stirred up old memories, if nothing else. As I began my work, he wheeled out of the room and didn't return.

The day passed, Kitty sitting on the rug beneath my feet for much of it. Just before I covered the typing machine for the evening, she disappeared. As Mrs. Wellington was away, our regular tea was suspended for the time being. This gave me unimpeded time to conspire with Owen. After gathering my coat and gloves from my room, I headed for the fields.

Since I continued to avoid the footbridge, I took the front road to the greenhouse in the pale moonlight. Owen had his back to me when my shadow announced my arrival. He turned with a half-hearted grin.

"You're right, Anne. No one is willing to talk about Eleanor's disappearance. Father was adamant. It appeared to genuinely trouble him. I'd be afraid to approach Mother." We moved through the rows of plants towards a bench at the back and sat.

There was no point in saying I told you so. "I'm sorry, Owen."

"I tried to see Aunt Martha twice, but she was in bed. I think she's come down with Father's cold."

I still had my doubts about how helpful Martha could be. Yet, I wanted to offer encouragement, some bread crumbs to follow out of the maze of questions we had. I said, "Well, that leaves Jonathan Cavanaugh for the time being. Have you any idea where we could find him?"

"Of course," said Owen. "Although he now resides in London, his youngest daughter Celia is a neighbor. We often see him here around the holidays and at local events during harvest. He'll be about sometime this month, and I can ask Celia exactly when. It wouldn't be unusual that I would inquire after Mr. Cavanaugh."

We left the greenhouse and wandered outside, our shoulders almost touching, to the fields now lying fallow. A tenant from one of the farms was gleaning in the distance. Owen whistled and raised his hand in greeting. The man stood and waved at us.

"My little brother could do that—whistle as if to wake the dead," I said.

"And you cannot?"

Hoping he hadn't seen the tears that had gathered in my eyes, I looked away. "No. No, of course I can't whistle." I didn't say what I felt, that it was not seemly for a woman.

"And why not? You appear to have the requisite anatomy."

I laughed in spite of myself. "Don't be silly."

"I'm not. Here," he said as he took my hand. "Touch your thumb to forefinger, making a 'v,' and place the tips of your fingers under your tongue."

I did so and watched him as he demonstrated.

"No, behind your teeth."

I felt awkward.

"Now close your lips over your fingers so that air can be forced through the hole between your fingers. Now blow."

I followed his instructions, laughing and self-conscious, creating only wet air.

Owen said, "Experiment with placement of fingers, tongue, and lips until it works."

I tried again and generated an anemic tweet. We both laughed as I tried and tried again. He showed me the process once more, letting out sharp, concentrated sound with ease.

At last, I got the hang of it and unexpectedly produced a loud warble that startled us both.

"I did it!" I squealed in an unladylike fashion.

"Now, just keep at it," Owen said, with pride in his voice.

After a few minutes of practice, I knew exactly how to place my fingers and blow. It was like riding a bicycle—once you got your balance, it was easy.

"See there?" said Owen. "You're a natural."

Indeed, he did make me feel natural, as though we belonged together, kindred spirits.

When we came in sight of the house, we parted with a renewed sense of anticipation. Owen vowed to plan a trip to talk to Mr. Cavanaugh. Once more, we had forward momentum regarding the mystery of Eleanor Granville.

Chapter 36

*T*hree days later, Owen and I were on our way to the home of Celia Cavanaugh Kellaway on foot. Mr. and Mrs. Wellington and Thomas had just left for Mass in Melling, and I declined to attend Sunday services with the staff, pleading a headache. Owen and I would not be seen or questioned about our Sunday walk to the Kellaway home.

The road was dusty, but wild asters and thistle festooned the hedgerows. Dappled sunshine paved our path through a canopy of overhanging branches. Owen appeared to be outfitted in his Sunday best, and I was wearing my most serious dress, the dark, serviceable one I'd worn to my father's funeral. In my bag, I'd stashed a small notebook and a fountain pen, as Owen had requested.

"You've known Mr. Cavanaugh all your life?"

"Of course. Before the war, his family rivaled my own in power and influence. Our families are well-known to one another. Father attended school with Jonathan's older brother."

"Have you never talked to Mr. Cavanaugh about Eleanor's disappearance?" I asked.

"No. Why would I? Our interactions have been merely social, our conversations focused on agriculture." Owen was pensive. "I never even thought about it, his relationship to her, what he might know. The subject of Eleanor Granville was never a topic of discussion at home or anywhere else. I don't even recall how I learned about it."

Owen had been like most children, even me—absorbing facts about our parents without recalling the lessons. I don't remember being told anything about Mother and Father, but I knew their history. They met standing on a railway platform, introduced by a mutual acquaintance. She was wearing dove gray and he his clerical collar. Within months, they were wed. A wave of sadness overwhelmed me. I shook it off and said, "How do you think Mr. Cavanaugh will respond to questions about those events?"

"I'm uncertain. He might be reticent. Maybe even offended."

"Your Aunt Martha said there was no question about his innocence. Is it conceivable either family lied about what really happened?" I had conceded to Owen's conjecture that it was entirely possible that wealthy families would hide an ugly truth to avoid disgrace and prevent the unfortunate gossip that would follow.

"Anything is feasible. But why would my family overlook an abduction, such a grievous crime, a hurtful act? Wouldn't they want justice?" Owen asked, questioning his own position.

I played devil's advocate. "Maybe she left willingly with Jonathan. And if their flight ended in Eleanor's death, what purpose would retribution achieve? Only humiliation."

"I find that implausible." Owen shook his head. "I can't imagine her parents being party to such a charade."

Of course, Eleanor's parents looked for her the rest of their lives. It wasn't credible that they kept up the search if they knew she was dead. The newspaper advertisements attested to their diligence, their desperation. But again, perhaps only the Wellingtons knew the truth. Yet, I couldn't accept they would have kept it to themselves. No one could be so heartless.

I peered up at Owen. "So, you have your interview all planned?"

"Yes. I know where to lead the discussion." Owen turned to me. "I'm ready for anything, rest assured."

"I'll be anxiously waiting for the walk back to hear what he had to say."

"But I want you there." He smiled. "We're in this together."

"How do we explain my presence? Will Mr. Cavanaugh not feel uncomfortable talking about this unfortunate bit of history before a stranger?"

Owen put his arm through mine. "Leave it to me."

At that moment, a large Georgian house came into view. It wasn't as grand as Northfield House, but was elegant and imposing, shaded by gnarled old trees. Owen and I immediately gave attention to our appearance, dropping our arms to our sides. I adopted a professional posture and took my tablet of paper out of my bag, realizing rather belatedly what role Owen expected me to play.

We were ushered into the house by an elderly butler. I at once sensed a soft, comforting presence hovering behind us in the entry hall. The images that came to me were bright pink ribbons and horse harnesses. I smelled wet newsprint.

"Good morning, Matthew. Mr. Cavanaugh is expecting us," Owen said.

"Yes, Mr. Wellington." The butler led us to a sun-filled room a few steps away. "I'll let him know you're here."

Jonathan Cavanaugh entered the room with a vigorous step. He looked much younger than Henry Wellington, although he must have been his junior by only a few years. He was slim and agile, with a thick shock of silver hair. The spirit crept into a corner behind him and waited there.

"It's good to see you, Owen." He had a questioning look in his eye. "I was delighted when Celia said you planned to call."

"Mr. Cavanaugh," Owen affected a little bow, "this is my colleague, Miss Chatham."

I nodded. Jonathan Cavanaugh took my hand while appraising me with an open stare. I lowered my gaze to my notebook, not knowing how to respond to his speculative eye.

After declining refreshments, we sat near tall windows with a view to a row of willow trees.

"Mr. Cavanaugh, I wish to speak to you confidentially and must trust in your discretion. Information has come to my attention regarding a certain matter I feel compelled to look into. As result, I seek your assistance. Please help me, if you will."

I poised my fountain pen over a blank sheet of paper.

Mr. Cavanaugh looked startled. "Of course, my boy. Anything I can do." He leaned forwards, giving Owen his full attention.

"New information has come to us regarding the disappearance of Eleanor Granville," Owen said with quiet dignity.

Jonathan Cavanaugh looked stricken.

Owen continued, "The only way to validate this new information is to verify the facts about that night."

Time seemed to stand still in the silence that followed. The weak sun must have found a cloud, for the room darkened. The lingering spirit was more evident in shadow. It shimmered with pale color.

Finally finding his voice, Mr. Cavanaugh said, "I must disappoint you. I know nothing about Eleanor's disappearance, as I told the authorities at the time. I was neither at the wedding nor, indeed, anywhere near Northfield. My wife, my fiancée at the time, would confirm it, were she living. As would her parents, who were with us that day." His mouth worked as if he might say more, but he merely stared at the floor.

The ghost, now behind his chair, quivered and darkened as if in response. I heard a buzz like that of fruit flies, which I knew was perceived by no one else.

Owen paused for a moment, as if rethinking his strategy. "We know this from the reports collected at the time, Mr. Cavanaugh. Please understand, we do not question your word or the conclusions of the police. But to evaluate this new evidence, we must seek different views, new answers. Please indulge me."

Mr. Cavanaugh's face had reddened, starting at his collar. Clearly, this line of inquiry was disturbing to him, even after all these years. He said, as if he were choking, "I will help if at all possible."

His form was now bathed in the colors of the specter that drifted behind him.

"I hadn't anticipated how difficult this might be for you, sir. Please forgive me. But for reasons that cannot be explained now, we must know what the situation was among the principals involved in this tragedy."

Mr. Cavanaugh stared at the blackened fireplace as if it were a tunnel into the past. I sat as still as the pattern in the carpet. A disorienting thought ran through my mind—Owen had not hesitated to lie to get what he wanted. It seemed easy for him. I was taken aback as I imagined how else this talent might be applied.

Owen continued, "Would you share with us details of your relationship with Eleanor? What had happened in her life prior to her wedding day?"

Mr. Cavanaugh cleared his throat with difficulty and, after a deep breath, said, "I was courting Eleanor. Had been for several months. I'd finished my education and returned from a year in Europe, and the time seemed right to take a wife. I began calling on her in the summer of 1891." He looked wistful, shifting his gaze about the room. "It seems like yesterday, rather than thirty years ago."

Mortified to see tears gathering in his eyes, I averted mine. I also declined to look at the spirit that throbbed with each word he spoke.

"We had not come to an understanding, but I had hopes. Eleanor was still a girl, and it wasn't prudent to rush into an engagement."

Owen's steadfast manner didn't waver in the face of this emotional confession. I wondered what was going through his mind.

"I escorted her to the harvest ball at Northfield." He looked directly at Owen now. "Your father hadn't seen Eleanor for years, probably since she was a child, and his first glance at her, glittering in silvery white, appeared to capture Henry completely. I was amused—until I realized she responded to his interest in equal measure."

"Your hopes were dashed, just like that?" asked Owen.

Startled by his heartless question, I swallowed and remained mute.

"I was surprised to learn how much it wounded me, taxed my pride. I hadn't fully realized how much I'd come to care for Eleanor until I'd lost her. I didn't know I was in love. Beyond her obvious physical charms, her stunning beauty, there was the alliance with the Granvilles. Men in my position took a rather calculated approach to marriage. Given that, I didn't expect to have my bruised heart handed to me." A rueful smile touched his lips.

"Did you continue to call on Eleanor after the ball, after my father took an interest?"

"No, I was rather cowardly in that respect. Perhaps I hadn't the confidence to battle with the likes of Henry Wellington, with his fame, wealth, and position, for Eleanor's hand."

An image of gray, frail Mr. Wellington, with his shriveled legs and distracted manner, came to mind. It was difficult to see him as a dashing suitor, ardently passionate, vying for the hand of a stunning beauty like Eleanor.

"I saw her only in social gatherings after that, and on those occasions, we barely spoke. It was clear she had set her cap for Henry. Although, for a while, he seemed to pay as much attention to Lavinia."

And Lavinia Granville lost the competition to her younger sister. A colorful picture emerged of the games played in an era when all the strategic moves were made behind a fan and a thin veneer of civility.

"By April, the banns were read, and I never saw Eleanor again. Shortly thereafter, I announced my own engagement to Jane Barrett."

I frowned, wondering at the suddenness of his decision. The wraith that had hung in the atmosphere was gone.

"I am pleased to say I kept my heart out of it, having learned my lesson. You may find that cruel, but in my defense, I came to love and respect my wife deeply. We had a happy life."

"You weren't invited to the wedding at Northfield?" Owen asked.

"I declined to attend."

"When did you hear of Eleanor's disappearance?"

"Soon after the wedding. I forget exactly when, or who told me." He looked directly at Owen. "But I wasn't surprised."

"No?" Owen was startled. "Why not? Do you know what happened to Eleanor?"

"Of course, I know."

Owen and I both gaped, our mouths hanging open.

"The devil, man! Tell us what you know," Owen cried.

"Henry killed Eleanor. As sure as I sit before you, Henry Wellington is responsible for the death of Eleanor Granville."

Chapter 37

Owen and I were both silent. It took several seconds for Jonathan Cavanaugh to calm his anger and for Owen to find his voice.

"Explain yourself, sir. Whatever do you mean?"

"Understand me. I say without reservation your father is responsible. Had he not pursued Eleanor, she would have been mine. Eleanor and I would have married and, God willing, she would be living today."

He was ascribing blame to Henry Wellington for an alteration of the natural chain of events. While it was true that Eleanor might still walk this earth if she had not walked down the aisle with Mr. Wellington, his conclusion was greatly flawed. Owen and I both took a relieved breath. I wanted to blurt forth that no one can know how any given action affects a reaction, but I felt pity for our host and allowed him his fanciful conclusion.

Mr. Cavanaugh spoke again, his voice harsh. "I felt it at the time, and I know it now. The moment Eleanor entered that house, she was doomed. And Henry Wellington doomed her. Don't ask me how or why, but if she hadn't agreed to marry Henry, whatever cosmic forces were at work would not have played out."

Owen said quietly, "When you heard of her disappearance, what were your thoughts?"

"I believed she'd changed her mind. That she'd fled from him, realizing her mistake." Mr. Cavanaugh bowed his head. "I thought she was coming back to me."

"And as time passed?"

"I never believed the abduction story. Had that really happened, she would have escaped eventually or somehow gotten in touch with her parents. Whatever happened that day, whether she fled or was abducted, after this many years, only one thing is clear— she died."

"How can you be certain?" I asked.

Mr. Cavanaugh turned a thoughtful gaze to me. "Women at that time, and of her class, were not like you modern females, Miss Chatham. Eleanor was a simple girl, she had no skills, other than to charm and beguile. She was close to her family. She knew only this county and this country. Where would she be?"

"Is it inconceivable," I said, "that she might have craved adventure?" The image conjured by Martha Langtry of Eleanor in buckskins or a simple printed cotton dress, a pioneer in the American West, flashed upon my mind.

"If you had known her, you wouldn't believe such a thing possible. She was barely more than a child at nineteen, and she did not take risks or flout convention. Furthermore, she was greedy and would have eagerly embraced all the comforts the Wellingtons or the Cavanaughs could afford her."

I understood. I would readily abandon my current circumstances, freedom or no, for a bit of security. Only my bad luck forced me into employment, where there was precious little protection or opportunity.

"And Henry was a coward." Mr. Cavanaugh spat the words. "Less than a week after the wedding, he closed up Northfield House and fled to London, lock, stock, and barrel."

"To London?" asked Owen. "Why?"

"To escape the disgrace. To avoid the pain her absence would require him to endure and explain. Can you image encountering your neighbors, your friends, if your new wife disappeared within hours?"

Owen looked puzzled. "I see what you mean, sir."

After a few more comments and the necessary departing pleasantries, Owen and I rose together and took our leave. As the door closed behind us, I felt deflated. The excitement that accompanied us to this place was displaced by disappointment.

"I agree with him. There's no question Eleanor is dead," Owen said after turning the corner on the path towards home. "And I'm convinced our ghost is Eleanor."

"I've never had any doubt."

The furrow in Owen's brow deepened. "And after all these years, Cavanaugh still feels the loss."

"Do you think he has told us everything, Owen? Or does his curious explanation hide a more sinister truth he dared not admit about his part in Eleanor's disappearance?"

Owen stopped and looked at me. "He did seem too emotional, after all these years. He still feels not only the loss but deep anger."

"But the anger is not about her disappearance, Owen. It's about her rejection of him. Was his anger at the time black enough for him to have abducted Eleanor?"

"I cannot imagine that, had he abducted her, his intention was to kill the girl he loved so intensely that it haunts him yet today." Owen shook his head.

"Perhaps her death was an accident, but he is loath to confess his role in it," I said.

"And he's kept this dark secret all these years? Such a thing would drive a man insane. No, Anne, I'm afraid we have yet to discover the truth. What do you make of his assertion that Father closed the house and went to London shortly after the wedding? Does that seem odd to you?"

"Not at all. He would want to escape the heartbreak that the house, which would have become their home, symbolized." I felt an overwhelming sadness. "How could he remain in the place where his hopes for the future had been destroyed?"

"I see what you mean. Also, he wouldn't stay here in the country, where there are no answers. My understanding is that he searched for her. A search would be better conducted where they are trains, carriages, and other means of escape. And pursuit, if a trail were to be found."

"That is so." It didn't seem amiss to me. "There would be so many more avenues to explore."

"But he had no success. Her disappearance remains a mystery."

"Still, someone knows the truth. Do you think your father harbors more information than he is willing to share?"

"No, I don't." Owen kicked a rock with the toe of his boot. "And how can we discover who knows what? We don't even have access to whatever the authorities discovered at the time. What do we do next?" He shook his head in frustration.

I was struck by a different thought. "Maybe there's another way." I faced him. "We should have thought of this before—wasn't there an inquest? Won't there be a public record?" I asked.

Owen sighed. "I don't know." He looked thoughtful. "Without evidence of a crime, what would the authorities do? They'd investigate, of course, at the request of the family. But those records wouldn't be public, even if they still exist."

"Maybe so. No body, no proof of a crime, no inquest," I said. "But Owen, we still might be able to talk to the detectives they employed. The newspaper announcement I dug up indicated that anyone with information should call a Michael St. George. There was only a post office indicated, not an address. But if we can find him, that's another thread to follow."

"Yes, of course. It's reasonable to pursue that path. But it's been thirty years. Shall I remind you of your own skepticism when you first unearthed those advertisements?"

"But it's a place to start. We can't let our investigations stop here."

We walked home among the rustling grasses. A chilly wind stirred the fallen leaves. I ignored the beings that beckoned along the way, the will-o'-the-wisp spots of color and light. Their yearning was something that I alone could feel.

I also dismissed my dismay at Owen's deception. As a parson's daughter, I was unused to such sly dealing, and therefore had been too critical. My faith in him unshaken, we walked companionably home.

Returning to the study, we consulted the record of our findings that I kept in my desk and took note of the limited information available in the newspaper announcement. Just the name and the town, nothing more. It appeared a thin strand to hang our hopes upon. We sat dejected for a moment.

"I cannot help but think our only option is to find Michael St. George in West Kirby," I said. "Or find out what happened to him. He could have left something behind."

"Right. That's exactly what we shall do. You must ask Father for a day off this week, and I'll make an excuse to go with you."

"I can do better than that. Your father has asked me to visit the library to complete some research. That might take as much as an hour, but afterwards we can see to this as well." I indicated the notes in my hand.

Owen smiled. We had a plan.

Chapter 38

*T*he following morning, Mr. Wellington agreed that Saturday would be a fine day to visit archives in West Kirby. Another two weeks would bring winter rains, making the primitive roads difficult to pass. The public bus was notorious for getting bogged down in bad weather.

Owen indicated his own plans for motoring through West Kirby on his way to a farm auction and would be pleased to have my companionship until he dropped me off. Fortunately, Mrs. Wellington, who might well see through our machinations, was visiting friends in Melling for the weekend. Thomas and Mr. Wellington were less likely to question our motives. When the time came, we embarked upon the journey without generating suspicion.

At noon on Saturday we were bouncing along the rutted dirt roads in Owen's old two-seater Wolseley. Owen drove at breakneck speed, while I held tight to the door. My headache and delicate stomach had eased at long last, enabling me to better tolerate the physical rigors of the trip.

"This is some car, Owen!" I shouted over the blast of air lashing at my hair and clothing.

"I'm lucky to have it," he yelled. "It was made for an army staff officer, but before it could be delivered, the war was over. It even has pneumatic tires."

Wolseley Motors had contracted to provide vehicles— including aeroplanes and ambulances—for the government, in support of the war effort.

"That explains the color!" I laughed. The car was army green.

Owen never slowed his pace. By the time we pulled up to the library in West Kirby, I felt as if I'd been rolled the entire distance. Pausing for a moment to tuck in my blouse and pin up my disarranged hair, I glanced at Owen. He was struggling to put up the top, as it looked like it might rain. His step was jaunty. I wondered what enlivened him.

Since he'd lived all of his life in Northfield House, his sudden interest in solving this mystery seemed odd. Perhaps it was no more than an exciting distraction. Or maybe, the impetus was an opportunity to spend time with me.

I chastised myself for entertaining such a daydream.

As he opened my door and helped me out, Owen wore an expression of genuine pleasure. His mood was so infectious that I dismissed my worries and stepped upon the curb with growing enthusiasm.

I spent the time necessary to look up material on behalf of my employer while Owen searched for anything related to Michael St. George. After completing my notes about agrarian policies and land reforms, I found Owen seated among the property records.

"Any luck?" I asked.

"I've looked from 1890 forwards and found no property listed for Michael St. George. No deeds, no contracts, no mortgages."

"Perhaps his home and office were rentals," I said, wondering how to track that down. "But maybe the business still exists, inherited by a relative. Are there other St. Georges?"

"Quite right." Owen perked up a bit. "We might get lucky."

He turned page after page of current property owners. "Only two St. Georges listed," he said. "A Gavin St. George on Dartmouth Street and John A. St. George on Andover Avenue."

I took a deep breath. "Assuming Michael St. George has either died or moved on to live elsewhere, let's hope one of these two men is related."

Owen shut the book and stood. "It can't hurt to ask. Shall we?"

Back in the motor car, we sped through the narrow streets towards the north end, slowing only to pass a lumbering horse-drawn ice truck.

We parked before a large Victorian home on Dartmouth. Our knock was answered by a middle-aged woman who led us to a solarium where a small elderly man, whom she identified as Gavin St. George, sat in the weak sunshine.

Owen said, "I apologize for disturbing you, sir. My name is Owen Wellington, and this is Miss Chatham."

Mr. St. George stood and shook hands. "How may I be of service?" He motioned to chairs across from him, and we sat.

"We're trying to locate Michael St. George," said Owen.

"I regret I must disappoint you," said our host. "Michael was my older brother. He died many years ago. In 1896 to be exact. Is there a question I may answer?"

"I doubt it. We're seeking information about a disappearance in 1892. It seems he had some involvement in solving the mystery surrounding it."

"I'm afraid I wouldn't know anything about my brother's work. He was a solicitor. Privacy, you understand." His yellowed skin looked like old newspapers. "He was legally restricted from revealing anything about his cases."

So the Wellingtons had hired a lawyer to seek information about the disappearance. This was, at least, a new wrinkle, even if I wasn't sure what it meant.

"Did your brother work with partners? Is the business still in existence? It might be possible for us to locate his files," Owen said.

"He did have a partner, but the offices were closed long ago. I don't see how you could track down anything pertaining to an old case."

Another dead end. My heart sank.

"Although," the elderly man brightened for a moment, "you could inquire of Michael's wife. About the files, I mean."

"His wife." This sparked Owen's excitement again. "That would be a great help. Do you know where we can find her?"

"She lives with her son, John."

We thanked Mr. St. George and were out again in the motor. Ten minutes later, we were being shown seats in a dim parlor while John St. George retrieved his widowed mother.

Mrs. St. George greeted us with warmth, her smile wreathed in wrinkles, but didn't have any idea what had happened to her husband's papers. She shook her head as Owen explained our quest to find Eleanor Granville. "He died more than twenty-five years ago. I'm certain his files were kept by his partner, but he's passed on as well."

"Thank you for seeing us," Owen said, his disappointment obvious. "We appreciate your time, Mrs. St. George."

Just as we rose and turned to leave, she adopted a pensive expression. "You could try talking to Harry Bedlow."

"Harry Bedlow?" Owen and I repeated in unison.

"As a solicitor, my husband often used an investigator," Mrs. St. George said, smiling. "You know. A detective? Michael wouldn't have done the legwork himself on a missing person case. He would have overseen the direction of the inquiry and the funds required, but not the business end of an investigation."

"Do you know where we might find Mr. Bedlow, Mrs. St. George?"

"I believe I do. He still has offices on Ashcroft Street, doesn't he, John?" She turned to her son. "Oh, I know." She fumbled through a drawer for an old address book and flipped through its tattered pages. "202 Ashcroft."

❧

At the corner of Ashcroft and Burrows, we pulled against the curb in front of a three-story building. The offices we sought occupied the first floor.

Mr. Bedlow, a florid, balding man in late middle age, was closing up for the day, but he reluctantly invited us to sit and ask our questions. Owen explained our purpose.

"I, for sure, remember the Eleanor Granville case," Mr. Bedlow said without prompting. "Most unusual, it was. I was young and just starting out. Never again did I work a situation involving so many toffs, you know what I mean?" He winked at me. "Even the rich have their troubles, don't they? You say Eleanor Granville was your aunt?"

"She was Mr. Wellington's aunt," I said, nodding towards Owen. "His mother's sister."

Owen spoke. "We were hoping to locate any files or records pertaining to the investigation. I understand Mr. St. George, the family solicitor, employed you to look into the disappearance?"

"Indeed he did. You understand, however, that we came to the investigation late, don't you now? The police had done their bit, and the family. It was months later that they employed the likes of St. George and me. The house where she vanished had been closed up since the wedding, and the trail was quite cold." He defended their lack of success.

"We're not here to criticize, Mr. Bedlow," said Owen. "We simply want information."

Looking at us sharply, Mr. Bedlow said, "Do you mind if I ask what would be your interest?"

"Just a family matter, Mr. Bedlow." Owen hesitated a moment. "As you might guess, they don't speak of it at home. Seems there might be more to it than meets the eye." He took my hand. "You see, Miss Chatham and I are planning to be married."

I started and looked down at my shoes, blushing. I must have looked for all the world like a shy bride.

"And she wonders," he nodded towards me, "I mean, we wonder if Aunt Eleanor's disappearance was what they say it is. After all, it doesn't sound quite right, does it? We had a thought. Miss Chatham is concerned that Eleanor might have been locked away for some reason. We want to know if you found any evidence . . . that is, do you believe she was of sound mind?"

Brilliant. I had to bite the inside of my cheek to keep from laughing.

"Insanity in the family?" Mr. Bedlow expressed genuine surprise. "No, son, we didn't dig up anything like that. Far as I could tell, it was a missing person case, plain and simple. I turned over all my notes to Mr. St. George, so I can't show you anything, but I assure you I talked to everyone in both families and all the wedding guests. I didn't detect anyone barmy among 'em. You're thinking a mite too hard."

"I know it seems excessive," Owen glanced at me, "but we want to have children, you see, and Miss Chatham here is a student of genetics."

Now he was going too far, as few people—including, I assumed, Harry Bedlow—had any idea what genetics was, but I played the part of the tongue-tied, soon-to-be-wed girl. I looked abashed and stuttered, "You see, the family history is important to my parents, Mr. Bedlow."

"You recall the case, Mr. Bedlow. At this late date, can you remember anything that struck you as odd? Anything at all?"

"You ask me, 'twas all odd, son. Young girl, disappearing on her wedding day, left everything behind without a trace. Not a thing about it was typical."

As if struck by an afterthought, Owen said, "Mr. Bedlow, do you remember interviewing a Mr. Jonathan Cavanaugh?"

"I do," said Bedlow. "Former suitor of the missing girl. Even though he wasn't at the wedding, the Wellingtons insisted, you understand. There was nothing amiss about his story. He was with his fiancée when the Granville girl vanished. Saw no reason to pursue that angle. If I recall rightly, the bride's family put their hopes on him, that Cavanaugh would know something."

"You yourself didn't think so?" Owen asked.

"My thinking didn't enter into the equation much. But we did a right thorough investigation, we did. No stone unturned, as they say."

I glanced at Owen, who looked at me. This didn't really clarify anything except that Cavanaugh wasn't at the wedding. He might have come to Northfield that night under cover of darkness and either met Eleanor to flee with her or somehow take her against her will. There was no way to be certain Cavanaugh wasn't involved in Eleanor's disappearance.

Mr. Bedlow asked, "She never turned up, Mr. Wellington, did she? Never contacted her folks?"

"No. She seems to have vanished like the fog at sunrise."

"Well, I'll tell you what did puzzle me a bit." Mr. Bedlow stared into the distance, squinting in concentration. "I talked to all the young people—the wedding party and the ones up past midnight. And it was queer. I asked each one, of course, when's the last time they saw Eleanor Granville. It was a surprise, and I still think so, that they all said the same thing."

"And what was that?" Owen asked.

Mr. Bedlow turned his puzzled eyes to us. "The last time anyone saw Eleanor Granville, she'd tied a blindfold on whoever was 'it' and run up the stairs in the great hall, playing a game of hide-and-seek. It appears she hid and has never been found."

Chapter 39

*W*e had stayed longer in **West Kirby** than expected. It was well past seven when we left Mr. Bedlow's office. The two-hour ride home gave us time to ponder the day's events. It was quite a stroke of luck to have found Mr. Bedlow, the only person still living who had personal knowledge of the private investigations into Eleanor's disappearance. However, neither Owen nor I felt any closer to solving the mystery.

Since it was dark, Owen drove with great care. The weak headlamps illuminated nothing but the front of the car. Even with the top up, the noisy motor made conversation impossible. The long day, steady hum of the engine, and repetitive rocking over rough roads lulled me into a pensive mood. I played over in my mind what it must have been like, that dark night of revelry, the evening's exhausting play, the wedding party scattering throughout the house during a feverish game of hide-and-seek. I could hear the careless shouts and trailing laughter, feel the anticipation of discovery, the throb of excitement. The moist air and heavy darkness were actually tangible for a moment. Then Owen and I crested a hill and the outline of Northfield House loomed against the starless sky.

As we approached the house, I saw neither welcoming lights nor signs of comforting warmth. There was no indication of life within. Something dark and silent in the trees seemed to be watching.

It was well after dinner, approaching ten, when we entered the house. Unfortunately, Mrs. Wellington had returned from Melling, and it was she and Thomas who greeted us in the shadows of the grand hall.

"Henry told us you'd gone into town," Mrs. Wellington said, "but we expected you home hours ago." She offered no affectionate kiss or warm hug to her younger son. She looked at me with suspicion. "How are you feeling, Anne?"

I was trying to tidy my windblown hair and said, "Better today, thank you."

Owen offered an explanation. "We stayed to see a motion picture show. I practically forced Anne. She felt she'd abandoned Father."

I was startled again by how easily Owen skirted the truth, how simply he fabricated not just a plausible explanation, but an outright lie.

"And what was showing?" asked Thomas, his piercing eyes probing mine.

I remained silent, an uncomfortably hot sensation swelling in my chest.

"*Nosferatu*," Owen said, lowering his voice and affecting a dramatic persona. "Murnau's film about vampires—the undead."

Mrs. Wellington's face wore a little moue of displeasure. "Isn't that German?"

"The intertitles were in English. Perhaps that's what defeat means. England gets to disfigure the Hun's art." Owen smiled.

"Art?" His mother sneered. "If that's art, I'm Queen Victoria."

"No wonder Anne looks like she's been frightened," Thomas said with a laugh. "Or maybe that was the plan, Owen. Did she take refuge in your arms?"

I was startled speechless, more than a little embarrassed at the image Thomas suggested.

"Anne was fearless," Owen said. "I'd wager she's a good deal braver than you."

I was pleased that Owen had come to my defense, deflecting a direct assault on my character, but still troubled by this unfortunate direction in the conversation. "Please excuse me. I need to place my library notes on Mr. Wellington's desk so he can review them first thing tomorrow." I turned and walked away.

Although buoyed by Owen's compliment, I was dismayed that Mrs. Wellington's suspicions were aroused by our trip and that Thomas had more fodder for his inappropriate musings.

A moment later, I opened the door to the vacant study.

Before I stepped into the room, I caught a glimpse of Mrs. Wellington and her sons melting into the shadows towards the other end of the house.

Chapter 40

*T*he next day was Sunday, my day off. After church services, I spent the afternoon in the garden with my father's Bible. Mr. and Mrs. Wellington attended Mass in Melling as usual, which meant I had the dried-up flower beds and bare bushes to myself. I worried about my work, since I'd been away from the study all day Saturday, and as a result, I couldn't concentrate on Psalms or other verses that usually soothed my soul. I didn't want to take advantage of Mr. Wellington. I vowed to get to my desk early on Monday to prepare a good many typed pages for him to review by the time he arrived.

This morning, a depressed mood had replaced my queasy stomach. It appeared I was destined to feel unwell. Wandering inside to the study late in the day, I shuffled through some papers, trying to shake my melancholy. I made an effort to focus on what Owen and I had discovered about Eleanor, entering facts in my notebook.

On reflection, precious little was learned from our trip. We already knew she vanished on the day she wed Mr. Wellington. No one had provided evidence of foul play or proof that Eleanor had abandoned her new husband voluntarily. Yesterday, we had discovered one simple thing: Eleanor disappeared while the young people were playing hide-and-seek and was last seen running up the stairs in the great hall. Not a person present had provided a different account.

I placed my personal papers in the center drawer and slid it shut, and then turned to find Mrs. Wellington standing in the doorway.

"I've come to say hello, Anne," she said, expressing no surprise at finding me at my desk on the Sabbath.

"Hello, Mrs. Wellington. Was your trip into town enjoyable?"

"Most pleasurable," she said. "Yesterday was a successful venture for you and Owen, I take it."

An icy trickle of dread slipped down my spine. "I cannot speak for Owen, but for me, I unearthed something of great importance." I turned again to my desk and located the notes I'd scribbled in the library the day before. "I found several records related to changing agricultural policies. It was such an exciting discovery I could hardly wait to share my notes with Mr. Wellington," I said.

"Henry is fortunate to have so dedicated an assistant."

I mustered up some enthusiasm. "I'm lucky myself, Mrs. Wellington, to have the opportunity to participate in such important work." I presented my pages of notes as evidence, holding them towards her.

She ignored them. "Well, you must now put it aside for today. It's Sunday. You work too hard. I should talk to Henry about it."

I wanted to protest, to defend myself against her implications that I had violated the religious observance of the Sabbath, but let it drop.

She took a step closer to my desk. "Come with me now, my dear. We'll take a walk in the gardens. You're so pale, and exercise will give you some healthy color."

"Of course," I said with a hearty smile. "Delighted." I steeled myself for another discussion about my leaving Northfield for a "vacation."

She took my arm, and we ambled towards the veranda. I had a fleeting glimpse of Kitty as we stepped across the threshold and into the late afternoon air. As usual, Kitty disappeared when Mrs. Wellington surfaced. I wished I could make myself scarce that easily.

We entered the garden, where the holly bushes and other evergreens were more prominent, now that the deciduous plants had died back and the annual flowers had been discarded. We contemplated the changing landscape in silence. Then Mrs. Wellington spoke again.

"I must say, I was surprised by your choice of entertainment, you and Owen. You enjoy tales of vampires, do you, my dear?"

As I feared, Mrs. Wellington wanted to continue questioning me about the day spent with Owen. "No. Not particularly." I didn't want to be caught in an untruth. I didn't know what more Owen might have said about the motion picture we were supposed to have seen.

"Or ghosts?" she asked.

"No," I quickly responded. I tried to plumb her train of thought. I wondered what she knew. Or what she had guessed. Wary, I tried to change the subject. "But motion pictures and photography have opened up new methods of inquiry."

"Indeed?" she said. "Are you interested in photography?"

"As an observer of its artistic value only." Glamorous shots of film actors and high fashion clothing popped into my head. "Not in the technical aspects. I'm afraid I have no head for that." Our steps crunched on the graveled walk as we passed fallow flower beds.

"And what has photography to do with ghosts?"

I racked my brain for the information she seemed to demand of me. "I'm not sure there's any connection at all."

"But I've seen those spirit photographs, where a ghostly figure floats behind a living person. It's very compelling. Some people seem convinced."

Anxiety dampened my brow. "Perhaps the unsophisticated are fooled, but I've read it's just some kind of mechanical malfunction. A double exposure of the negative."

She looked satisfied. "Just as I suspected. It looks like carnival-sideshow flapdoodle to me," she sniffed. "I'm glad you see through it, that such things are nothing but a charlatan's trick."

"Of course, I believe you are quite right."

I heard swift footsteps behind us and was relieved, for once, to see Thomas striding down the path. Hopefully, he would lighten the burden of conversation by taking the center of attention.

"There you are, Mother." He put his arm across her shoulders and fell into step with us. "Did you ask her?"

Again, apprehension washed over me. They had been talking. About me.

"I'd forgotten," she said with a sly glance in my direction. "Thomas found a board game in the library. A Ouija board. Does it belong to you?"

"No," I answered truthfully.

"You see, Thomas? Anne is much too rational for such nonsense. Ask your brother. He has an adventurous nature, and I've no doubt he would plunge into the supernatural and other silliness."

"I don't know." Thomas was amusing himself. "Seems to me Owen and Anne are kindred spirits. They saw *Nosferatu* after all," he said, looking at me. "Do you believe in all that mumbo jumbo about communicating with the dead?"

"I believe the Great War awakened a desire for connection with lost loved ones," I said. "I find it quite natural that grieving parents and wives would explore the possibility of communicating with spirits. Séances, Ouija boards, and fortune-tellers are all part of the inability to let go of the dead."

"And how does *Nosferatu* figure into that?" he asked.

What they were trying to get me to say, I couldn't begin to guess. I said, "Not at all, as far as I know. It is pure fantasy, the work of people who wish to create on film what exists only in the imagination. How does one explain German expressionism?" I wanted this conversation to end.

"You must teach me all you know of expressionism, Anne, German and otherwise. I'm all ears." Thomas grinned.

"I must direct you to the nearest library, Thomas, for I know but little. You could see *Nosferatu* first."

Mrs. Wellington, suddenly bored, changed the subject. "I'm chilled, Thomas. Please take me inside."

Thomas drew her closer as we turned towards the house. I walked a step behind, and their conversation did not include me. But one thing was clear. They had been talking about Owen and me. They were curious about what we'd been up to. We were being watched.

Chapter 41

*L*ate the following afternoon, I spied Owen pulling up to the front in his Wolseley and slid away from my typing machine to meet him at the door.

Glancing behind me, I whispered, "Owen, you've gotten me into a bit of a jam."

He looked surprised. "How is that so?"

"Your mother *and* Thomas quizzed me about the film we were supposed to have seen. Then they asked about the Ouija board."

"Fear not, fair damsel, for I shall keep your secret," he joked as though I was the one who told the lie.

"You can make fun, but you've put me in a difficult position. My reputation depends upon my honesty. My employer cannot find me telling tales."

"You didn't lie. I did."

"But I've condoned it by saying nothing to correct it."

"Aren't you making a bit much of this?" he asked.

"Owen, I feel cornered, especially by your mother. Since Charlotte's death, she's watched and judged me. I'm a paid employee and can't afford a misstep."

He looked at me as though just realizing how serious I was. "I can see how Mother comes off more like the Inquisition than Florence Nightingale, but she intends to be generous. After all, Mother's responsible for your well-being while you're under her roof."

"And she can dismiss me any time she wishes."

He shook his head. "You work for Father, and he thinks you're a gem. She can't convince Father to let you go because you fibbed about something having nothing to do with your work."

I remembered my mother dismissing a charwoman because a trinket went missing. Later the lost item was found, and the servant exonerated, but how easy it would be to create such a situation. I was vulnerable in ways that Owen could not possibly understand. "Maybe not, but she can fabricate something else."

"You worry too much. I'll own up to the Ouija board."

I tried to keep the frustration out of my voice. "Not unless asked, Owen. Otherwise, they'll know we've talked. They'll think we've conspired."

He paused and peered at me with a puzzled expression. "Anne, are you quite all right? You look very pale."

I withdrew into my shell of self-sufficiency, realizing that Owen could never understand how precarious my position was. "You're right, of course. Thank you, Owen. I should get back to my work."

Instead of returning to the study, I fled to the veranda and sat on the steps in the shadows. I leaned against a pillar on the far edge, out of sight.

From nowhere, Kitty stole to my side and took my hand. She looked up at me with her wide eyes.

"You and me, Kitty," I said. "We're kindred hearts, two out-casts set upon the world alone." But Kitty belonged in a way that I did not. She would always have a home at Northfield House.

Two years ago, I was the beloved, last-remaining child of a prosperous, well-respected man of the cloth. I had a home and knew my place, despite the tragic loss of my mother, sister, and brother, all dead of influenza. What was left to me was torn asunder when Father was found, seated at the desk in his office, one lifeless hand upon his open Bible. He left little savings and no insurance, no support for me, a young woman of limited means and with meager prospects for marriage. At twenty-three, I was already considered a spinster.

Yet, I was reminded I had possessed the wherewithal to arm myself with skills to provide for my future. Should I lose my position at Northfield House, these skills remained at my disposal. And I might also have a recommendation from Mr. Wellington.

These thoughts comforted me. I could not control the vagaries of Mrs. Wellington's temperament, but I could manage my own interests. I was strong and independent. I gazed across the meadow towards the footbridge. Having avoided it since that terrible night, I now felt compelled to solve the mystery buried inside my head.

The sensation that I knew something—a suppressed memory, a hidden fact—about Charlotte's death worried at my mind. I found myself on the familiar path, plodding my way there, around the fields, past the trees, to the jagged rocks through which the dark waters rushed. Revisiting the scene might have the palliative effect of unlocking the deep recesses where secrets lay concealed. Kitty walked behind me until disappearing somewhere along the way.

I took my first tentative step upon the boards, reliving once again the discovery of Charlotte's body lying broken on the rocks below. The churning water was hypnotic. I moved to the center of the structure. The broken railing had been repaired. A new piece of bright wood, braced by a bridging joist, marked the spot where Charlotte had fallen.

I experienced a flash of memory. Something sinister and frightening slithered away before I could grasp it. I felt faint.

Steadying myself with a deep breath, I watched the falling water strike the rocks like solid glass shattering, sending shards of spray into the air. The mist swam upwards to swirl about me, chilling my skin. The sound of the rushing stream drowned out other night sounds and made me uneasy. I forced myself to remain on the bridge while I concentrated, waiting for that buried memory to resurface. I stood alone, while the sky darkened and the stars rose, for what seemed a very long time.

Movement caught my attention. On the other side of the ravine beyond the footbridge, I saw a shadow, a backlit form, unmistakable and menacing. Someone was watching. When the figure disappeared, I imagined it moving towards me. My mouth went dry. My resolve disappeared. I stepped backwards, turned, and fled from the scene. I struggled up the embankment and stumbled towards the path. Pulling my slim skirt above my knees, I ran to the narrow passage through the woods.

I darted through a valley hooded with trees. A crescent moon hanging low over the horizon provided weak light as I hurried past the dense undergrowth. Brambles and bushes tore at my hair and clothing.

At last, I was in the open, stumbling past the fields and onto the grounds surrounding the house. As I approached the veranda, I slowed my step and took a shuddering breath. But someone stepped out of the shadows and grabbed my arms.

I cried out.

"Anne!" said Owen.

I took deep, gasping breaths, my lungs burning, and collapsed against him.

Owen folded me into his embrace. "What's happened? You're frightened. What are you doing out there in the dark?"

I looked behind me towards the footbridge. I saw no dark form. No one had followed me. The shadowy figure must have been a figment of my imagination. "Owen," I was breathless. "I don't know what's happening to me."

He held me while I tried to explain.

"I've always been . . . stalwart. Capable. Sensible. But lately," I said, shaking my head with disbelief, "I've felt so alone, so hopeless and desperate. I'm tormented by waves of nausea and headaches. This is so unlike me—I've never been sickly."

"Please forgive me, Anne. I should have been more aware. You tried to tell me, but I've shown little consideration for your feelings." He tightened his embrace and pressed his lips upon my forehead. "Instead, I've pulled you down a rabbit's hole of intrigue. Ghosts, a fatal accident, all the family conflict. Anyone would feel threatened."

He tilted my chin upwards and peered into my eyes. "Anne, I . . . ," he said, then seemed to lose his train of thought. He gently touched my cheek and smoothed a lock of hair behind my ear.

"No, you've been more than kind." I felt his beating heart beneath my palms, his arm around my waist. "You are the only one I can talk to . . . the only person I trust."

His face stilled above mine, and I was suspended in time. For a moment, we hovered, lost in a secret place, insensible to the surrounding world.

Without warning, someone loomed over us. We both started and looked up.

"Owen," Mrs. Wellington said, her piercing eyes seemed to look through me. "We wondered where you were." She towered above us from the top step, her silver rosary glinting in the moonlight. Owen stepped away, and I felt my face heat with shame.

"Anne isn't well, Mother," Owen explained as if he felt my discomfort. "She was out here wandering in the dark."

"Oh, my dear," Mrs. Wellington said. "Come inside. Allow me to pour you a cup of tea, and we'll sit for a while." She turned to Owen. "Your brother is looking for you."

"I will see you tomorrow, Anne," Owen said and vanished in the darkness.

I watched his shadow until it disappeared, then followed his mother into the house. She put her arm about my shoulders as we strolled towards the library.

"Come now, Anne. Calm yourself. You've become entirely too nervous."

"I'm sorry to be such a bother," I said, putting my hand to my head. "It's unlike me, really, to be anxious."

"Were you at the footbridge?" she asked.

"Yes. I thought, perhaps, if I visited the scene of . . ." I struggled with the right words to use, ". . . the accident, I could conquer my agitation and face my fears, as it were. I dream about it, about things I can't recall."

"You need to forget what happened there, Anne. Your *agitation*, as you call it, will result in mental fatigue and physical ailments. Can you not see that? Trust me. You should see Dr. Termeer. He can give you something to soothe your nerves."

We sat in the library once Maddy had come with the tea tray. As Mrs. Wellington busied herself with the service, I nestled with the thought of Owen's caress, burning it into my memory.

"Here you are, my dear," she said as she poured. "Now, relax for a few moments."

"Thank you, you're very kind." I looked into the steaming cup that she handed me. Its amber liquid reminded me of something else. I glanced up into Mrs. Wellington's eyes. They were the same amber color as Charlotte's. I hadn't noticed it before, a distinct family trait. I looked at the tea steaming in my hand once more.

The tea.

My stomach rolled at the delicate fragrance of bergamot. I brought the cup to my lips, then hesitated. A seed of suspicion started to grow in a dark place in my mind. Was Mrs. Wellington putting something in the tea?

No, I told myself. It wasn't possible. No, of course not. I was letting my imagination run wild again, just like I had at the footbridge. Still, I placed my untouched cup on the tray.

As Mrs. Wellington prattled on about her day, I further considered the possibility that she had been dosing me with something. That might explain the fatigue, headaches, and nausea. Perhaps she had decided that there was more than one way to dispatch an unwelcome competitor for her sons' attentions. Her warning about Northfield being unhealthy for me and the suggestion that I needed a vacation took on a whole new layer of meaning.

When Mrs. Wellington paused, I spoke up. "I'm feeling much more settled now, but weary. If you don't mind, I'll go to my room."

"Of course, dear," she said. "I do hope 'sleep that knits up the raveled sleeve of care' embraces you."

Afterwards, on the way to my bedchamber, I wondered if I would be able to sleep at all. The quotation from *Macbeth* did nothing to relieve my dark thoughts. Too many questions surrounded Charlotte's accident and the odd behavior that followed. I remained frustrated by my inability to remember what had been clutched in Charlotte's hand. I hadn't solved the mystery of how and why her skullcap ended up in the fireplace in the boot room. And now I suspected Mrs. Wellington of slipping something into my tea. I had no way of knowing whether my intuition was reasonable or merely the product of my growing paranoia.

Only one thing was certain in my mind. I had fallen in love with Owen. Despite all my caution, and the impossibility of a relationship between us, I had succumbed to his innate goodness. He was everything I admired in a man.

As I lay on my pillow and watched the stars in the heavens pop up one by one, I relived the touch of his lips upon my brow, his arms about me, the warmth and nearness of him.

I knew it was hopeless, even if he shared my feelings. The wealth, status, and power of his family and the desires of the Wellingtons to secure an appropriate match created a gulf between us. One that, even together, we could not breach.

Chapter 42

*M*artha Langtry is dead," said Mrs. Hadley, dabbing at tears. "Dolly found her in bed this morning. Gone in the night, she was."

I stood rigid, swamped by sadness. "I've no words to express my sorrow." I looked through the kitchen window at the frosty view outside. "I liked Mrs. Langtry."

"Dolly knocked at seven, as usual, with her breakfast, and there she was. Eyes staring at the ceiling."

"Poor Dolly."

"She dropped the tray, soiled Miz Martha's Axminster Rose. She loved her things, all those reminders of her youth. I don't think the stain will come out." Mrs. Hadley's voice caught.

I took her hands in mine. "Come and sit. Tell me what I may do to be helpful."

"Take care with Mr. Henry, is all. He and Mrs. Langtry weren't close, far as I could tell, but they were kin. And following Miss Charlotte's death, it's bound to be a blow. A death like this, of natural causes due to age, can't help but put you in a mood to consider your own mortality."

As if the Great War hadn't made us all feel the tentative quality of life. "Of course, Mrs. Hadley. I understand."

Mrs. Hadley, Dolly, Maddy, Kitty, Cook, and I huddled in the kitchen like the outsiders we were, while the family absorbed the loss. By late morning, I ventured upstairs to find Mr. Wellington in the study.

"Mr. Wellington, my deepest condolences," I said, standing in the doorway, eyes downcast. "All of us feel the loss of Mrs. Langtry. She was well liked." I stumbled about uncomfortably. "Please tell me what I can do—what you expect of me."

He looked up and appeared to see right through me. "Anne." He frowned and turned to the window again. "Just . . . carry on. I'll be busy with notifications and the arrangements. I won't be available this week for our work. You know how to proceed." His limp hands lay upon the wheels of his chair, a reflection of his helplessness.

"Yes, sir."

A hush fell over Northfield House. I was able to convey my sympathies to the members of the family personally, making an effort to see Mrs. Wellington first, and afterwards, Thomas and Owen. Each withdrew into that deep, hollow place where grief resides.

The kitchen was the only place humming with activity as the staff prepared for visitors. They assuaged their sense of loss in a flurry of baking, cooking, and making a grand table for the funeral guests who would come from across the county to pay their respects.

I was grateful for the break from normal routine, since it took me out of the sphere of the family. No more questionable tea with Mrs. Wellington, no more snide remarks from Thomas, and a respite from the intense work with my employer. Sparing his increasingly frail father, Owen took upon himself the responsibility of making the funeral arrangements, so we had no opportunity to speak privately until the middle of the week.

Walking in the gardens and enjoying the unseasonably mild afternoon, I saw the Wolseley returning to Northfield, top down. Owen must have spotted me as well, because he soon appeared, his hair windblown.

He approached, and I grasped his hand. "This is such a sad time, Owen. I am, again, heartbroken for you. Mrs. Langtry was much loved. I regret I hadn't spoken to her once more before her death."

"I'm sorry about that too, Anne. The last time I tried, Mother was there with her tea service." He whispered like a conspirator. "Now we'll never know what Aunt Martha might have remembered about Eleanor's disappearance."

I was aghast. "My remorse has nothing to do with our ghost hunting." Disappointment must have shown in my face. "I wasn't thinking of myself or of our plans."

He blinked, and his posture stiffened. "Of course not, Anne, I . . . forgive me." He looked ashamed.

"It's not my forgiveness you should be asking for." I withdrew, taking the opportunity to join the servants in the kitchen once more.

Later, I regretted our exchange. Owen had taken on the lion's share of preparations for the funeral. His week had been spent immersed in the reality of his aunt's death as he assisted his grieving family. I was certain he had handled this responsibility with grace and gravity.

Perhaps, with me, he had let his guard drop, although he was not a man who usually acted with impropriety. But his irreverence had caught me unawares. Sometimes my strict upbringing caused me to judge others too harshly. I shouldn't have been shocked at the turn in the conversation. Under the strain of recent events, I, too, had not acted well.

❧

Two days later, Martha Langtry's body lay in the parlor. White lilies and orchids surrounded the coffin and filled the great hall with their cloying sweetness. For Martha's funeral attire, the family had chosen the Victorian velvet she'd worn at the masquerade ball, the dark, heavy dress she couldn't wait to shed.

A long line of motorcars rumbled down the graveled lane on the day of the service. People from the village and surrounding community came on foot. Silent mourners sifted into the house, past her bier, and to seats draped in black crepe.

Members of the household, including Kitty and me, followed the family to the cemetery in a black limousine. At the grave site, I stood at the rear, not wanting to intrude. Martha's two sons led the procession following the coffin to its final resting place. Mr. Wellington, pushed in his chair by Martha's oldest grandson, and Mrs. Wellington trailed behind. Owen, tall and slim in his formal attire, and shorter, broader Thomas stood by their parents, with Martha's other grandchildren.

The lugubrious party, trussed in black and dripping with veils, stood in the incongruous sunshine. Martha's grave was between that of her husband, George Delbert Langtry, who'd died almost a decade ago, and her daughter, Mehitable Cordelia, interred in 1884 at the age of twenty-two months. Beyond it was Charlotte's plot, recently a raw scar upon the ground, now scabbed over with fledgling grass.

The priest from Melling, his medieval vestments and Latin words foreign to me, committed Martha Langtry's body to the earth. As the subdeacon from the local parish held the processional crucifix high above the casket, I had a disconcerting sense of déjà vu. The deaths of Charlotte and Martha Langtry had followed one upon the other all too soon. I felt faint.

Not wanting to make a scene, I left the crowd without anyone noticing. Taking refuge behind the draping limbs of a gigantic fir tree, I supported myself against a marble angel at the entrance to a mausoleum. Short of breath, feeling a heavy weight upon my chest, I swooned, my mind going blank.

I came to myself, slumped against the mausoleum. The angel loomed over me, her spreading wings monstrous and intimidating. *Martha. The cemetery.* Sweat dampened my brow as I leaned against the statue to remain upright. A sense of impending doom seized me, making my limbs weak.

Glancing towards the silent body of mourners, I stumbled to the limousine and collapsed in the darkened interior, awaiting Mrs. Hadley and the others. All I could contemplate was escape. I needed to quit this place and find refuge elsewhere. The shadows crowded in and threatened to suffocate me. I closed my eyes, which made the claustrophobia worse. My panic subsided only when the others joined me in the car, their familiarity easing my feelings of despair.

During the slow ride home, we sat in silence while Dolly chattered between sobs about how horrifying it was to encounter a corpse first thing in the morning.

"As God is my witness, 'twill haunt me all my days, it will," she stuttered. "Poor Miz Langtry, poor dear." She dissolved into a fresh bout of tears.

During the hour before dinner, I was able to convey my condolences to Martha's sons, both of whom had traveled great distances, and to her six grandchildren. Owen, serious and handsome in his mourning garb, stood at the edge of the crowd. I sought him out, moving closer. My gaze held his. He stood still for a moment. Then he turned away to speak to Martha's oldest granddaughter.

I retreated to the buffet table and watched as he addressed his young cousin, Arabella, a girl of nineteen, just coming out into society. She was lovely and graceful, born to his class. With a start, I realized she was a good match for Owen, a distant relation, a girl of the right background with all the charms to attract a man.

The barriers between us loomed in my head as I watched them commiserate. Arabella turned her doe-like eyes to Owen, a sad smile on her lips. Her light brown hair made a pleasing complement to her delicate skin. Her mourning dress only emphasized her youth and beauty. He spoke to her, words I could not hear, his head bent near. She placed a hand on his forearm and leaned closer. I recognized the delicate dance of courtship.

Tears stung my eyes. I felt more isolated than ever. Sweeping my gaze across the crowd of mourners, I questioned who these people were, and whether all of them were insensitive and merciless. If an elderly aunt could garner no kindness, it was certain a humble wage worker could expect no compassion. Preferring not to join the guests for supper, I went to my room. The family would share stories of Martha's life and once again get to know one another.

No one would miss a lowly employee whose life had brushed so briefly against their own.

Chapter 43

*E*arly the following morning, before the ritualistic process of dismantling Martha's rooms began, I slipped upstairs to stand in the place where she'd died. I said a last prayer as bright light streamed past heavy draperies drawn wide. The room possessed an incandescence absent during the time I'd known her. The shadows were dispelled, and Martha's precious belongings, starkly exposed and unprotected in the pitiless sunshine, stood waiting to be discarded or given away, dispersed like chaff in the wind. The tea stain in her lovely carpet perhaps spoke most eloquently of life's vagaries.

Lined up on the table beside Martha's rocking chair, the photographs met my gaze once more. With silent faces and frozen smiles, they told of a life passed and a past abandoned to the shadowy fog of time.

I frowned. Something was missing. I looked about the room. The image of Eleanor was gone. The picture capturing the demure, delicate Charlotte look-alike against the backdrop of the footbridge was nowhere to be seen. I was puzzled for only a moment. I suspected Mr. Wellington had taken possession, and it now resided in the bottom desk drawer with the other cherished photograph.

One thing I knew for certain, however. Martha Langtry was no longer here. Not a trace of her spirit remained behind to haunt the halls of Northfield House.

❧

By the following week, everything returned to some semblance of normal. Mr. Wellington and I delved anew into his scholarly work, and I felt a keen sense of accomplishment, having recorded information regarding three hundred and fifty acts of Parliament authorizing enclosure of agricultural land. Our piles of documents and files covered every surface in the study. The downstairs corridors were filled with our voices in deep discussion or the tapping of the keys of my typewriting machine.

"I'm pleased with our progress, Anne."

It was good to see him smile. "As am I, sir. Shall I visit the archives in West Kirby next week? There's a wealth of material there." At the mention of the little village where Owen and I had had an adventure, I felt a deep pang of longing.

"If the weather permits, my dear."

Mrs. Hadley and the other staff went about their business, except for Dolly, who took a few days' vacation to visit her parents. She returned to take up her duties, now solely as Mrs. Wellington's maid. Although it was mean-spirited of me, I believed Mrs. Wellington would be happier with Dolly's full attention.

"Don't forget to keep Mrs. Wellington's closet in order now, Dolly," Mrs. Hadley reminded her. "And maintain her gloves in pristine condition."

"'Course I will." Dolly bristled a bit at the direction. "You don't need to say."

Dolly seemed rather full of herself now that she was full-time maid to the lady of the manor and could dispense with her other responsibilities. The regular duties of all the servants shifted a bit with the loss of a member of the household.

And something else belatedly occurred to me. Mrs. Wellington was not close to Martha despite all they had in common. Either that or Mrs. Wellington had no capacity for grief. She had Martha's belongings boxed up and sent to the church charity store, permitting no trace of sentimentality. Afterwards, as she went about her daily routine, no lingering shadow of Martha Langtry appeared to darken her thoughts or dampen her spirit.

Pondering the loss of Charlotte as well, I wondered about Mrs. Wellington and her reaction. Perhaps I had only imagined her despair, and sorrow was not an emotion she possessed. Desolation was so clearly etched upon her husband's face and those of the rest of the family.

Two days after the funeral, Owen travelled to London with his cousins. His plan was to stay with his Aunt Martha's oldest son—Jeremy, Arabella's father. The two young cousins seemed to be fond of one another, and it might be supposed they had a good deal to catch up on.

It hurt that Owen hadn't sought me out to say good-bye. Instead, he'd dashed off a quick note and slipped it beneath my door the morning he left.

Dearest Anne,

I fear I've disappointed you, and for that I am truly sorry. Beyond careful consideration of my failings, which I feel keenly, your steady heart and my poor circumstances have convinced me to pursue an opportunity to secure something approximating a reasonable future. I will return to Northfield when my fortunes have been settled.

Owen

I felt the sting of loss, and a hollowness in my chest beyond mere heartache. Owen had left to court Arabella. An alliance between them made perfect sense, of course. I knew Owen could never be more than a friend, no matter how dear he was to me.

How fortunate Arabella was! I'd never felt jealousy before, but now I understood why it was termed a monster. I found myself hating the girl, regardless of her youth and innocence. I reproached myself for feeling as I did. I had no business brooding over Owen. He would always remain outside my reach, regardless of how much I cared for him.

Thomas, on the other hand, visited the study almost daily, and we took up our acerbic banter. He seemed to enjoy our encounters, while I tolerated him, making the best of it.

"Anne, you should get out more. Your face is drawn," he said, perching on the edge of my desk as I typed.

"You don't have to look at my face at all, Thomas. Don't you have something to keep you busy elsewhere?"

"Nothing could keep me from your side, dear Anne. Unlike Owen, who has a great affinity for plants but none for women, I like looking at your fair features."

As if he'd guessed my unfortunate attraction to Owen, he made a good job of punching my bruised feelings. I did my best to ignore him.

"Wouldn't you like to take a walk in the gardens?" he asked one afternoon.

"I prefer to walk alone."

"You must have heard of polite society." He leaned close with this reproach.

I looked at him pointedly. "That depends upon what you mean by polite."

For the next few days, I plodded on. I rose with the sun and worked until darkness fell. I preferred to take my evening meal in the kitchen or my room since Owen was not at the dinner table, and Mrs. Wellington continued to keep her eye on me as we resumed our daily spot of tea.

She gathered me each evening, and we sat in the library with her delicate china cups and ornate silver service. Her motives remained unclear, and I continued to be wary. Rather than give in entirely to my paranoia, I conducted a rational experiment. I now added a good dollop of sugar and cream to my tea and drank only half. Each morning, I recorded how I felt upon waking.

Mrs. Wellington did not fail to notice my changing habits. She watched me closely and revealed herself during our casual chats.

"Are your labors nearing completion, Anne?" she asked. "I understood Henry to say this latest manuscript would be finished in two months or so."

I understood her intent was to encourage me to seek employment elsewhere, planting the seed that my work at Northfield would arrive at its natural conclusion when the manuscript was ready.

"Mr. Wellington has had some great success," I said, mentioning nothing of the outline he and I were already making for his next treatise. "He is rightly very proud."

I maintained a cheerful façade despite her intimations. When I failed to become distressed, she spoke often of my state of mind, her concern taking on the quality of a veiled threat, as though my being there might be unsafe. "Have you been resting well? I hope our tragic circumstances do not continue to haunt you. I'd hate to think Northfield had unpleasant associations or was a danger to your fragile constitution."

In response to such inquiries, I would sit up straight, look directly into her eyes, and say, "I appreciate your concern, but I'm fine, thank you."

"You should be around suitable people your own age, my dear," she chided one evening. "Have you thought of frequenting the attractions in Melling or the village?"

"I don't know what attractions you refer to, Mrs. Wellington." There was precious little with which a single woman could occupy herself in the nearby communities.

"Your church surely offers opportunities for volunteering," she said. "You might find a beau. A good-looking and accomplished girl such as you ought to make an effort."

Finding a mate among the homeless veterans, orphans, or widowers I was likely to encounter working for the church seemed farfetched. "How kind you are to suggest it, Mrs. Wellington."

I maintained a dependable routine despite my sorrow over Owen's absence, Thomas's unpleasantness, and the misgivings I had about Mrs. Wellington. My fatigue and melancholy did not improve, so I questioned my concerns about the tea. Mr. Wellington was interested only in my work with him, which went well, and Mrs. Hadley, Dolly, and Cook offered the refuge of genuine friendship. And, of course, Kitty was one upon whom I could lavish my other talents. I participated in the group-mothering that supported this dispossessed child. In her hand-me-down clothes, she made herself useful in the kitchen and the gardens. And I knew, as I went about my own work at Northfield House, she was always there, watching.

Chapter 44

Christmas Day came and went, and Owen still did not return. Although the holiday wreaths went up, they were draped in black crepe as befitted a house mourning two recent deaths. The loss of Charlotte and Martha Langtry required the family to dispense with the typical celebrations. Recognition of the holidays had been limited to hours in church and mince pies. There was no kissing bough, no tree decorated with feathers, and no carolers.

As a parson's daughter, I felt this was no sacrifice. As was usual, I spent both Christmas Eve and the day of our Lord's birth in prayer. The family and staff permitted themselves a cup of wassail on Twelfth Night, the only occasion for a bit of cheer.

I was shocked when Owen came looking for me upon his return. I had taken a walk along the creek bank and was making my way towards the house when he intercepted me. His sudden appearance hit me like a lightning bolt.

"Owen!" I cried.

Stepping off the veranda, he grasped my hands in his. I drank in his presence like parched ground absorbs the rain.

He swept me into a shadowed corner. "Anne." His serious face hovered over mine. "I've missed you so."

"Have you?" The emotional distance I'd planned to maintain at this moment melted in his company.

"You know I have." He drew me closer. "It took longer than I expected, but things have finally fallen into place."

An image of Arabella flashed before me. I was desolated at the thought of them together and then, at once, felt guilty. I was selfishly mired in jealousy, not considering Owen's needs and feelings at all. Still, I wanted to delay his revelations for as long as possible and changed the subject. "It hurt me that you left for London without saying good-bye."

"You got my note?" He looked puzzled.

"Yes, of course."

"It was vague, I realize, but I expected you to understand."

"Understand what?"

"I hesitated to get our hopes up. I didn't know if I could accomplish my plan."

"What plan?" I tried to steel myself for his explanation, certain that it included his lovely cousin.

He looked over his shoulder at the veranda, then took my elbow, moving me into a secluded spot in the garden where we couldn't be seen from the house. "We must talk, Anne."

I didn't think my heart could bear news of his impending marriage. "Can we do this tomorrow?" I said, although I didn't want him to go.

"No, it can't wait. I won't sleep." He held tight to my hands and spun me about, laughing. "I'm a wreck of a man."

I was instantly dizzy. "Owen! Stop. I'll faint."

"Go ahead, collapse with joy. I want you to feel as I do," he said, swinging me faster.

"I must sit!" I pulled us out of our spin and sat upon a nearby garden bench, trying to catch my breath. "What are you going on about?"

Owen dropped beside me, shoulder to shoulder. "I've wanted to speak to you, so many times, but didn't feel I had the right. Now that I am free to do so, I . . ."

His yearning expression pierced me to the heart, and I looked away.

He placed an arm around my shoulders and pulled me close. "Anne, I have something for you." He reached into his vest pocket and brought forth an iron key with a white ribbon tied to it.

I took it from him, the weight of it heavy in my hand. I looked from it to him. "I don't understand."

Owen said, "In her bequest, Aunt Martha left a small farm in Lancashire to her sons. Neither of them wants it, and they are willing to sell. I was in London seeking a small loan to add to my savings, so I'll have a place to call home." A tentative smile spread across his anxious face. "This is the key to the farmhouse. It's yours if you want it."

"Mine?" I was bewildered.

"I'm asking you to marry me, Anne."

I was dumbstruck. "Marry *me*?" Tears gathered in my eyes.

"A more traditional man would have bought you a ring, but . . ." He shrugged and grinned.

I began to cry in earnest.

He frowned and turned me to face him. "You know I love you."

"You love me?" An indelicate hiccup punctuated my question.

"And I need you. Surely you've expected this."

"No." I stared at the key in my palm. "I'm stunned. A house?"

"And sixty acres of good land, outbuildings, orchards, and a garden."

"You bought me a house?"

"Yes, our house, if you'll have me."

As we embraced, I felt the warmth of his body through my lightweight shawl and thin blouse. "Owen," I whispered as his lips sought mine.

His kiss swept me to heights of emotion quite foreign to me. I thrilled at his touch, his hands about my waist. I was both excited and shocked by his familiarity, and my modesty struggled with the intensity of pure physical desire.

"Anne," he breathed into my hair. "Tell me you feel as I do."

"You know I do," I said. "I love you with all my heart, Owen."

"Then we'll marry as soon as the banns can be read."

This stopped me cold. I shook my head. "Is that really possible?"

"Why not? I now have something to offer you. It isn't much, but it's mine, and we can build on it. We love each other. What else is there?"

"To marry you, Owen, to be yours forever and always, is my heart's desire." Emotion swelled my throat. "But it's easier said than done." I felt the futility of it all fall like a weight upon my breast.

"Why, Anne, if you feel as I do?" He pulled me to my feet and wrapped both arms around me, burying his face in my neck. "What's to stop us?"

I forced him to unhand me and took a step away. "Owen, this is folly. There's more to marriage than just our feelings. Your family would never agree. I'm nobody."

"As am I . . . the second son with no money and no inheritance. Even now, what I have is mostly debt."

Although feeling altogether irrational as well, I tried to reason with him. "No one will accept me, Owen. Your mother and father would object, stand in the way."

He raked the fingers of both hands through my hair and cradled my face. Without hesitating, he kissed me again. His lips pressed upon mine and then moved to my neck and throat until I was breathless. He caught the top button of my blouse in his teeth. A jolt of excitement shot through me, and I experienced a violent longing to be completely, utterly part of him, to lose all sense of myself.

"Owen. This is madness." I struggled out of his arms, remembering something far more important than the family. Even now, I needed reassurance that he wasn't pining over the loss of Charlotte. "Am I really the woman you want?"

"Yes! Who could possibly be your rival?" he asked, looking perplexed.

My cheeks stung with the memory. "Are you forgetting the night of the masquerade ball, not so many weeks ago? Were you in love with me that night?"

"Love? Maybe not. But mad with desire." His arms encircled me once more. "When I saw how men looked at you, I raged with jealousy." He was only half teasing. "You danced with one, then another, giving no thought to me, until I believed I would go insane."

"But I believed you were at the time in love with Charlotte. I felt sure of it. And if so, you must long for her, ache for her, even now."

"Charlotte?" He laughed bitterly. "That ended long ago. She was a childhood affliction overcome after enduring cruelty upon cruelty. She was more Thomas's type."

"So you *were* following me to the footbridge that evening," I said. The image of a panicked, breathless Owen from the night of Charlotte's death resurfaced.

"I've already told you so. I thought you'd gone to meet a man. I had to know whom you preferred to me."

"But what of Arabella? She is certainly a more appropriate match."

He looked at me, baffled. "Arabella? She's my cousin."

"Once removed."

"Anne, believe me." Owen took my hand in his. "I have no interest in Arabella or any other woman." His eyes searched my face. "Oh, my darling, what a dunce I've been. How heartless and cruel I must seem to you. I had no idea."

"Loving you has always seemed so out of reach," I said, "Everyone spoke of your feelings for Charlotte. And she was so beautiful. And I imagined Arabella a more likely match. I assumed you could care for her."

"You are wrong!" He shook his head. "I assure you, you are mistaken."

"I don't doubt you—not now—but you must understand how I need to put my worries to rest. I'm sorry for being so obtuse."

"You've no need to be sorry. I've been faint of heart and careless with yours. Forgive me for the hurt I've inflicted through my thoughtlessness."

With that, every muscle in my body relaxed. I dared not breathe. "You? Thoughtless?"

"Forgive me, Anne. I've been a fool, all along imagining obstacles to our happiness because I had nothing to give. But now, with the farm in Lancashire, I see my way clear. I stand before you a man bereft if you choose not to love me."

I embraced him in a moment of abandon. "Owen! I do love you. And I love this." I held up the beribboned key. "But this can never be. We must consider your—"

"Mother? You're living in the last century, Anne. I'm not inclined to follow my mother's wishes in the matter of matrimony."

In that moment, I realized that, even in my happiest dreams of Owen, I had dreaded an imagined future at Northfield House with Mrs. Wellington as my mother-in-law. My stomach knotted at the thought. But a home in Lancashire would take us hours away. With wonder, I looked at the key, a symbol of freedom and happiness.

Owen took it from my hand. "You're supposed to wear this, you know," he said, pulling the white ribbon over my head so the key sat upon my bosom. "Say yes, Anne! Please, say yes!"

"Of course, Owen. Gladly! Lovingly, wholeheartedly, yes!"

I could have wept for joy, but we laughed instead. We could leave this dark house with its tragic history and its ghosts. Owen was no longer held captive by circumstances beyond his control. He could pursue his experiments and operate his farm without interference from his old-fashioned father or selfish Thomas.

And I would have a home of my own.

Chapter 45

*T*he **following morning,** I heard Owen whistle from the bottom of the stairs just as I left my room. I responded with quite a competent whistle of my own, which made us laugh.

He said, "You appear to be a very able student. I'm quite proud."

"Of me or yourself?" I scolded him as we embraced on the bottom step. He planted a chaste kiss upon my forehead as he hooked a thumb in the waistband of my skirt.

I swatted at him playfully. "Stop. You're shocking. Someone will see."

"But I'm your intended. And I *intend* to take full advantage." He winked at me. "We must tell Father and Mother today, Anne."

I blanched at the thought of facing the Wellingtons. "Why such a hurry? Shouldn't we keep this to ourselves for a while? We can savor this secret between us."

"For what reason?" He asked, leaning close. "I'm afraid you'll change your mind and refuse me. Once it's announced, if you cry off I can sue you for breach of promise." In a more serious tone, he said, "Unless you've thought better of it."

I shook my head as I nestled against him. "No, of course not. Since last night, I have thought of nothing but marrying you."

"I want everyone to know, now. I want to start my life with you," he said.

We took the corridor towards the grand hall together, our hands clasped.

"And Mother will want all the time in the world to plan, so we should tell her as soon as possible. I may not be the favored son, but I'm the first to marry. She'll pull out all the stops."

Although I chose to say nothing, I was sure our announcement would find no favor with Mrs. Wellington. But I also knew she would put on a brave face, as would I. Nonetheless, I was deeply grateful that our married life would begin far away from Northfield House.

He whisked me to the dining room where we poured coffee and waited for the others. Thomas entered first. He looked at me with surprise, since joining the family in the morning was contrary to my habit.

"Anne. You're with us for breakfast?" He looked at Owen.

"For every meal, Thomas."

Before Thomas could respond, Mr. Wellington wheeled in with Mrs. Wellington at his side. Owen gave them no time for questions.

"Father," said Owen as he took my hand, "Mother. We've come to ask your blessing. Anne has agreed to become my wife."

I blushed furiously. Mr. Wellington immediately beamed a broad, genuine smile.

"My boy!" he said. "Well done, sir! Delighted." He shook Owen's hand.

Displeasure flickered across Mrs. Wellington's face but was at once replaced by a mask of enthusiastic joy. "My dear," she said as she placed a kiss upon my cheek. "How lovely."

It couldn't really have been a shock. She must have realized Owen and I had feelings for one another, as very little escaped her notice. This seemed the obvious reason for her thinly veiled encouragement to find my fortunes elsewhere and to banish me from the dinner table. However, I had been uncharitable towards her as well. Although suspicious about the tea, I found no evidence of skullduggery. My condition had not improved, even after I diluted it with milk and consumed only half a cup. Since my experiment did not support my fears, I tried to lay them to rest.

"I've always wanted a sister!" bellowed Thomas, as he clapped a hand on Owen's back and embraced me in a bear hug. "Imagine Owen interested in something that isn't green."

There were general well wishes, and we were joined by Mrs. Hadley and Maddy once they heard the commotion in the dining room.

"Miss Anne, how lovely," said Mrs. Hadley. She had tears in her eyes.

Maddy, looking disconcerted, only managed an awkward curtsy.

After breakfast, Owen and I went directly to the kitchen to present ourselves to the staff below stairs.

Cook was as excited as the birds on the first warm day of spring and twittered accordingly, but Dolly wore an expression of astonishment, as though it should have occurred to her to marry one of the sons of the house.

Kitty was the surprise. She embraced me about the knees and hugged me tight.

"Why, Kitty, my little one." Now tears welled in my eyes. This was the most overt affection she had yet paid me, which let me understand I had her full acceptance. Her little face beamed with all the joy I myself felt.

Tragedy had weighed upon the occupants of Northfield House for as far back as the current inhabitants could see. I hoped, with all my heart, my union with Owen would break that unhappy spell.

Chapter 46

*W*ith Owen's simple declaration of commitment, everything changed. Setting aside our interests in ghosts and ancient secrets, he and I found ourselves in a dizzying whirl of activity for the rest of January. There were family and friends to be notified, the banns to be read, and the dates to be set. I was suddenly folded into the family in a way that was completely unexpected.

Although I insisted on continuing my work with Mr. Wellington—I was as committed as he and wouldn't abandon him—he did not demand it.

"My dear, Lavinia will never forgive me for keeping you here. You must help her plan your nuptials. You shouldn't be bogged down with my research," he said, as I typed away.

"But I like being here in the study, helping you."

"You are very kind. Don't spend too long at the machine now."

Thomas became even more flirtatious—but in a less threatening manner.

"Anne, how did you do it?"

"Whatever do you mean, Thomas?"

"Get Owen to notice that hair and those eyes. You must have bewitched him."

"Nonsense," I said.

"I'm certain you did something quite underhanded."

"I'm innocent of all charges."

"Well, you enchanted me, didn't you? All that time I spent in the study pursuing you was for naught."

"Don't be absurd." I couldn't help but smile.

Owen was cheerful and affectionate, participating in every way possible in mapping out our future.

"How is the lovely bride-to-be today?" He kissed me on the forehead one cool morning after the family filed out of the dining room.

"Exhausted. I've never looked at so many fabric samples. I swear your mother is only trying to confuse me. Why don't you choose the pattern for the wedding linens?"

"Gladly. Is there a wrong choice?"

"No. Not as long as you pick something white."

"Blindfold me, and my hand will be guided by our resident ghost."

At this happy time, it didn't occur to me to feel uncomfortable with Owen's lighthearted reference to the tragedy of Eleanor and her last act before disappearing.

The household staff accepted me and my new status as well, but Mrs. Wellington was the real surprise. She warmly embraced me as her future daughter-in-law. I began taking all my meals with the family and was included in every conversation, social event, and evening discourse. When Owen and I decided upon March 28 for our wedding day, as he refused to consider a longer engagement, she appeared to be delighted—although a bit panicked that the wedding would take place in a little more than eight weeks.

All of Northfield House was open to me. Mrs. Wellington showed me the fabulous silver service and the damask linens that would be mine upon my marriage. I was made privy to nearly every room and corner of the estate. It was notable that the south wing did not figure into my education.

As part of my induction, Mrs. Wellington shared family lore. "The Wellingtons have always been related to the Granvilles. The families have been united by marriage for two centuries."

I listened, adding murmurs of appreciation.

"The original Wellington estate doubled in size in 1821 with the marriage of Cornelius Wellington to Elizabeth Granville." She never touched on the sad details of her own marriage. "The Granvilles include magistrates, peers of the realm, and shipping magnates." She demonstrated understandable pride in her family heritage.

She introduced me to the portraits hanging in the great hall as though I would meet them regularly at weddings and funerals. "This is Owen's grandfather, William. He made his fortune in imports from India."

My own family history included nothing remarkable. The Chathams had made little mark upon the world, so I had nothing to add to her accounting of wealth and accomplishment.

"This is Mathias Wellington. We won't discuss how he made his millions, as the slave trade is something we don't speak of," she said, her voice lowered to a whisper.

My future mother-in-law and I continued our early-evening chats to discuss our plans—Owen's and mine—for the future. She now brought the best tea service to our little tête-à-têtes. And still, I harbored dark suspicions about her feelings towards me.

"Are you still struggling with fatigue, my dear?" she asked, her eyes lowered, as she carefully placed the milk pitcher at my right hand.

I knew she had noticed I was adding ever larger dollops of milk to my tea. I was still nervous about consuming it, even though my little experiment had yielded no improvement in my condition. In fact, I often felt worse, with no explanation at all. Surely, I was being absurd, but I couldn't help myself.

As we lifted our cups to our lips, her gaze was steady and untroubled. I left most of my drink untouched.

I shared my misgivings about the tea with Owen.

"You're daft, darling," he chuckled, hugging me. "Mother can be a pill, but she's quite harmless. You're overwrought, with all that's going on. Ghosts and deaths, your experience at the footbridge, not to mention all the excitement weddings create. Overwork can affect us in odd ways."

"Your mother doesn't like me, and this marriage is but a trial for her, no matter how she tries to hide it."

"Well, mothers and their boys. There's always a bit of jealousy there, don't you think, no matter the woman?"

Despite Owen's dismissal, I remained uneasy. And besides that, with the impending marriage, the social order had been shuffled. I no longer had to cater to my employer's wife in order to keep a position. The following evening, I took the bull by the horns.

When Mrs. Wellington entered the library at the appointed hour and sat, I spoke without preamble. "Please don't think me ungrateful, but I'm afraid I must ask that we dispense with the tea."

She regarded me steadily. "Why, my dear? Have you tired of my company?"

"Not at all," I quickly reassured her. "But I believe a stimulant this late in the evening each day has interrupted my sleep. That, combined with the excitement about the wedding and all the planning, has exhausted me. Surely you don't mind taking a break? We will have ample time together as we make decisions about the marriage."

She was gracious, and we parted amicably, knowing we would spend hours over wedding invitations and place cards. But she could not mistake the message that I was no longer dependent upon her good will.

Over the next few days, I began to feel a bit less fatigued, which buoyed me. My improvement may have been the result of simply avoiding an unpleasant and anxious hour with Mrs. Wellington at the end of each day. I still fell into bed exhausted every evening after being inundated with so many decisions and future plans. Maybe Owen was right, and that my exhaustion wasn't due to his mother at all, but the enormous task we faced of making a life for ourselves. Surely it didn't matter, as Owen and I would be leaving soon and both of us would spin outside her orbit.

A month before the wedding, Owen and I traveled to Lancashire to see the farm and the house where we would begin our married life.

I was giddy with excitement as we set out in the Wolseley. Cook had thoughtfully prepared a picnic lunch to sustain us as we made our way. After several hours of bone-jarring travel, Owen pulled to the side of the rutted road.

"We're about halfway there. Good time to stop," he announced, jumping out to help me from the motor car.

My legs wobbled. "Let me catch my breath! Good gracious." I pulled my wrap close as I looked across the monochromatic landscape.

We drank in the bare trees, the fallow fields, and a tumbling stone fence on what was an unusually warm day for late February. The sky was a misty blue.

"Owen, how lovely this is." I didn't give voice to my relief that our new home would be over six hours from Northfield.

We laid a blanket under a gnarled black walnut and lunched on cold chicken and fruit. Once sated, we were loath to move and lay side by side on the cold ground, embracing to keep away the chill. We stared upwards into the snaking, bare branches of the ancient tree.

"You make me deliriously happy," Owen said, as he turned his body towards mine. He caught my earlobe between his teeth.

I laughed. "Owen, you'll make a fallen woman of me."

"I sincerely hope so," he said, nuzzling my neck. His fingers traced my cheek, my nose and chin. His lips pressed against the bare flesh of my throat.

"And if I allow you to have your way, you'll leave me. Refuse to marry me."

"Not on your life," he said. Emboldened, he undid the ribbon on my blouse.

I trapped his hand in mine and pulled away. "We're not married yet." I laughed at his stricken face.

"But we are to be," he said. "What's the harm? No one will see us." He moved closer. "No one will know."

I stood, smiling, and put my hands on my hips. "*You'll* know. And your mother will see it in your face, and I won't be able to show mine for shame."

Owen grabbed my wrists and forced me to my knees. "Hang it all, Anne." He pulled me tight against him and kissed me.

He released me, and I laughed as my heart soared. "Oh, Owen, I do love you." I sat back on my heels and looked at him seriously. "And you do understand what you're giving up for me?"

"No, I don't." He shook his head. "I'm gaining everything."

"Blather. You know that's not true. With your family connections, you could make a better marriage. A girl with money." I thought about my conversations with his mother. "Isn't there a marriageable Granville beauty out there with your name engraved upon her delicate heart?"

"You may not have noticed, but Wellington-Granville marriages have been less than successful. We need some new blood in the family."

"Will you mind leaving the grand estate, your birthplace, to live on a farm? Won't you miss Northfield?"

"Filled with bad oil paintings and weeping ghosts? Not a bit."

I frowned. "Owen, we've forgotten about Eleanor these past weeks. What will become of her?" I thought of the heartbreaking wraith that had materialized in the south wing, more an object of pity than of fear, as we sat in the watery sunshine.

"She can haunt Thomas and the poor, unwitting fool who agrees to marry him," said Owen.

Dismayed, I searched his eyes with mine. "Then we're to abandon her, are we?"

His mood sobered. "You feel it, as well? That, in our happiness, she's been shoved aside after all her efforts to engage us."

"I'm glad it isn't just me," I said. "You, too, sense the sadness pervading the halls of Northfield. Perhaps there's nothing to be done after all."

"Maybe not, my dearest. If the love that fills our hearts cannot dispel the gloom, nothing can."

We picked up the blanket and basket and returned to the car. The humming engine and buffeting breeze from our leaky windows precluded conversation as we bounced onwards to our destination. I could not help but think of Eleanor and what I believed was her tragic life.

Where are you, Eleanor? Where are you now? Will Northfield House ever release you or you it?

Chapter 47

*W*e finally reached our journey's end, the small quaint village of Preston, where we were to spend the weekend. It was all quite proper, as I was to stay the night with his aunt and her daughter, who lived just outside of town.

Their charming cottage sported a roaring fireplace and diamond-paned, beveled-glass windows, glazed with frost.

"Aunt Georgiana, this is Anne," said Owen, grinning.

She took my hands in hers. "So Owen is to be wed," she said, her gray curls bobbing, joy shining in her eyes. "Welcome, my dear. It will be wonderful to have you as neighbors, won't it, Samantha?"

Aunt Georgiana and her daughter, Samantha, wore simple calico dresses and woolen shawls, as sufficed country folk. I'd seen them both from afar at Martha's funeral, but they'd been almost indistinguishable from other veiled mourners. Owen's aunt looked just like Henry, her older brother, but Samantha was blonde and petite, and I could discern no familial resemblance. Both were gracious and warm, as I'd come to expect from the Wellington side of the family.

"We've kept an eye on the place for you, as we did for Martha," said Aunt Georgiana, a wistful sadness darkening her small face at the thought of her departed sister. "The last tenants left six months ago, but Mr. Lamb has seen to the yard and kept the wildlife out of the house. It's a grand home, and I'm sure it will prosper under your care."

꧁

Early the next morning, Owen drove the Wolseley deep into the countryside. We passed hedgerows and elm groves, sped over bridges and past glens in a soft, watercolor world. After half an hour, we pulled down a tree-lined drive to a small red-brick Queen Anne-style house. Its trim needed fresh paint, but the building looked sturdy, the roof sound. A center turret flanked by several gables topped a wraparound terrace.

"Why, Owen," I said, awed. "It's lovely. I can't believe this is to be my home." My heart felt full. Here was a place to belong at last.

"Mr. Wellington," said an elderly gentleman who came from somewhere in the back. "It's right good to see ye." He extended his hand and turned to me as he removed his cap. "Miss."

"It's good to see you, too, Lamb." Owen placed a possessive arm about my shoulders. "My fiancée, Anne Chatham. Anne, this is Walter Lamb, our caretaker."

I was barely able to acknowledge the roughhewn watchman, so taken was I with the house. Mr. Lamb unlocked the door while chattering about problems and repairs.

"The house wants paint inside and out. The dining room fireplace draws air. Water's good, though. 'Twere a new well we sunk last year."

"Owen, it's more than I ever dreamed." I pirouetted through the downstairs, laughing. There were two front rooms off a large, oval-shaped reception area with a curved double staircase. In the back, space was occupied by a formal dining room and a dismal kitchen with an airless larder and storage closet. It looked like heaven to me.

"I was right sorry to hear Mrs. Langtry passed," said the caretaker.

"Thank you, Lamb," said Owen.

"I guess it'd been nigh on twenty years since she stepped foot on this place. Good to have family living here again," he said as he followed us from room to room. "Right glad I am of it."

I scampered upstairs where the chill was more pronounced and a broad hall led to four large bedrooms, a linen press, and a rather dreary bath. Each room had multiple windows with views of rolling hills, broken-down outbuildings, or the overgrown apple orchard.

Sweeping down the broad staircase, I imagined myself living here with Owen and our children. I looked from ceiling to floorboards and from the front to the back of the house. Although the walls were streaked with soot, the plaster and crown moldings were solid. The dusty woodwork, creaking and dull, showed no evidence of rot. The downstairs rooms were of gracious proportions, and each had a fireplace and a bay window topped by a stained-glass half-moon. The sunshine filtering through the colored glass cast blues, greens, and purples across the floor.

My excitement quite overcame the queasy stomach and light-headedness that I'd felt all morning. While Mr. Lamb and Owen went over the foundation from the cellar, I stood in the center of the reception room and turned round full circle. This was a good house. Spirits sparkled in the corners, bright orbs danced through the air, but they were cheerful sprites all. No evil or sadness penetrated this home.

Owen and I spent hours looking into closets and cupboards. The only major renovation required, could we afford it, was the kitchen, where a corroded metal sink with a hand pump and a wood-burning cookstove dominated the space. After exhausting our curiosity about the house, having gone over every square inch with critical eyes, we took a long walk through the fields. Rolling tracts of stubble, separated by dilapidated stone fencing and overgrown berry patches, spread out behind a thickly treed yard and two separate structures—

a horse stable and a milk barn. We paused in the stable yard, drinking in the fragrance of baled hay and rich soil that penetrated the cold.

"The land is leased until next year, but the income is mine as soon as the papers are signed," Owen said. "After that, I'll work the land in a manner that suits me. That is, if you agree."

"Yes, of course, Owen," I said, embracing him. "This is beautiful. More than I ever hoped for."

He kissed me, and our dreams seemed well within reach.

"I can get the painters started right away on the inside. We'll have to wait for the weather to turn before getting to the exterior."

"May I choose the colors?" I asked, as it occurred to me I had a say in how my home would look.

"Anything you like," Owen said, "but it will take a couple of years of good crops to do anything major, like the kitchen."

Evening was falling before we once again started the army-green Wolseley and bounced towards Northfield House.

The full moon was high by the time we swung past a curve in the road, and I spied the roofline through the bare trees. All was quiet as we pulled near the stables and stole up the path towards the veranda. It struck me anew, the dark weight of this house. I smelled stagnant water and heard the soft fluttering of wings. An oppressive atmosphere pervaded this place, making my breathing labored. I again felt ill, my head muzzy, my limbs heavy.

"Anne, are you all right?" Owen put his arm across my shoulders and peered into my eyes.

"Please, I'm fine. Just fatigued. The excitement of encountering our future has exhausted me." I tried to laugh it off. I didn't want to spoil this perfect day by worrying him over my fit of nerves.

He kissed me tenderly. "Anne, my love, rest well. I'll be gone before you get up tomorrow. I'll return before you know it. Three days at the most."

Owen was going to London to make final arrangements for the purchase of the farm. I would be busy during the week with fittings for my wedding gown and the selection of china, crystal, and other household necessities. It tired me to think about it. I watched as he disappeared towards the back of the house.

As I turned towards my room, I spied Kitty lurking in the door to the study, waiting in the shadows.

"Why, Kitty, whatever are you doing up at this hour?"

She stood quietly in her outgrown nightdress, her feet bare. I knelt in front of her and gave her a hug. It had been days since I'd spared any time for her, and I at once felt guilty.

"My sweet little girl." I feared I had neglected her in my happiness. "How are you, little Kitty?"

Mrs. Wellington's devotion to me these past few weeks had the effect of distancing Kitty, who'd kept to dark corners, out of sight. "Come. Let's sit for a moment before we go to bed. We can talk, just us two," I said.

We cuddled in the large chair behind Mr. Wellington's desk. I laid my cheek against her fine hair and warmed her toes with my hands. "You'll catch your death, no slippers on your feet. What have you been up to, Little Seedling?" I asked. "Do you remember that Mr. Owen and I are planning to marry?" My heart caught in a little lurch at the thought.

She nodded her head vigorously and, with a shy smile, produced a small package from the folds of her gown.

"For me?" I asked.

She held it towards me in the palm of her hand and nodded.

"How lovely that you thought of me, Kitty. How sweet." I took the object from her. With a gesture, she encouraged me to open it.

"Shall I?" It was wrapped in a piece of misshapen brown paper and tied with the blue ribbon I'd once seen in her hair. "A wedding present?"

I removed the paper to reveal the little box she kept with her always. Tears gathered in my eyes. Kitty had made a gift to me of the only possession she had.

I hugged her close. "Oh, Kitty. My precious girl. My little friend."

She returned my hug but tapped on the box with her index finger.

"Shall I look inside, Kitty?"

Again, she nodded.

I lifted the lid.

The box contained a tiny, delicate white feather, a red marble, a silver foil gum wrapper, carefully folded, two intricate seed pods, and a rhinestone button. And on the bottom was a piece of darkened paper. I lifted it gingerly with a fingernail and, turning it over, focused my tired eyes upon a charred piece of photograph. I recognized it at once as the picture of Eleanor at the footbridge. Only the oval of her face and the collar of her dress had escaped the flames.

"Kitty, where did you find this?" I indicated the scrap of photograph. As her puzzled eyes questioned mine, I remembered the last time I'd seen it—on Martha's table, next to her chair, in a silver frame. A poignant sorrow descended upon me at seeing the image once more. It had obviously been thrown into the fire. I could only imagine that Mr. Wellington was so full of grief that he destroyed it in a fit of disconsolation. I frowned.

Kitty hung her head as though she'd done something shameful.

"No, Kitty, my love. You've done nothing wrong," I said, as images of Eleanor's ghostly figure formed in my mind. "We'll talk again in the morning. We both need to get to bed." It wasn't wise to invoke spirits this late at night, especially after a day full of happiness and hope.

I was at once overwhelmed with fatigue. I walked Kitty to her little room next to Cook's on the other side of the kitchen, tucked her in, and took the back stairs.

I hesitated in the corridor leading to my bedchamber. A deep sense of menace engulfed me. The darkness, the silence, the very atmosphere of Northfield House was forbidding. My limbs were heavy, and my heart raced. I gasped for breath, smelling the delicate scent of roses. For a panic-stricken moment, I wanted to flee, to escape this place and the peril hovering in the shadows.

I managed to make it to my room before collapsing on the mattress. *Too much excitement. I've really overdone it.* I slid Kitty's little box beneath my bed and then slumped into unconscious darkness but would not call it sleep. Drifting in and out of awareness all night, I was burdened with an unaccountable fear.

The ghosts of this bleak, cheerless place weighted my dreams. A specter I knew to be Eleanor beckoned me to the south wing. I clutched my sweat-dampened sheets and cried out in the night. I dreamed, too, of Charlotte and her broken wings, the answer to the mystery of her death clutched in her hand. Hovering shadows loomed, and I was threatened by unfocused images.

Martha Langtry appeared and held me, whispering comforting words as I rose from a shallow, fretful slumber. No, not Martha. I frowned and felt a cool cloth upon my brow.

"Anne, dear. You're dreaming. Wake up."

It was Lavinia Wellington, sitting with me, next to my bed. She'd brought a bowl of cool water and pressed a dampened handkerchief to my face.

I rose with a start. "Mrs. Wellington!" Morning light was streaming through my window. "What time is it?"

"After nine, dear. We thought we'd let you sleep. You must have returned late last night, you and Owen. You're overly tired. You must relax and take care of yourself, Anne. Have a bit of nourishment." She raised a glass of milk to my lips.

My mouth felt parched. I took the warm milk and drank it, then handed her the glass.

"That's better, isn't it?"

"I have to . . ." I couldn't think of what I might have to do.

She put a gentle hand on my shoulder, and I lay down again.

"No. You need rest. There's no reason to rise," she said.

"Where's Owen?"

"He's gone to London, remember? To make arrangements about the farm? He's seeing his banker and will go to the registry office about the deed. He meets with his lawyer to complete everything. He'll be back in three days."

Three days?

"Yes, Mrs. Wellington. I remember." I realized I'd slept in my shift. Sometime in the night, I had removed my skirt and shirtwaist but never managed to pull on my gown.

Mrs. Wellington comforted me, covered me with a sheet, and left after saying, "You sleep, now. I'll see you when you're rested."

Chapter 48

I awoke in the silent darkness and fumbled for my watch. It read seven thirty-five. I must have slept all day. Turning my face to the window, I saw the stars emerge in the heavens, one by one. After a while, the unnatural quiet struck me. I listened for the evening hum of the house. I tried to detect the hustle of living, the staff preparing dinner, the swift footsteps upon the stairs, or muffled chatter from the kitchen, but all was still.

I climbed out of bed and dressed. My reflection in the mirror showed a thin, pale woman with no vigor or vitality, someone who had been ill for a long time. After pinning up my hair, I blew out the flickering candle and crept down the corridor.

At the head of the stairs I stopped abruptly, startled. At the bottom, a murky shadow darkened the passageway. The silence deepened as I strained to hear anything familiar, holding my breath. My heart began to pound.

The dark shape blocking the stairs stirred, moving closer. The shadow took on a familiar form as it came nearer, and Mrs. Wellington's face appeared in a pool of moonlight from the window, as if floating up from the bottom of a well.

I breathed a sigh of relief. "Mrs. Wellington."

"Anne, dear," she said. "I was just coming to see to you. Are you feeling better?"

I made my way down the stairs. "I do feel better, thank you."

She linked her arm with mine, and we made our way towards the great hall.

"You must eat, now," she said. "I had Cook prepare something light. It's in the library."

"That's very considerate. I'm afraid I made extra work for you."

She patted my hand. "Nonsense. I thought you shouldn't have anything heavy since you've been ill. Some tea and milk, and an egg custard."

"Where is everybody?" The eerie silence in the house was unnerving.

"Since Owen is in London, and Henry and Thomas went to Melling for the week, I gave the staff the evening off. There are musicians on the green, a local tradition, and I believe it will be good for everyone to get away. They've all gone into the village. I stayed to watch over you. We'll be fine by ourselves, don't you think?"

"Of course. Thank you," I said. Dolly had mentioned taking Kitty to the Winter Carnival celebrations. I had been looking forwards to going, too.

Mrs. Wellington opened the door to the library. "We two can just rattle around in this old house like school chums." The room was bathed in the soft light from an oil lamp.

We sat next to the tea cart, and she poured. I held the cup as if to drink. It warmed my hands, yet I felt an icy chill run through my body. Mrs. Wellington looked at me with a smile, and our eyes locked. I pretended to sip and then set the teacup aside.

"You need nourishment, dear," Mrs. Wellington said as she handed me a small bowl of custard. "You look so peaked. Anne, you must recover your strength. Tomorrow we meet with the Reverend Hollis, and we've scheduled an hour with the florist. I do wish you and Owen had given us a bit more time." She handed me a spoon.

Cook made the best custard, and this was no exception. It was soft and cool and slipped across my tongue like silk. After three bites, I sagged against the couch, relaxed.

"I'm afraid this is the last of our hothouse roses, Anne. I picked this one just for you." Mrs. Wellington touched the blood-red blossom gracing the tea tray.

"You're so kind," I said. "It's lovely." I took another bite of custard, and the rose began to waver as if under water. I closed my eyes for a moment.

"I regret the wedding plans must be so rushed. Blame Owen, Mrs. Wellington." I heard myself speaking as if from some great distance. "Had it been up to me . . ." I couldn't remember what I was going to say. I blinked, trying to keep my eyes open.

"Owen was always impetuous," she said. "You should have seen him as a boy."

A bit of custard dribbled out of my mouth as I said, "What kind is this? It tastes . . . different."

"Cook made vanilla this time. She did right by us with this batch. But I prepared the rosewater sauce myself. Just for you."

" 's good." I tried to get my mouth to work.

"Really, Anne, you must get more rest. You can hardly hold your head up."

As she spoke, I slumped forwards and rolled off the couch. The room tilted sideways and spun. I closed my eyes. When I opened them again, Mrs. Wellington was bending over me, her ever-present rosary beads swinging across my line of sight, gleaming in the lamp light.

The rosary. The black one she carried after Charlotte died. The blue one Eleanor had carried on her wedding day had been put away.

"You're heavier than Charlotte, Anne, but if you help me we can make it upstairs." She had an arm under my shoulders, lifting me to my feet.

Charlotte. I heard her laughter first and remembered her slim, pale form wafting through the trees towards the footbridge.

Mrs. Wellington struggled to hold me upright, both arms around my waist. "If you would just help me, Anne. Charlotte was so much more cooperative."

Charlotte! A vision flashed like a bolt of electricity. An image of that night under the footbridge swam before me, the rushing water grasping at Charlotte's red hair, her white gown rippling, her twisting gossamer wings, and my perilous effort to pull her from the raging stream. I suddenly remembered what was coiled in Charlotte's hand.

It was Lavinia Wellington's blue rosary, twisted about her fingers like a snake with golden, cruciform fangs.

I stood, reeling, and stumbled. Teacups crashed to the floor. The shattering sounded like the distant tinkling of a bell. "I'm so sorry, Mrs. Wellington. I don't know . . . what's wrong with me?" Any sense of real danger skittered away like ashes caught in a draft.

"You're overly tired. You and Owen should both be resting rather than running all over the countryside, looking into things that don't concern you." Her voice took on a menacing, singsong quality. "Don't think I don't know what you've been up to."

"Please," I begged and clung to her to keep from falling. "Please, we meant no harm. Please, help me."

"Your candle burns at both ends," she said. "It will not last the night."

Before I lost consciousness again, I had a single odd, random thought. Quoting Millay seemed out of character for a cold-blooded murderer.

Chapter 49

I focused on the pattern in the carpet, struggling to pick up my feet, as Mrs. Wellington dragged me to the top of the grand staircase in the moonlight. "Come on, Anne, you can do this." Her breathing was ragged and labored.

Or was that me?

I shook my head to clear it. "Owen," I said.

"Has gone away, remember?" She grunted with exertion.

The black-bead rosary, one end tucked in Mrs. Wellington's waistband, swayed from side to side. Once more, I pictured Charlotte's body broken upon the rocks below the footbridge. "Charlotte. Your blue rosary."

"You've remembered something, have you?" She chuckled. "I wondered what you'd seen, and what you'd suppressed. I feared it was just a matter of time before details of that night came back to you. It's a pity, really."

"Charlotte's dead. You killed her." *Had I said this aloud?*

"I'm afraid so, dear. A necessity." She gripped my arm as she pulled me upwards. "It didn't take much effort. She was full of champagne and trussed up in that stupid costume and couldn't defend herself."

I struggled to speak. "Your own niece."

"And the very image of her great-aunt, my sister Eleanor." Mrs. Wellington spat the words. "Eleanor took what should have been mine. And Charlotte was a constant reminder of that painful memory. And the way she treated my boys was despicable."

We reached the second floor, and I nearly collapsed. Mrs. Wellington propped me against her shoulder as we swayed at the top of the stairs.

"Owen was in love with her, did you know?"

"Love?" I squinted and tried to clear my blurry vision.

"Of course, they were children, but still. It was painful for a mother to watch. But when she set her sights on Thomas, I couldn't bear it any longer."

We caught our balance, and she kept me upright and pulled me forwards, leaning against her.

"The night of the masquerade ball, it was shocking," said Mrs. Wellington, her voice hard. "Charlotte in that unspeakable costume, flirting and teasing. I knew the game she was playing. She wanted to make Thomas jealous, send him into fits of rage and desire, so he'd propose. He'd do anything to have her."

"But poor Charlotte. Why did she go . . . there?" I gasped and started to cry.

"For someone so devious, she was easy to fool. I sent her a note, supposedly from a mysterious devotee—not Thomas—asking to meet her at the footbridge. *Important*, I wrote at the end, with exclamation points. She was a girl addicted to a life of exclamation points. A clandestine meeting? A secret admirer? Charlotte couldn't resist the intrigue."

"She was meeting someone. Not Thomas?" I said, my tongue thick.

"The laudanum is making you stupid. Of course, it was I who waited for her. She was featherlight compared to you, Anne." She grunted as she supported my weight upon her shoulder. "Pushing her through the handrail was simple, although she fought me. I was

306

so angry I'd have snatched her bald given the chance, but all I came away with was that hideous skullcap. I burned it with the boys' costumes. I'd do anything to rid them of the stench of that whore and to destroy any memory of that night. I didn't miss my rosary until later, when you started babbling about something Charlotte had clutched in her hand. I feared the worst."

"Yes." *I remembered the blue rosary, at last.*

"That's why I kept you close. All those boring little tea parties. The laudanum made you fuzzy-headed and weak, but it merely delayed the inevitable. You finally remembered." She sighed with world-weariness, as though it couldn't be helped.

Laudanum. I felt a wave of nausea. I had been right. The headaches and fatigue that plagued me these past few months were the result of being drugged.

"Of course, I put it in the tea, but you got suspicious, didn't you? You thought you were so clever, thinning it with milk, drinking but a sip. So I put it in the milk, too."

I tried to raise my arms but couldn't.

"But now, you've forced my hand. Accepting an offer of marriage from Owen! So I took no chances tonight. The rosewater sauce for the custard was carefully prepared, just in case. I'm lucky you were so gullible."

I blacked out for a moment, and when I came to, I didn't know where we were. With effort, I concentrated. Mrs. Wellington supported me as we staggered down the long passageway past Martha's rooms.

"Martha!" I cried out.

"Martha's dead, dear. She can't help you. And it's your fault."

"My fault?" I began to breathe heavily with the effort of staying upright.

"Stirring up that old history about Eleanor. Asking all those questions. I couldn't have that. Martha was here when Eleanor disappeared, and I always wondered if she knew. She might have, but she also knew the Wellington name was too valuable to foul with a scandal."

Lavinia Wellington was stronger than I ever imagined, and she held me with a tight grip. The front of my dress was damp and smelled of vomit. I struggled in vain to free myself.

"And Martha saw Charlotte run to the footbridge that night. Had she seen me go as well? She should've thought better of taunting me with what she knew and teasing about what she'd guessed." Anger weighted her voice. "And she kept that picture of Eleanor on her table just to mock me, to remind me of the shadow that clouded my life."

"You threw it into the fire? Not Mr. Wellington?" I said, faltering. In my fuzzy vision, Eleanor's face swam before me, suddenly becoming Charlotte's, staring, lifeless, into the night sky. I felt another wave of sickness.

"She was hateful, that old woman. I couldn't take the chance her last act wouldn't be to hang me. Her sewer of a mind might spew out all sorts of filth before she died."

"You? You killed Martha?"

She startled me with a rasping laugh. "I gave her no more laudanum than I was giving you. But you're young and healthy, and her heart was weak." She turned to me, pleading. "Believe me, Anne, I never meant to kill her. I only meant to keep her quiet."

"Dear God," I whimpered. Owen had tried to see his aunt for days before her death, but she was either sleeping or having tea with his mother. The roadblocks strewn across our path were so obvious now that I knew. "Poor Miz Martha," I said, propped against Mrs. Wellington's shoulder.

"It wasn't my fault. *You* did it, can't you see? You kept asking questions. Martha was never the problem, but you pestered her. But the real villain, the cause of all this misery, was Charlotte," she said, seething with anger. "Charlotte the harlot. That's how I thought of her."

"Poor Charlotte?" My mouth was dry, and it was difficult to speak.

Lavinia Wellington tightened her grip as her anger rose. "She deserves no sympathy. If they married, she would have become mistress of Northfield House when Thomas inherits the estate. I would have lost my son and my home. I couldn't see her take my place. It would be like Eleanor returning from the dead to haunt me. I've already paid a high price to be what I am."

I looked into her glassy eyes, burning with purpose. She expected to remain mistress of Northfield House always. She believed no one could ever replace her in Thomas's life. An image flashed upon my mind of Thomas and his mother linked arm in arm in the garden.

A savage wildness had replaced her gracious calm and given her the strength to force me, an unwilling captive, through the house. The faintest light from the windows paved our way down the long corridor.

I didn't know where we were. I blinked to clear my vision and focused on the floor and the wallpaper. Suddenly, I knew. We were headed for the south wing.

Chapter 50

*A*t the end of the long, dark passageway, the doors to the south wing were standing open. With labored steps, we stumbled through them. The palest of moonbeams spilled from the tall windows into the gallery, and the ghostly figures in the portraits stared, their eyes following us as we swayed the length of the room. Leaning against the door at the other end, Mrs. Wellington pushed it open, and we crossed the threshold into the darkness beyond.

All was black, clammy, and cold. Deep silence surrounded us. Something was waiting at the end of the corridor.

Mrs. Wellington produced a small torch from her full skirts and snapped it on, keeping a firm grip on me. As shadows bounced around us, the lamp's unsteady beam darted across the ceiling and settled on the door at the very end. I found it difficult to breathe and tried to rally my strength. Limping forwards, we started our slow dance once again, Mrs. Wellington breathless with exertion.

"You and Owen have been exploring here."

I should have known she was aware of everything.

"You can't hide from me, Anne. Very little happens in this house that I don't see." She was perspiring now, and her slick face had taken on a deathly pallor. "It's your fault. You had to push and prod at old memories. You threatened to bring Eleanor back to life."

My throat constricted, and I tried to swallow.

"In the beginning, she haunted me as I took up residence here with Henry. I saw her in every shadow, heard her voice in the very air that stirred, sensed her step in every sound. Those fears had faded after so many years." Her voice hardened. "Then you arrived. It all started up again."

"I meant no harm," I barely whispered.

"Would you like to know the truth at last? Would you like me to reveal the great tragic secret of Northfield House?" she said.

I couldn't speak. I moaned as my mouth worked, but no words came out. I kept my eyes riveted on the last door. My heart pounded. I gasped for air.

"Eleanor never left Northfield," Mrs. Wellington said, crowing. Her hideous laughter echoed off the bare walls. "That's what she wanted, and I granted her that wish. A final benediction."

Mrs. Wellington's breathing was heavy as she struggled to keep me upright, pulling me in the direction of the last room.

"I was 'it' during a game of hide-and-seek. I heard Eleanor take the stairs in the great hall after she blindfolded me. She couldn't stop giggling like the silly child she was." Her eyes narrowed. "She was so competitive that I knew she'd try to find a place I'd never discover. Eleanor always had to win."

Mrs. Wellington spoke with loathing, but as if in a trance where she inhabited the distant past. I imagined she was once more at the wedding, the scene of her desolation. She no doubt heard the haunting strains of a waltz as she went back thirty years to another time, another place. Perhaps for her, this house was once more full of revelry, laughter, and her own heartrending disappointment.

"After searching every chamber on the upper floor, all the guest rooms and closets, I realized the doors to the closed-off south wing were unlocked."

"They were unlocked?" I repeated her words, my voice barely audible.

"Why should that be? I wondered. I learned later. An elderly grandmother had come for the wedding. Henry's father opened the south wing so she could view the portraits in the gallery." She gave a derisive snort. "They'd forgotten to lock it. As many times as I'd been to Northfield House, I'd never been in the south wing. I opened the doors and saw the footprints in the dust. Only one set—Eleanor's, as it happened—went beyond the gallery into this hall. I added my own following hers to the end of this very passage."

She never left, she never left, she never left, echoed in my mind. Fear crawled up my spine.

"I was very clever," she said. "When we searched the house later that night, I asked for the key to the south wing. No, no, they all protested. She couldn't be hiding there. It's locked." She spoke in a mocking falsetto. "Leave no stone unturned, I insisted. But I locked the doors, rather than unlocked them. When they searched the house again, as I felt sure they would do the next day, everyone would assume I had made the footprints while searching the abandoned rooms for my beloved sister."

Mrs. Wellington pulled me along, forcing me towards the door at the end of the long corridor. Icy dread spread through my chest. The torch beam danced wildly, throwing grotesque shadows as we staggered forwards.

Reaching the room at last, Mrs. Wellington swung the door open to a gust of musty air. I summoned my remaining energy. Lurching against her, I knocked the torch from her hand. It came to rest against the far wall, its yellow beam blooming upon the ceiling, illuminating the room in pale, otherworldly light. I looked for the specter that had beckoned Owen and me here.

Help me, I appealed to her in silence. *Help me.*

"Eleanor brought it upon herself, actually," Mrs. Wellington whispered, her face close to mine, her breath ragged. "I was sure they'd find her eventually, but meanwhile, she'd endure the agony that tortured me." She began to cry. "Henry and Northfield House were mine, and she took them from me, and I was helpless to change that. She deserved to suffer."

I cried out, the effort exhausting me. "*Please.*"

"How was I to know?" Mrs. Wellington expelled her words on a hushed breath. "How could I know that no one would bother with the south wing again? That Henry, in his grief and distress, would close up Northfield almost immediately and take the servants to the London house, staying there for months while he searched the world for her?" Her voice broke with heartache. "After a few days, it was too late for me to say anything. Too late." The sweat on her face now mingled with tears.

She dragged me towards the dusty bed dressed in faded embroidery and rotted lace. At its foot was the large, heavy trunk to which Owen and I had paid little attention. Mrs. Wellington let go of me. I collapsed to my knees as she lifted the jointed metal strap from the staple.

She heaved the top up, its rusty hinges groaning as the faint odor of stale decay escaped from the interior.

"Eleanor hid in the perfect place," Mrs. Wellington said. "She climbed into the trunk, but the hasp fell and the lid couldn't be opened from inside. And my clever little sister couldn't get out."

Stupefied, I stared into the trunk—at the hollow sockets and joyless grin buried in shreds of yellowed lace. It occurred to me, just before I lost consciousness, that the search was over. *Here was Eleanor, found at last, in all her bridal finery.*

Chapter 51

I drifted, mindless, in an all-encompassing darkness. My muscles were slack. My head throbbed, but I felt no pain. I willed my body to waken. I sensed a lift, something shifting. Consciousness returned as if it were a radio being tuned to the right frequency. I felt my senses come alive, one by one, the first being touch.

My shoulder lay against something smooth and round. It seemed I'd settled myself upon sticks and stones, their hardness digging into my back, my hips. I shifted my shoulder and explored the object with my fingers. A skull. Eleanor's skull.

Awareness struck with a jolt. I snatched my fingers away. The hideous truth paralyzed me with fear. I'd been trapped in the trunk with Eleanor's corpse.

The horror of that moment flooded through me. Mrs. Wellington and I had grappled at the edge of the open trunk. Her madness gave her almost superhuman strength, endowing her with the savage power to lift and push my slim frame, drugged and helpless, into it. The bones of Eleanor Granville shattered under my weight, as the dust from years of desiccation billowed into the air. The lid slammed closed, the hasp fell into place, and I was engulfed in claustrophobic black.

I'd tried to scream, but terror closed my throat, and I emitted only anguished gasps. My scant cries echoed against the walls of my trap and filled my own ears, but they would reach no one else's. My sluggish limbs were too weak to mount a struggle with the sturdy sides of the trunk.

How long have I been trapped? It is cold. Airless. The only sound, my labored breathing.

My dread subsided. I felt myself slipping into an addled unconsciousness once again. *No no no no no!* I struggled to stay awake. Losing control of my body would doom me. I must stay lucid, focus my mind upon escape. I wrestled, frail and ineffective, within the confines of my prison.

Then suddenly, a kind of trance settled over my mind like a blanket. Hopelessness was like a drug. My body stilled, my mind quieted, and I whispered prayers until I slipped into visions of the past. My parents. My little sister with her sketch book. My young brother whistling to call his mates. And Owen. *Owen . . .*

Then there was nothing.

After . . . moments? . . . hours? I awoke in a sluggish stupor. Something as delicate as a spider web brushed my cheek. I batted at it before becoming fully aware. It was fabric that fell apart at my touch, my nose stinging with old dust.

Where am I?

Fear jerked me out of the haze.

I'm trapped in a trunk in the abandoned wing of Northfield House.

Not a pinprick of light pierced my prison. I lay on my back, my knees bent, my feet crammed against one end of the trunk. Both hands explored, feeling the top, bottom, and sides, desperately searching for purchase, for joints and seams, for some weakness by which I might free myself. I swallowed bile as I swept aside Eleanor's bones.

Panic seized me, driving away the last of my torpor, and I did battle. I pushed, fierce and wild, using hands and feet and shoulders, refusing to accept this as my tomb. With every fiber of my being, I strained against the narrow confines of the trunk, struggling to get out. In my terrified thrashing, the rotted silk of Eleanor's wedding dress disintegrated, smelling sharply of mold and decay.

Owen! Owen! I cried in silence. *Help me! Find me!*

I smelled my own blood as I tore at the trunk with my fingers. They traced the claw marks of another desperate girl, trapped and terrified.

For how many hours did Eleanor scream? For how many days did she lay here, growing weaker and weaker? I wondered how much longer I had before her fate became my fate. I couldn't imagine how many tears were shed before her body was depleted of all moisture and all life, before she perished, her flesh finally withering away.

Eleanor must have hoped that Henry would find her. I prayed that Owen would find me, that he would look until he made his way to the south wing.

How long was he to be in London? Three days. Maybe he would return sooner. How long have I been here? What day is this? I must reserve my strength until he returns.

He will look, and he will find me.

My head swam between bouts of kicking and thrashing. An image of Lavinia Wellington wavered in my tears. She was a clever adversary. I imagined her packing my bag with all my belongings and telling everyone I'd gone home to Liverpool. No one would look for me until suspicion dawned. By then it would be too late. *Too late!*

Owen! Help me! Find me!

I calculated the cost of our naiveté, our guilelessness, for Owen and me. His mother stood before us all along. It was astounding that we had not seen her madness. I had deemed myself a powerless employee, at her mercy. I had been convinced that I was unable to call her out on her efforts at controlling, belittling, and shaming me, even as I chafed beneath her slights. Owen had been oblivious to the fact that his mother's social status allowed her to poison and kill. Her need to control and her belief in her superiority made her a monster.

Owen! Help me! Find me!

"Eleanor?" I whispered, "Are you here? I dredged up the past, stirred up old memories, trying to understand what happened to you. And now I know. Perhaps Lavinia didn't intend for you to die, but she could have saved you and did nothing. This drove your sister insane." I recalled that long, last trek to the south wing. "She admitted your ghost taunted her with a truth she alone knew."

Owen! Help me! Find me!

"Poor Charlotte," I cried out to the spirit. "Young and beautiful and cruel, she unwittingly stepped into Lavinia Wellington's web of madness. Looking like you, Eleanor, come to life and threatening to marry Thomas, to become mistress of Northfield House." As if her bones could hear me, I spoke to the girl whose fate I feared I shared.

Owen! Help me! Find me!

My mind raced over other clues and opportunities we had missed.

Befuddled Martha, steeped in her memories and her losses. Her puzzle of a brain could have pieced together what really happened. In her senility, she must have blurted out menacing words after connecting jigsaw pieces of knowledge. Mrs. Wellington was right to fear her.

She had also feared me. At any moment, I might have remembered the blue rosary grasped in Charlotte's dead hand. That was the impetus for the tea laced with laudanum. It must have forced her hand, my decision to dispense with the tea. And she had to do something to prevent the marriage to Owen, which would make of me a menace forever within her sight.

❧

I screamed for Owen, again and again, until my cries became whimpers, sweat and fear drenching my clothes. My throat ached. Pain seared my bruised head, hands, and feet. Thirst twisted my gut, and dread flooded my soul. But I promised myself I would not die. Not here. Not as a result of Lavinia Wellington's evil machinations. Truth will out. Owen *would* find me. Clenching my fists and my teeth, I made a vow to myself, speaking it aloud. "When I get out of here and depart Northfield House, I will never allow another to have power over me. I will do more than survive. *I will prevail.*"

ॐ

I woke with a start. Had I heard something?

Someone is coming. They have found me.

Nothing.

But they must be searching. Unless Mrs. Wellington had convinced them I had gone.

I imagined the hum of activity about the house, the inhabitants of Northfield going about their daily lives, unthinking, unknowing, and unaware. Perhaps Mrs. Hadley polished silver as Dolly repaired the hem of a curtain, and Maddy prepared a tea tray for her mistress. I could see Kitty, even now, sifting through the pebbles on the creek bottom or gathering twigs.

Is it day or night? I had no way to know how many hours I'd agonized in this trap.

My lips felt dry and cracked. I didn't know how much more I could scream without entirely losing my voice along with any hope of discovery. Perhaps I would soon haunt Northfield House, I thought, seeing myself drifting down the hallways and up the stairs, a soulless wraith, lost between worlds, unable to find my way.

ॐ

My father touched my cheek.

318

"Sweet daughter, come with me." He cradled me in his arms.

My mother's face hovered above mine. Planting a kiss upon my brow, she wrapped me in soft weightlessness.

&

I felt myself floating in the dark, like the stars in the heavens.

"Eleanor," my whispering voice rasped, "come find me. You've come to me before. Show me how. Come show me how to die."

I flickered in and out of consciousness.

&

Where am I?

Pounding. I heard pounding.

My flailing was useless. My mouth and throat were so dry I was unable to swallow. I tried to scream again, but nothing came from my cracked lips. I fell into a dream instead. Owen and I were in the beautiful house outside of Preston, knowing our children played in the fields, preparing food we'd grown in our garden. As I watched the sun go down, I saw my dreams disappear along with it.

&

Every time I awoke, I prayed. *Dear God in Heaven, help me.* The lessons of childhood swept over me. *In the name of the Father, the Son, and the Holy Spirit . . .* in the name of all that is sacred . . . come for me. Save me. End this agony.

&

My blood. I swallowed my own blood, its metallic taste like honey in my throat. I bit at my own flesh, at my fingers and forearms, desperate for moisture to slake my thirst. Bitter shreds of fabric, laden with aged cobwebs, choked me.

᪥

Another dream. Distant voices drifted towards me. Pounding again.

Or perhaps it is footsteps.

A voice. Owen's voice!

And his mother's. "No, Owen, no. She's gone. Look again at this note she left in her typing machine. She didn't love you. She couldn't stay here."

"I don't believe it, Mother. I don't."

"She's left Northfield behind, you fool!"

I heard them clearly. They were moving towards me down the hallway in the south wing. Coming closer to the last room. The room where I was trapped.

Owen. Find me. I'm here.

"No one saw her leave. She spoke to no one, not even Kitty. She wouldn't have left without saying good-bye to the girl."

The voices came closer yet, and I heard angry words, garbled words as Owen and his mother talked over one another.

Owen, find me! I opened my lips to scream. But I made no sound. I was unable to speak any longer.

The footsteps came nearer. They were very close now.

"Owen. You must accept the truth. Forget that girl. She's nothing. She was harmful, bad for you. I'm your mother . . . I know these things."

"Be quiet, Mother. Shut up, for God's sake."

"You may not speak to me in that manner!"

I tried to call out. I no longer had the strength to kick or pound my fists or feet on the sides of my cage. I had nothing but the breath in my body. I heard the footsteps recede.

No! Don't go! I'm here!

In my panic, I found the will to lift my hand from my throat to my mouth.

I cannot call out, but I do have air in my lungs still.

I placed thumb and finger beneath my tongue and closed my lips over them.

I tried to force sufficient air through but only a weak hiss of sound escaped. I wanted to swallow but could not. I tried to signal again to no avail. And again.

The footsteps became fainter.

Dear God in Heaven, help me.

I gathered every shred of strength remaining to me. I positioned my fingers once more and blew.

A shrill whistle reverberated in the trunk.

Everything stopped.

Then the footsteps, running this time, came towards me once more. The slam of a door against a wall. Clatter and clank. The rusty hinges of the trunk squealed.

All of a sudden, I was suspended in air, Owen's arms lifting me up, the light stabbing my eyes.

I heard Owen, his voice choked with tears. "Anne! Oh, Anne, my beloved!"

I closed my eyes against the searing brightness. Darkness descended again.

Am I dead?

Chapter 52

S he's evil! She's a liar! They were against me, all of them. Charlotte, Martha, and this nobody!"

His mother paced about screaming, as Owen cradled my head and shoulders. I tried to speak but could not. Owen smoothed the hair from my face and murmured words I couldn't understand. His voice, soothing and hypnotic, lulled me.

I started to slip once more into darkness, but fought back. I forced my eyes open.

"Anne, drink this. Drink!" He held his flask to my mouth. Something alcoholic stung my lips and burned my throat, but the moisture revived me, making me feel alive once more. I swallowed too eagerly and burst into a fit of coughing. As my body calmed, I found myself splayed across the corridor floor, just outside the bedchamber where the trunk sat, now filled with nothing but old bones.

I am safe in Owen's arms.

Mrs. Wellington stood above me, pointing an accusing finger. "That witch wants me to hang!"

Her face was contorted with madness as she hissed, "She's plotting against me. It's all her fault. She's the reason Martha is dead.

And Charlotte's death, it's not true, what she says. She's . . . she's . . ."

"*Mother*," Owen said. "Calm down."

"It's a lie! She'll tell you she saw my blue rosary in Charlotte's dead hand. I gave it to her, that's why she had it. This filthy wench," she flung her arm towards me with a sneer, "will tell you I pushed Charlotte off the footbridge. And Martha was old. I gave her laudanum to calm her, to help with her ague. If the dose was too much, well, that was an accident."

"Mother, what are you saying?"

Even in my weakened state, I could see awareness dawn in Owen's face. *My mother has gone mad.* It was terrible to see the sadness and horror in his eyes.

She babbled and screeched in turn, giving excuses, justifying her actions, alternatively pleading and demanding. Her ravings amounted to a confession. She was responsible for the deaths of Eleanor, Charlotte, and Martha Langtry.

Owen and I huddled on the floor, watching in frozen silence.

Suddenly Mrs. Wellington jerked backwards as if physically struck. She took a step away. Her eyes widened, and her mouth worked like she was struggling to speak. Her gaze had shifted beyond the two of us to the room where the trunk lay open to daylight at last.

The pale light dimmed. The air became unnaturally still. The door crept open.

As silent moments passed, I saw it, too. Something hovered there in the dark, and the air began to vibrate as if breathing.

A heavy, smothering weight enveloped me.

A chilling cold descended.

Shadows gathered.

We three stared at the miasma forming at the threshold to that horrible room. I heard a faint buzzing. The scent of decaying roses filled my head. Then the sharp stench of death caused me to cover my mouth and nose with my hand. Owen did the same, but his mother only whimpered.

The darkness thickened. The thing pulsated, quivered, and coalesced into the outline of a human form. With a swirl and a twisting motion, a face and two hands appeared out of the nebulous gloom. As we watched the spirit materialize, the face and hands sharpened and resolved in perfect clarity, while the rest of the figure remained unformed, but shining like gleaming ink.

Mrs. Wellington emitted a guttural groan. Owen gasped. Inside my head, I heard a high-pitched wail—a scream of anguished outrage.

The wraith swayed towards us, fluid, lissome, menacing, her long-fingered hands beckoning to us from the murky depths of her amorphous robes. Her red tresses floated on the air, suspended as if in still water. Her face bloomed with the freshness of youth. Blue eyes seemed lit from within, and every feature was distinct. If there had ever been any doubt that Eleanor Granville haunted Northfield House, it was now dispelled.

Lavinia Wellington mouthed a strangled cry. "Eleanor? Eleanor! I was young and foolish. And insanely jealous. I never meant for it to happen."

I gaped at her, grasping the arm Owen had wrapped around me.

"Henry was mine," she sobbed. "Northfield was mine. You took them from me. *You* got into the trunk on your own. How was I to know they wouldn't find you?"

The ghost of Eleanor Granville opened her mouth in a soundless howl. She flew past Owen and me in a blur. The wraith swept directly through Mrs. Wellington. Then she disappeared into the gallery and the corridors beyond.

Lavinia Wellington cowered, groping the air. A raw, rasping cry fell from her lips. She twitched violently and clutched her bosom with both hands, took a faltering step, and collapsed.

Chapter 53

I **dreamed once more.** Mrs. Wellington bathed my brow with a cool cloth and suddenly pressed it hard against my mouth and nose. I lifted my head and tried to scream.

"It's all right, Anne, you're safe," said Owen, his voice desperate. "You're here. You're with me." I felt his gentle hand on my cheek.

I became conscious gradually, finally understanding where I was. I lay in bed in Martha's room, soft sunshine filling all the corners with subtle light. My gaze darted everywhere, seeing everything at once. Relief flooded through me.

"Thank God!" I cried. "Owen!"

Grasping my shoulders, he pulled me close and held me tight. "You're back, at last. I thought I'd lost you forever."

"Lost me?"

Owen released me from his embrace to look at me. "We thought you'd lost your mind and might never recover. Do you know me, Anne?"

"Owen. Yes, Owen." I sobbed. My hair spilled across my shoulders, and my arms and fingers were bruised and bandaged. I was wearing a white, lacy shift that wasn't mine, and I lay upon deep pillows.

"How long . . ." My voice caught. "When did you . . ." Tears wet my face.

"You've been in bed almost a week now," he said.

I saw medicine bottles and sickroom detritus scattered on the bedside table. I felt the weight of soreness in my limbs and aches and pains in my feet, legs, and arms.

"Dr. Termeer was here until this morning. He'll be back in a few hours." Owen swept his gaze over my face, his eyes awash with concern.

"Help me sit up," I said.

Owen put his arm around me, lifted me, and repositioned the snowy pillows. Once I was propped against them, he held onto my hand.

I struggled to speak, my voice hoarse. "I mean, how long was I there . . . with Eleanor?"

"Darling," Owen gasped, shaking his head. "Don't think of it. How terrified you must have been." Heartache mixed with anger contorted his face.

"How did you find me?"

"Let's not talk about that," he said.

"No. No, Owen, you must tell me."

"Must it be now?"

"I need to know, Owen. You must share everything, or I cannot rest."

I pleaded until Owen relented. He settled beside the bed in a low chair to tell his story, holding my bandaged hand all the while.

"I returned from London a day early. I'd finished my business more quickly than expected and had little reason to tarry. And I couldn't wait to see my love." He leaned forwards and pressed his lips against mine. "The house was in order, everyone bustling about. But you weren't in the study or in your room. I felt uneasy, believing you'd be anxious for my return, so I asked Mrs. Hadley."

He struggled to continue, and I pressed his hand between mine.

"Mother had informed her that you'd gone to Liverpool. She told Mrs. Hadley she didn't know why you left but assumed you'd gone to see friends or do some shopping. This didn't immediately strike me as troubling, but by evening, I went to your room again. Not until that moment did I realize everything was gone. Your bag, your belongings." Owen's voice broke. "Everything."

"You knew I had nowhere to go," I said.

"Yes, I was keenly aware of that. And you'd never even spoken of friends, let alone taken a holiday to visit them. And I knew you would have left me a note. Something just wasn't right. Father seemed oblivious, so I sought out Mother."

"Your mother!" The words caught in my throat.

"I found her in the garden in a dazed sort of mood. At first, I thought she'd taken ill. She wasn't herself at all."

I imagined Mrs. Wellington coping with the knowledge of her crime, trying to maintain the appearance of sanity. Perhaps she heard me screaming inside her head, choking for air in the south wing.

"Mother said you'd gone, that you'd taken the opportunity provided by my absence to pack your bags and leave. She even produced a typewritten note, insisting that she'd found it in your machine." His voice cracked. "The note said you couldn't pretend any longer. You didn't love me, had never loved me, and were returning to a man from your past."

"Oh, Owen," I said, clasping both his hands. "You couldn't have believed that."

He looked at me longingly. "Not for a moment."

Owen groped for words through thick emotion and leaned close, putting his face against mine. "But she hadn't seen us at the farm in Preston. She didn't know how happy we were, about the plans we'd made." He smiled at the memory. "I knew it wasn't true."

"My darling." A pain stitched my heart.

"You were right. Mother had been pretending to accept our marriage. And she feared you'd remember about the night Charlotte died, about seeing her rosary. Nothing could have been more damning. Poor Charlotte. In her mind, Mother thought she was saving Thomas and, in the bargain, saving Northfield House from a monstrous indignity."

"What made you start looking for me here rather than in Liverpool?"

"It was Kitty," he said.

"Kitty?"

"I went again to your room to search for anything that would give me answers. I was looking for a sign, a note I might have missed, something to help me. I found only Kitty's box upon the floor under the bed. I sought her out to return it." Owen kissed me once more. "Anne. I almost lost you."

"Never, my love. Not in a thousand years. But how did Kitty know where to find me?"

"She didn't. But she provided the clues. Kitty was always afraid of Mother, never entered a room if she were present. But when I returned her box, she took me by the hand and pulled me to the boot room off the scullery. She opened an old closet, and in the bottom was your bag, all your things. Kitty hadn't seen Mother trap you in Eleanor's tomb, but she'd seen her hiding your belongings."

"Bless little Kitty," I said. Just like Mrs. Wellington herself, Kitty always knew what was going on at Northfield House.

"My first thought was Charlotte, and how she died. I raced to the footbridge, but found no sign of you. It made me sick with anxiety," Owen said. "Frantic, I called the tenants and the authorities and had them out in force, looking downstream and combing the countryside."

"Just like they did for Eleanor," I said.

"Yes, exactly like Eleanor. That's what prompted me to consider our own search for her. And the haunting in the south wing." Owen hung his head. "I only wish I'd done that sooner."

"Oh, Owen. In a way, Eleanor saved me."

"Yes, she saved you from her own torturer."

A sudden vision of my rescue from the south wing flooded over me. I recalled Lavinia Wellington's anguished confession about Martha, her denial regarding Charlotte's death, and something else. She'd made an apology to her sister for failing to save her life. Eleanor's chilling wraith spun like a dervish in my mind's eye. So Owen must know everything.

"I'm so very sorry, Owen. I know how hard it is to accept—your own mother. How painful the truth must be. And your poor father. How terrible for him, discovering what really happened after all these sorrowful years." I wiped away tears. "Whatever will happen to her?"

"Mother's dead, Anne."

My breath caught with the shock. For a moment, I couldn't speak.

"She died right there in the south wing."

I conjured my last moments in the south wing, recalling Mrs. Wellington's collapse in the moonlit hallway. Then a swarm of people had whisked me away. "It must have been too much for her, having to confront what she'd done."

"It was more than that," said Owen. "Eleanor's spirit exacted her revenge at last."

I remembered that fearsome wraith with the starkly beautiful face, howling as she flew past us and through Lavinia Wellington like dark smoke.

Owen squeezed my hand. "We called Dr. Termeer to attend to Mother, but it was too late. Heart failure."

Chapter 54

*A*fter more than thirty years, Eleanor Granville Wellington was laid to rest in the family graveyard, her parents on one side and Charlotte on the other. Efforts to keep the story out of the papers came to nothing, and the family suffered the unwelcome attention of the yellow press. Not until headlines appeared regarding another more famous interment—Howard Carter's opening of King Tutankhamen's tomb in Egypt—were the Wellington family troubles forgotten.

Although my physical wounds healed in good time, the recovery of my mental balance lagged. But by spring, when lilac blossoms scented the pale air, Owen and I married quietly in London. Given the circumstances, we avoided the fanfare that typically surrounds the marriage of a member of an important family. Henry Wellington, Thomas, and Mrs. Hadley attended. And, of course, Kitty was there, dressed in sugary pink and glowing with smiles.

Taking Kitty, our little talisman, with us, we began our lives on the farm near Preston where the rooms were filled with light, love, and the restful dead.

Carrying me across the threshold, Owen asked, "Are there ghosts in residence, my dear wife?"

"There are always ghosts, my beloved," I answered. "Our peace and comfort depend only upon whether they have secrets to share."

PHYLLIS M. NEWMAN

Acknowledgments

*A*s with most books, mine was not created in a vacuum. I had the help and support of an amazing writing group, Company of Writers of Columbus, Ohio, which has taught, nurtured, and supported me throughout my writing career. The members are honest, direct, creative, and perspicacious. My enduring thanks go to Pat Brown, Jamie Rhein, Erica Scurr, Leslie Robinson, Elizabeth Sammons, Lacy Cooper, Ken Leonard, Dianne Moon, Kath Giblin, Angela Palazzolo, and Sue Rudibaugh. Another member, Gretchen Hirsch of Midwest Book Doctors, gets a special shout-out for her invaluable professional advice and expertise.

My heartfelt thanks go to members of my art group, who have provided sage advice and moral support: Kathie Houchens, Deb Linville, Julie Osborn, and Gail Evans.

I am grateful for family and friends who read my work, carve out and preserve valuable time for me, and provide feedback. But above all, I am beholden for the inspiration they provide: John M. Newman, Alexis D. Newman, Gregory A. Newman, Lisa Johnson Newman, Sharyn Talbert, Amy Millsap, Douglas Millsap, Kathi Godber, Deedy Middleton, and Alexandra Glover.

I am fortunate to have an excellent partner in PageSpring Publishing and Cup of Tea Books, and wish to thank particularly my editor, Katherine Matthews, for her taste, patience, and superb intuition. She has made my writing fuller, richer, and deeper.

Any merit this novel has is due to the contributions of many people. All shortcomings are mine alone.

About the Author

Phyllis M. Newman lives in Columbus, Ohio, in a rambling house surrounded by a yard full of weeds, with three perpetually unimpressed cats (ghost watchers all), and a husband that's easy on the eyes.

Learn more about Phyllis at *readphyllismnewman.com*.

63011229R00205

Made in the USA
Columbia, SC
07 July 2019